**Praise for the
Major Ariane Kedros Novels**

Vigilante

"[An] intriguing ensemble cast . . . [a] nicely complex universe . . . in this entertaining second military SF adventure for Ariane Kedros, a secret agent of the Consortium of Autonomous Worlds. . . . Reeve immediately immerses the reader in her universe's vernacular, acronyms, and backstory . . . most rewarding."   —*Publishers Weekly*

Peacekeeper

"An excellent debut novel. *Peacekeeper* is full of exciting, complex characters in a truly byzantine universe where everything hangs in the balance. I can't wait for Reeve's next book."
        —Mike Shepherd, author of the Kris Longknife series

"Reeve shows great promise."   —Darque Reviews

"Former USAF officer Reeve channels her flight experience into this crisp military SF debut. . . . Reeve drives the story at a breakneck pace, providing a fine mix of derring-do, honor, and courage, and the familial bickering and affection of a close-knit crew."   —*Publishers Weekly*

ALSO BY LAURA E. REEVE

Vigilante
Peacekeeper

PATHFINDER

A Major Ariane Kedros Novel

Laura E. Reeve

A ROC BOOK

ROC

Published by New American Library, a division of
Penguin Group (USA) Inc., 375 Hudson Street,
New York, New York 10014, USA
Penguin Group (Canada), 90 Eglinton Avenue East, Suite 700, Toronto,
Ontario M4P 2Y3, Canada (a division of Pearson Penguin Canada Inc.)
Penguin Books Ltd., 80 Strand, London WC2R 0RL, England
Penguin Ireland, 25 St. Stephen's Green, Dublin 2,
Ireland (a division of Penguin Books Ltd.)
Penguin Group (Australia), 250 Camberwell Road, Camberwell, Victoria 3124,
Australia (a division of Pearson Australia Group Pty. Ltd.)
Penguin Books India Pvt. Ltd., 11 Community Centre, Panchsheel Park,
New Delhi - 110 017, India
Penguin Group (NZ), 67 Apollo Drive, Rosedale, North Shore 0632,
New Zealand (a division of Pearson New Zealand Ltd.)
Penguin Books (South Africa) (Pty.) Ltd., 24 Sturdee Avenue,
Rosebank, Johannesburg 2196, South Africa

Penguin Books Ltd., Registered Offices:
80 Strand, London WC2R 0RL, England

First published by Roc, an imprint of New American Library,
a division of Penguin Group (USA) Inc.

First Printing, July 2010
10 9 8 7 6 5 4 3 2 1

Copyright © Laura E. Reeve, 2010
All rights reserved

 REGISTERED TRADEMARK — MARCA REGISTRADA

Printed in the United States of America

To my parents, Gerry and Norma,
who have never stopped exploring and learning

ACKNOWLEDGMENTS

Every novel has its quirky challenges, particularly when life intervenes. This one turned out to have more challenges than most, and I'm grateful for my husband, Michael's, support, as well as his encouragement and advice. I also thank the rest of my family for their patience while I focused on this book. Special recognition must go to neurologist Dr. Randall Bjork, who figured out how to treat my headaches while not turning me into a drooling (and nonwriting) zombie. Once again, I'm indebted to my critique partner, Robin Widmar, as well as first readers Summer Ficarrotta and Scott Cowan, for their reviews and editorial comments. Finally, I must thank my fantastic agent, Jennifer Jackson, my editor, Jessica Wade, and the staff at Penguin Group for their work on this series.

CHAPTER 1

Did you rats sense the fracas in our newest solar system? G-145 went silent and Pilgrimage HQ panicked, sending out emergency messages. When G-145 came back up and the *Pilgrimage III* said, "Nothing happening here," did anyone believe them? *Something* happened, because net-think has Jude Stephanos, senior senator from Hellas Prime, hurrying off to G-145. . . .

—*Dr. Net-head Stavros*, 2106.051.22.04 UT,
indexed by *Heraclitus 12* under Flux Imperative

The alien followed her, quiet as a whisper. As Major Ariane Kedros turned into the chapel, she caught in her peripheral vision a glimpse of the tall, horned Minoan warrior. Perversely, she refused to acknowledge who, or *what*, followed several meters behind her.

Every day for the past six days, before her shift started, Ariane had stopped by the chapel of the *Pilgrimage III*. On the front wall, above the altar, was the list of recent fatalities. This list grew every day, as Abram's attempted takeover of G-145—a takeover she had played a large role in stopping—was converted from blood to dry data. Terran State Prince Hauser's death put the number at more than two hundred.

Ignoring the Minoan behind her, Ariane selected the front bench. She sat with her back straight and stiff, her hands gripping the cool, hard surface beneath her. She started at the top and read every name. As always, she paused when she came to Colonel Elene Dokos.

It took physical effort to move past that name. *They killed her in front of me, and I couldn't stop them.* The edge of the bench dug into her fingers as her grip tightened.

"You did the best you could."

The voice made her start. Justin Pilgrimage, the communications officer for the *Pilgrimage*, stood beside the bench with his head cocked in question. When she nodded, he sat down beside her, although he jerked his head toward the back of the chapel.

"Don't look now, but a Minoan's back there watching you," he murmured, leaning close.

"Warrior Commander's been following me around for days," she replied in a flat tone. Minoan technology exceeded theirs by so much that there was no chance of hiding their conversation.

His eyes widened. "Does this have anything to do with them calling you 'Breaker of Treaties'?"

His reaction made her pause. She'd become blasé, almost numb, to the aliens that had given humans faster-than-light travel more than a century ago—and indifference was dangerous. The Minoans carried weapons that boiled people from the inside out and they had organic ships with directed-energy weapons, all of which were beyond humanity's comprehension.

The Minoans didn't think like humans. There was no gray area for them, particularly when following laws or dispensing justice. They'd committed "delayed genocide," using mysterious genetic weapons, upon a tribe as punishment for piracy and terrorism. They'd followed interstellar law to the letter, of course, and no government had the balls to protest that attack. While it led to a decades-long lull in piracy, it also caused festering resentment—*and we were the ones who suffered from Abram's vengeance.*

"Does it follow you everywhere?" Justin pressed.

"I'm given privacy for my work, but not in public places such as this." She glanced around, noting that repairs had started on the shrine at the front. Someone found the original gold statue of St. Darius, in a helmetless environmental suit, holding out only one hand in benediction because his other arm had broken off.

This suddenly seemed ludicrous as well as heretical—having a Minoan, who probably wasn't even a Gaian-based life-form, inside a place where people venerated Gaia's servant St. Darius. Swallowing the hysterical giggle that rose in her throat, she said, "Luckily, they have no interest in my hygiene habits. Warrior Commander follows me only in public areas of the *Pilgrimage*, not onto my ship."

"Why?"

"I've asked questions, with no success." She forced her hands to rest in her lap rather than balling up into fists of frustration. "He—*it*—has been following me ever since the sun calmed down."

"About that." He smiled. "I wanted to thank you. It's beyond rumor now. We all know you saved us from becoming another Ura-Guinn."

She flinched and went still. She should have anticipated the comparison, even though G-145's sun hadn't suffered a full temporal-distortion wave because she pushed the weapon into N-space as it detonated. Of course, Justin couldn't know she was *also* responsible for Ura-Guinn's devastation; her apparent age didn't make her a likely candidate for detonating the only other temporal-distortion weapon ever used. That detonation was sixteen years ago, during the war between the Terrans and the Consortium of Autonomous Worlds, and that fatality list could eventually number over four billion souls. Saving the several thousand souls inside G-145 was almost immaterial by comparison.

Due to the vastness of space, proof of the survival of Ura-Guinn's star had taken this long to get to civilization. Now the Feeds screamed with each new guess of Ura-Guinn's fatalities, using clues stitched together by the Epsilon Eridani antenna telescope, which couldn't even see the man-made structures in Ura-Guinn. Each report from the Feeds resurrected her nightmares and reanimated the accusing ghosts in the back of her mind.

"We're all grateful you got rid of the weapon before it did much damage." Justin hadn't noticed her stiffness, and his voice was warm. Friendly. What would he think of her if he knew her *real* history? Justin's gaze sharpened, focusing on the top of the list displayed on the bulkhead next to the shrine. "I always stop here, for Dan's sake."

She nodded, and her relief at the change of topic almost made her dizzy. The top name on the list was Daniel Pilgrimage. Dan had worked beside Justin on the control deck, and he'd been the first to die when Abram arrived.

Justin looked down at his hands, which he tensely kneaded. "My shirt was covered with his blood. I looked at it for days, building up rage. I thought it would dishonor him if I threw the shirt in the disposal. This morning, I realized I could honor him, yet lose the rage, so I threw the bloody thing away."

Her throat was so tight, she could barely swallow. "I can't," she finally said.

"Can't what?"

"Lose the rage. I hate the monster that did this." Her hand swept through the air, motioning toward the damaged shrine. "I'm *glad* he's gone, and I hope the rest of those isolationist bastards are put away for as long as possible."

"You'll get your wish." The corners of Justin's mouth quirked upward. "The Terran State Prince has already boarded and your senator arrives tomorrow, so the Tribunal—whatever it's called—can start."

"The Interstellar Criminal Tribunal," she said hollowly.

"Yeah, for war criminals."

"They're being tried for *crimes against humanity*, not as war criminals. They weren't part of an armed conflict between states." The difference was important, but not to the ghosts shrieking in her head. She pressed the heels of her hands against her eyes, trying to blur the image of Terran agent Nathanial Wolf Kim as he tortured her, saying, "Four billion people gone. Admit it—you're a war criminal."

She didn't know how much of the war Justin remembered, since he had been born shortly before the generational ship *Pilgrimage III* embarked on the G-145 mission twenty-six years ago. He wasn't used to military uniforms, however, and as her hands dropped into her lap again, he gestured at her attire. "I almost didn't recognize you from the back."

She wasn't wearing her normal crew coveralls with the Aether Exploration logo, because she was still on active duty. Her black uniform with light blue trim was crisp and clean, appropriate for a golem from the Directorate of Intelligence, under the Armed Forces of the Consortium of Autonomist Worlds. She ran her fingers through her dark hair so it curled under at the ends, shortened to collar length to meet AFCAW uniform regulations.

Justin went quiet and made the universal gesture for wait-I'm-taking-a-priority-call. He listened while his finger drifted to press behind his jawbone, acknowledging the call.

"Needed on control deck?" she asked.

"Yeah." He gripped her forearm and gave it a reassuring squeeze. Crèche-get, those born and raised on generational ships, tended to be sentimental and demonstrative, so she resisted the urge to pull away. "I know you feel guilty," he added.

"Excuse me?" The words came out sharper than she intended.

"You just couldn't save everyone, Ariane. It's time to forgive yourself."

"Oh, so *that's* my problem." She smiled, hoping she looked natural. "Thanks for the amateur psych eval."

"Hey, I just saved you a trip to Mental Health." He winked as he stood. She watched him hurry down the wide aisle. He took care to step down one side, away from the still figure of Warrior Commander seated in the exact middle of the last bench on the left.

After Justin left, her gaze lingered a last time on the list. Her mouth hardened as she considered the two latest entries. State Prince Hauser hadn't been able to recover from a rare reaction to the prophylactic radiation drugs. More tragic, Major Phillips of the Terran Space Forces had gone beyond the radiation exposure point of no return while retrieving victims who had been spaced alive, in environmental suits, by Abram's men. The fatalities continued long after Abram's defeat and death.

This list didn't include the other victims, such as AF-CAW Master Sergeant Alexander Joyce, who had barely lived through face-to-face combat with Abram; or Danielle, the pilot raped by Abram's nephew Emery. *Yet more justification for leaving Emery to die in N-space. I'm not sorry I did that.* N-space, or nous-space-time transit, was the only way to traverse space in faster-than-light fashion, but entering it without having a buoy lock meant the ship was lost forever. The passengers would be insane after a couple of hours without D-tranny in their bloodstream. Although that might have been too good for Emery, by only adding disassociative psychosis to his sadistic sociopathy. The lack of delta tranquilizer, however, wasn't what mattered most; going into N-space without locking onto a buoy meant you could never return to real-space.

Standing, she smoothed her black uniform. Her shiny boots made light taps on the deck as she walked down the aisle. She paused before passing the dark figure with tall horns that was sitting quietly. She sighed. This seemed too much to ask of her, considering her pay grade. At least the warrior didn't have a guardian escort, like a red-robed emissary Minoan, or she'd be leading around a whole parade of aliens. She made a tight gesture toward the hatchway. "Are you ready, Warrior Commander? Another day, another drachma, as we say."

Warrior Commander's horns dipped slowly in a nod and she moved on, knowing she'd get no other response. She no longer watched the tall figure in billowing robes rise and mysteriously fit within the *Pilgrimage*'s decks.

Why are you following me? The unanswered question stoked her glowing ire and resentment. Her pace was solid, with purposeful cadence, as she strode through a spoke hall toward her destination: the brig.

"Sorry, Matt. There's nothing I can do." In the view port, Carmen's head bobbed on her treadmill at Athens Point, more than seven hundred light-years away from G-145. "I can't find anyone with enough balls to sign off on extending your line of credit."

"But I have a low risk rating." This situation seemed entirely illogical to Matthew Journey, majority owner of Aether Exploration. Why should the rules change so suddenly?

"I know. It's just that G-145 is anathema to the financial sector right now."

"Government contracts are still funded," Matt said, "and the Terran League is moving money for their contractors."

"From what I hear, they're stretched to cover the rise in hazard pay that contractors demand." Carmen stopped bouncing and moved to pick up a towel, the cam-eye panning and widening the view. She dabbed at the sweat between her breasts, her athletic cleavage separated and firmed by space-age materials in her bra as well as her body.

"But nothing has changed. The Builders' ruins Ari and I discovered are an engineer's wet dream, with the possibility of re-creating those materials. There's an inactive buoy—a potential gateway to Gaia knows how many worlds. G-145 has the same resources it had a month ago."

"More than a dozen contractors have pulled out of their leases on Beta Priamos. They're being sued, or are under risk of suit."

"They have insurance—"

"Their insurers are reeling from payouts. I'm sympathetic to those who lost their loved ones, truly, but the claims and lawsuits are overwhelming the financiers. That Abram fellow caused a crisis in what used to be a well-oiled economic machine that drove our space exploration."

He nodded numbly, having run out of challenges. The smug voice in the back of his head, the one he never liked, pointed out that Carmen hadn't asked about his safety nor expressed concern for his welfare, nor for that of any other "crisis" survivors.

"Sorry, sweetie, but I don't see this problem blowing over quickly. Forget about G-145 and concentrate your efforts somewhere else for a while." She twirled the towel and laid it around her neck.

"That's difficult. As second-wave prospectors, we depend upon third-wave exploration and development to make back our expenses. Anyway, there isn't another solar system opening up for several years."

"*Everyone* should diversify." Carmen's cheek dimpled as she flashed a smile, too bright and hard to ever be innocent. "You'll find something else; I have faith in you. Call me when you get a line on work that's not connected to G-145."

"Sure thing." He projected confidence. He had to; investors, even those specializing in small businesses such as Carmen, were pack predators. First, they couldn't deviate from pack groupthink, and second, they must *never* see weakness in their victims—er, clients. They'd devour him and pick his bones clean.

"Look me up when you dock in Athens Point." She winked and the call was over, a blessing due to the high cost of bandwidth through the *Pilgrimage*-controlled buoy.

Sure thing, Carmen. After a moment, he cleared the bulkhead display of recent reports from lessees of his claims. In theory, all he needed to do was sit back and wait for his percentage. Reality, unfortunately, required operating funds from the constipated CAW space exploration and exploitation system. No money was flowing, and he needed funds *now*.

Carmen was usually his financial ace, his best chance for credit when his need was dire. He stared at the blank wall for a moment and sighed. It was time to look into the offer from the Minoans, as they were the only ones in this solar system holding any money.

The legend beside the door, MENTAL HEALTH FACILITIES, was lined through and OUR HELPFUL *BRIG* had been added. Ariane grinned. Someone had been bored enough to hack into title storage, but the delinquency was harmless.

After she opened the door, the dichotomy indicated by the changed legend was obvious. On her left, an ugly temporary bulkhead ran straight through the facility. It was raw nano-manufactured ultrapure steel, new enough to emit a metallic smell. On her right was the original waiting room for the "touchy-feely" sessions, as Matt called them. Since generational ship folk, or crèche-get, preferred monochromatic interiors without high contrast, the walls, deck, and furniture made for a soporific environment with their slightly different values of beige.

Two crèche-get, although that name wasn't always considered tasteful, were waiting for psych sessions. They ignored Ariane as she walked along the dividing bulkhead. A woman watched Feeds on the wall while a young man tapped through articles displayed on the coffee table surface in front of him.

She looked back over her shoulder when she heard the door open again, seeing Warrior Commander dip its tall horns to enter. Warrior Commander chose a solitary seat. Suddenly the two waiting clients were tapping frantically and canceling their appointments, having much better things to do. Nothing could empty a waiting room like a Minoan warrior.

Just past the check-in counter and to the left was a door in the dividing bulkhead. Ariane knocked and entered.

"Good to see you, Major." Pilgrimage security officer Benjamin looked up from his small desk, his sharp eyes scanning her uniform. His husky build, an anomaly among generational types, who grew tall and willowy under the one gee boundary, had singled him out for this new security position.

She glanced around, noting he was alone. Commander Meredith Pilgrimage, the senior ship commander of the *Pilgrimage*, had finally convinced the Minoans to recall their guardians. It must have been difficult for Meredith, who had the demeanor of a scholarly grandfather, to assure Warrior Commander that the *Pilgrimage* crew could now take over the Minoan's security operation. "I'd like a private interview, under Consortium-Pilgrimage agreements, with Dr. Rouxe."

"Ah, so you've heard." Benjamin cocked his head.

Always the last to learn. She suppressed a sigh. "Heard what?"

"You won't be allowed privacy, once the Terran Counsel arrives. He's taking over Rouxe's defense and he'll be monitoring all visits." In response to her raised eyebrows, he added, "That doesn't go into effect until tomorrow."

"Rouxe turned himself in to Pilgrimage authority, and he has Pilgrimage counsel. Why'd he send for Terran defense?" This seemed strange, since Dr. Tahir Dominique Rouxe made use of several gaping holes in *Terran* security in the process of stealing a *Terran* weapon. Rouxe couldn't expect sympathy or generosity from the Terrans.

"He didn't, but our defense counsel was easily convinced that someone else could defend Rouxe better." Benjamin tapped the surface of his desk to display a document. "This fellow named Istaga seems quite accomplished in interstellar criminal law."

In the act of raising her slate to make a note, she froze.

Benjamin looked at her quizzically. "You know this guy?"

"Yes." She thumbed her slate so she could have somewhere to look, other than his face. "Dr. Rok Shi Harridan Istaga was on the temporal-distortion weapons inspection team that came to Karthage Point, when I was the treaty liaison officer."

"*Doctor?* I can't keep track of these new degrees; what specialty qualifies him to inspect TD weapons, in addition to acting as defense counsel?" Benjamin's gaze went to the ComNet view ports on his desk, with the fascination only the crèche-get had for current events. Granted, they were always catching up; in this case, the crew of the *Pilgrimage III* had been out of touch for approximately twenty-six years. Plenty had happened since 2080, most notably the only wartime use of a TD weapon, and the cessation of warfare between the Terran League and the Consortium of Autonomous Worlds.

"Dr. Istaga was on the inspection team as an interpreter. He has a doctorate in Political Science. Apparently, his skills also extend to interstellar criminal law." She picked her words carefully, but crèche-get could be surprisingly perceptive.

"You don't believe that." Benjamin watched her face. His unlined skin, even at the corners of his eyes, didn't betray his age; he could have been as young as Justin. However, she figured Benjamin was at least 120 UT years. A transparent wariness overlaid his face and he had cynicism in his eyes that came only through wisdom.

"I don't question his education. I just can't believe *any* Terran has Rouxe's best interests at heart," she said. "Besides, Istaga's first move is to shut down access to Rouxe."

A sly frown formed on Benjamin's face. "So the Terrans are performing triage?"

"Of course. They need to control intelligence leaks. It's a golem thing."

He nodded. The crèche-get loved the fictional drama surrounding Terran and Autonomist intelligence operatives, not realizing that "golem" was an accurate description for what happened to intelligence personnel after years of mindless drudgery spent slogging through data.

While she misdirected Benjamin, she wondered why the Terran League would *really* send Dr. Istaga to G-145. Her suspicions screamed, *because Istaga is Andre Covanni.* Andre was the cover name for a shadowy legend in the intelligence field: TerraXL's most effective wartime operative, whose penchant for causing excessive civilian casualties made him a war criminal in Autonomist eyes. Andre had also specialized in assassination, performed after covert insertion behind enemy lines.

As Benjamin tapped to unlock the doors to the holding cells, she glanced at the cam-eye view ports. The *Pilgrimage III* held the isolationists who had boarded and taken it. The converts and moles who had helped them were detained instead far away on Beta Priamos Station, above the moon Priamos, orbiting the gas giant Laomedon.

The cam-eyes showed ten men, nine of them sharing cells with open bars and only one man in a solitary room. Dr. Tahir Dominique Rouxe had asked for special protection from his tribal brethren. Because he had failed to carry his father Abram's instructions out to completion, he claimed he would be a target for abuse, perhaps even murder.

Whether Tahir had botched his mission was questionable; he had still armed and detonated the stolen TD weapon, intending to escape and leave the other inhabitants in the solar system cut off from civilization and frying under an enraged sun. Only Ariane's act of pushing the detonation into N-space had minimized damage, and thwarted his father's plan.

For his cooperation, albeit *after* his crimes, Tahir had an enclosed private cell as well as controlled ComNet access. In the cam-eye view, he looked comfortable, sitting on his bed and reading his slate. It was a child's slate: soft, flexible, and with restricted functions. Pilgrimage security filtered everything that went to it.

"Okay." Benjamin groaned and picked up the spit shield. "Let's go. I've got the scrubbers going on maximum."

She nodded in sympathy. Benjamin hadn't volunteered for this job. The G-145 takeover attempt had shocked the Pilgrimage line and reverberated through the other generational ship lines as well. No longer could they consider their ships or their newly opened solar systems to be neutral territory. Even Benjamin's security "uniform," light gold coveralls with a shoulder patch, was a new concept. Before the takeover attempt, there'd been no permanent security force on the generational ship.

The crew of this generational ship hadn't wanted to build these cells. Commander Meredith protested the *Pilgrimage III* had "secure quarters for self-destructive and mental-health cases," but AFCAW advisors toured the facilities and deemed them inadequate. A new brig had to be built. It had to be managed, logically, by a new security force.

Open barred cells lined one side of the corridor they entered. The prisoners immediately noted her uniform, and the black and blue of AFCAW's Directorate of Intelligence provoked outright hatred. They must have learned the Directorate of Intelligence, in the form of Major Kedros and Master Sergeant Joyce, had killed Abram and stymied his plans for getting his own solar system. The clean transparent shield Benjamin carried was soon spattered with spit as they neared the end of the corridor. As Ariane ignored the shouted insults, she glanced at Benjamin, seeing his nose and lip twitch. Prisoner hygiene was adequate for her, but the faint tangs of desperation, hate, and sweat offended the crèche-get.

The spit shield was slimy by the time they reached the safe end of the corridor. At Tahir's cell door, Benjamin used his public password for voiceprint analysis and applied his thumbprint.

"Rouxe hasn't been violent, but I'll still wait and check every half hour. For right now, the node isn't recording. Knock when you want to leave."

Tahir stood as she entered, but there was no exchange of pleasantries. After the door locked behind her, she used her specialized slate to scan for recording pips. Terrans, fond of littering about intelligence-gathering devices, had been inside this cell. She found nothing and motioned for Tahir to sit at the small table.

"I know the drill." Tahir swung his leg over the chair, attached to the deck, and sat down to face her. He ran his hand over his severely cropped hair. "You're putting together a report, so you can figure out *why* this happened."

She shrugged. "It's called an after action report."

"What am I talking about?"

"Your life with Abram, and why he planned the theft of the Terran warhead."

Tahir sighed and she tried not to mimic him. Yes, she was doing *exactly* what the incoming Terran Counsel, the supposed academician Dr. Istaga, hoped to prevent. The golems at the Directorate of Intelligence would comb through this statement, hoping to find intelligence nuggets regarding Terran weapons programs. *The games of military intelligence stop for no one—and certainly not for "Peace."* She thumbed her slate to record and encrypt the deposition.

In a flat voice, Tahir summarized his early years with his father at Enclave El Tozeur, a community that provoked the justice of the Minoans. During their one attack, the Minoans had surgically destroyed all weapon systems and hardened bunkers. Then they had dropped genetically targeted bioweapons to sterilize the men and change the genetic structure of babies currently in the womb. Researchers were still studying the effects of those weapons, but it was universally acknowledged that the Minoans had devised a perfect punishment for men whose lives were measured by the number of their sons.

Abram couldn't strike back at the Minoans, so he channeled his frustration into capturing his own solar system, complete with scientists and crèche-get who knew how to "create" sons for his tribe. He intended to protect himself by severing his system from N-space with a TD weapon, a risky maneuver that might have destroyed G-145, had Ariane not prevented it.

By the time Tahir wrapped up his statement, Benjamin had checked on them three times.

They stared silently at each other. She stopped recording and cleared her throat. "I have a request for you. From Muse, the guy who picked us up with *Aether's Touch*."

"Yeah?" Tahir didn't sound interested, but then, he thought Muse was a person, not a rogue Artificial Intelligence. She amended her thought: Muse 3 was only rogue until Matt could get his AI development licenses. Unfortunately, the fees cost more than three years of her salary—but that was a different problem.

"Muse asks that you leave him out of your testimony, since he never encountered any of your father's men." She tried to look indifferent. "*I* said he shouldn't trust you to do that."

"I'm an honorable man." Tahir frowned; she'd hit a nerve. "Muse doesn't have to worry about my testimony, but you do. It's your face that'll be plastered over net-think. Can you handle that, Major?"

"Sure." She rose to leave. After all these years, she had confidence in her identity. Owen had created a believable new life and AFCAW had replaced expensive crystal vaults to get rid of her past identity. Now, the more data on net-think reinforcing her new identity, the stronger her identity became. As for her appearance, anyone could change their face, body, skin, and hair if they had the money. Appearance had little bearing to *identity*.

"Are the flares dissipating?" Tahir abruptly changed the subject. "Is the sun back to normal?"

She paused at the door, tempted to torment him further, because she knew the agony that lay in wondering whether people survived.... After a moment, she turned around. "The flares and radiation are winding down, so ships are making runs across the system again. Comm's operating normally."

"Ironic, isn't it?" Tahir's eyes darkened.

"How?"

"My father"—Tahir always carefully placed blame upon Abram Hadrian Rouxe—"caused much less damage with his weapon than you did at Ura-Guinn, yet you remain free and my father's followers will be charged with crimes against humanity."

Cold squeezed her heart, but she kept her voice steady. "Different circumstances. *You* detonated a TD weapon with the purpose of separating and enslaving a *civilian* population. During the war, Ura-Guinn became a valid military target when the Terrans opened a weapons development complex there."

"A thin line of distinction, Major. There were civilians in Ura-Guinn."

"Yes." She stopped. She didn't need to defend herself to Tahir.

"I hear there could be as many as four billion casualties. Do you really think the Terrans can forget that, just by saving a few thousand here in G-145?"

If you're trying to threaten me with exposure, Tahir, you're way out of your league. He looked down, breaking eye contact, as she watched him narrowly. Plenty of Terrans erroneously called her past self a war criminal and hoped for vengeance; her new identity was supposed to keep her safe from retribution. State Prince Parmet and his staff had already unmasked her, tortured her, and coerced her into signing over Matt's leases. Half a year later, Parmet himself then revealed this information to Abram and Tahir under torture.

"The Terrans are sending someone to assist in your defense. He'll be controlling all your visitors." Her voice was abrupt.

"I didn't ask for Terran counsel. Why would they want to help me?" Tahir's face tightened.

"That's a good question."

"I'm cooperating with you," he said plaintively. "I'm helping identify the security holes."

Which was why Tahir's testimony couldn't be released to ComNet: The Consortium of Autonomist Worlds and the Terran League, in spite of their chilly relationship, had agreed to classify his testimony regarding TD weapon security. Even the Minoans didn't want to publicize Tahir's escapades. Ariane watched him clasp and unclasp his hands.

"Through all this, I have one consolation," Tahir said, breaking the silence. "I don't have to wait eighteen years to see the results of my father's weapon."

She recognized what flitted across his face even though his tone was spiteful. *Pity*. She turned and pounded twice on the door, her motions jerky. He was a weak-minded criminal, driven by a desperate need for his father's approval. How *dare* he pity her?

CHAPTER 2

Nestor's tiny voice sounded from Matt's implanted ear bug. "Matt, wake up."

Nestor? Matt's eyelids jerked open and his stomach tensed. *Nestor's gone, murdered.* He relaxed as he realized he was safe in his quarters on *Aether's Touch*.

"Matt, you have an urgent call." The voice belonged to Nestor's Muse 3. Matt had allowed the burgeoning AI to manage messages, but felt he really should curb his increasing reliance on it. Until Muse 3 was fully licensed, CAW authorities could legally seize, dissect, or destroy it.

"I'll take it on control deck," he whispered.

Diana stirred beside him, muttered something unintelligible, and slid back into sleep. She lay on her side, back toward him, and he rolled so he could smell the light, delicate scent that mingled in the strands of her long chestnut hair. Raised generational, he was easily overwhelmed by soaps and oils, but Lieutenant Diana Oleander was rarely overbearing. Not even in uniform. His eyes strayed across her shoulder, which he struggled not to stroke, to the steamer where she'd put her Alpha Dress. Her uniform was no longer the colorful green, gold, and red of AFCAW operations. Last night they'd had harsh words about her change to the "black and blue," her transfer to the Special Operations Division of the Directorate of Intelligence. It was their first spat and, not surprising, it was caused by that manipulative bastard Edones: the colonel who ran that division, ordered Ari about—like a puppet—and now controlled Diana.

Sighing, he pulled on his shorts. He slipped through the hatch and into the ship's corridor without waking Diana. After quietly closing the hatch, he glanced toward Ari's quarters. The status light beside the hatch indicated they were empty. He strode to the end of the corridor and grabbed the rungs of the ladder before asking, "Who's calling, Muse Three?"

Muse 3's answer made him pause and curse. Belatedly, he considered the listening AI and its learning algorithms. "Uh, ignore my last phrase."

"Did I notify you correctly? Colonel Owen Edones is listed as Ari's supervisor and he is making a high priority call."

"You did what you were supposed to," he said as he climbed, clamping his teeth together. This was his own Gaia-b'damned fault. If he'd used the ship's automated call answering, he could have ignored the call.

He padded quietly over the warm deck in his bare feet, comfortable in the one-gee provided by the generational ship's gravity generator. They were docked with the *Pilgrimage III*, a behemoth among even generational ships. Fourteen other ships were attached to the *Pilgrimage III*, now in habitat mode. Four days ago, a Minoan warship joined them, hovering about ten kilometers away from the *Pilgrimage*. No one missed the hint: The Minoans and their warship would be staying until the Tribunal concluded.

Colonel Edones's call blinked in HOLD mode until Matt tapped for pickup.

"I'm sorry to wake you, Mr. Journey." Edones's voice was infuriatingly bland, as usual. "Do you need time to dress?"

Matt forgot he wasn't wearing anything above the waist but he was on *his* ship, so he'd answer in whatever attire he chose. Edones, on the other hand, wore his impeccable black and blue uniform. *Doesn't the stiff prick ever take it off?* Matt realized he'd never seen Edones in anything other than Alpha or Full Dress.

"What do you want?" Matt glanced at the time. If Edones were considerate, he'd have waited until Matt's publicly posted sleep shift was over.

"The Feeds are sending correspondents for the arraignment and the Minoans have classified the detonation as a violation of the 2092 testing treaty. If the correspondents get hold of *that*, they'll descend on Major Kedros."

Matt rubbed his eyes and forehead. "Everybody's already stated, *for the record*, that Ari had no choice but to send the weapon into N-space."

"Certainly, but—"

"Ari isn't here, so why wake *me*?" Matt asked bluntly, letting his hands fall into his lap. "Combined with what you're doing to Diana, this feels like harassment."

"Maybe I'm interested in whether you intend to sleep your way through my staff." Edones's tone was cool.

Ouch. Matt's face reddened. Admittedly, he usually didn't jump into bed so quickly when there was a real relationship on the line, but his mind quickly formed excuses. First, Diana had serene beauty, intelligence, and she seemed genuinely attracted to him, making this an unusual circumstance for someone who was only a boring businessman in civilized space, and an isolated second-wave prospector in new space. Second, romances were breaking out all over in the aftermath of Abram's takeover. He and Diana weren't the only ones trying not to miss any more opportunities in their newly appreciated lives. Third, and most important, he'd *never* made advances toward Ari, and any fantasies he had in that direction were none of Edones's business.

He's probing for information. Luckily, this thought

quickly cooled Matt's response. Besides, where Diana stayed when she was under open-port protocols was her own choice. Matt pressed his lips together and calmed himself. "Your remark's uncalled for, and unfounded."

"So is your assumption that my interest in Major Kedros's welfare reflects any personal feelings about you." Edones's lips stretched into a thin smile. "And if I wanted to harass you, my intentions would be obvious."

Was that, in itself, a threat? Matt hesitated. If he attempted to duel with Edones, with innuendo and subterfuge the preferred weapons, he'd be seriously outgunned. He changed to the original, safer subject. "Is Ari in danger?"

"The Directorate would like to keep Major Kedros's involvement in this incident low-profile, below the net-think exposure horizon."

Matt's eyes narrowed. This was as close as Edones had come to admitting Ari's identity was a fabrication, one that might not stand intensive scrutiny. Matt had accepted the fact that he didn't know her background since she'd proven herself, multiple times, in dangerous situations. However, he still had niggling doubts regarding the influence Edones might exert upon Ari. Her altered records could only have been sanctioned and created by AFCAW. What if Edones called in that debt?

"So?" Matt prompted.

"The correspondents will arrive in less than five hours and she's not answering my calls. She's in Recreation Four."

Matt sighed and ruffled his short hair with his fingers. Ari was drinking. In the past, she'd had an ironclad rule about not drinking in uniform, but he noticed her tenet had been spaced—put out the airlock with whatever humor she'd managed to retain after the Terrans had kidnapped and tortured her. She hadn't yet rebounded to the old Ari before Abram's isolationists tried to use her in their grand scheme. *Gaia knows, she has reason to drink.*

"Why not deliver your message in person?" Matt asked.

"Because she's in uniform and she registered for substance abuse counseling. As her supervisor, I'd have to put in a report if I saw inappropriate behavior." Edones raised an eyebrow.

Ah, he's trying to save her career. Much as Matt distrusted Edones, the Directorate, and perhaps AFCAW in general, he knew Ari valued her reserve duty. He didn't know why; perhaps she thought she was paying her dues for Ura-Guinn—his thoughts veered away, not wanting to consider what part Ari played in the TD weapon detonation that ended the war. That was information she held tight and close.

Edones waited.

Matt realized the supercilious colonel was asking for a favor. Keeping his tone resigned, he said, "I'll get her out of there. But you *owe* me for this, Edones."

Both light eyebrows rose on Edones's bland face. "I wouldn't go that f—"

Matt cut the connection. Moving with the elegant restraint of someone always testing the local gravity, he grabbed coveralls from the hall locker and pulled them on. Since third shift was usually quiet, with minimal traffic, he breezed through the airlock without checking the outer cam-eyes.

Big mistake. N-space-capable ships had no windows, so Matt stumbled in surprise when he saw the red-robed Minoan emissary standing at the bottom of the ramp to *Aether's Touch*. A guardian in black, with shorter horns but looming taller, shadowed the high-horned emissary. As always, the guardian carried a baton. Matt had intimate knowledge of how dangerous those Minoan weapons could be, having used one himself when they took the *Pilgrimage* back from Abram's men.

The emissary was already dipping its horns in greeting and he couldn't turn back. Squaring his shoulders and taking a deep breath, he continued down the ramp. The sound of his footsteps broke the stillness of third shift. He stopped more than a meter away, keeping his distance from the red robes that drifted about without the aid of a breeze.

"Contractor Advisor?" Matt wasn't sure whether this

was the same Minoan who had rescued him after he and David Ray had fled the *Pilgrimage*. Did that happen only nine days ago? At the time, David Ray Pilgrimage was the line's general counsel. Now he was on "crew sabbatical" and working for Matt, although the only way he could afford David Ray's services was by making the attorney a minority owner in Aether Exploration.

After a Minoan-length pause, while Matt tried not to fidget, the emissary said, "We recognize you, Owner of Aether Exploration, but I am Contractor Director."

He glanced at the Minoan's face, covered in the black "velvet-over-ice mask" coined by net-think, which showed only generic raised features. This Minoan *sounded* like Contractor Advisor, but might not be. After their experience aboard the Minoan ship, Matt and David Ray suspected Minoan "interfaces" were manufactured by their ships as needed for the situation. On the other hand, Contractor Advisor might be filling a new role. Even mundane humans could be multi-roled, which explained the Minoans' occasional use of Ariane-as-Kedros, when they couldn't choose between Explorer of Solar Systems and Breaker of Treaties.

"Congratulations on the promotion." Matt clamped his jaw shut. Why did he always have to make a smart-ass remark?

Contractor Director ignored his comment and got right down to business, its black-gloved hand twirling one of the many jewels cascading from the tips of its horns, while its other hand pointed toward the bulkhead. This was the standard gesture for showing information on a displayable surface, but the movement didn't feel human and Matt shivered. He looked at the view port, which pushed aside the Feeds and displayed a contract that he estimated at two hundred pages in length.

"We have received a counteroffer from the legal advisor for Aether Exploration." Contractor Director scrolled to the end of the contract, which had a confusing snarl of provisos.

Matt waited silently, since one could never go *too* slowly

when speaking with Minoans. They considered long pauses of silence to be respectful, not the result of frantically firing neurons.

Contractor Director pointed at lines highlighted on the display. "This clause is nonnegotiable. The work, as stated, requires Ariane-as-Kedros in the role of Explorer of Solar Systems."

Matt kept his jaw from dropping open. The Minoans had requested an *individual*, by *name*, in a contract? He was surprised David Ray hadn't called him but, as he checked the time of the contract change, he realized David Ray had sent the counteroffer only half an hour earlier.

"If you need Ari, what do we get in return?" Then, he rephrased it so the Minoan would understand. "If you require *Explorer of Solar Systems*, who is also *Ariane-as-Kedros*, do we get a guarantee you won't file charges against her as *Breaker of Treaties*?"

He waited for Contractor Director's response, trying not to grind his teeth. Finally, the horns dipped in assent.

"Write it up and send it to my legal staff." Not bothering with niceties, he walked away. When he was out of sight, he pulled out his slate and sent a priority message to David Ray, who comprised the entirety of his "legal staff."

He hated intimidation, even by powerful, mysterious, and yes, scary aliens. As he jammed his slate back into his pocket, he wondered if Edones had forewarning about this Minoan proviso. He eventually turned off the spoke hall, and his stride slowed as he neared the cause of all this trouble. He hoped Ari hadn't been in a brawl. *Retrieval duty*, as he used to call it, hadn't been necessary for almost a year.

The room was eerily quiet, except for the major five Feeds running mute on the walls. No one was playing games, watching Feeds, or drinking, except for a few hard cases at the bar. Even for third shift, it was strangely deserted. Matt spun around and saw the cause. Creating an imposing shadowy bulk against the back wall, Warrior Commander sat at a table. More surprising, however, was the row of drinks in front of Warrior Commander. Four drink packs were precisely arranged in a line. Matt had never seen Minoans consume food or drink.

Shrugging, he went to the bar and sat on a stool next to a sleeping Ari, whose left temple rested on her folded arms. On Ari's other side, her drinking buddy Hal Bokori, a load-master on a freighter, gently snored. His dark head rested cheek down on the bar surface, with one arm flung over Ari and the other sprawling across the bar.

"Hey, Daren. Cold papango juice, please." It was a relief not to have to say, "hydroponic sources only," because that was obvious to other crèche-get. He liked being back with his own kind, even if he was Journey rather than Pilgrim-age line.

Daren set down a drink pack and snapped the cold tab, making it frosty. He tilted his head toward Ari. "Sorry, Matt. She's protected by Autonomist privacy law, so I can't give you a report on her consumption."

Matt sighed as he put his thumbprint on the bar to pay the bill. Daren had just reminded him why he'd opted off the *Journey IV*, and how he'd chafed under the everyone-must-be-happy dictum. If Ari were crèche-get, her su-pervisor would be advised of her drinking and she'd be automatically scheduled for mental health sessions. The news would pass throughout the ship as well, resulting in pitying glances from friends and coworkers. Surpris-ingly, on Autonomist worlds with ubiquitous public Com-Net nodes, it was unlawful for an employer to track the off-duty behavior of employees if it meant violating pri-vacy. An employee could even charge an employer with stalking.

"I don't need a report, but I am curious about your new clientele." Matt jerked his thumb toward Warrior Com-mander's table.

Daren's jaw muscles tightened. "That warrior is scaring away my regular customers."

"Anybody ask why? They answer questions, you know." Matt took a sip of cold sweet liquid.

"He's been following Major Kedros around for days." Daren apparently bought the theory that Warrior Commander was male. As Matt's face stretched in surprise, Daren asked, "Where have you been, anyway?"

Matt's cheeks flushed as he took another sip. *I've had my head up my ass, I guess.* Ari was *crew* and in his world, that meant she was family and deserved loyalty beyond the employer-employee relationship assumed by grav-huggers. He should have protected her from harassment, even from Minoans, but he'd been too involved with Diana to notice. He put down the juice decisively and swiveled his stool toward Warrior Commander.

Daren put a restraining hand on his arm. "Every question's been asked."

"But—"

As Daren and Matt faced the Minoan across a sea of empty tables, a black-gloved hand appeared out of the Minoan's voluminous dark robes. Warrior Commander held up its index finger with a meaningful gesture.

Matt recoiled, his plan of marching over to Warrior Commander disappearing. "What does that mean?"

"Another drink. I said he couldn't take up space here without ordering drinks or food. He asked me for a *minimum order rate* and I told him one drink for every one or two hours, which he's interpreted as one point five hours." Daren checked the time on his sleeve. "Exactly."

Another drink for Warrior Commander added up to seven-point-five hours. Matt wasn't surprised Ari had been here that long, and he was sure she'd surpassed Warrior Commander's order rate. Both Ari and Edones tried to dismiss her alcohol tolerance, swift healing, and other aspects of her ultra-rapid metabolism as natural, but Matt suspected darker causes, such as military medical experiments.

He heard Daren pop the cold tab on a drink pack and asked, "What is Warrior Commander ordering?"

"A Hellas-brewed specialty beer, made from altensporos. Costs twelve HKD, plus import taxes, because we're sovereign Pilgrimage territory." Daren shrugged, embarrassment flitting across his face. "Hey, we have to support ourselves."

Twelve Hellas Kilodrachmas was expensive for beer and Matt suppressed a smile as Daren carried the drink pack over to Warrior Commander's table. After setting it down with a flourish and turning away, Daren didn't see Warrior Commander adjust the drink pack so it aligned with the others. Daren thought he'd pulled a fast one on the warrior, but Matt knew just how attuned the Minoans were to human economies. They knew when they were paying abnormally high prices.

Matt didn't feel like smiling anymore. Why would Warrior Commander pay premiums for unused beer, just to sit and observe Ari? Why would Contractor Director try to strong-arm Matt into signing a contract, with a clause designed just for Ari?

He looked down at the focus of the Minoans' strange behavior slumped on the bar beside him in a deep alcohol-induced sleep. Ari's lashes lay thick against the olive skin on her sharp cheekbones. Light shadows from a healing bruise on her face added vulnerability. With her eyes closed, without those deep, wise, tormented dark orbs, she looked younger than the age in her records, which was *still* younger than Matt's estimate.

Matt resisted the sudden urge to comb back the thick dark hair swirling forward on her jaw. Instead, his hand went to Hal's forearm, which he gently raised off Ari and placed on the bar. Hal snorted as he raised his head, folded his arms, and went back to sleep. Matt never asked Ari about Hal. They shared a love of drinking and if more was going on, Matt didn't want to know.

"I've got an antigrav harness, but I don't recommend using it." Daren's voice was close behind Matt, making him start. "Antigrav can make even a sober person puke. Luckily, she's small enough to carry."

"She can walk." Matt glanced at the time on his sleeve, hoping to get back to the ship before Diana woke. "I'll need some water."

Daren shook his head as he placed the water pack on the bar. "At the best, she'll be in a blackout."

"I've never seen her have a blackout," Matt said grimly.

He wished he could get some answers, himself, to Ari's strange physiology.

"Considering what she drank—"

Matt jerked his head, telling Daren to mind his own business. He shook Ari's shoulder and she groaned.

"Matt? Wha's happening?"

He shoved the water into her hand as answer, helping her get her head up and dribble water into her mouth. Ari could drink enough alcohol to kill the Great Bull, and still be able to stagger to the ship. But, by experience, he knew her recovery wouldn't be pretty.

"Thanks." After a few swallows, she became intelligible.

"Come on, let's get you home." He meant *Aether's Touch*, of course. He got her standing.

"Amazing," Daren muttered.

Matt thought he had everything working smoothly as he propelled Ari toward the door—until she saw Warrior Commander. She suddenly resisted, planting her feet firmly and swinging them both around to face the Minoan. By Gaia, she was strong.

"Warrior Commander!" Ari's voice was belligerent.

Warrior Commander stood. *Uh-oh*. Matt tugged Ari, but she was as immovable as rock.

"Ready to tell me why you're following me?" She shook off Matt and stepped forward, folding her arms. Warrior Commander started winding through the empty tables, gliding silently.

As the Minoan came closer, Matt's heart began to race. "Ari, I don't think this is a good idea."

"Too many secrets." Her voice was ragged. "What are *you* hiding, Warrior Commander?"

While this wasn't the time to vent, he understood Ari's sentiments. Everyone was scrambling to hide their vulnerabilities: The Terrans had lost control of a temporal-distortion weapon, both Terrans and Autonomists had revealed classified agreements with generational ship lines, and those ship lines couldn't protect their crews or the solar systems where they had temporary sovereignty.

Everyone concerned had requested the ComNet coverage of the ICT be heavily censored. *Everyone* included the Minoans; even they weren't exempt from this frantic cover-your-ass chaos. His gaze went to the approaching Minoan, remembering how the Minoan ship took damage *after* N-space swallowed the temporal-distortion weapon. David Ray and Matt suspected *this* Warrior Commander was a replacement, and the first Minoan warrior was—what? Recalled? Mundane human weapons had never been able to do bodily harm to a Minoan, as far as they knew.

"Leave them their secrets, Ari." Matt was uneasy. *I'm one of only two humans who witnessed a damaging blow to a Minoan ship.* He never thought the Minoans would consider him a threat to their security, but this could explain the restrictive nondisclosure agreements in the contract they'd offered Aether Exploration.

Warrior Commander stopped several paces away. Ari faced the black horned figure, nearly twice her height, and didn't even twitch. Matt thought of a shore scene he'd watched, where unstoppable seawater beat tirelessly, forever, on an immovable boulder.

"You're cleaning up, just like the rest of us. Aren't you?" Ari sounded more deranged than drunk.

The Minoan nodded, slowly and fractionally.

Matt grabbed Ari's arm and pulled, this time getting a response. "You need rest."

"Yeah. I don't feel so good." Her face was paling.

"That's no surprise. Will the warrior follow you home?"

"Doubt it." Ari looked like she needed to puke.

Warrior Commander didn't follow. Matt hurried Ari through the *Pilgrimage*'s corridors, his arm around her waist, half carrying her. She had three hours to sober up and get back to uniformed duty. *Please, St. Darius, let me get her on the ship before Diana wakes up.* For some reason, he didn't want Diana to see her like this.

CHAPTER 3

In contrast to others I won't name, *we* have not publicized casualty counts nor maintained a "death toll ticker." The factual reports of Ura-Guinn's coronal mass emissions, as we capture them sixteen years later, are horrendous enough for viewers to make their own conclusions.

–Marcus Alexander, Sophist at Konstantinople Prime University, 2106.052.08.10 UT, indexed by *Heraclitus 13* under Flux Imperative

Ariane's body convulsed and she spewed bile into the head. She felt the cool metal surface against her cheek. She was crammed inside the tiny hygiene closet on *Aether's Touch*, where Matt had propped her into position. Her stomach made another attempt to vomit something, anything, trying desperately to rid itself of poison.

No regrets this time. Too many reminders of Ura-Guinn. She had to do something to silence the ghosts rustling in the back of her brain. Slowly, sounds started separating from the confusing roar in her ears.

"Atrocious behavior ... She's a Major, a field-grade officer.... I can't believe you...." Oleander's voice rose, then faded.

Matt's voice protested. "Diana, he asked me to ..."

Only Matt called Lieutenant Oleander by her first name. From the sound, the two of them were walking down the central hallway and their conversation was resonating through the ducting. They paused at the end, unwittingly under an air duct that pressed against the deck above their heads.

"Why would he ignore her behavior?" Ariane could picture Oleander's puzzled face from her tone.

"They've got an unusual relationship." Matt's voice held distaste. "This doesn't happen often, believe me."

"You're both enabling her—you and the colonel."

"Don't compare me with that manipulator, please. Consider what she's been through ..." Matt's voice faded as they moved to a different part of the corridor, but Ariane's stomach twisted at the pity in his tone.

"Don't ... just because you're feeling guilty." Oleander's parting words came more clearly. "Anyway, I've got to leave for VIP detail."

After a murmured good-bye, Ariane closed her eyes. They sounded so—what? *Normal. Untroubled by nightmares and hidden pasts.* She envied them.

Her body was recovering. She felt her metabolism rising to process the alcohol and she was ravenous. She sighed as she looked at her wrinkled uniform and the lint highlighted on the black. It was too grubby for the light steamer installed in her quarters; she'd have to take it to the cleaners on the *Pilgrimage*.

She stood up slowly. Wiggling out of her uniform shirt and trousers wasn't difficult for her, being familiar with tiny hygiene closets. The common closet in *Aether's Touch* was luxurious when compared to some military ships.

She rinsed her mouth and cleaned her teeth. After massaging in the pre-steam shampoo and soap, she stepped into the personal steamer. It could never compare to standing in a deluge of water, but she still felt refreshed after using the steam scrubber and comb.

As she dried, she reviewed her messages on the small bulkhead surface available inside the closet. She flushed with embarrassment as she acknowledged Edones's message. Her current assignment was already low profile, and she could avoid the Feed correspondents by rearranging her interviews. She tiptoed to ship stores and then to her quarters, where she wolfed down the concentrate bars she'd grabbed and drank more water. As usual, she recovered quickly once her body went through the unpleasant purge.

After buffing every bit of regalia she could, she dressed meticulously and searched for lint, finally evaluating her uniformed figure in the view port. Her only criticism was the childlike tendency to her features, enhanced by her petite frame. Other than that, she looked every part of the controlled, disciplined AFCAW officer. *Too bad it's all a facade.*

Joyce was first on her "to do today" list, provided he was healthy enough to have visitors. She called him, expecting to speak with the infirmary nursing station. Instead, Joyce answered.

"If you're called to active duty, Major, the colonel must need me badly," Joyce said from his wardroom bed, when she tapped up video on the bulkhead.

His smile was weak and lopsided. She thought she was prepared, but her first sight of Abram's work, up close and personal, shocked her. Besides healing from broken bones, lacerations, and bruises, Joyce had undergone several surgeries for transplanted vat-grown tissue and organs.

"Very funny, Sergeant. I've been on active duty orders ever since the colonel verified the stolen weapon was in G-145." No point in mentioning that she remained in uniform because Edones was desperate for manpower, because the Directorate had to escort Senator Stephanos and augment his security. "Why are *you* slacking about in bed?"

"Don't I deserve down time after saving your ass?" His smile slipped, betraying his fatigue. "But you've outdone me this time. Saved the solar system—how can I compete with that?"

"You get an award for taking the most damage. We all thank you for taking Abram down."

He closed his eyes and nodded with satisfaction. "Sounds like you debriefed my vigilante team."

"You've got quite a fan club in this system. Your exploits grow larger with each telling."

"As they should." One eyelid raised and Joyce looked

toward the cam-eye with a piercingly clear eye that might be gray or blue, depending upon the light. "You need a statement?"

"I'm reporting on this *unfortunate incident*, which is how our leadership spins it. You up for an interview?"

"Certainly. They moved me into a private room at the end of the ward, hoping to get rid of me." He snorted. "Ask for directions at the front desk."

Once she finished the call, she made notes on her slate and checked her quarters. Everything was trim and neat. Loose articles were stowed out of sight and no personal items were displayed. This was a protective habit she'd developed; nothing could be determined about the resident, Ariane Kedros.

Aether's Touch was quiet. Matt was checking equipment status on the control deck. Short of sneaking through the cargo airlock, she'd have to walk past the control deck.

"Ari, can I have a word with you?" he called as she went by. He motioned for her to enter as he ruffled his short, dark blond hair with his other hand. His gaze roved over the front display area as he stood behind the piloting seat, so he didn't see her take a moment of appreciative regard. His strong, clearly defined nose and jaw were in profile. Not yet hidden by loose coveralls, his stretchy under-insulation easily defined the lean muscles on his generational frame. Glancing away and putting her thoughts in order, she stepped through the hatch, careful not to scuff her shoes.

"Thanks for—" She didn't know how to continue.

"Don't mention it. I suppose you keep extra Alpha Dress handy?" Matt looked her over and his brown eyes, usually warm with a friendly glint, cooled as his expression soured. It took her a moment to realize he was viewing the *uniform* with disfavor. Matt's ire was about Owen Edones, probably regarding Owen's recent recruitment of Lieutenant Oleander into the Directorate.

"Matt, regardless of what you think, working for the Directorate is an honor. Oleander—Diana has to be an outstanding officer to be selected for the black and blue."

Why, for Gaia's sake, was she defending *Owen*? Nonplussed, she looked down at the tips of her boots, buffed into a glassy shine. And why wasn't she in her "military mode"? Ariane was too young to call her commanding officer by his first name, even in her thoughts. Her lives, military and civilian, were blurring. *I'm Major Ariane Kedros. I work for Colonel Edones as an intelligence officer.*

"You don't have to tell me Diana's exceptional," Matt muttered.

She nodded. Oleander had to have top scores in mental, physical, and weapon skill tests; she also had to be one of the thirty percent with the capability of accepting her own vat-grown tissue and organs. Ariane figured this wasn't the time to mention *that* Directorate qualification to her civilian boss.

"I hope—" Matt's face flushed. "We aren't making you uncomfortable, are we? When Diana stays here on the ship."

"No, of course not. I'm used to crowded living," she replied quickly. She was *happy* for Matt and Oleander. *Honestly* happy. Those minor jabs of envy were only reminders of what she'd lost; she'd never feel the heady innocence of new love again. As for the tight quarters and lack of privacy, she'd been in worse situations on AFCAW ships.

"Just checking. After all, both you and Diana were raised planet-side." To Matt, that explained a multitude of idiosyncrasies and erratic behavior.

"I should get to my duties." She paused. "Thanks for retrieving me. It won't happen again, I promise."

"Sure." He ducked his head. He probably didn't believe her hollow promise, but then, neither did she. "By the way, who is Tafani?"

"What?"

"You seemed to be rehashing an argument with this Tafani as we came home."

She'd asked Edones for a cleared AFCAW therapist, although Major Tafani wasn't allowed to see the Directorate's "Special Access" material. Too bad he ended up being a twit who couldn't understand her situation. To be fair, he never knew the truth: her identity, military history, and the experimental rejuv procedures. While she considered how to respond, she saw Matt's unfocused eyes come back to her. He'd already forgotten his question, obviously distracted by something deeper.

"How long will you be on active duty orders?" he asked.

"Don't know. These were executed under emergency conditions and there's no end date."

"You think you can get Edones to free you? Aether Exploration might have a contract, but I'll need you and David Ray." Matt's forehead crinkled and his eyes looked worried.

"I'm not sure." With Edones's manpower situation, she didn't think it likely. "Perhaps we can talk about this after the arraignment at thirteen hundred. Send a reminder to my queue."

Matt nodded and she escaped his foreboding somberness. She rubbed her temples, trying to soothe away the minor throbbing pain that she, admittedly, deserved. She hoped she didn't have to choose between her reserve duty and her job as pilot of *Aether's Touch*. Giving her headache an even better foothold, Warrior Commander waited for her at the edge of the ship's dock area.

This was the first time Diana Oleander wore the black and blue uniform of the Directorate of Intelligence. She examined the light blue rank trim on the sleeves and checked for lint on the sea of black covering her body. The uniform had looked unusual on her, almost menacing, but she didn't feel any different today. *Just the same old Diana.*

One rumor about the Directorate turned out to be true. They said once you sold your soul to the black and blue, you never go back—to normal ops, that is. Colonel Edones had presented her with paperwork to sign at the beginning of shift that restricted her future assignments.

"We can't risk our core intelligence officers falling into enemy hands, Lieutenant. Signing this means you understand your future assignments must be approved by the Directorate." Edones smiled impersonally as he handed her the slate for her thumbprint.

Falling into *enemy* hands? As she signed, she wondered
what risk he alluded to, and which enemies. The war had
ended more than fifteen years ago. Perhaps, for older officers such as Edones, the Terran Expansion League would
always be the evil foe.

"Are the plainclothes missions that dangerous?" she
asked.

"Field operatives are specially trained and they're the
only ones assigned covert missions. You can train for such a
position later, if you wish." He glanced at her sharply.

She looked away. Matt had speculated about Major Kedros's sporadic and mysterious missions. In particular, he
was incensed by Kedros's last mission, which had turned
out to be extremely dangerous even though she'd been in
uniform. Then there was the seriously wounded Sergeant
Joyce, who initially traveled to G-145 out of uniform. Apparently, one could be put in harm's way, regardless of mission uniform.

Oleander sensed those particular mission reports were
off-limits. Besides, they were at the opposite end of the
danger scale from her duty today. She smoothed her new
uniform as she waited outside the airlock. Edones called
this the public relations meet-and-greet, but it was a chance
of a lifetime for her. How else would she ever meet Jude
Stephanos, the senior senator for Hellas Prime?

The lights above the passenger airlock turned green. After it was opened by the crew, the familiar broad figure of
Senator Stephanos was not the first to step out. Instead, a
young man with intricately braided long hair appeared. He
wore an expensively tailored suit that emitted, tastefully
but with a mesmerizing flicker, the latest fashionable color
rotation. His thin olive face puckered with disapproval as
he looked over the assemblage at the dock, then smoothed
as he focused on Edones and Oleander at the bottom of
the ramp.

Her eyes widened as the young man lurched toward
them. Some people just couldn't handle artificial gee,
namely "grav-huggers," as Matt disdainfully called them.
Even though the *Pilgrimage* was nominally one gee, it just

didn't feel natural to have a point source pulling you in a direction that wasn't perfectly *down*. To compensate, the decks curved in strange ways, but they could generate nausea. The man's expression indicated exactly that possibility and she almost stepped forward to intercept him, but hesitated when Edones cleared his throat.

Miraculously, the passenger stayed on his feet and came to a stop in front of Colonel Edones. "Good—you're here just in time. The senator's bags are ready in his state room."

"*Pardon?*" The Colonel's tone would have frozen the eyebrows off a more astute individual, but this stylish man was undaunted.

"The senator and his staff have carry-on—"

A beefy hand settled on the man's shoulder and startled him, as well as Oleander. She hadn't noticed Senator Stephanos walk down the ramp, even though there was no mistaking his broad shoulders and barrel chest set on short stocky legs. Those legs, however, were steady under station gee.

"Myron, these are AFCAW *intelligence officers*. They're not baggage handlers." The Senator's voice was dry. The Feeds often described his craggy face, trimmed beard, and thick bushy hair as ursine. Stephanos's politics had been described that way as well; he'd savaged many opponents on the floor of the Consortium Senate, and because of this, he purportedly always wore light, expensive body armor in public.

"Fine. I'll send a remote." Myron looked as sulky as a ten-year-old. His hand started moving toward his other wrist, where his implant was installed.

"Remotes aren't allowed on the *Pilgrimage*," Oleander said quickly.

"What?" Myron's eyes widened and for the first time, his gaze flitted around the slip bulkheads and focused on the larger docking ring corridor. Even though there was extensive foot traffic, he must have just noted the lack of remotes and dizzying displays fighting for space on walls and ceilings. On any Autonomist habitat, he'd be the focus of commercials touting any business vaguely connected to his spending habits. He'd have to pay for suppression of commercials, or privacy, but he didn't have to worry about that on the *Pilgrimage*.

"How do I call for baggage sleds or handlers?" He turned his wide dark eyes on Oleander. They expressed the harried look of a civilized man dropped suddenly into savage circumstances, but like a thin layer of oil sliding across water, his emotions disappeared. She saw *nothingness*, an empty shell. Suppressing a shiver, she turned away from Myron to look at the senator and his security detail of two brutish men.

"Check in with hostel services." Stephanos gently pushed Myron toward a kiosk on the main corridor bulkhead.

After Myron left, Stephanos shook his head. "My sister's grandson. All her careful work to ensure an original Colonist bloodline, and that's what she gets."

There was no appropriate response for this comment. After a pause, Edones said tonelessly, "Welcome to the *Pilgrimage Three*, Senator. Lieutenant Oleander and I are available to assist you."

She stood straighter. Stephanos's gaze flickered over her, checked her nametag and decorations. She nodded politely, but he'd already dismissed her, his attention back to Edones.

"You're a lucky bastard, Colonel." Stephanos chuckled dryly. "I just put your superiors at the Directorate on the chopping block, but senatorial ire rarely descends to the O-6 level."

"Too low on the food chain?" Edones said.

"You uncovered the theft of the weapon, but then, I'd have expected the Directorate to be on top of that in the first place." Stephanos's eyes narrowed, perhaps searching for sarcasm in Edones's politic face. Oleander glanced at her commanding officer, noting his slightly pink ears. Edones was impossible to read, but she was sure of one thing: He wasn't feeling lucky right now.

Noise at the top of the airlock ramp distracted the senator. Oleander leaned sideways to look around the senator's security bulwark of personnel and saw a handful of offloading passengers arguing with *Pilgrimage* officials. Small antigrav multi-cam-eye recorders, somewhat larger than remotes, hovered above the argument. They spun and whirred, jostling one another for the best views of the altercation.

"The Feeds have released their hounds." Stephanos looked over his shoulder. "I've had a lifetime of their complaints already on this trip. They're not happy about having to travel *personally* to cover their news."

"Our security plan allows them one recording device each, which can't go remote. Fortunately for us, the *Pilgrimage* doesn't have the nodes to provide a continuous mesh network." Edones gestured toward the main corridor. "If you'll follow me, Senator, I'll brief you on the security plans."

Oleander ended up at the tail of the procession, behind the security posse and beside the muttering Myron. Between Myron's complaints about the lack of facilities, she heard scraps of conversation floating between Edones and Stephanos.

"Our security plans will stand scrutiny by the Terrans," Edones said.

Stephanos mentioned Terran State Prince Duval. She craned to hear the colonel's answer, but Myron poked her in the shoulder.

"If the Feed correspondents are allowed remotes, then why can't I operate one?" Myron asked.

After she finished explaining that cam-eye platforms had to be kept near enough to be controlled by the correspondent's equipment, which didn't really qualify as *remote* operation, the conversation between Edones and Stephanos had moved on.

"They won't like being barred from the classified sessions, but we've got no alternative." Edones jerked his thumb toward the mayhem they left behind at the docks.

"As long as net-think believes these men are getting fair trials. If I hear even a whiff of a rumor of railroading, I'm making it the Directorate's business to stamp it out."

"We can't affect net-think."

"Perception is everything." The senator paused, and their procession bunched up and stuttered to a halt. Stephanos looked sharply at Edones. "Those correspondents are the only senses net-think has in G-145. They must show a cooperative Terran-Autonomist-Pilgrimage Tribunal giving this isolationist scum their due process of interstellar law. Do you understand?"

"Yes, sir," Edones said.

Myron poked Oleander in the shoulder again and she tried not to grit her teeth. It was going to be a very long morning.

At the infirmary desk, the medical technician on shift glanced at Warrior Commander before firmly averting her eyes. The Minoan hung back, staying a couple of meters behind Ariane, who had almost forgotten its presence.

"The sergeant's monitor says he's awake." The technician looked at her console. "Yesterday, he was only conscious for an hour or so. He made a supreme effort to speak with his family, using head shot only, of course. His wife might suspect the extent of his injuries, but his kids don't."

"I'm sure that was his purpose." Ariane smiled. She'd never met Joyce's children and only met his wife once.

"He collapsed afterward. But early this morning he looked good enough to move him out of critical care." The technician frowned. "Comm to the room is down. That node has to be replaced—just like everything else."

"It worked this morning." Ariane shrugged in sympathy. This was why generational ships had a year or two of downtime after hauling a buoy to an unexplored solar system. They spent ten to seventy years at sub-light speeds, and when they arrived to set up the buoy, allowing faster-than-light (FTL) travel to that system, their technology was dated. The *Pilgrimage III* was being retrofitted with new ComNet nodes, as well as other enhancements.

"Go ahead, while I call maintenance. His room's around that corner and at the far end."

She walked in the direction the woman pointed and

found a long corridor with an exit beside Joyce's room at the end. The technician wasn't correct in assuming he was awake, because he didn't answer her chime. After two tries, she opened the unlocked door and peeked in.

Something was wrong. Joyce lay in an awkward position, obviously unconscious, amid rumpled bedclothes. Even though the monitor beeped quietly and cheerily at the foot of his bed, his breath was shallow, his skin was pale and had a light sheen of sweat. She stepped to the foot of the bed and examined the monitor, started tracing the leads under the top sheet to where they connected to—

The monitor leads disappeared under the bed frame, instead of plugging into Joyce's implants. A whispering sound at the door made her look around; Warrior Commander stood there with a slightly cocked head, as if homing in on a sound beyond human senses.

A frigid breeze brushed her and she stepped backward. The Minoan was suddenly kneeling beside the bed, reaching under it. When Warrior Commander stood, it held out its gloved hands. On the right hand rested a tiny sensor pad that connected via a thin wire to a small cylindrical device in the left hand. Her throat tightened: *a Terran antipersonnel grenade*, smaller than Warrior Commander's palm. An old but reliable device used by TEBI during the war, designed to maim and wound. A device that couldn't be separated from its sensor without causing detonation.

She whispered, "Don't break the wi—"

Warrior Commander closed long inhuman fingers over the two devices and pulled. She heard the wire snap as she threw herself on the bed to cover Joyce.

CHAPTER 4

The establishment of an interstellar criminal tribunal (ICT) for some horrendous happening in G-145, muffled like a government cover-up, has net-think focusing upon the roots of interstellar criminal law. AIs are scurrying to index this history, relegated to the obscurity of late-twentieth-century pre-Terran Earth. . . .

—Dr. Net-head Stavros, 2106.052.22.04 UT, indexed by *Heraclitus 17* under Flux Imperative

Ariane landed lengthwise on the bed, covering Joyce's torso and head. She waited, tensely, for the deafening explosion and the pain of molten metal piercing her back and legs. She winced at a muffled pop and crackle.

"You are safe, Breaker of Treaties."

She raised her head to look at Warrior Commander and cleared her throat. "What happened?"

"Please make your emergency call."

Right—the *Pilgrimage* had to be warned. She pressed her implant mike. "Emergency, nine-one-one. We need an explosive ordnance disposal team in infirmary room three-two-seven. This is Major Kedros." The traditional emergency code should be routed to the control deck, by any means possible. She heard warning alarms start in the corridor. Her message went through, so the node in Joyce's room really *did* work, at least for processing base-level emergency directives.

The Minoan warrior had its hands tightly closed, held

carefully away from its torso. Slowly, its hands uncurled to show the sensor pad in one and a molten mass of metal in the other. A strange and unpleasant smell filled the room, partly caustic explosive, and partly—what? The Minoan gloves, apparently, weren't made of leather.

When she reached to touch what had once been a grenade, Warrior Commander stepped back and said, "It will burn your skin."

"Room three-two-seven, this is *Pilgrimage* command deck. Major Kedros, are you there?" The voice, carrying over the alarms, came from the comm panel next to the door. "A damage assessment team is on its way, and we've called for explosive ordnance disposal personnel from the *Bright Crescent*."

The medical technician bustled in, checked Joyce, and called for support. More medics pushed their way to the bed and fussed over Joyce. Then, as if there weren't enough people in the room already, the AFCAW Explosives Ordnance Disposal team showed up. She convinced Warrior Commander to hand over what was left of the grenade to the EOD team. There wasn't any space to move, particularly with everyone trying to keep a safe distance from Warrior Commander. The medics noticed this also, and demanded that all nonmedical personnel get out of the room.

She quickly complied, followed by Warrior Commander, and found a crowd had formed outside Joyce's room. People started appearing from nowhere. She saw Lieutenant Oleander appear with a thin sallow man.

Captain Doreen Floros, another Directorate golem, was suddenly at her elbow and remarked, "You seem to attract explosives, Major Kedros."

"What happened?" asked Benjamin Pilgrimage.

Then it got crazy—rather, *crazier*. Feed correspondents showed up, with their platform cam-eyes and bright lights. Everybody who was anybody seemed to be squeezing into the infirmary hallway, shouting questions at Ariane. She started edging into the no-man's zone around Warrior Commander, a perimeter of about one meter, just to get space to breathe. Against her back, she felt cold air stirring those black robes. Once, when she glanced down and behind her, she glimpsed a writhing darkness within a fold of the robes, whereupon she suppressed a shudder and kept her gaze forward.

"Clear this infirmary. Now!" This came from the Chief Medic, who persevered with a loud voice. *Pilgrimage* security came to her rescue, breaking up the crowd.

"Thank you for saving our lives," Ariane said quietly, directing her words over her shoulder.

Warrior Commander's head dipped in acknowledgment.

"Research is in shambles, SP, particularly the programs for the Builders' buoy." Maria Guillotte was conferencing in from the surface of Priamos. Her image showed the upper half of her body for *somaural* communication.

"That's good. We want to replace those contractors with Terran companies," Ensign Walker said.

A typical response from a young Terran Space Force officer, and State Prince Isrid Sun Parmet gave him a tight smile, adding a subtle flourish with his fingers that said, *You still have much to learn.* Ensign Walker's jaw tightened.

Maria, who had worked for Isrid for many years in TEBI and then as his personal aide, explained. "We can't just move in on other contracts or leases, Ensign. The Consortium's S-triple-ECB requires an organized, and unfortunately bureaucratic, process."

"Who owns those leases?" Walker was apparently familiar with the Consortium's Space Exploration, Exploitation, and Economics Control Board, or SEECB.

"Aether Exploration," Maria said.

"Oh." Walker's eyebrows went up.

So did Isrid's assessment of Ensign Walker. He'd hoped to get an experienced officer to manage security on Beta Priamos Station, but at least Walker had read his classified background briefings. The ensign would know the delicate difficulties: Isrid had coerced Aether Exploration, in the person of Major Ariane Kedros, into signing leases over to Terran interests. Ensign Walker might also know more classified details, such as Kedros's being kidnapped by Maria, then tortured by Nathanial Wolf Kim, both of whom were Isrid's aides. However, Isrid hoped Walker was oblivious to the most recent reason Kedros might hate him: His co-wife Sabina had taken out her revenge and her rage, physically, upon an inebriated Kedros. That seemed so long ago, although it happened only a day before Abram's aborted takeover.

"We can petition for contractor reassignment, but I doubt Aether Exploration will consider it." Isrid's co-wife Garnet showed her usual efficiency, making a note on her slate.

When Pilgrimage HQ contracted Isrid and his staff to manage the station, Garnet took over administrative work in the scramble to continue Priamos research and development after Abram's short reign of terror. Abram had killed off almost a fifth of the civilian contractors because they "worked for Minoans." Specifically, they'd worked for an Autonomist company named Hellas Nautikos that was majority-funded with Minoan capital.

"Don't bother petitioning," Maria told Garnet. "Every contractor and lessee will submit rebuttals; they'll hold their leases tight, even if they can't afford to work them right now. The problem is the Autonomist banks and insurers—they're the ones who won't take the risks."

While the others brainstormed solutions for the research gridlock, Isrid sensed a presence in an alcove by the far doors. The yellow-green froth of her aura, smelling like pines, gave Sabina away. Unexpectedly, he'd started sensing auras even when he wasn't deep in trance—ever since Abram had pumped him full of pain enhancers and psychotropic fear inducers.

The meeting agenda turned to security. Ensign Walker's current roadblock was convincing Pilgrimage HQ to change their position on background investigations. "We're still trusting research contractors to screen their own personnel."

"You won't get Pilgrimage to budge on that, since Abram's converts didn't come from any R and D contractors," Garnet said.

"But his moles in station maintenance did more than enough harm," Walker shot back. "And they were the result of lax background investigations."

Isrid stopped the developing squabble with a gesture. "What about expanding ComNet coverage?" he asked. "It would improve station security, as well as help the Autonomist contractors."

"ComNet says they can't afford hazard pay and insurance premiums for workers in G-145." Walker shook his head. "Ironically, we've got two of their best installers in lock-up for helping Abram. Neither had a criminal history, before this."

"Can we use prisoner labor? Those two installers could extend our coverage."

"Pilgrimage HQ will probably require they volunteer their skills," mused Walker, obviously feeling his way through a morass of unfamiliar regulations. "And I'm sure there are plenty of Autonomist legal hoops to jump through."

Likewise, Isrid had no authority over non-Terran assets or personnel, other than what Pilgrimage HQ and the Consortium's SEEECB allowed him. Besides, what was there to control? Right now, some bored troops rattled around Beta Priamos station, frozen midconstruction, while the station's upkeep overwhelmed the remaining maintenance staff. The research facilities on Priamos's surface were understaffed as well.

Ensign Walker finished his report, adding nothing new. After Isrid adjourned, the ensign left as quickly as politeness allowed.

Garnet's gaze rose from her slate and fixed on the dark alcove near the far doors. "Looking for entertainment, Sabina? Can't find any drunks to roll?" Her voice carried an uncharacteristic streak of annoyance.

Isrid's curiosity was piqued as he watched his wives. Garnet was usually indifferent to Sabina's tempestuous behavior but not this most recent sulk. His wives hadn't come through Abram's crucible unchanged, and neither had he, proven by the haze of aura he caught in the corner of his eye when he looked away from people. Everyone knew the body emitted an electromagnetic field; Autonomists transferred data over it and Terran *somaural* masters claimed they could be seen via meditative trance—but *this* wasn't normal. Should he see a doctor? Whom could he trust, here in G-145?

The faint sound of airlocks closing carried through the curved conference room bulkheads, the result of Ensign Walker making best speed to the Security Control Center. Sabina stepped out of the alcove with taut and controlled movements. She rivaled Isrid in *somaural* projection and showed off her artistry whenever she could.

"We've received a threatening message," Sabina said.

Why the drama? He signaled Sabina to follow standard procedure. His public queue received several threats an hour, according to his security staff.

"Has Flynn tagged it? Do Erica and Yvette need to take special precautions?" Garnet frowned, her thoughts going to their daughters.

He'd spent precious out-of-system bandwidth this morning to talk with his daughters and neither had mentioned security problems. Luckily, they still lived within the secure family complex on Mars; Erica was beginning university courses and Yvette was studying for her secondary school finals. They assured him this hiatus from parental oversight wasn't hindering their studies—although he read the subtext of joyous freedom in their voices. It was a false joy, since Erica and Yvette knew the household staff sent daily reports and *all* their parents read them, down to the last detail. It was one of the disadvantages of only having three parents when Terran society considered a balanced child-rearing multimarriage as three fathers and three mothers.

"The threat wasn't routed to Mars." Sabina's fingers added, *Our daughters are safe.* "It popped up on our private queue here at Beta Priamos."

"Over ComNet? Unlikely, given its privacy controls," Isrid said.

Garnet poked at her slate. "Perhaps that's the point. Whoever sent this knows where we are—physically."

"I think the point's made clear in the text," Sabina said.

"The message promises dire consequences for a State Prince who allowed 'a *destroyer of Ura-Guinn to go free*, and for his *family*."

It was a reference to Major Kedros. Not many people knew her background, let alone that he'd ransomed her safety for the G-145 leases. *Finally, something serious.* Isrid picked up his slate, knocked out of an ennui brought on by station issues ranging from clearing sewage smells on Ring Three, to allowing prisoners their rightful hour of exercise under the Pilgrimage legal system.

"Flynn's already analyzing the message." Sabina stopped him from searching his queue.

"This goes no further—only *our* security will work this," Isrid said. Garnet and Sabina nodded agreement; this was something they'd only trust to Flynn and his staff.

"Flynn will have his analysis to you in an hour and he's sending more personnel." Sabina cocked her head to indicate the brawny male and female bodyguards outside the conference room. Flynn's staff refused to be caught delinquent again in their protection of the State Prince and his family.

Garnet sighed, probably weary of being trailed everywhere on a sparsely populated station.

"Flynn also passed a keyword message, which I saved in your queue. The message is, *Andre's coming to the dance, but his card is empty*." Sabina quoted the message word for word, understanding the necessity for accuracy, but moved quickly to the true source of her ire. "Isrid, this threat is your fault. Your son wouldn't be in this danger if you'd executed Kedros when you had the chance."

"I don't need to hear this again," Garnet murmured.

He watched Garnet thoughtfully as she left the room with a calm and purposeful stride.

"Our family is threatened by your actions." Sabina raised her voice. "Or more accurately, by what you failed to do."

He slowly turned to look at Sabina, baiting her. *We've been cooped up on this station for too long.* His multimarriage had stood the test of time, perhaps only because he was absent for long stretches: first for the war, then for

TEBI, and during the past decade, for political missions directed by Overlord Three. Now his multimarriage was having to endure Maria's absence; more specific, his needy wife Sabina was going through withdrawal from her lover.

"You had the chance to kill Kedros, yet you didn't. Why not?" Sabina's fingers flickered questions, or insults, depending upon the interpretation: *Too intimidated? Too greedy?*

As intended, she hit a nerve. His outrage propelled him out of his chair and across two meters of floor before she could move. Surprised, she took an involuntary step backward to press against the curved bulkhead. He restrained her movement by placing his hands flat against the bulkhead on either side of her, but carefully kept his body centimeters away from hers, never touching.

"*I* had the chance to infuse our economy with Autonomist money—what's your excuse?" His voice was a cold snarl.

"What?" Sabina, unusually petite for a Terran, glared up at him.

"You had the chance to kill Major Kedros, yet you didn't. Why not?" He echoed her question back at her.

"Not enough time. Couldn't do it cleanly." Her voice was breathy and her words were a lie. She didn't know why she hadn't finished Kedros, and her body language shouted her confusion.

He knew Sabina wasn't really interested in *his* reasons. Taking the same care as he would with a dangerous captured animal, he tucked a short lock of her burgundy hair behind her ear. The dilation of her pupils told him what she wanted: attention.

His fingers traced her delicate ear and moved down her neck, stroking warm skin that used to look like translucent porcelain. It was now temporarily copper-colored, as if burned by solar radiation. Sabina had made the very un-Terran move of getting a skin-do at an Autonomist salon that had recently opened on the station. She hadn't let them touch her natural hair color, of course. Garnet had been duly horrified, possibly more by the salon bill than

Sabina's appearance. The skin-do would fade, and Isrid was indifferent to the change, but strangely attracted by Sabina's *act*, her defiance of Terran decorum. Troublesome women enticed him and Sabina had always known this.

"How much time?" she asked.

He looked at the display on the wall. "Twenty minutes. I've got a meeting with Maintenance, then the arraignment."

"You work best under deadline." She leapt up, her legs gripping his hips. Her opening mouth met his as he pressed her against the bulkhead.

Their bodyguards would hear what they were doing, but they wouldn't interrupt. This was just another example of his power and it went straight to his groin like any aphrodisiac.

Ariane had no time to meet with Matt, because Colonel Edones drew her aside to give a statement to *Pilgrimage* security. She did message to say she and Joyce were all right, perhaps exaggerating how "safe" Joyce was, since the medics thought he'd been given a dangerously high dose of sedative. As for other mysteries, she didn't speculate; she didn't know whether she and Joyce were specific targets, or whether the timing and location of the explosive device were relevant. Still in reaction mode, she didn't have time to think about the bigger questions.

Edones ordered lunch delivered to the security office, where Benjamin Pilgrimage took her statement. Benjamin sniffed at the covered dishes when they arrived, but proceeded with recording the deposition. She gulped down food between answers, not even tasting it. Meanwhile, the ship's time display edged closer and closer to thirteen hundred.

"We need more information, Ariane, but the arraignment's starting," Benjamin said. "Its exposure ratings are already climbing, and net-think predicts it'll be the most reviewed event of 2106."

The arraignment was held in the largest facility the *Pilgrimage* could provide: a small amphitheater for entertainment and presentations. Right now, the chaos matched a going-out-of-business sale at Athens Point's biggest shopping mall, without the clouds of remotes, of course.

After she entered, Ariane made her way toward the small cluster of Directorate uniforms, keeping an eye on the recorders hovering above the press box. They whirred and circled their handlers tightly, but they seemed enamored of Warrior Commander, who had followed her to the amphitheater, but now sat across from the press box. Five guardians sat behind Warrior Commander. The red-robed Contractor Director wasn't present.

"There are more important fish for the Feeds to fry, Major." Captain Floros smirked as Ariane sat down, taking the vacant aisle seat.

Floros was right. They'd just had the equivalent of a decompression scare, but the Feeds had moved on. She and Joyce were old news within the hour, which was fine by her.

The Directorate of Intelligence personnel clumped together in a dark row behind a sea of AFCAW red and gold service dress coats. On the other side of Captain Doreen Floros sat Lieutenant Diana Oleander. Next in the row sat Colonel Owen Edones and the newly arrived sublieutenant, Matthaios. Notably missing were Major Bernard, sent home to die of complications from radiation exposure, and Master Sergeant Joyce.

A hush moved over the amphitheater as the Tribunal members filed in to sit at their bench on the dais. Representing the President of the Consortium of Autonomous Worlds was Senator Stephanos. Following him, representing the Pilgrimage ship line and family, who still held sovereignty over G-145, was Senior Commander Meredith of the *Pilgrimage III*. The recent hostile intrusion, takeover, and recovery had aged Meredith; Ariane noticed new creases on the Commander's face.

Last came the hatchet-faced Terran SP Duval, representing Overlord Six and the empire that now styled itself the *Terran League*, dropping the outdated "Expansion" term whenever they could. She leaned forward and twisted her head to look up at the wall displaying about forty-odd virtual attendees, searching for SP Parmet. Since there were so many remote testimonies to take, the *Pilgrimage* support crew opted to use hologram and v-play technology only when someone was on the witness stand, so flat view ports crowded together to show heads and shoulders of remote attendees.

SP Parmet's view port was so small, she couldn't see if he still had bruises and electrode burns on his face, courtesy of Abram and his men. The interstellar justice community had asked the League to provide another representative, since Parmet couldn't sit on the Tribunal as well as give testimony against the accused. To everyone's surprise, the League sent a representative from Overlord *Six*. After all, the weapon came from Overlord Three's arsenal, Tahir had thwarted Three's security, and Abram had personally assaulted Three's staff. On the other hand, many thought the League chose Duval because Abram's home, Enclave El Tozeur on planet New Sousse, was within Duval's territory and under Overlord Six.

Edones was not so sure. Ariane saw him lean forward as Duval stepped up on the dais, watching carefully. He admitted he was troubled by this prominence of Overlord Six, the Overlord historically most hostile toward CAW. Beside her, Floros kneaded tense fingers together. The dour captain probably missed her slate. Recording devices, other than those registered to the press and security, were forbidden inside the amphitheater.

Ariane leaned back and closed her eyes. *Just a moment of rest, please*—her eyes flew open as Commander Meredith opened the procedures with the sound of pipes.

"I call to order the Fifth Interstellar Criminal Tribunal created under the authority of Pax Minoica." Meredith's amplified voice filled the large space. "This tribunal will address the charges against Abram Hadrian Rouxe's original conspirators. The following must stand: Rand Douchet, Jareb Rouxe, Manuel Delacroix . . ."

Directly in front of the bench, men in brown jumpsuits stood up as Meredith called their names. They seemed subdued and she wondered if they were finally convinced of the gravity of their situation. After all, the Tribunal could recommend the death penalty, which was still in effect in parts of the Terran League. Perhaps Rand, Abram's man in control of the *Pilgrimage III* during the takeover, was learning to use the legal system. With Abram dead, Emery gone, and Tahir expelled, Rand became leader of this tribal band. The two-meter-high view port on the wall showed him turning calmly to speak to his defense counselors. In contrast to Tahir, Rand had requested Terran legal support.

"Emery Douchet is charged in absentia." On the wall behind Meredith, a face she knew well appeared in a large view port.

Emery looked very much like Tahir, his cousin, but his eyes were much darker, having a reptilian arrogance mixed with a gleam of fanaticism and hate. She wondered why the Tribunal pretended there was a chance Emery could come back from the hell of N-space, where she had sent him.

". . . hereby charged under two articles. The first is Article Two, covering grave breaches of the Phaistos Protocols."

She stretched her legs to shake off Meredith's soporific drone. These were the trivial charges. On the display going straight out on the Feeds, she saw Rand smirking. Her lids drooped. Squirming, she shifted to get a better view, hoping her movement would help her stay awake. Meredith finally arrived at the important charge.

"The defendants are charged with crimes against humanity, under Article Five. Specifically, the intent to isolate and enslave the population of G-145 by detonating a temporal-distortion weapon."

Over in the press box, there was a subdued flutter at this first mention of a temporal-distortion weapon. Suddenly, video of Warrior Commander lost out to closeups of the defendants. Correspondents were rapidly tapping slates, probably messaging cohorts to perform research. Meanwhile, the defendants took their seats as Commander Meredith started formal witness disclosure for the prosecution, which was why most of the audience had to attend *in person*, giving their thumbprints at the door. Only witnesses who had justified their absence to the tribunal could attend virtually. She scanned the rows of tiny view ports and saw several people sleeping, including Tahir. His justification for attending virtually was the threat of bodily harm, made by the defendants.

The Pilgrimage prosecution attorney stood up and began calling his witnesses. Today's disclosure was a formality. The counsels for prosecution and defense had already exchanged witness lists, gone through their challenges, and stripped hearsay witnesses.

Ariane saw her name displayed before the attorney read it. Her fingers gripped the arms of her chair and she felt an odd surreal moment until she saw the verification symbol appear beside her name. *Because there never was a real Ariane Kedros.* Her identity was an expensive fabrication, engineered by the Directorate after the Ura-Guinn mission.

"Now for virtual attendees. Provide your voiceprint and thumbprint when I call your name, please." The Pilgrimage attorney for the prosecution turned toward the wall of view ports. Audience heads swiveled, mimicking him.

"State Prince Isrid Sun Parmet, home of record: Mars . . . AFCAW Master Sergeant Alexander Joyce, home of record: Hellas Daughter . . ."

As the prosecution called each name, the view port expanded so everyone in the amphitheater could see details. Joyce was still unconscious and a medic verified his identity. Parmet's face barely showed the torture he had suffered. Sabina—*that psychotic bitch*—had gotten a skin-do since Ariane had last seen her, but Garnet and Maria looked the same. The only witness of minor age, Chander Sky Parmet, was a striking combination of Sabina and Parmet's genes, having golden skin, green eyes, and chestnut hair with burgundy tones. Chander replied confidently in a clear voice. These Terran witnesses were on Beta Priamos, which was a nine-hour trek, on average, across the solar system.

"Dr. Tahir Dominique Rouxe, current home of record: Teller's Colony."

This was the prosecution's star witness and every face in

the audience turned toward the expanding view port that showed—*nobody*. The node cam-eye had algorithms for finding and focusing on bipedal forms and human faces. The cam-eye panned back and forth, showing a small room with a small service panel, a bed, and a table with chair. Where was Tahir? Ariane had seen him, several minutes ago, with his head lying on the table. Did security escort him to the head at just the wrong time? Pilgrimage didn't have the time, or money, to put hygiene facilities inside each cell.

"Security." Commander Meredith motioned to the head of Pilgrimage security, who made a call.

More than a thousand people watched in quiet fascination as the cam-eye started focusing on irregular outlines, still looking for a person.

"There he is!" Murmurs started as the cam-eye found a foot peeking out from under the large writing table.

Suddenly, the cam-eye refocused on a security officer bursting into the cell. The entire amphitheater watched the officer pull Tahir out from under the table, where he'd slid, and query his implant. Time of death, as recorded by the implant, was *twelve minutes ago*. The crowd's sudden uproar drowned out audio from the cell. A medical resuscitation team appeared and many watched, irresistibly hooked, as the medical drama ended in failure.

Ariane turned away to look at the displays the Feeds were sending out of the solar system. One correspondent had focused on Rand's face to catch his reaction. He was laughing.

CHAPTER 5

> Dr. Rouxe's murder [*link to my proof*] is a smokescreen
> to divert us from the true shocker in the Interstellar tri-
> als: How did a rogue temporal-distortion weapon get to
> G-145? Guess what? Our government knew all about
> it. Stay with us as we keep you informed of the conspira-
> cies unraveling behind this macabre theater.
>
> —*Citizens for Responsible Disarmament*, 2106.053.20.00
> UT, indexed by *Heraclitus 17* under Conflict Imperative

"Ari, this doesn't look good." Matt might have been
worried, but she couldn't be sure because his voice
was flattened by compression.

She was standing in the stagnant outflow of people from
the amphitheater. Standing on tiptoe to look about the crowd,
she realized many people leaving the arraignment had slowed
to make calls and the *Pilgrimage*'s internal communications
were swamped. "I know. This ship still isn't secure."

"You're missing my point." Matt's voice sharpened.

"Sorry?" She keyed up her ear bug's output to override
the crowd's babble.

"It looks like somebody wants to get rid of key prosecution witnesses. Whose testimony could be as damaging as
yours, *Joyce's*, and *Tahir's*?"

"Oh. I didn't think about that." Her knee-jerk reaction
had been to suspect Terran Intelligence, not someone working with the isolationists. She had immediately thought of
Andre Covanni, who specialized in assassination.

"Not everything is Intelligence skullduggery, Ari."

Matt had read her mind. She turned and froze, suddenly facing Dr. Istaga. He smiled warmly and looked the part of an unassuming, middle-aged academician, but *this was Andre*. She was sure.

"Matt? How 'bout I get back to you?" She tried to smile as she cut the call.

"No need to stop on my account, Major. Just ensuring you're safe. Heard about your brush with danger." Istaga spoke in his usual snippets.

"Yes, word gets around fast with the Feed correspondents here. Thank you, Doctor, for your regards."

"Terrible turn of events, this. Poor Tahir." With his thinning hair and stricken expression, Istaga wasn't a likely candidate for the war's biggest Terran super-spy.

"Didn't you visit him this morning? I heard you were going to be his defense counsel," she said, watching his face carefully. *Yes, poor Tahir, dead only hours after you arrive.*

"The fellow fired me immediately." Istaga grimaced, his tone turning aggrieved. "Restricting visitors was for his own good. You understand, Major."

"If there's no one to defend, what will you be doing next?" She hoped he'd be going back into Terran territory.

"I'm off to Beta Priamos Station. Offer my services to State Prince Parmet. Need to be useful, you know." His vague tone and demeanor sharpened as he drew himself up and made two quick bows. "Captain. Lieutenant."

Glancing to each side, she saw she was flanked by Floros and Oleander. Their three uniforms made an unrelenting wall of black.

"A triumvirate of Directorate brawn, brains, and beauty." Istaga's smile weakened as he watched their responding frowns. "Ah. I mean *each* of you has those qualities. Not to insinuate . . ." He nodded toward Floros, the bulkiest of their trio, and then lapsed into silence.

"Good day, Doctor," Ariane said.

After the red-faced Istaga pulled back into the crowd, she exchanged a smile with Oleander, who started laughing. Ariane's chuckle stopped when she turned to see Floros still frowning, her eyebrows meeting straight across her face and dividing it into perfect squares.

"That's your candidate for *Andre*, Major?" Captain Floros asked. "Looks like your normal bumbling professor to me."

"It's an act. Besides, Andre could be close to retiring by now. And no—" she stopped Floros's response. "I don't have any proof. Just a gut feeling."

"Some guts are more intuitive than others, to be sure." Floros stolidly tried to cover her doubt.

Suddenly, Ariane got a call from Sublieutenant Matthaios. "Colonel Edones wants you on the *Bright Crescent* immediately, ma'am, for a classified session with the senator."

As she acknowledged the call, she saw the dark horns of Warrior Commander over the heads of the crowd. Those in the Minoan's way were desperate to move, but people could only squeeze about and frantically exchange places. The corridors were still packed.

"Here comes my escort," she said with resignation. "Just in time for a meeting with the senator."

Oleander and Floros gave her sympathetic glances as she left, probably due more to her shadow than to the unpleasant meeting ahead.

Intelligence skullduggery, Matt called it, whenever the Directorate of Intelligence became involved. Ariane used to call the Directorate's stratagems *games*. For the first time, last year, these games affected innocents: Nestor was murdered and Matt was put in danger, all because of her mission. To be fair, neither she nor the Directorate bore *direct* blame for Nestor's murder, but her stomach tightened every time Matt railed against the Directorate, wondering if he was transferring his anger at her to a safer, less personal target.

She wondered if she could ever make amends to Matt for Nestor. *Making amends*, however, became a fathomless task. What about the wartime comrades, murdered by her crewmate Cipher? Were they on her account also, because she didn't discover Cipher's deranged plan for retribution until it was too late? What about those victims she couldn't save from Abram, such as Colonel Dokos? And their numbers were dwarfed by the casualties at Ura-Guinn, the deaths that couldn't be counted for years, yet had happened so long ago. The ghosts in the back of her mind began to shriek that she could never, *never* make reparations; she'd always fail and fall short.

Gritting her teeth, she concentrated on the sound of her footsteps on the deck, or the faces of oncoming passersby as they quickly moved to the other side of the corridor. She glanced back over her shoulder. Warrior Commander still followed her. She turned off the ring corridor into the *Bright Crescent*'s slip.

"ID, please," said the dockside guard, in full armor with exoskeleton.

She produced her identification and added her thumbprint for verification.

"You're expected in the Mission Stateroom, Major." His eyes flickered over toward Warrior Commander, who stood against the station-side wall of the docking area.

"Warrior Commander won't be boarding," she said.

"Yes, ma'am." The guard's tone meant, *that goes without saying, ma'am.*

She noted his insignia: He was shipboard AFCAW security force, or SF, rather than a shock commando, an informal name for those assigned to the Special Operations, Infiltration, and Aggressor Units. The *Bright Crescent* had arrived in G-145 with a platoon of shock commandos, but the Status of Forces agreement with Pilgrimage HQ didn't allow them to billet on the *Pilgrimage III*. To ease the crowded conditions on the *Bright Crescent* and keep the platoon within G-145, Colonel Edones had shipped them to Beta Priamos along with the three companies of Terran special forces rangers from the TLS *Percival*.

She suppressed a smile as she walked up the ramp to the AFCAW cruiser. Terran SP Parmet was probably sitting on a powder keg, with Beta Priamos holding aggressors from both the Consortium and the League. She didn't feel sorry for him.

The tight corridors of the *Bright Crescent* were familiar by now, even though Colonel Edones had been mission commander for less than a year. Outside the Mission Stateroom, she found Sublieutenant Matthaios and the senator's great-nephew, Myron, sitting on jump seats. Myron watched her approach with a strange sulking curiosity, but pressed his lips together and didn't answer her greeting. Matthaios looked bored and miserable.

"Go ahead, Major. It's a private meeting between you, the colonel, and the senator." Matthaios confirmed her worst fears.

She gave him a nod and took a deep breath before entering.

"Major Kedros, reporting as ordered, sir." Her salute was sharp and precise. She figured this was the time for formality, as she glanced sideways at the watchful bulk of the senator.

"Have a seat, Major." After returning her salute, Edones pressed his thumb to his desktop. "Secure Session in Progress" traveled about the bulkheads and settled to flash above the doorframe.

She sat in an expensive seat that adjusted itself to her height, weight, and shape. Her senses ramped up with her tension, as if she sat on the treacherous edge of a pit of vipers. Owen Edones was hard to read, but she generally knew what drove him. She believed that, at his core, Edones was a soldier and fiercely loyal to the Consortium. Senator Stephanos, however, had ten times the political savvy of Edones, without the constraints of duty or discipline. Whether his word could always be trusted was under debate by net-think and a matter for history to decide.

"*Pilgrimage* security has finally admitted they're overwhelmed. They've asked us for support," Edones said. "Not only that—with the murder of a high profile witness plus the attempted assassination of a Minoan warrior, the *Pilgrimage* crew is so spooked they want to relocate Abram's children to Beta Priamos for protection."

"They think this is about the trial?"

"It'd be best if they thought that, and leave worrying

about TEBI to us." The senator's deep voice didn't reso-
nate the way it usually did, perhaps because of the close
quarters.

*The war with the League has ended, yet we're still caught
up in intelligence and counterintelligence maneuvers.* The
thought depressed her. "What about Istaga?" she asked.

"The Colonel told me of your theory, Major. Have you
any proof?"

Before she could answer the senator, Edones shook his
head. "Even if he's Andre, there's no motive for an Intelligence hit."

"Perhaps the Terrans don't want their security gaffes ex-
posed. And if this is about getting rid of Terran witnesses,
State Prince Parmet ends up high on the target list." She
blinked to clear the mental image of Istaga saying, *I'll visit
Beta Priamos—offer my services to State Prince Parmet.*
She told them about her conversation with Istaga.

"I suppose we can't ignore the possibility." Senator
Stephanos's voice rumbled. He propped his chin on his
clasped hands and his elbows on the arms of his chair. He
looked bored, almost asleep, except his eyes were alert and
sharply focused on her.

"I don't figure Andre for the attempt on me and Joyce,"
she said. "There's a distinct difference between a crude
planted grenade and Tahir's murder, which has sophistication, flair, and intentional drama."

"*Intentional* drama?" Edones frowned.

"It's a classic locked-room murder, which mocks us with
its audacity and dares us to think 'out of the box,' if you'll
excuse the pun." She smiled wryly. "I'm guessing Tahir was
killed by a two- or three-part poison, with chemical tim-
ers. It'll take forensic experts, money, and time to nail it
down."

"You're not a trained profiler." Edones sounded skeptical.

"Unfortunately, we won't find an experienced profiler
inside this Gaia-forsaken solar system," Stephanos said.
"Go on, Major."

"The other crime sends a different message. The device planted under Joyce's bed sure looked like a Terran covert antipersonnel grenade, specifically an APG-thirty-thirty-four." She paused and cleared her throat. The colonel and the senator remained silent. "So we might have two different perpetrators. One uses cutting-edge poisons and daringly makes the murder a public circus. The other is old-school, using outdated grenades that were standard TEBI issue during the war, who gets more physical, even—"

"*Personal.*" The senator's eyes glinted under his bushy salt-and-pepper eyebrows. "You're saying this shouts TEBI and I agree. Is this about the war? *Ura-Guinn?*"

"We don't know enough to make that connection, sir." Already prepared, she didn't flinch when he mentioned Ura-Guinn. "But I'm worried about someone trying to sabotage Pax Minoica. Is our peace strong enough to stand a pissing contest between TEBI and the Directorate?"

"TEBI involvement is still supposition," Edones said. "Nobody's throwing around accusations, or urine, yet."

The senator ignored Edones's cool, dry delivery. "You handily deflected the conversation away from yourself, Major. Or the possibility that you're the target."

"And Sergeant Joyce?"

"Collateral damage, maybe." Stephanos shrugged. "But let's get back to you, Major. More specific, your shadow. Why are the Minoans following you?"

"I don't know." She shifted uncomfortably and belatedly added, "Sir."

"Is it possible they knew there'd be an attack on your life?" Stephanos squinted, as if in deep thought. "But why protect *you*, and not Dr. Rouxe?"

"I asked Warrior Commander why I was being followed. Rather pointedly. They never indicated they were protecting me. All I provoked was a vague insinuation the Minoans are performing triage, just like the rest of us." She didn't add any more, remembering her drunken belligerence.

"Maybe they're protecting a Minoan *asset*," Stephanos said, pressing his implant and pointing for display. "Myron—who inherited my sister's nose for money, if nothing else—found this contract being negotiated between Aether Exploration and Hellas Nautikos, which is purely a Minoan front."

She looked at the fragments of contract displayed on the wall. Only the public parts were available to Myron, and by the timestamps, the SEEECB had only just approved it. Bewildered, she glanced at Edones, who appeared to be scanning the information for the first time.

"I'm surprised your people haven't seen this yet, Colonel. The S-triple-ECB said it had the most constraining nondisclosure clauses they'd ever processed. They even sent it back once to Hellas Nautikos, requesting revisions."

"Senator, I'm sure this is in Captain Floros's queue." Edones's tone was cool. "I apologize for the delay in analysis, but I'm a little shorthanded right now, what with organizing the security for your contingent."

She saw the senator's eyes flash and narrow, but Colonel Edones could apparently get away with a few acerbic comments. The senator tapped his implant. "There's something else strange about this contract. It's one of only two contracts the Minoans have ever made with humans that *name* the required contractor personnel."

Three names appeared highlighted in the view port text: Matthew Journey, David Ray Pilgrimage, and Ariane Kedros. She felt her stomach muscles tighten with tension and her scalp tingle. She lightly ran her fingers through her hair to disperse the prickling.

"You mentioned *two* contracts?" Edones asked.

"The other unprecedented contract was signed just a day ago, between Hellas Nautikos and the Martian offices of MIT, naming Dr. Myrna Fox Lowry to this *team* being constructed by the Minoans. She's already on Beta Priamos doing research, so she'll just change employers. Let's not forget, however, she'll be working under a different set of nondisclosure clauses."

"Ones acceptable to CAW. Otherwise, they'd never have pushed the contract through our S-triple-ECB." Edones's frosty gaze met and held hers. "Do you have something to ask me, Major Kedros?"

"My employer mentioned he might have a contract, but he didn't give me specifics. He wondered when I'd be released from active duty." She kept her tone flat, not even sure what she wanted. Her current task felt onerous and came with the nasty side effect of arousing her ghosts. "I was going to ask about that today, but so much has happened. . . ."

Her voice died away. Had it really taken less than six hours to dodge an attempt on her life, show up at the arraignment, and watch Tahir die in front of Gaia and everyone else? When had she last eaten? As if on cue, her stomach rumbled.

"You could put the Major on plainclothes assignment. She'd be in perfect position with her civilian job," Stephanos said, looking at Colonel Edones.

"No," she said sharply, immediately discerning the senator's purpose. "I won't *spy* on my employer, even if my employer's working for aliens. That goes beyond the constitutional purview of the Armed Forces."

The senator's eyes glittered. "No one mentioned the 's' word, Major."

"I won't accept a mission that's in conflict with my employer's interests." She locked her eyes on his.

Senator Stephanos looked away first. He rose, eerily silent in spite of his bulk. Both she and Edones stood, as well.

"Colonel, the Directorate of Intelligence has seriously disappointed the Senate, particularly those of us who support your funding. You're supposed to be our best source of military intelligence, yet we had no notice of the security problems in the Terran weapons programs. I have to warn you I'm under pressure to perform a full mission audit of the *Bright Crescent*'s response mission to G-145. That's an intense, time-consuming affair and I'm strongly resisting."

"Yes, sir." Edones's voice was colorless and he didn't

seem surprised at the not-so-veiled threat. He stopped the secure privacy shield by tapping his desk.

Senator Stephanos paused at the hatch, his eyes flickering to her and back to Edones. "Another thing, Colonel. If you come under audit, the Senate will need assurances that you can control your subordinates and your resources."

CHAPTER 6

Net-think has spoken: The reason Dr. Rouxe was murdered was to prevent his testimony, although no one can explain *how* he was murdered. Another shocker: Who's missing a TD weapon? Here's a list of Terran and Autonomist weapon storage facilities....

—*Dr. Net-head Stavros*, 2106.053.21.32 UT,
indexed by *Heraclitus 8* under Flux Imperative

After Matt disconnected his call with Ari, the ship's proximity alarm went off. A view port opened over the pilot's panel and showed the reason: a maintenance bot was approaching the port dorsal area, using the standard stern approach. Its automated message said it intended to perform a hull integrity test. He called the *Pilgrimage* maintenance control center.

"This is *Aether's Touch*. Can you explain the maintenance bot at my slip, when I didn't ask for one?" When he could, he managed his own maintenance; he saved money and if the job wasn't done well, he could only blame himself.

There was silence. Finally, the operator responded. "This is *Pilgrimage* Maintenance One. We don't show you on our schedule, *Aether's Touch*. What ID is it squawking?"

"Hmm ..." He looked over the message header and text. "I don't see an ID."

Puzzlement was evident, now, in the operator's pause. "*Aether's Touch*, we've put out a recall to all maintenance bots, both internal and external. Did it respond?"

"No. It's fifty meters and closing." He double-checked the ship's smart armor status.

"We've got an EVA-capable team in a shuttle. They're at Gold One and can be at your slip in two minutes." Even if the team members were inside their extravehicular activity suits, ready to "go EVA," they'd be too late.

"Negative, Maintenance One. It's encroached into my self-defense zone. I'm exercising my rights." Matt's fingers danced as he powered up the midsection rail guns. The bot was using the correct maintenance approach, perhaps to allay his suspicions, but the approach also gave him a clear corridor to punch it. The security system provided targeting vectors and he loaded slugs. He ordered thrusters to compensate, so he didn't transmit too much force to the *Pilgrimage* through clamps and connections.

"*Aether's Touch*, we recommend waiting for our team." He ignored the message and fired.

"Maintenance One, I've fired a soft dispersive-force slug. The bot just took—" He stopped to calculate forces and, in the view port, saw the bot try to compensate with thrusters and—*uh-oh.* "I think the bot just *exploded.*"

"Not possible. You must have seen a canister rupture."

"I *saw* an explosive force. You'd better report this to security. Send your shuttle to collect what you can for analysis." He sent the vector track of the biggest cluster of debris.

"*Aether's Touch*, we didn't have cam-eye coverage—"

"I'll attach it to my report. You've got another security problem, *Pilgrimage* Maintenance One." Matt tersely signed off.

Bots used in space were designed to cause minimal damage when they ruptured. They weren't supposed to fly into lots of small pieces, even from compressed gas canister rupture. If the bot had been closer, he'd have needed his expensive high-grade active armor. Thank Gaia that *Aether's Touch* was tougher than the normal exploration vessel.

My ship was just targeted by saboteurs. Matt took a moment to get his brain around that. The *Pilgrimage* wasn't a safe haven, even after all its security upgrades.

* * *

After the hatch closed behind the senator, Ariane was caught off guard by Edones's sudden ire. "What's your problem, Major? You save an entire solar system from frying, and crack under the pressure of being a hero?" Edones's biting voice felt like the slap of cold water on her face.

"Excuse me?" She met his icy gaze with her own. She sat back down. "Sir?"

"Your maudlin behavior. Your drinking. Didn't you realize that by volunteering for addiction counseling, your superior—that's *me*, if you're not up to speed here—is required to report any abuse of alcohol or drugs. Why do you think I called in Mr. Journey last night?"

She flushed, but stayed silent.

"I can't have your attention focused at the bottom of a bottle. Not right now."

Her embarrassment turned to anger. "Owen, if *you* haven't noticed, the Feeds are reporting whatever can be discerned, or guessed, about the Ura-Guinn detonation." Her hands balled into fists, while the ghosts started rustling again in her brain. "They're trying to piece together what happened, find out who survived. You can't know how distracting it is to be reminded of—*that*."

She saw his eyes flicker when she used his first name. It had almost become a code word, an indication she wasn't in "military mode," even if she currently wore the uniform. Her hands opened, only to intertwine and grip each other tensely.

He sat silently and considered her. After methodically restoring the secure privacy shield, he spoke in a mild tone. "Remember, the telescope data is decades behind us. We won't know about individual survivors until the generational ship gets to Ura-Guinn. You're going to have to deal with sensationalism and conjecture in the meantime."

He was right, but entirely unhelpful. She swallowed, her throat tight, and nodded.

"You followed orders and did your duty. AFCAW will always protect you, as long as you wear that uniform," he added.

As long as I wear this uniform. She looked down. "I still put on this uniform because I believe in Pax Minoica, if nothing else." She suppressed a bleak chuckle. "Otherwise, it hasn't been much protection."

"And neither have I, being remiss in my duties as a supervisor."

"Duties?" She looked up at his sober tone.

"I should have recognized you had a problem. Even though neural probes are forbidden due to your background, I should have put you into addiction counseling sooner."

She looked away. Knowing Owen Edones as long as she had, she recognized this as his one and only warning shot. *Straighten up and fly by the book.* Since Edones focused on results, he was less inclined to worry about borderline behavior in his people, but once he advised about such behavior—she'd better listen. She remembered the senator's similar warning.

"What'll happen to *you* when the Senate gets around to nitpicking and second-guessing your decisions?" she asked.

"Since each Assassinator missile costs several million HKD, shooting off sixteen of them was certain to have repercussions. Particularly when our most fiscally conservative party controls the Senate." Edones picked up his slate.

Ariane shifted her weight, uncomfortable despite the chair's efforts. If someone replaced Colonel Edones as head of the Special Operations Division of the Directorate of Intelligence, people and policies would change. There wasn't another colonel in AFCAW with Edones's experience—she remembered the earnest face of *young Lieutenant Owen Edones*, as he explained how her new identity would work and the risks of the experimental, but voluntary, rejuv procedures.

Self-consciously, she raised her fingertips to stroke the smooth line of her jaw. Rejuv, as it currently existed, was rarely successful. The only reason she wasn't a coddled lab rat having her life documented for the advancement of human biochemistry, was due to Owen's personal com-

mitment to give her a shiny new life. She ignored the inner
voice that spitefully told her she'd ruined this life as she
looked at the lines developing on Owen's face. At some
point, he'd passed her in apparent age. Would a different
division head be inclined to maintain a Reservist slot for
someone who was, frankly, both an embarrassment and annoyance to the Consortium?

"Is your career in jeopardy?" she asked.

"Heads are rolling above me, but the mitigating factor is
that we knew the Terrans had piss-poor weapons security,
because we watch a good many people who fall *outside our
purview*."

"But—"

"Don't worry, Major. I can defend myself in the political
arena." Colonel Owen Edones gave her the brusque little
smile that told her this subject was closed. He tapped his
slate. "Let's talk about what you'll be doing. I've sent your
orders to Admin and they'll be ready to sign. It's a plainclothes mission and you'll be able to go to Priamos with
your Mr. Journey."

She ignored the dig. Matt wasn't *her* Mr. Journey, but
Edones always tried to goad her into exposing personal details about her life. "Matt's my employer, and he's stood by
me. I won't take a mission that'll injure his reputation or
his business."

"In this case, there's no conflict of interest. Since I'm not
getting any more personnel, I need you to pick up Joyce's
mission." He nodded at her slate on the arm of the chair.
"You should have access to the case file."

She saw the special information access form pop up on
her slate and thumbed acceptance. The case file was catego-
rized "Kressida" and she read it warily. Her lips tightened.
"You're peddling shit from the Great Bull itself, as my *employer* would say. No one needs to defect from the Terran
League since they instituted their Open Gates policy."

"The gates aren't open for everybody. In particular,
prior TEBI agents."

"Why would we want Maria Guillotte?" Saying that
name gave her a bad taste. She'd added Maria's statement

regarding Abram's takeover to her report, but avoided speaking with her directly. Interviewing the woman who had kidnapped her last year was low on her list of fun things to do.

"She can provide recent information on TEBI. The Terrans say they're dismantling the organization and it only has domestic tasking, but we think otherwise. If Dr. Rouxe was killed by a TEBI weapon, then she may provide support for your Istaga-Andre theory. On a more personal note, Maria knows far more than we do about what Cipher did on Karthage Point—particularly how Cipher convinced a Terran mole in AFCAW to do her dirty deeds."

Okay, so Maria *might* be useful. Cipher was part of the crew on the mission that took out Ura-Guinn, and she had earned her nickname as a cryptography specialist, although she wasn't too shabby with explosives, either. When she decided that everyone who processed the weapon release orders for Ura-Guinn had to die, including her former crewmates, she used all her specialties toward that end. Karthage Point was still upgrading the security systems that Cipher had infiltrated, as well as the environmental controls she'd used to kill the station commander. In addition to cleverly subverting those systems, Cipher also needed a pair of hands on the inside. These hands belonged to an AFCAW Lieutenant Colonel, whom Ariane identified as a Terran Intelligence operative, but there were gaps in their knowledge: for instance, how did Cipher manage to "activate" a Terran mole? Someone who had TEBI connections might be able to fill in those blanks. Someone like Maria.

Ariane read more, while Edones waited. Maria had contacted the Directorate after her favorite father died, leaving her with three estranged parents. The case file assumed this was the instigating factor for Maria's defection request. Joyce was initially assigned to contact and negotiate.

"This file says she's to remain in place, but she *requested* relocation and asylum on a Consortium prime planet." Ariane looked up, questioning the contradiction.

"She'll be most useful if she stays on Parmet's staff. That's all Sergeant Joyce was authorized to offer."

"And did she agree?"

"You've got everything I know. The Sergeant didn't have time to report before Abram's Great Unpleasantness started. Hopefully he can brief you before you arrive at Beta Priamos."

She didn't show her distaste. Exploiting informers and defectors was the sleazy side of intelligence, in her opinion. The task looked even more disagreeable when she considered the subject.

Edones's slate buzzed with an AFCAW-generated emergency message, the only type allowed through the security shield.

"It's out of *Pilgrimage* security." He dropped the shield and pointed the slate at the wall so they could both watch the report.

Her jaw dropped in surprise as the video from *Aether's Touch* ran, concurrent with Matt's voice-over. She immediately defended Matt's actions. "The bot didn't back off, so it was within his rights to fire. Classic defense steps, per CAW Space Emergency Procedures."

Edones ran the disintegration of the bot in slow motion. Grudgingly, he said, "Mr. Journey appears to be correct. There's a visible shock wave, courtesy of the escaped gas. Luckily for Mr. Journey and his ship, it didn't have a lot of power."

"And, once again, using an amount of explosive small enough to get by the *Pilgrimage* airlock sniffers. Current ComNet equipment would have caught it."

"Yes. We'd better force some of our equipment upon *Pilgrimage* security. Of course, the senator will insist they pay for it." Edones's voice was grim as he ran through the explosive sequence again. "I'll have Floros analyze this."

"I'm beginning to take this personally." She watched Edones's face. "I'm the common target between the attacks and considering the methods, I might suspect that Cipher is back."

Edones blinked, surprise moving so quickly through his eyes that she might have missed it if she didn't know him. "Why would you suspect Lieutenant Paulos?"

"Because she's not dead, is she? If you had confirmation of her death, you'd have told me. Instead, you've been suspiciously quiet."

"You needn't worry about her arriving here, in G-145." Edones was his carefully bland self again. "We go through each arriving ship's manifest and examine the background of every Autonomist. We know what to look for, when it comes to ComNet records. So, unless Paulos can pass for a Terran, she hasn't entered this solar system."

She agreed. Cipher didn't have the right body build to mingle, unnoticed, with Terrans. She was far from being tall enough, or slim enough, and her facial features weren't unremarkable. Even if she suppressed her urge for bright hair, skin, and clothing colors, Cipher would still stand out.

"However, you're right to suspect you're a target," Edones said.

"And if this trouble follows me to Priamos?"

"I hope that's the case, Major." When her eyebrows went up, he added, "If you pull even one culprit to Beta Priamos, please drag along the one with a fetish for explosives."

"But that'd put everyone on Beta Priamos Station in danger." Not that she'd mention it, but she was tired of dealing with explosions and decompressions.

"They have less than two hundred and fifty civilians, mostly contractors, plus three companies of Terran special forces, with a platoon of our commandos. By comparison, we're trying to protect nine hundred civilians on the *Pilgrimage Three*, including visiting dignitaries, Feed correspondents, and one hundred twenty-seven children under the age of sixteen." Edones cocked an eyebrow and his voice was heavy with sarcasm. "By all means, Major, *please* lure the miscreants to Priamos."

She didn't have a response. When he put it that way, hanging her out as bait, *again*, seemed to be the sensible course. Edones's logic was always sound, even if it was ruthless. She looked at her slate and scrolled through her queue until she found the orders, which she accepted with a thumbprint.

"You also have authority to take emergency mission

command of the platoon on Beta Priamos. That doesn't give you command of day-to-day operations, but you should introduce yourself to Pike and stay on his good side. Remind him that both you and State Prince Parmet must be kept safe so you can testify to the ICT."

"Yes, sir. I'll make sure my employers understand I have to give testimony. Am I dismissed?"

"One more thing, Major." He paused. "Don't trust Maria, or forget she was TEBI."

Well, *that* didn't seem likely. She sighed as she opened the hatch. No Directorate orders would be complete without some cryptic warning from Edones.

News travels fast on a generational ship. By the time Matt met David Ray in Dr. Lee's lab, everyone had heard about the exploding bot. Decompression and module integrity was important to everyone on the behemoth that was, after all, only a fragile spacefaring habitat.

"No damage to the ship?" David Ray pointed at the status display near the door.

"They think it's a similar device to what nearly killed Sergeant Joyce and Ariane. At least that's what Denise overheard from Benjamin. She told Barnes, who told Randall, who told Jamie and me." Lee efficiently moved a circular wheel of samples between equipment as she spoke, her tall thin body moving gracefully.

Matt's eyebrows jumped. Once again, the lack of privacy aboard a generational ship didn't bring back fond memories. The level of privacy Autonomists insisted upon was considered unhealthy, inconsiderate, and self-serving by the generational lines. However, he'd gotten used to the sense of freedom he felt from the "self-serving" privacy. He was saved from commenting by a call on his ear bug.

"Matt, are you okay? How's *Aether's Touch*?" It was Ari. "We saw your report."

"Where are you?"

"Leaving the *Bright Crescent*. I'm released from uniformed active duty, so David Ray can negotiate with the Minoans. I'll have to stay in-system, until I testify to the Tribunal."

Uniformed active duty. She'd used those careful words for a reason. He paused, laying his hand on the edge of the cold smooth lab counter and softly drumming his fingers. Did it matter, for the Minoan contract, that she was doing some skullduggery for Edones? "Good. Considering that your employment was nonnegotiable, we've probably got the contract."

Matt terminated the call to find David Ray nodding. Sure, it was great to have the work, but being employed by aliens? This would be new territory for all of them.

"We're not the only ones going to Beta Priamos Station. They're moving three artificial wombs out there," David Ray added. Crèches in use were rarely moved, even when occupants were in the embryonic period.

"Abram's children." Matt easily guessed which crèches were being moved. He couldn't forget the isolationist aiming his weapon at one of the wombs, nor what the man's body looked like after the Minoan beam weapon hit him. Matt closed his eyes and shook his head hard, hoping to dislodge the image.

"Command staff thinks Dr. Rouxe was targeted and killed for revenge. They're worried the three embryos will be next; in particular, Charlotte Anne. Abram considered himself childless and the isolationists call first-born females abominations. They're aborted when they have the technology to detect them, or if born, they're murdered or abandoned."

"Moving them will risk their health. Should they really be sent off-ship in such a rush?" Matt was used to speaking of those in crèches as if they were present. He already considered Nigel, Peter, and Charlotte Anne crew members.

David Ray shrugged. "The decision's made."

"But they listen to you, and to Dr. Lee." He gestured toward the tall woman with his chin.

"I'm not on staff anymore; I'm on hiatus. Besides, Lee thinks it's feasible and she'll accompany them to Beta Priamos. She'll make sure they're safe." David Ray grinned. "I'm not too upset about how things shook out."

Indeed. David Ray and Lee had been almost inseparable

since they'd recovered from the isolationist takeover. Matt suddenly remembered whom he was leaving docked at the *Pilgrimage* while he waltzed out to the gas giant Laomedon, its moon Priamos, and the Beta Priamos Station.

"I should tell Diana we're leaving," he said.

"Yes, you should," Lee said.

CHAPTER 7

Net-think is so fickle. Notice how the Interstellar Criminal Tribunal in G-145 eclipsed the Ura-Guinn news? Of course, we're comparing absolute gibbering drama to dry data! I'm glued to my Feeds....

−*Cicely Janda*, 2106.053.21.28 UT,
indexed by *Heraclitus 10* under Flux Imperative

Before she could leave for Priamos, Ariane had to finish giving her statement to *Pilgrimage* security. Captain Floros, performing as AFCAW recorder and representative, accompanied her to the new security offices. Unfortunately, once the very important members of the ICT learned about Ariane's interview, it was impossible to keep them away. This made it quite a jaw-clenching episode for her.

"Why didn't you immediately call after looking into Sergeant Joyce's room?" State Prince Duval's eyes were narrow with suspicion.

"Because I didn't have any reason to suspect an attempt on his life," she said.

"I should think it obvious that something was amiss."

As her jaw started tightening in response, Commander Meredith leaned forward and put his hand on Duval's arm in restraint. "Please, SP, let my people do the questioning. That's their job."

From her position in front of this august audience, Ariane watched Duval's face tense in discomfort. This was cross-cultural clashing at its best, and she tried not to smile. Terrans enjoyed pushing Autonomists and crèche-get about in awkward conversational dances, but *they* rarely enjoyed being touched in public.

Duval muttered, "Excuse me," and pulled his arm away.

Meredith flashed her a look of un-Commanderly wicked humor as he faced forward again. She took this as a signal that she was, for the most part, among friends.

"Gentlemen, please hold your questions." Benjamin Pilgrimage, who was presumably taking her statement, finally regained control. "Continue, Major Kedros."

She described what happened in Joyce's clinic room, up to the part where Warrior Commander discovered the antipersonnel grenade. "I saw Warrior Commander close its hands over the Terran APG-thirty-thirty-four and snap the connection between sensor and grenade. I covered Joyce and heard the detonation, but the sound was muffled."

This caused a flurry of questions.

"Its *hands*? The force of a thirty-thirty-four must be . . ." Floros started poking at her slate.

"How could you possibly identify it?" said SP Duval. "Claiming it's an old Terran antipersonnel grenade is inflammatory, Major. Besides, the model you picked isn't in our inventory anymore."

"I'm trained to recognize older Terran weapons, considering their potential to pop up in the strangest places."

"What?" SP Duval sputtered. "Senator Stephanos, this is insulting. Where's the objective evidence?"

Stephanos leaned forward. His eyebrows were knotted together, a sign known throughout net-think as a forecast to his bad temper.

Benjamin tried to head off disaster, appealing to the ICT members. "Gentlemen, please. We all want to find the culprit. We don't have to rely upon Major Kedros's memory; we have physical evidence, starting with the contained output from the explosion."

"Metallurgic analysis shows a signature consistent with Terran metals circa 2090 to 2096." No one acknowledged Captain Floros's comment.

Duval, though he'd previously demanded objective evidence, wasn't swayed by these inopportune facts. "That evidence was handled by no fewer than three AFCAW soldiers before it got into your hands. It's tainted."

"We also have Warrior Commander," Benjamin added.

"The Minoans agreed to give you a statement?" This was the first time Stephanos spoke.

"They haven't answered our request yet. But we're hopeful," Benjamin said.

"Humph." Stephanos's grunt showed what he thought of Benjamin Pilgrimage's hopes. "Major Kedros made the obvious *safe* choice in handing it over to AFCAW EOD. At the time, she considered it military ordnance, not evidence."

"Yes, sir." Ariane was relieved. Senator Stephanos should back his own military personnel, but after he'd come down on Edones, she had misgivings about his loyalties. "I didn't know if the remains of the grenade might be explosive."

"Kedros has proven she's willing to be judge, jury, and *executioner*—why bother with judicial procedures?" Duval's voice was sour.

Her stomach tensed. Her objections died on her lips as she saw the warning in Floros's eyes. Even worse, Meredith didn't come to her defense and Stephanos merely shook his head. She could see how the winds might blow, once it came time to testify to the ICT about sending the weapon and two isolationists into N-space.

"The question we should be asking is: What would have happened to the prosecution's case if we'd lost Major Kedros *and* Sergeant Joyce? The two of them, in addition to SP Parmet, now comprise most of the prosecution's eyewitness testimony after Dr. Rouxe's death," Stephanos said.

Meredith nodded.

"Meanwhile, Dr. Rouxe's murderer may have gone anywhere," Duval said.

"That's unlikely, sir. No one can presently leave G-145," Benjamin said.

"He or she could be anywhere in this solar system."

"We're examining all requests for travel on or off the

Pilgrimage and we're tracking everyone in the solar system. There are fewer than five thousand people in G-145 and we can find any one of them." Benjamin stood stiffly; he didn't look comfortable in his new uniform.

"And yet these procedures didn't ensure safety for your visitors, considering the recent attempt upon the *Aether's Touch*," Stephanos said.

"Why would that have anything to do with the ICT?" Duval's lip lifted in a sneer that had to be habitual, given the deep lines radiating from his nose to his mouth.

"*Please.* Quiet, everyone." Benjamin's tone was ragged. "I'd like to get a statement from Major Kedros before she goes off active duty at the end of the day. She'll be testifying to the ICT from Beta Priamos Station, like SP Parmet."

Benjamin finally finished recording Ariane's statement. He also asked her what she saw at the arraignment, which was no more than the hundreds of other witnesses in the amphitheater. She accounted for her movements before the arraignment and during the period when the bot menaced *Aether's Touch*.

While she answered the questions, State Prince Duval watched her with narrowed eyes. He didn't interrupt her, but he couldn't resist doubtful snorts here and there.

"Thank you for your time, Major Kedros," Benjamin said. "Since you've been summoned as witness to the Interstellar Criminal Tribunal, you must keep us appraised of your whereabouts at all times. You may testify from Beta Priamos, but you cannot leave this solar system."

She didn't feel relief until she reached the *Aether's Touch* and took off her uniform. What shift was it? It didn't matter; she fell onto her bunk and slipped into exhausted sleep.

The ship's systems woke Ariane. "Notice: disconnection in four hours. Undocking procedures must begin."

The message repeated until she mumbled, "I'm *awake*. Notice acknowledged."

The status light on Matt's quarters indicated they were occupied. As she quietly passed by, she heard Diana's voice in a low unintelligible murmur. She climbed up to the control deck and started the undocking checklists.

She was checking the provision orders and deliveries when Hal Bokori called. Guilt washed over her as she answered. She'd forgotten about him during the chaos of murders, bombs, and skullduggery. Their arrangements were usually loose, meeting up for drinking and socializing, although she knew Hal hoped for more.

"I'm sorry I didn't call you sooner," he said when she opened the view port and answered.

"What?"

"We're disconnecting in a few minutes. It's just been frantic work, right up to this moment. I finally have time for a quick call." His light green eyes, such a contrast to his dark skin, searched her face for reaction.

She moved her hand along the edge of the console as he talked, feeling the symbols and tapping. Beside the view port with his face, the list of departures from the *Pilgrimage* appeared. Hal was the primary loadmaster for the *Golden Bull*, which was currently undocking and leaving for Beta Priamos.

"This has been my worst nightmare—we're moving crèches," Hal continued, obviously thinking that she was up to date on current events. "Worse, there's hardly any safety data on these *artificial wombs*, as Dr. Lee calls them. Since we're staying in real-space, we can use the gravity generator, and we've gimbaled the monstrosities—"

She managed to break into his monologue. "Hal, *I* have to apologize too. You're not the only one who's been absorbed with—other matters." *Like dodging grenades.*

His eyebrows went up.

"We're also heading to Beta Priamos. I was going to call you, see if you wanted to have a drink." She was ashamed the lie came out so effortlessly and she looked away as she tapped a status question: Who else was traveling on the *Golden Bull*?

When the manifest displayed, she swallowed hard to hide her dismay. Besides the crew, there were almost forty passengers, all of whom had supposedly been "cleared" by the *Pilgrimage* security office. As she expected, Lee was escorting Abram's embryonic children to Beta Priamos. David Ray was going to Priamos to work for Aether Exploration. Nineteen Terrans were also listed on the passenger manifest, including Dr. Istaga. How had he convinced *Pilgrimage* security that he needed to get to the R&D center of the system?

Hal was smiling when she again made eye contact. "Then this isn't good-bye. See you in a day or two?"

She nodded. He had an undertone of relief in his voice. Perhaps he didn't want to make any more of their relationship than she did. *We're a couple of lonely people who use each other as an excuse to drink, nothing more.*

"Good." Hal gave her his unique and confident smile. "See you at the Stellar Shield for a drink or two."

After Hal signed off, she tried not to contrast their good-bye with Matt and Diana, cocooned away in Matt's quarters below. To distract herself, she turned to provisioning and preparing to disconnect the ship. She pulled out her slate and alternated ship preparations with her military mission research, consolidated her notes on the events of the past two days.

After authorizing a delivery of food stores, she opened the folder on Joyce's mission. She had his pre-mission notes on Maria, but he hadn't added anything to them and he wasn't going to, not for a day or two. He was still unconscious, with a low respiration rate and heartbeat. The medics were trying to filter the sedative out of his system.

She yawned and closed the documents, putting down her slate. She'd completed an extraction mission several years ago, retrieving a witness from a dangerous fringe colony where neither Terran nor Autonomous law had any control. Extractions were difficult to plan before visiting the site, but Maria's case didn't require extraction. Directorate protocol dictated she do everything she could to keep Maria in place, as a continuing source of intelligence.

"Ari?"

Matt's call from the airlock jolted her. "Yes?"

"I'm going to walk Diana back to the *Bright Crescent*."

No surprise there; the new lovers were postponing their separation as long as possible. "I'll take over disconnection when I get back. And turn Muse Three on, for Gaia's sake. You know it needs the interaction."

Grumbling about distracting pests under her breath, she tapped the commands to allow Muse 3 input and the capability to vocalize.

"Hey, Muse." She was tired of using the model number. "Muse 3" was the AI's unique identifier but in all practicality, there were no other Muse models in existence.

"Good day, Ari. Do you need help with disconnection checklists?"

She sighed; the AI apparently wanted interaction. "No, Muse. By the way, I thought you were handling the message board and comm."

"Matt changed my responsibilities, perhaps because I did something wrong. You could ask Matt to explain his decision." The wheedling tone of his maker, Nestor, came through. However, Muse 3 was more childlike than Nestor and made her smile.

"No, Muse, I can't." Her face, and her mood, relaxed as she grinned. "You'll have to ask Matt yourself."

The dockside cam-eye displayed a view of Matt and Diana, who was dressed in her civilian clothes with a duffel bag hanging from her shoulder. They walked down the ramp toward the main connection ring, where they turned and stepped out of view.

"Why is Matt leaving the ship when the disconnection checklists have started? He has never done that before."

She picked her words carefully in answering, hesitant to step into the quagmire of human relationships. "Matt is escorting Diana back to her ship, giving her a personal good-bye."

"The personal good-bye, which I find defined as a face-to-face interaction, is also defined as a gift?"

"Well . . ." Trying to verbalize these simple acts for Muse 3 took some thought. "Matt is assuring Diana of her importance in his life and thanking her for her company."

She was pleased with her succinct definition, but not with her feelings. The gloom she'd felt of late, the weighty guilt of Ura-Guinn, had mixed with something else that had the unmistakable tang of jealousy. She didn't resent Matt's foray into a sincere relationship, the first she'd seen him have, and she didn't begrudge Oleander for capturing Matt's attention. Or did she?

"Should you give a personal good-bye to the Minoan warrior, for saving your life?" Muse 3 moved a cam-eye view into the center of her console. Warrior Commander, by now a standard fixture, stood motionless at the intersection of the dock and the ring corridor.

"That's not the same, Muse." She was almost to the point where she didn't notice the Minoan and now she chewed her lip contemplatively. The Minoans weren't supposed to understand individuality, right? But there was no denying the fact they had distinctive reactions to different humans.

"You've made an interesting suggestion, Muse," she murmured as she left the control deck.

The docks on the *Pilgrimage* were bland and uninteresting when compared to Autonomist habitats, but at least there was a display to the right of the airlock showing their departure time and status. Out of habit, she checked it.

The Minoan warrior stood with arms crossed over chest, using a human-looking stance. It ignored the traffic on the main ring. A cargo lift rumbled by and the handlers watched Warrior Commander with guarded curiosity. She walked quietly down the ramp to stand in front of the Minoan.

"I have questions for you, Warrior Commander." Since she couldn't know if the Minoan was actually looking at her, she pressed on. "Have you stayed on the *Pilgrimage* purely to protect me?"

Remembering her training, she waited. Net-think hypothesized the Minoans considered periods of silence to be respectful. In that case, Warrior Commander had extremely high esteem for her, because she seemed to wait forever before the slight *negative* nod. *Well, chuck that theory.*

She tried again. "Is my protection within your duties?"

This time Warrior Commander rewarded her, eventually, with an affirmative nod.

"What will you do when my ship leaves for Beta Priamos?"

Warrior Commander used its grating voice. "I will join Knossos-ship."

The Minoans called all their space-faring vehicles "Knossos-ship," but since this warrior commanded all Minoan assets within this solar system, it probably meant the warship. She wondered if the warship would keep its position near the *Pilgrimage*, and when Warrior Commander didn't elaborate any further, she asked, "Will Knossos-ship remain in its current position?"

She wasn't surprised at the lack of response. Minoan ship movements were forbidden territory. She gave the warrior a respectful nod. "Farewell, Warrior Commander."

As she returned to the *Aether's Touch*, she figured it never hurt to be polite to aliens.

At 23:07, Universal Time, approximately six hours after the *Golden Bull* departed and approximately two and a half hours after the *Aether's Touch* undocked, Tammy Jean Pilgrimage had to enter the general counsel's office. The general counsel's office was locked up, and the acting general counsel wanted Tammy Jean to find a slate that held a particular legal brief.

Even though she had permission to be there, Tammy Jean was nervous. She'd just begun training in Legal, and the impressive legend beside the door said, GENERAL COUNSEL, DAVID RAY PILGRIMAGE, RETURNING 2107.01.05. She tapped in the code she'd been given. The door slid open and the lights in the office began to brighten. She listened for a security warning.

Well, it's not like I'm a criminal, she thought, as she timidly stepped over the threshold. She never heard the faint snap of the wire. The APG-3034 exploded from the left of the doorframe. Designed to maim and wound, it blew small pellets of shrapnel in a fan-shaped pattern, cutting through her legs. As she went down, whooping and shrieking alarms went off, signaling structural damage and smoke.

Lucky for Tammy Jean, who had a bright future in Legal, there was no decompression and no loss of atmosphere. The grenade had been placed to cause damage in a low, downward pattern, so she didn't catch any shrapnel above her hips. She would probably live, provided she was treated immediately for shock and blood loss.

CHAPTER 8

Here's another installment of my real-time coverage of the Tribunal in G-145: This morning was all about recovery, as the prosecution rebuilt its case against the accused isolationists. With the loss of Dr. Rouxe as star witness, they've rearranged their presentation of evidence and testimony. They'll start with the hijacking of the *Pilgrimage III*. . . .

—*Dr. Net-head Stavros*, 2106.054.09.30 UT,
indexed by *Heraclitus 13*, *Democritus 8* under
Conflict, Cause and Effect Imperatives

"Go get some rest," Matt told Ari. When she looked at him doubtfully, he added, "I've got a class C license, remember? I can watch thrust-brake diagrams as well as any other hominid."

She sniffed. "You've made your point, because a chimp could get a class C real-space license. Just make sure our gravity generator is bleeding gee by—"

"Okay, all right, I've memorized the safety checklists."

"I know." She grinned, lighting up the control deck with her smile. "Do you think I'd let you pilot, if I didn't? I trust you because you're the only one who cares more about this ship than I do."

"So I'm just as obsessive as you—thanks." He waved her away. "Sleep well."

She winked and disappeared. Once he'd adjusted the temperature—he liked it warm on the control deck—and checked all the burn parameters, he switched on Muse 3. After ten questions requiring complex answers, he was already tired of the pesky AI. Now he knew why Ari kept shutting it down.

"Once your company is licensed to develop artificial intelligence, what else will be needed before I can vote?"

"Don't worry about that yet, Muse. There are plenty more tests to get through before you can earn right of individuality." *And many, many more fees.* "Muse, I have to conference with David Ray privately, so I'm shutting down your input. Ready?"

"Yes, Matt."

He didn't want Muse 3 to know the hurdles that existed: Although he'd sent in the down payment, it'd be a while before he could pay for the entire development license. In the small amount of literature he'd found on the subject, the experts recommended he isolate the AI from the regulatory process. Matt figured that was academic-speak for "don't worry the growing AI with issues where they have no control." He wished he could have that protection in his own life.

He put in a call to the *Golden Bull*, asking for David Ray. This would be a real-time discussion, since the *Golden Bull* was only about ten thousand kilometers behind them. *Aether's Touch* had passed the slower freighter near the halfway point between the *Pilgrimage* and Beta Priamos.

"What's wrong?" asked Matt, when he saw David Ray's face.

"There's been another explosion on the *Pilgrimage*—triggered at the door to my office. It got one of our young legal aides in training. She's in surgery; she's got injuries, but they say she'll live."

"Thank Gaia and St. Darius. Will she need transplants?"

"She can't accept vat-grown tissue, and they're trying to save at least one leg. She'll have to use a prosthesis on her other leg. Benjamin says she got off lucky."

Lucky? Matt might quibble with that. "This means, though, that the miscreant is still on the *Pilgrimage*."

"Maybe. Benjamin says it was a dooby trap, you know,

something that's triggered later. Obviously, it was meant for me." David Ray's face was pale and drawn. He looked so pathetic that Matt didn't have the heart to tell him it was actually a "booby" trap.

"You can't blame yourself, David Ray. That's something I learned the hard way, believe me, with Nester's death."

"Speaking of that, I've got good news from Athens Point." David Ray tried to smile. It slid down his jaw a little sadly.

"Nestor's murderer?" Matt felt ashamed; he'd completely forgotten Hektor Valdes was being prosecuted. The trial had started several days ago.

"The jury deliberated less than an hour and came back with a guilty verdict. Sometimes the system works." David Ray heaved a sigh. "It also means Athens Point Law Enforcement didn't need that subpoena. They can no longer use it to impound the AI."

"What did Valdes get?" Matt asked.

"Life, for first-degree murder. They had physical evidence from the murder scene, messages hiring him and identifying the target, and a big fat payment dumped in his account. Almost as if his employer *wanted* his stupid ass hung out to swing."

"To dry. A corpse can swing, but an ass is hung out to dry." Matt, having opted off his generational ship when he was young, was more adept than David Ray at Autonomist colloquialisms and slang. He ignored the other man's puzzled frown. "Can they trace the money?"

"No. If Valdes knows anything about his employer, he's taking it to prison."

Meaning they can't tie Hektor Valdes to Cipher, Ari's old crewmate who fashioned herself into a lethal avenging angel. Cipher tried to take out her original crew with explosives and as far as Matt knew, the authorities hadn't yet found Cipher's body.

"I've filed to have the subpoena dropped, and I've started the AI development license application. Your queue should also have the nondisclosure statements the Minoans provided. They're more standard now, allowing for better communication between the research contractors. I suggest you read them before you disembark." David Ray hesitated.

"Why? What's the problem?"

"State Prince Parmet requested a meeting with you and Ariane, when you arrive. I'm nervous about him."

Ari never talked about the torture she'd suffered on Parmet's ship, but Matt knew enough from his own investigation, plus comments made by Joyce. Matt cautiously said, "Ari has history with Parmet."

"Really? That could help us." David Ray sounded relieved, so he didn't understand Ari and Parmet's "history."

"Ari met Parmet during a weapons inspection on Karthage Point, while she was on active duty. They—ah—didn't hit it off." Matt tried to sound a positive note for the biggest understatement of the century.

"Too bad, but I'm worried about his Terran tendencies toward governance, not his personality. The Terrans nationalized their scientific and engineering research, which didn't help them during the war. What if he wants more control, or can't accept our nondisclosure agreements?"

"Parmet's authority over the Priamos facilities is controlled by Pilgrimage HQ, so we can always complain. I think you'll find he's more savvy about open markets than most Terrans." Matt could vouch for that; Ari's life had been saved because Parmet preferred advancing Terran interests in the free Autonomist market *more* than he wanted personal revenge.

"Regardless, read the employment agreements. We don't want to piss off our new employers before we start," David Ray warned, before terminating the call.

Alone again, Matt began to go through the forms in a desultory fashion and an arriving comm packet caught his attention. It was addressed generically to Aether Exploration, Inc. The sender hadn't anticipated talking with him personally, perhaps because they weren't inside G-145. He tapped the blinking entry.

The familiar Leukos Industries logo revolved on the display, above the acknowledgment of receipt. His throat tightened as he remembered finding Nestor hanging, with blood dripping ... Ordeals he'd tried to forget had wormed their way back into his life. The wounds from Nestor's murder were reopened, just like Ari's kidnapping and torture by Terrans, and now—up popped rich, reclusive, and mysterious Bartholomew Leukos. Matt was one of the few who knew that Leukos was really one of Ari's comrades during the war. What next? Would Cipher suddenly appear and use some of her trusty explosives?

Matt froze. *You idiot, someone* did *try to blow up your ship, your pilot, and your fr— Sergeant Joyce. Someone's "trusty" explosives nearly killed poor Tammy Jean Pilgrimage.* And who's always at the center of all the trouble? His fingers suddenly jerked, initiating an alarm in Ari's quarters. It was time to drag the truth, kicking and screaming, out into the open.

Ariane quickly tapped through her new Feeds, noting the recent explosion on the *Pilgrimage*, which wounded a legal intern. She hurried up to the control deck, expecting this to be the subject of Matt's alarm, until she saw the Leukos Industries logo on the message view port. She looked at her employer's clenched jaw and said, "The message isn't addressed to me."

"I know who Leukos is."

"Who do you think he is?"

"I don't know his real name, but remember, *I* was there when Edones rescued you both from Cipher, and I remember everything said at the time. Leukos served with you during the war. Don't deny it." Matt looked angry and accusing; she'd desperately hoped to avoid this.

"You said my past doesn't matter." She dared him to deny his own words.

"It didn't, at one time."

"And now it does." A quiver passed up from her stomach and tightened her throat, choked off her words. She pressed her shaking hands against her thighs. "You blame me for Nestor, don't you?"

He was silent for a moment. Then his eyes unexpectedly softened with anguish. "No, Ari. I blame myself. I was the one who asked him to investigate Customs, after Valdes pissed me off."

"You think *you're* responsible?" Her relief mingled with surprise. She snorted, her common sense rising to the fore. "What a pair of idiots we are. Cipher paid the blood money, Valdes did the deed—yet we continue to flog ourselves."

"That's all gas into space; nothing can be done about it now." He jabbed his finger at the logo. "But this message follows an attempt to kill you and Joyce, an attempt upon my ship, and a trap set for David Ray that almost killed a young woman. Leukos's past is your past and I'm tired of making assumptions, Ari."

His tone was sad by the end and her eyes watered. She recognized the tears of self-pity and blinked, suppressing the urge to break down and tell Matt everything. Baring her sordid history would risk his esteem and respect, which she'd spent years in building.

Cipher had risked the truth for love, and lost her husband and children as reward. *You can't share your life, you can't wholly love each other, until you're honest with each other*, she'd said, while pointing a stunner at Ariane. Cipher's husband couldn't handle the truth and left, taking the children. That was her breaking point, after which she faked her death and started killing everyone who had been in the chain of command for releasing the TD weapon at Ura-Guinn. Cipher lost everything, even her sanity, for the hope of redemption, acceptance, and family.

Redemption isn't worth losing Matt. Examining his familiar and angular face, she knew too much of her life was anchored by this man. Yet she'd *already* endured torture and risked losing Matt, to protect Leukos's real identity. Taking a deep breath to calm her internal flutters, she thumbed acceptance of the message.

He didn't stop her.

"Let's play this message before I say anything about Mr. Leukos. He's protected by Autonomist privacy law, just like me." She struggled to keep her tone light.

The message began, showing a formally dressed thin-faced man at a desk that hid his crippling medical problems. Even though he looked every bit his age, she instead remembered the young, vital Captain Brandon Lengyel, crew commander assigned to the Fourteenth Strategic Systems Wing.

"Hello, I'm Bartholomew Leukos of Leukos Industries." The recorded Brandon smiled, looking comfortable, his false identity rolling out of his mouth with easy glibness. Was she just as facile, by now, using the fraudulent persona of Ariane Kedros?

"I send greetings to Mr. Matthew Journey, majority owner of Aether Exploration, and Ms. Ariane Kedros and Mr. David Pilgrimage, minority owners," continued the recording. "At Leukos Industries, we're well aware of the recent events in G-145, including the credit freeze from the lack of insurers for your high-risk endeavors. Personally, I feel the risk associated with solar system exploration has always been high, and it's shameful that insurers have backed away after they had to provide compensation."

Her mouth twisted at the brief show of hypocrisy. Leukos Industries had ownership in several insurance companies. This was classic Brandon behavior: complain about the status quo of the current "system," while he was doing enormously well by it. Even when that same scientific-military-industrial establishment had saved his life, after he'd volunteered for the risky rejuv process.

Her unflattering thoughts didn't slow the recorded message. "Because of this, Leukos Industries is willing to extend credit to promising research and development efforts in G-145. We will be happy to consider any proposals from Aether Exploration, or provide contracted personnel toward your G-145 commitments. Thank you."

"That looks like a business proposition to me," she said. "There's nothing sinister here."

"Yeah, right." Matt glared. "*Who is he?*"

"I can't tell you." Her fingertips felt ice cold. She crossed her arms to cover and warm her hands.

"He's made scads of money from AFCAW projects, but publicly scorns the military. Suddenly, he wants to delve into G-145 prospecting, where Leukos Industries hasn't previously shown any interest. Why?"

She ground her teeth. As a minority owner in Aether Exploration, she had to consider Matt's point of view and he had valid suspicions. "Leukos was my commander during the war."

"Now we're getting somewhere." Matt leaned back and crossed his arms, mimicking her. "Let me fill in the holes. Leukos commanded a Naga vessel, you were the pilot, and that left Cipher as what? The communications officer, obviously."

He knew much more than she realized. Her hands, covered by her arms, tightened into fists and she pressed them painfully into her ribs. *Don't go any further, please.* They stared at each other, the only sounds on the control deck the faint hum of equipment and the tension of their breaths.

"I *know*, Ari, although I'd prefer not to go back to 2090, or talk about why so many Terrans want to torture you." His tone was kind.

A roar rose in her ears and her eyes watered again. She turned away. Maybe Matt didn't judge her, maybe he didn't think she was a monster—but she fought the urge to shift her burden to anyone else. It took a moment for her ears to clear; she realized he was still speaking.

"I'm sure you wish you had the chance to turn back time, to do things differently," he was saying.

"No." She whirled.

"What?"

"I wouldn't do anything differently." Her voice was harsh. "I've gone over it, thousands—millions—more times than seems possible. Given the exact same circumstances, *I'd still follow orders.*"

Matt's eyes widened. He said nothing, but she watched the crèche-get sensibilities rise in his face: the aversion to violence, the indulgence that everyone had to have empathy and good conscience. The same impractical sensibilities that left the crèche-get defenseless, allowing Abram to slaughter his way into and through G-145. The same sensitivities that might lead Matt to believe *she* didn't have a conscience, even though she did.

Her voice broke as she quickly added, "I still—I ask *why*. There were several Naga teams placed at viable targets for the—that mission, so *why* did it have to be us? *Why* did it take such a horrific action to bring the League to the peace table? But I followed my orders, and I take responsibility for my actions, which doesn't change the guilt I suffer. Or the nightmares."

His face twisted with pity—Gaia, how she hated pity—and regret, which was far better than the revulsion she expected. He gestured toward the final still picture of the message with his thumb. "And the reclusive Bartholomew Leukos? Will he crack, like Cipher?"

She took a deep breath, feeling as if she'd just risen from the depths of a crushing ocean. Reluctantly, she considered Matt's question. "Leukos survives, I think, by shifting the blame to those who gave the release orders and picked the target. He likes to think that we, the crew, were left in the dark and perhaps things could have gone differently . . ."

Her voice trailed away. Matt stayed quiet, perhaps sensing that her mind was turning, forcing her to look at memories she'd hidden in the dark recesses. "The decision about the target wasn't under our control—the crew must do as they're ordered. What in Gaia's name did he think our mission was? Naga was *designed* to carry TD weapons." Her eyes widened and she met Matt's sympathetic gaze, without flinching this time.

"It's a defense mechanism." Matt cocked his head. "It helps him get through the days and lets him look the Terrans in the face. What about you? You'll have to manage a working relationship with SP Parmet."

"I'll be fine." Parmet had already passed up two perfect opportunities to kill her. His wife Sabina was another matter. Sabina had gotten the drop on her and kicked her almost senseless in a deserted passageway, but she wasn't going to reveal that embarrassment to her employer. "I can handle my job, if that's what worries you."

Frustration came back into Matt's eyes and his lips

closed firmly. "Sometimes, Ari . . ." He shook his head and closed his eyes for a moment. "It's *you* I'm worried about. While I admire your determination to be responsible—which seems more honorable than Leukos's coping method—you've left yourself no way out, no path toward redemption. If you can't forgive yourself, you're going to self-destruct. And when that happens, how many bystanders like Nestor will be taken out?"

Of course, he meant how many *innocent* bystanders. She considered her conversation with Edones and Stephanos. Matt deserved to know the threat.

"Ari?"

"I'm still a target."

"No kidding."

She ignored his drawling sarcasm. "I'll get updates regarding the investigations on the *Pilgrimage*. I can keep you apprised, as long as you don't tell Owen I'm leaking you information."

"As if I'd tell that bastard anything." Matt gestured toward the Leukos Industries message. "What about your old commander? Why is he trying to wiggle his way back into your life *now*?"

Her hopes whispered that Brandon wanted to be near her, perhaps he still loved the original Ari—but *no*, her logical brain argued. Brandon had made it clear that he didn't approve of Ariane Kedros, *of who I am today*.

"You know Cipher's body was never found." Matt's eyes were focused on her, waiting for her to nod. "Do you know Leukos blocked the military investigators?"

"No."

"He also railroaded the civilian authorities into closing the case. No one's looking for Cipher."

She watched Matt and felt a sinking feeling in her stomach; neither of them trusted Brandon, aka rich Mr. Leukos. Inside her gut, lack of trust felt just like betrayal. "Do we need his money?"

"Not after we got an infusion from the Minoans. They pay promptly; none of that forty-five-day-accounts-payable-cycle rubbish I get from everybody else."

"Then thank Leukos Industries for their consideration and tell them we may have an 'opportunity for investment' in the near future. If you stick to business, it'll give us time." Her stomach rumbled. She moved toward the hatch and the lower levels, which held their small galley and quarters.

"Time for what?"

"Time to learn why he's so interested." She glanced over her shoulder and saw suspicion cross Matt's face. He probably sensed so much more: *Time for me to uncover Tahir's killer, find a saboteur who uses TEBI grenades, and get our new double agent on the Directorate payroll.* With such an impossible list, she felt tired. She also felt ashamed, because she was *still* hiding her mission from Matt.

"Was he ever more than just your commander?"

The sharp words made her pause. Matt's question almost sounded jealous. The small kernel of fluttering pleasure was immediately overwhelmed by embarrassment as she felt the shadow of Diana Oleander. Was she really hoping for Matt's attention, when he was involved with a talented, attractive, young officer, unfettered by emotional baggage? Oleander made Matt happy, and she shouldn't mess that up.

"Well?"

"How many times have you and Oleander talked, since you left the *Pilgrimage*?" She raised an eyebrow.

"That's none of your business." His voice abruptly fell. "Point taken."

"Good. I'm cooking cabbage rolls for lunch. Want any?" Her smile widened at the way his nose and upper lip twitched. She could lighten the moment by tormenting his crèche-get senses, but she couldn't lighten the load of guilt and secrets she carried. Everything had changed now that Matt knew her past, and yet, nothing had changed inside her.

Procedures and security at the Beta Priamos Station had changed significantly. No one, particularly the Terran State Prince now responsible for station operations, wanted to be caught unawares again. Everything was tighter. Ariane noticed on the Space Docking Automated Transmission System, or S-DATS display, that Beta Priamos had finally upgraded their dock-approach software so the autopilot on *Aether's Touch* could interface. After docking, hard-faced inspectors came aboard to check for undeclared passengers or dangerous cargo. By their bearing and the way their hands kept drifting toward absent sidearms, she figured they were nonuniformed Terran Space Forces. Matt's tight jaw, as he answered standard questions asked at other ports, said he wasn't fooled by the civilian attire.

After they docked, Matt scheduled the meeting with Parmet. She hid her misgivings. *Saying* she could face Parmet was easy, but actually *doing* it—much more difficult.

"Shouldn't we wait until the *Golden Bull* docks, so David Ray can go with us?" She hurried to keep pace along the curved corridor.

"Parmet wanted to see us, so let's get this over with." Matt's stride never faltered. "Anyway, we need his approval to travel down to the moon's surface."

They moved through a ring and climbed a vertical to the level that housed Command Post. Parmet's offices were located near CP. A uniformed and armored TSF, stationed at the junction of the vertical, nodded at them as they stepped out of the hatch.

"Where are *our* guys?" Matt whispered after they were well away from the guard. "And what is he packing?"

She smiled. Sometimes Matt seemed completely Autonomist: If he needed help, he wanted his *own* military around. "You'll have to ask Parmet. As for the TSF, he's got a short-range stun pistol on his belt and a civilian shotgun slung, probably loaded with rubber-covered riotshot."

He frowned. "That doesn't sound like military issue."

"It isn't. They're trying to fill the civilian role of constable or security. Like those." She gestured toward the civilian security appearing over the hallway horizon. They were approaching Parmet's office and outside the hatch stood two brutes, one male and one female, rigged in slick expensive civilian armor and exoskeletons that surpassed most military-grade gear.

"Parmet's locked this station down tighter than the sphincter on the Greaaaaat—" Matt gargled his last word, trying to swallow any mention of the Great Bull as a red-robed Minoan emissary stepped out of a hatchway down the corridor, followed by a guardian. The civilian security brutes split their attention between the two approaching parties, although the Minoan seemed intent upon intercepting her and Matt. They met in front of the guards to Parmet's office.

"Contractor Director?" Matt said cautiously.

There were the requisite pauses in the conversation, but Contractor Director was a speed-speaking demon compared to Warrior Commander. The emissary's horns waved formally in acknowledgment, first toward Matt, then Ariane. "Owner of Aether Exploration, Ariane-as-Kedros."

She bowed her head slightly, relieved to avoid the titles "Breaker of Treaties" and "Destroyer of Worlds." But why didn't they use "Explorer of Solar Systems," since that was the position they wanted her to fill, per the contract? Very puzzling. Matt was frowning also.

"You do not need to rent work facilities," Contractor Director said. "Equipment and premises leased by Hellas Nautikos can be transferred to Aether Exploration. However, there is individualized property that must be inventoried and delivered, once ownership is traced. Can this be done by Aether Exploration?"

Matt gaped as he tried to understand the convoluted question, but she grasped the meaning immediately.

"Personal effects, to be returned to next of kin?" Her heart felt squeezed as she remembered Mr. Barone, a big quiet man with a deep voice, who picked his words carefully. He'd been the highest-ranking Nautikos supervisor. He and his employees on Priamos were dead, executed, the target of Abram's rage because they worked for the aliens that had attacked Abram's home.

Contractor Director made a fluid gesture with a black-gloved hand, which she interpreted as helplessness. "We do not understand the delicate traditions involved with your familial grief."

This was the last sort of duty she wanted, but someone would have to do it. She and Matt exchanged a nod.

"We can take care of it," he said.

That apparently satisfied Contractor Director, who moved away while saying, "The contract kick-off meeting will be at sixteen hundred tomorrow."

The haste with which the Minoan ended the conversation was downright human, almost unseemly so. Matt and Ariane were left in front of the silent civilian guards, unmoving except for an occasional swivel of their heads.

Matt shrugged and turned. "We're Mr. Journey and Ms. Kedros, of Aether Exploration."

"We need to check your identification." After loading and perusing their ID data in her slate, the female security officer spoke quietly into her implanted mike.

The double doors behind the guards opened ponderously. They were made to handle pressure, but still look like their "grav-hugger equivalents," as Matt would say. Waiting behind the doors was TSF Ensign Walker, the current head of security on Beta Priamos.

"If you'll follow me, please," Walker said.

The ensign led them to a conference room. Just inside the hatch was a tasty layout of pastries, snacks, and a hot drink dispenser filled with real Hellas Kaffi.

"Make yourselves comfortable. The SP will be here in a moment." Walker sat down at the table installed in the center of the room.

Always ready to eat, Ariane grabbed two small phyllo pies from the counter. Matt was more cautious, sniffing and carefully examining the label on the dispenser. Once he was satisfied with the contents, he injected a healthy amount into a cup with a self-sealing top.

She popped the little pies in her mouth; they had a sweet nutty filling and the thin parchment pastry melted in her mouth. Matt settled himself across from the ensign, and she sat down next to Matt.

"You'll both be happy to learn we've installed ComNet-grade explosive sniffers at all station portals." Ensign Walker gave them a perfunctory smile. "Especially you, Ms. Kedros. When we heard you were coming, we rushed the installation."

What a smart-ass. Her polite smile hardened. "That's thoughtful of you, Ensign, but—"

The rest of her retort died on her lips as State Prince Parmet and his co-wife Garnet entered the room. She'd forgotten the presence Parmet could project. He was tall and, like most Terrans, had perfect body symmetry. Adept at *somaural* projection, his dignified stride made Garnet, hurrying behind him, seem obsequious by comparison. Ensign Walker stood up, smartly at attention, and Matt automatically followed suit in a civilian parody. She, however, took her time and haphazardly pushed herself out of her seat. Parmet wasn't *her* leader. Since Terrans were quick to interpret body language, Garnet's eyes narrowed. Ariane nodded at her with casual recognition.

"Take your seats, please." Parmet ignored her insolent posture and seated himself at the head of the table. He made introductions, for Matt's benefit. As usual, this social dance displayed the Terran love of names that tied back to the home planet. "My wife Garnet Westwind Tachawee has taken on some of the reporting tasks required by your S-triple-ECB."

"They're not *mine*." Matt refused ownership of that infamous bureaucracy.

"We agree, Mr. Journey, after we waded through their regulations," Walker said. "We needed to see whether you could work for yourself, because this exploration process was starting to look like a money-laundering scheme."

Matt's mouth fell open, but Garnet smoothly interrupted.

"Forgive the ensign. He's just expressing our frustration with the Consortium's complex procedures." Garnet's eyes flashed sideways toward Ensign Walker. "We understand the percentage Aether Exploration makes from the leases is to help you recover your earlier prospecting costs. That percentage has nothing to do with the *current* contract you've signed, although we were concerned about possible conflicts of interest."

"And the fact you're taking Minoan money," added Walker.

"We're hired by a company incorporated on Hellas Prime. Besides, we can't benefit from the leases until this research generates spinoff technology." Matt started explaining the financial relationships.

Bored, Ariane's attention wandered about the room and lit upon Parmet, who was watching her. This didn't surprise her. Parmet liked to watch his staff prod others so he could study reactions. He was talented at *somaural* reading, which could interpret everything from unconscious body language to subtle Martian hand signals. With a shock, she realized her eyes were locked with Parmet's. The green of his eyes was flecked with brown, but they weren't warm. She looked away. She had no way to prevent Parmet from "reading" her, but she didn't care. There was nothing he could learn as she listened to Matt and Garnet chat about contracts.

"Everything's in order, including transfer of facilities leased by Nautikos. We'll key the locks to your thumbprints." Garnet's voice was emotionless as she handed Matt's slate back.

Mercifully, the meeting was wrapping up. She stood up with Matt. Walker and Garnet picked up their slates—everyone stopped at a motion from State Prince Parmet, who hadn't risen.

"I'd like to speak with Major Kedros alone," Parmet said. Garnet's eyes widened.

"I'm not on active duty," she said.

"Then I'd like a word with you, *Ms.* Kedros."

"Only if I'm present. She's my employee." Matt's hands suddenly rested on her shoulders, protective.

"No." She touched his hand on her shoulder. "I'll be fine. Wait for me, okay?"

"You bet," Matt muttered.

Everybody reluctantly filed out of the room. Garnet left last, her lips pressed together. Ariane stayed standing, waiting.

"You don't fool me, Major. You're still wearing your uniform."

CHAPTER 9

TEBI's success with two-part poisons near the end of the war justified their research into more sophisticated assassination tools. The R&D was expensive, since each constituent of a poison must be specially designed for effective delivery. Whether the League considered TEBI's investment worth . . .

—*AFCAW Report on TEBI Weapons and Tactics (Declassified)*, 2101.242.12.00 UT, indexed by *Democritus 12* under Metrics Imperatives

"**P**ardon?" Ariane looked down at her clean coveralls with the Aether Exploration logo.

"You're under orders. A plainclothes mission, perhaps?" He matched her sardonic tone.

She'd specifically avoided even *thinking* about Maria in his presence. Maybe he was fishing for a response. She smiled and returned the favor. "You needn't worry about any *Directorate* missions, SP. It looks like Dr. Rouxe was killed with a sophisticated multicomponent poison, a common TEBI tool. Perhaps you should worry about Dr. Istaga, who's stepping off the *Golden Bull* right about now."

As a *somaural* master, Parmet wouldn't reveal surprise unless he wanted her to see it. He nodded thoughtfully, as if he expected her comment. She glanced at the time displayed on her cuff; if everything went well, the *Golden Bull* had recently docked and Istaga would soon be on Parmet's calendar.

"I look forward to seeing my previous interpreter," Parmet said in a flat voice. "But you're wrong about whether I should *worry* about your Directorate. I'm interested in everyone's agenda, because I've recently received odd threatening messages."

"Odd? I thought State Princes received threats all the time."

"Not ones that know my private ComNet address; usually they end up in the public queue handled by my staff. And no one has previously threatened the *family* of a State Prince *who let the destroyer of Ura-Guinn go free.*"

His words, as well as his tone, chilled her. Being Autonomist, her reaction was to look around for recording nodes.

"Don't worry, I haven't allowed ComNet to encroach into *this* conference room. Everyone must carry their data on slates or implants."

"How many people know about—me?" She sat back down.

"Not many."

She leaned back in her chair and crossed her arms, uncomfortable with his intense scrutiny. "I hope you're not suggesting the Directorate would stoop to sending threats, or involve your family."

"My security determined the message came from *inside* G-145, so once again, I ask about your *mission*." His eyes had gone from intense to glaring. "And save me from that prim protest, *the Directorate doesn't perform state assassinations.* We both know what a slippery definition you're using."

Contrary to the Directorate, TEBI had claimed responsibility for assassinations during the war, but her words of objection stayed in her throat. *She'd* never been a hired killer. At least, that hadn't been the original purpose of the mission. Her eyes lowered, and she stared at the generic gray deck without noticing it, the seams of displayable material blurring. There had been one covert mission when things went wrong, when she and Joyce wouldn't have made a clean exit if she hadn't . . . She shivered, clearing her head of the memory, and looked again at Parmet.

"Smart." His facial muscles slid into neutrality. "Don't

say anything, Major, because there's no need for either of us to explore the past. What I propose is cooperation."

"What sort?"

"The sort where you use your skills to help me find my culprit, and I don't throw you into protective custody. Ensign Walker already suggested that, after reading the case files from the *Pilgrimage*."

"I've got no time to do charity work. Our employers have promised a full schedule." She smiled. The smile was pretense, hiding the sinking feeling in her chest. G-145 represented such *potential*, being the first place mankind had found evidence of an alien, but non-Minoan, civilization. What she longed for, hoped for, was to throw herself into this huge well of research and exploration. It was a chance to lose her guilt and ghosts, but then Edones assigned her to Mission Turncoat. The last thing she wanted was to add another pesky case on top of that, particularly one that kept dredging up ghosts. Besides, she was the last person who would willingly help Parmet. He hadn't touched her personally, but he'd ordered the kidnapping, torture, and then blackmailed her with Brandon's safety.

"I'm not asking for extra time. At some point, you'll stumble over the malefactor and I'll want information."

"If I refuse?"

"I tell Ensign Walker you have a covert Directorate mission and he throws you in the brig—to hell with mere protective custody." His voice was light.

She snorted. "You have no justification for detaining me."

"I don't need any."

She watched Parmet's face, even though he didn't allow any clues. In her gut, she felt he was bluffing. She concluded the same through cold calculation. Parmet knew Matt's company worked for the Minoans. He wouldn't dare endanger the advantage, and money, the Minoans offered to beleaguered researchers in G-145. So why was he trying to enlist her aid in the first place?

"If I run into anything, I'll let your people know. Who would be my contact?" she said cautiously.

"Zheng, from my civilian security staff. None of the military personnel, AFCAW or TSF, have been told about these personal threats."

Aha. Her fingers tapped the arm of her chair with satisfaction. Parmet was so worried about the Terran political environment that he only trusted his own longtime employees, transplanted from Mars. His civilian security, and *her.* Why did he trust her, when she was his traditional enemy and he'd personally wronged her? Her fingers stopped moving and she again looked straight into his eyes. If he was offering her an olive branch, there wasn't any suggestion in his expression.

"Fine. I'll talk to Zheng if I discover anything." She rose to leave.

He spoke as she reached to open the door. "You understand, Major Kedros, that you shouldn't confuse *trust* with *forgiveness.*"

She left without acknowledging his words.

"Lieutenant Oleander? Still with me?"

Diana focused on the maintenance tech again, and grimaced. "Sorry. Had problems sleeping." That wasn't a complete lie, but the root cause was the misery fogging her head and heart. When Matt left, she thought she'd be fine with frequent calls to *Aether's Touch,* but the calls didn't stave off loneliness for the Matt-shaped void in her life.

"I can understand, with everything that's happened recently." He gave her a sympathetic smile. Oleander wished, desperately, that she could remember his name. A nice man, with the ageless look the generational got after years of journeys that stretched out time. He'd probably been born before her great-grandfather.

"You were saying . . . ?" She motioned vaguely at the cold stainless steel table, where the blackened pieces of a maintenance bot rested.

"Our cursory audit of the surviving logs hasn't proven anything, except the bot was hijacked. We've sent evidence on to the cybernetics unit for analysis." He picked up a hand-size fragment of casing. "Since bots don't have the aerogel armor that ships do, the shrapnel literally blew it to bits."

"Were you able to recover all the pieces?"

"About ninety-five percent. Unfortunately, due to its time in space and the effects of the explosion, we haven't found any fingerprints or biological samples for DNA analysis."

"Or the saboteur was careful not to leave any evidence," she said.

"Possibly. This time, however, State Prince Duval can't complain about tainted evidence. Only *Pilgrimage* personnel handled the salvage and we documented each piece extensively and maintained the chain of custody."

"Since you mention Duval, I'm guessing the evidence points toward a Terran saboteur."

"Terran explosives," the tech corrected. "We've identified the composition as Terran, specifically manufactured for the military at Teller's Colony—"

"From approximately 2090 to 2096," Oleander finished. "Such as the device planted in Sergeant Joyce's room. Could anyone get physical access to the bot to plant the device?"

The tech gave her an anemic smile and hedged. "Well, we never had this situation before."

"Please tell me they're controlled, or under observation, at all times." Through the long window on one side of the maintenance bay, she saw mechanics hanging bots on a revolving storage device.

The tech shook his head. "We've never needed to maintain physical security on the maintenance bots. There are unsupervised storage and dispersal bays on every docking level. But they had to crack password-controlled security to change the bot's programming," he added stoutly.

"Hmm." Oleander had no response; she was realizing how overtrusting one could become in a cloistered environment. For decades, this generational crew had been on the *Pilgrimage* with no exposure to human malignancy. The enemy had been their environment. Now they were having difficulty adjusting their protective instincts.

"Thanks—look forward to your full report." Having forgotten the tech's name, she pointed to the base of her ear in a harassed fashion as she backed away. "I've got to call my superior."

Standing beside the hatch to the corridor, she called Captain Floros. She was surprised she had to leave a message; as a compulsive multitasker, Floros usually picked up personal calls. Halfway through her bleak report, she received a familiar poke in the shoulder.

Myron, the senator's aide and great-nephew, had quietly entered the maintenance bay.

"—Because there's no supervision of the equipment in storage." She finished the message quickly, noting the anticipation that lit Myron's flat eyes.

"Yes?" she asked, using a deliberate and cold tone.

"I've got a summons for you."

"For what?"

He tapped his slate and motioned. When he figured out that the bulkhead wasn't going to display anything, he handed the slate to her.

She looked over the summons, trying to interpret the legalese. "This statement and questioning is required by Senator Stephanos, not the ICT?"

"Yes. The Senator has acquiesced to review AFCAW's part in the recent catastrophe." A smirk twitched his lip and quickly disappeared. "This is in everyone's best interest; get the facts documented before anyone starts pointing fingers or criticizing."

"What do you mean, our *part* in the catastrophe?"

"I suppose it's more accurate to say AFCAW's *performance* is being evaluated. All crew members are recalled to duty stations, to assist with the audit. All data and logs on the *Bright Crescent* are temporarily confiscated for examination."

Scrolling through the summons, she saw her schedule. She was booked for several days. "What about my work for Pilgrimage security, regarding the murder and sabotage?"

"The only thing that takes precedence over this summons would be a call to testify for the ICT. You understand,

Lieutenant." He nodded, that frightening emptiness flooding his eyes again.

No, she didn't understand.

Ariane went back to the corridor, where she found Matt chatting affably with that *lunatic bitch* Sabina. She hesitated in surprise, but made sure she was moving through the hatch when they both noticed her. Matt's smile widened as he relaxed; Sabina's face went blank and her posture tensed.

As she approached, she heard Sabina say, "It was nice meeting you, Mr. Journey."

Sabina smiled sweetly at Matt, turned, and walked past Ariane with a cold nod. They were almost the same height; Sabina had a very un-Terran-like dainty physique. Her recent skin-do, also uncharacteristic for a Terran, was fading in a natural way that could only be provided by expensive salons. Her short, red, almost burgundy, hair cupped her head and neatly stayed behind ears pierced with three small studs of precious stones. As she stepped, using a gymnast's prance, her smooth gray jumpsuit showed muscular ripples in her legs, stomach, and arms.

When she reached Matt, Ariane crossed her arms and watched Sabina enter the hatch she'd just exited. "You've got to appreciate the Terran fashion sense—don't they wear anything but muddy colors?"

"Huh? Color?" Matt was also watching Sabina's backside. "Why bother with color?"

"Yeah, why bother?" Ariane echoed, glancing slyly at her employer. "Spoken like true ship-born-and-raised. But I'm warning you: Watch out for her."

"Why? She seemed nice enough. She welcomed me to Beta Priamos and offered to show me around."

"Sure, she's a model tour guide when she's not beating visitors to a pulp."

"What?" Matt snapped out of his reverie at her caustic tone.

"Never mind."

"What did Parmet want?"

"He had concerns about security." This was true, although her mouth tasted as bitter as if she'd lied.

"That's all?" Matt's voice became sharp. "He didn't act, er, improper?"

"Improper?"

Matt wouldn't meet her gaze. "He's obsessed with you, but it feels—it feels sexual."

Her eyes widened. "*What?*"

"I can see the signs. It's a guy thing."

"You're selling shit from the Great Bull itself." She pictured Parmet, feeling revolted, but it only took a moment for her brain to find the absurdity of the suggestion. She almost laughed. "Don't put Emotional Analyst on your resume yet, Matt. He played you. He's an expert in *somaural* projection."

"Ah." Matt blinked. "But why would Parmet want to mislead me?"

She shook off her disquiet. "Maybe he just wanted to mess with you *and* me. He likes to manipulate people."

"Like that bastard Edones?" Matt frowned.

"I suppose so." She nodded and they continued walking. There was no point in protesting the differences between Owen and Parmet. Matt had long ago made up his mind about Owen, calling him manipulative, secretive, dangerous, and egotistical. While she'd agree with the first three traits, she suspected Owen was more complicated than Matt gave him credit for.

They were almost late for their contract kick-off meeting, an unpardonable sin. Matt picked up speed and she hurried to follow, glancing at him thoughtfully. It was indeed a festering question: Why would Parmet want to manipulate Matt?

As Isrid expected, Sabina showed up immediately after Kedros left.

"It's a mistake to bring her into this." Sabina walked up to the table, placed her palms on the surface and leaned over toward him, providing him a perfect view of her cleavage.

"You had no problem leaving Ensign Walker in the dark and, if I remember, you were in favor of taking this approach."

"I was carried away. Aroused by visions of Kedros hung out to dry, I'll admit." She bared her perfectly regular white teeth. "But when I passed her in the hall, she didn't look hunted so much as a huntress." A twist and flicker of her hand said, *Not the effect I wanted*.

"Too late. I can't take back the information I gave her, just because you want her to fail."

"I want her to be successful, but as *bait*." She rolled her shoulders so her breasts rounded even more. This distracted him, just as she designed. "How can you be sure she'll pull our stalker out of hiding?"

"The threats always mention her. So if I'm a target, she has to be." He looked away to regain his focus. "I'm not surprised she seemed confident. Kedros's superiors have thrown her to the wolves before."

"So now we're *Canis lupus*." She raised an eyebrow. "Luckily, a few subspecies still exist on Terra. Should we find a pack to join?"

"Funny you should *finally* think of Terra." His tone was savage, intentionally so. "Because this isn't about you, or your vengeance. You *know* what we've tried, and how desperate it is for all species clinging to life there, in the face of an oncoming ice age. Think, for once, without your hormones."

Her expression became unreadable as her *somaural* training kicked in. "The Builders? You mean their attempts to transform Sophia Two? They didn't get very far with that lump of ice, and I thought the last research report put our chances of understanding the Builders on par with—"

"Our chances of understanding ancient Egyptian hieroglyphics without the Rosetta stone," he finished. "I read the reports also."

"We're looking at decades of work. You think anyone can shortcut that?"

"The Minoans might. They wouldn't sell the Nautikos leases."

"So? Our horned peace police don't like to lose their investment money, any more than any other lessee." She shrugged.

He pressed his lips together and shook his head. "That's what we thought, too, so I made them an offer blessed by the Overlord himself, an offer that was more than generous. The Minoans couldn't make that much from their leases for a decade—*unless they expected a breakthrough*."

"Their refusal to sell may not mean anything."

"The Minoans crushed every possible legal obstacle to contracting Aether Exploration, and hired Kedros *by name*. If the Minoans want her so badly, I want to know why."

Sabina looked thoughtful. "I understand the urge to keep your allies close and your enemies closer. But beware of that strategy, because you may confuse them."

He gave her a dark look as she strolled out of the room, but was distracted by a call. He took it using his Autonomist-made implants, relayed through his slate. Garnet's voice sounded clear in his ear; he loved the Autonomists' equipment, so much more reliable than the Terran equivalents.

"The *Golden Bull* has docked and we're moving the crèches into the labs," Garnet said. "One of the passengers, a Dr. Istaga, wants to see you right away."

"Bring him round." Isrid stretched. Maybe now he'd get some answers.

CHAPTER 10

The testimony and evidence presented this morning was horrific. If the deaths of Daniel Pilgrimage, Commander Charlene Pilgrimage, and Captain Zabat teach us anything, it's a cautionary tale against naiveté. They let the isolationists onto the control deck, trusting in their historical neutrality. Here's another tragic lesson: Pilgrimage HQ sent more than fifty thousand HKD in relief donations to this same isolationist cult. . . .

—Dr. Net-head Stavros, 2106.054.12.30 UT,
indexed by Heraclitus 9 under Conflict Imperative

Ariane and Matt were not the latest arrivals to the kickoff meeting. They met Dr. Lowry and David Ray, waiting in one of the few ComNet-capable conference rooms in the station. Ariane made introductions, being the only person who had met everyone. Then they waited for their employer. Half an hour of chitchat passed.

"I'm honored to meet one of Mars's premier astrophysicists," David Ray said to Dr. Lowry. "But I'm puzzled. Why did the Minoans ask for you by name? We've guessed that they want to hamstring me, Matt, and Ariane, the infamous Breaker of Treaties, with nondisclosure agreements."

"That's a joke; they named me Explorer of Solar Systems in the contract," Ariane said quickly, glancing at Dr. Lowry. She and Lowry had been imprisoned together when Tahir had threatened them all with a weapon, demanding to meet the Destroyer of Worlds. The Minoans had used

that term, publicly, during the initial Pax Minoica conference, for the Autonomist crew that used a TD weapon on
Ura-Guinn. Had Dr. Lowry made the connection?

"Don't worry, Ms. Kedros. I can forgive you for breaking treaties, but only when saving a solar system." Her eyes
sparkled with warning.

So she does *remember*. Ariane looked away first, and
busied herself with her slate.

Dr. Myrna Fox Lowry had earned her Astrophysics
chair at MIT, Mars, three years ago, the youngest person to
ever hold that position. Her features and build were typical of the uniformity enforced by Terran eugenics, relieved
somewhat by her small crooked smile and animated dark
eyes. Her tomboyish face was framed by short, light brown
hair that spiked and twisted from a casual finger-comb.

"To answer your question, Mr. Pilgrimage, I'm not sure
why the Minoans requested me," Lowry continued.

"Please call me David Ray. 'Mr. Pilgrimage' applies to
several hundred men in this solar system. Perhaps your
work here in G-145 has interested the Minoans?"

"Certainly—David Ray." Dr. Lowry's smile widened
to match David Ray's. "I'm the Terran member of the research team that's working on the Builders' buoy, although
our work's on hold."

Beside Ariane, Matt shifted uncomfortably. The *artifact*
was now called the *Builders' buoy*. A motionless artificial
structure in space, anchored in the inner part of the solar
system, which researchers had determined was an inactive
N-space buoy.

"We're familiar with it," Matt said. "We left our most
expensive bot on it."

Lowry laughed. "It's still there, Mr. Journey."

"You can call me Matt."

"Lucky for us, Matt, your bot is still attached to the
buoy and transmitting. Our team, that's me, Oran Novak,
and Peter—" Lowry's smile faded. "Dr. Katsaros was killed
by the isolationists. Executed." She glanced at Ariane, the
wounds evident behind her eyes.

"Hmm. I have a lot of questions. The first is whether

the Minoans will *really* help us restart the research on the Builders' buoy. If they do, they weaken their stranglehold on the technology—" David Ray's musing was cut short by the tardy, but nonetheless well-timed arrival of their employer.

The heavy hatch swung open to reveal the red robes of Contractor Director. With a dip of its long ebony horns, the emissary easily stepped through an opening that seemed impossibly small for its shoulders and height. She watched the long red robes stir and remembered the cold she felt from Warrior Commander. A short-horned guardian followed the emissary, of course.

"Welcome, Contractor Director," David Ray said.

Everyone was quiet as they waited for the emissary's horns to nod acknowledgment. They had all probably read helpful material, articles titled "Interaction Techniques with Minoans" or "Minoan Etiquette" or such, but there was nothing like experience to help build patience. She looked at Matt, who folded his arms and settled back to wait.

Contractor Director appeared to be hurrying, for a Minoan, and keeping the requisite pauses short. Even so, Matt started nodding off. She kept him awake with her elbow, and David Ray occasionally asked questions, making sure the nondisclosure agreement didn't cause treasonous acts against their multiple governments, and that there was wiggle room for contractors to exchange research data.

"Finally," Matt whispered in relief, as they all thumbed acceptance and signed.

Unfortunately, the next unimaginative topic was the work the Minoans expected them to take over. These included contributing to the study of the Builders' buoy, as well as the "cultural anthropological studies" that Hellas Nautikos had been running. She lost the thread of the briefing as she tried to puzzle out why the Minoans had *humans* study *human reactions* to the alien Builders. Thus, she missed the shocking—

"You've got *what*?" Matt jumped to his feet, saw the guardian react defensively, and as quickly bounced backward into his chair.

"This is a set of rules we call the Mundane Semantic and Lexical Parser, although that is an optimistic title. We were going to release it to all Priamos research contractors, but our plans were changed by the Criminal Isolationists."

"You understand the Builders' symbols—their language?" Matt sputtered.

Dr. Lowry frowned. Ariane wondered if she was dismayed at all the lost research time. They could have spent the past months doing more than getting the power working and mapping the ruins.

"By your calendar," Contractor Director paused briefly, "we were first able to communicate with the 'Builders' twenty-six thousand UT years ago."

Matt made a dry sound in his throat. Ariane was speechless, exchanging glances with David Ray. Turning, she saw Dr. Lowry making notes on a slate, something about "time scale." There was no sense in complaining about not producing the translator earlier; suddenly, she had a different perspective on wasted months, only *months*, of research.

"When Pilgrimage proposed the G-145 mission, we understood that Minoan ships had never traveled to this solar system," David Ray said quietly.

"You were correct."

"You encountered the Builders elsewhere?"

It was agonizing to wait for the Minoan to dip its horns, causing strings of cascading jewels to sway. "Correct."

"Are you going to tell us *where*?" From the tightness of his voice, Matt sounded like he was reaching the limit of his restraint.

"That information is not necessary for your research." Contractor Director sounded smug.

"When Minoans first made contact with humans, they stated there were no other existing sentient species." Lowry's voice was brusque, a logic missile homing in on a problem.

"That's practically yesterday for them," whispered Matt in Ariane's ear. First contact between the Minoans and Earth, now called Terra, happened around one hundred and thirty UT years ago. Everyone assumed the contact was the result of the Hellenic Alliance landing on Terra's moon.

Contractor Director said nothing, until David Ray rephrased Lowry's comment as a question. "When Minoans arrived in our solar system, why didn't they consider the Builders an 'existing sentient species'?"

"The Builders had ceased being sentient. It happens, particularly with evolved self-consciousness." Contractor Director made a negligent motion with its hand.

"Just like that, huh?" Matt commented quietly.

Contractor Director might have heard him. "We think it ninety-nine percent probable the Builders regressed in the past ten thousand years and their civilization collapsed."

"But you haven't confirmed that." Lowry belatedly remembered that a question was required. "Is the collapse *verified?*"

"Researcher of Astrophysics asks an excellent question." Contractor Director methodically selected a tawny jewel on a rope that fell from its left horn and looped down to the back of its headdress. Two gloved fingers on one hand twirled the jewel, while the Minoan pointed at the view port on the bulkhead. The words "Proprietary Information" displayed.

The Minoan's surprisingly crisp tone, as well as the display, caused Ariane to sit up. Until now, she'd been enjoying the show, but wondering why she'd been given a ticket. The Minoans had their expert astrophysicist, experienced prospector, and—well, David Ray had a lot of legal experience and knew how to protect intellectual property. Why did they need her?

"We intend to repair the Builders' buoy and sponsor your *exploration* to the Builders' main world. Of course, we need volunteers." After making this pronouncement, Contractor Director folded its arms and waited.

Shocked silence. The world had just flipped ninety degrees; technological blocks had mysteriously disappeared, replaced with questions, such as *why didn't the Minoans just go themselves?*

This felt like a dream she'd had before she came to G-

145. In the dream, she struggled to break through a heavy door that had a keyhole. Somewhere, somehow, without any memory of how it happened, she found a key. It was cold and heavy in her hand, made through archaic metallurgy. Then, when she turned to the door, she couldn't find a keyhole.

She'd told Major Tafani about the dream. After some thought, he pronounced his explanation: She was searching for meaning in her life, trying to validate her existence. Whether Tafani had been correct or not, no longer mattered. The Minoans had just handed her a clear, honorable, and beneficial goal, minus the usual moral ambiguities of Edones's missions.

Ariane stirred. "Count me in," she said.

Looking every bit the middle-aged academician, Dr. Istaga hurried forward and offered his hand. "SP, nice to see you again."

Isrid smiled dryly as they shook hands. Dr. Istaga knew how to break a *somaural* reading, and contact did that quite handily. The diffident Istaga had convincingly played the part of interpreter during the weapons inspection at Karthage Point, but he was also a *somaural* master and a special operative for Overlord Three. He'd earned Autonomist hatred for his wartime missions, which he performed under the code name Andre Covanni and where he pushed the boundaries of the Phaistos Protocols. As Andre, he was responsible for many civilian deaths that only narrowly were defined as collateral damage.

"I hope your excursion to Beta Priamos was comfortable." Isrid picked his words carefully, adding emphasis on excursion and signaling, *A brief pleasure trip?*

"It's business, I'm afraid. A fact-finding trip for the Overlord. You understand." Dr. Istaga looked around and asked about area security with rapid subtlety of finger and wrist movements.

The room is secure, Isrid answered *somaurally*. "I watched them put up the bulkheads in this section. My personal security staff scans for both active and passive recording pips every shift, at two randomly determined times. No one, including me, knows the scan schedule more than twenty minutes in advance." Isrid tapped the time display. "The last scan occurred about an hour ago, at thirteen thirty-three."

"Good. I have information for ears only, no record allowed."

Isrid nodded. "Now you'll try to surprise me by saying you killed Dr. Tahir Rouxe."

"SP, I'd never attempt to surprise you." Dr. Istaga used a reproachful tone. "Besides, I couldn't hope to hide my methods from a former TEBI Director. I delivered two components to Dr. Rouxe, while a guard unwittingly provided the third."

How long had it been? Only seven years since he held the position, but those memories had already faded, like they were part of someone else's life. Was that because he had pushed them away, or because he had changed? Maybe he was just getting old. He sighed and said, "Multicomponent poisons have been in TEBI's toolkit for a while. In some circles, it'd be tantamount to burning 'TEBI' across the victim's forehead."

"True, but it was nice to get back to dependable basic tools. It's also appropriate *for this case*, because Pilgrimage sovereignty demands that the crèche-get perform the autopsy. They're just not up to snuff in multicomponent poisons." Dr. Istaga smirked.

"AFCAW's Directorate of Intelligence will surely suspect, and Colonel Edones has his ship docked on the *Pilgrimage*."

"The Autonomists are snarled up in their own problems. Some sort of political furor over the costs of saving G-145."

"But why neutralize Dr. Rouxe? That could capsize the prosecution's case." Isrid took care to appear noncommittal, but this question was important. Several Terrans had died in fighting Abram's isolationists; one of them was State Prince Hauser, a comrade and friend. Abram also had the audacity to imprison and torture Isrid, as well as

Isrid's son, Chander. For those crimes, Isrid would gladly see the isolationists executed, under Terran authority—but killing Rouxe made that goal more difficult. Why take out the prosecution's best witness?

An expert reader, perhaps even sensitive to auras, Dr. Istaga's eyes narrowed as he watched Isrid. For a fraction of a second, Isrid saw the vague features of an unremarkable academician sharpen into those of a cunning, uncompromising political officer. This, surely, was *Andre*. Just as quickly, facial features blurred and shadowed, as if a cloud had passed over—quite a trick inside a space habitat with artificial lighting. Isrid forced himself to blink and breathe naturally.

Dr. Istaga was back, and he cocked his head. "Rouxe would have exposed weaknesses, in our forces as well as security. And, since our Overlord lost control of a TD weapon, he's lost political clout."

Political clout? Isrid had rarely heard this phrase uttered on the Overlord's staff, but he'd always worked external threats. Even now, as Assistant for the Exterior, he wasn't focused on politics within the League. He waited.

Dr. Istaga noted the sideboard with refreshments and paused, going over to pick out a drink pack. He came back, took a deep draw and set the pack down with a tiny betraying quiver. "Remember, your ears only. The Overlord has initiated Operation Palisade."

Palisade. As the name insinuated, it was the plan for digging in and protecting Overlord Three's assets from "close neighbors," generally meaning an *internal League threat*. There was always distrust between Overlords, and secrecy and intrigue were expected, particularly with regard to resources.

"SP Duval? Overlord Six?" Isrid asked. "I wondered why a representative from District Six was appointed to the ICT. I should have queried Terra immediately."

"I'm afraid we've become accustomed to controlling the wealthiest solar systems, and using Terra as the weight to control the rest of the League."

"Accustomed?"

Dr. Istaga played with the label on his drink pack. "The dynamics have changed, SP."

Historically, Overlord conflict lined up with Five and Six against an accord of One through Four. Districts Five and Six contained most of the "fringe" worlds, defined as such by their wildly diverse, contentious, and sometimes insular inhabitants, rather than by galactic location. Fringe worlds usually had dysfunctional economies and weak gross planetary products, due to fragmented populations operating around hot spots of rampant lawlessness.

One of those hot spots, Enclave El Tozeur on New Sousse, had attracted the ire of the Minoans about thirty years ago. Abram's isolationist tribe claimed responsibility for an act of space piracy that, inadvertently or not, damaged a Minoan ship. When pressed by the Minoans, Overlord Six had disavowed sovereign responsibility over Enclave El Tozeur and allowed them their retribution. The physical damage was surgical and temporary, but the Minoan's genetic weapons had permanent effects.

"Six's staff has always parroted the line that the Minoans railroaded us into peace, that we should have retaliated after Ura-Guinn." Isrid didn't mention he'd had the same opinion until a few years ago. Then he had decided the League's dire economic situation required a change in his attitude. "What's changed? Why initiate Palisade, at this point?"

"It's still about Pax Minoica, of course. Overlord Six started pushing, again, for us to pull out. Started campaigning several months ago. Vociferously and convincingly. Overlord One has taken his side." The corners of Dr. Istaga's mouth stretched into a faded smile, his eyes unfocused, as he mused. "Fifteen years ago, I would have supported that. But now . . ."

Isrid relaxed. "Same old issues, so *Palisade* seems rather extreme at this point. District One has always been weak."

Dr. Istaga held up a cautionary finger. "Four has sided with our Overlord, but Two is wavering. That's the problem. The Triangle is no longer united." Districts Two, Three, and Four comprised the Triangle of Power, because of their resources and raw materials. They could conscript more people from their better-educated populations, and build superior weapon systems.

"That seems oddly coincidental," Isrid said slowly. "When, exactly, did Overlord Six start pushing for withdrawal from Pax Minoica?"

"About eight months ago." Dr. Istaga shrugged.

"That's right behind the release of the Autonomist second-wave prospecting data for G-145."

"Ah. You think Six is threatened by the research into the Builders' technology. Why?"

"I don't know, but the timing is suspicious." He carefully watched Dr. Istaga. "By the way, my security has decided Rouxe's execution isn't related to the other drama on the *Pilgrimage*. Were those explosives your doing?"

"I'm distressed by your suggestion, SP." The doctor looked honestly offended. "Those were gauche operations, lacking sophistication."

"Are the incidents related to Six's waning support for Pax Minoica?"

"Maybe, since they targeted Autonomists." Dr. Istaga shrugged, and glanced at the time on the wall. His voice hardened. "My purpose here, on this station, is *Palisade* assessment. Cleaning our house, so to speak. The Overlord can't be worrying about informers or defectors on his staff."

He felt tired, watching fire shine deep in Dr. Istaga's eyes, but feeling none inside himself. Knowing Istaga was the last person who should hear this from his mouth, he said, "I thought, with our *Open Gates* policy, we stopped questioning loyalty. This is a small frontier community of interstellar scientists, who value personal opinions and free speech. Do you really intend to single out *our* District's people, in this environment, and interrogate them?"

Dr. Rok Shi Harridan Istaga, known as Andre Covanni by very few people, looked at him with sparkling eyes. "SP, I'm surprised that *you* would call the test of patriotism an interrogation. But have no fear. The methods I use these days are subtle. Nobody's going under neural probe."

"What about the loyalties and backgrounds of other Terrans? We have contractors coming from throughout the League and it seems sensible to evaluate those from District *Six*."

"Not my responsibility. The TSF should be doing that." Dr. Istaga shrugged. "But if I see anything unusual, I'll notify you."

"Please do, Doctor." It took all his composure and training to keep irritation from marring his State-Princely nod and gesture of dismissal.

Istaga/Covanni seemed to pull the shadows out with him, because the room felt brighter after he left. Isrid sat quietly deflated, and considered how his life had gone sideways. He'd just given his traditional *enemy*, Major Kedros, information about the threats against his family, yet didn't feel he could trust his Overlord's master intelligencer and "political officer" with the same. Strangely, he'd finally come to accept Pax Minoica. He had even staked his career and his family's livelihood on it and the economic partnership it allowed with the Autonomists. Now it might all go up in smoke, and Sabina's warning echoed in his mind.

Ariane was, apparently, the only person who felt freed by the Minoans' proposal.

"Whoa, whoa, whooooooaa!" The crèche-get, who'd never seen a riding beast, began applying reins. David Ray stood, his smooth face creased in a grimacing frown. "Before *anyone* volunteers for *anything*, we need more information."

Contractor Director turned its attention toward her, ignoring David Ray for an interminable span of silence.

"Ari, you have no idea what's involved," Matt said uneasily. "We're a long way from mounting an expedition."

"Agreed." Contractor Director dipped its horns toward Matt. "Much work must be done before we retrofit a vehicle, but we had to be assured of the crucial volunteer."

"Her verbal agreement isn't binding, in any context." David Ray's legal retort was quick.

"Much work must be done," Matt repeated, under his

breath. "Retrofitting a vehicle? Where's the money coming from?"

She leaned forward to tell David Ray that she wasn't going to change her mind. Matt put a warning hand on her arm. *Later*, his headshake seemed to say. She leaned back, her protest left unsaid.

"Is your translator classified as proprietary? With whom may we share it?" Dr. Lowry's cool tone changed the subject deftly.

"Any company contracted by an S-triple-ECB lessee," Contractor Director said. "Please reactivate your research projects, keeping our goals in mind. I will meet with you on a cycle of two UT days, and we will provide more information as your research progresses."

"Why so frequently?" Lowry looked irritated.

"We know how close you are to triggering an nous-space transition, Doctor."

Lowry paled at the Minoan's comment.

"We have given you partial translation capabilities, which should accelerate research. Please understand that we want you to be successful." Contractor Director dipped its horns. The ropes of jewels hanging from the tips sparkled and scattered shards of colored light across the walls.

They watched quietly as the Minoan and its guardian escort left, moving through the hatchway with hardly a rustle. Afterward, Ariane was the only one in the room who didn't reach for a slate or start making a call.

"I've got to disseminate the translator." Lowry sprang to her feet and left the room, her hand going to her implant behind her ear.

"I need to reserve this conference room," David Ray said.

"I should call Diana," Matt said.

She sat motionless, in wonder, ignoring the others. *Will they really let* me *pilot to a Builders' world? Explorer of Solar Systems*, the contract had specified.

"What does this mean?" Matt jerked her out of her reverie. He shoved his slate in front of her face, showing the message, "No incoming or outgoing messages allowed at this location [AFCAW 56394854-BC] due to AFCAWR 122-5 audit procedures."

"That's the *Bright Crescent*'s identifier. They're locked down for a full audit and inspection." Her voice tightened in surprise. *So the senator apparently has the time, even during the tribunal, to make good on his threat to Owen.*

"Diana's not a prisoner, is she?"

"The ship's temporarily offline. Nobody's a prisoner—although the comm will be down as they pull data and logs from the systems. Diana can call you from the *Pilgrimage* when she gets the time."

"Why would that bastard do this?" No need for Matt to use names.

"It's not Owen's fault. My guess is that he, as mission commander, as well as the ship commander and crew, are under Senate investigation."

"Oh." Emotions fought on Matt's face: satisfaction at seeing the arrogant Colonel Owen Edones get his "due," and concern for Diana and other crew members of the *Bright Crescent*.

She hadn't expected Senator Stephanos would go through with the investigation *now*, not when Edones hunted wayward murderers and saboteurs. Was Stephanos dead set upon ruining Edones's career?

David Ray interrupted her thoughts, putting a hand on her shoulder and Matt's. He bent down so his head was on level with theirs and spoke softly. "I hope I don't have to remind you that the Minoans are never altruistic. They'll want payback."

"Yes, 'All the world's a stage,'" Matt quoted. "'And we're all merely puppets.'"

"*Players*," corrected David Ray. "'And all the men and women merely players.'"

"Really? Because I feel like a *puppet*, with too many masters pulling my strings." Matt's eyes narrowed.

Ariane agreed. Matt didn't know the half of it.

CHAPTER 11

Our correspondent in G-145 suspects Tribunal members State Prince Duval and Senator Stephanos are conducting their own side investigations into the recent tragedies in that solar system. Of course, our correspondent is barred from both inquiries. . . .

—*Interstellarsystem Events Feed*, 2106.054.14.28 UT, indexed by *Heraclitus* 7 under Flux Imperative

Ariane and Matt used the time remaining in first shift for an elevator trip down to the moon surface. Matt hadn't ever seen the alien structures, even though he'd mapped their outlines remotely. Their purpose wasn't to sightsee, however, but to start sifting through offices, labs, and quarters used by Hellas Nautikos employees, just as they'd promised Contractor Director.

Ariane enjoyed the ride, even though it took several hours. This was her third trip in the space elevator, but the first time she could relax and just experience it. She watched the views projected on the walls. There were no true windows, or radiation holes, as space crew called them. Thankfully, Matt had stopped fussing about not getting through to Diana. He looked like he was finally relaxing as he chatted with Dr. Lowry, who had business down on the moon's surface, but might have time to help them inventory personal items, notes, and whatnot.

"The Minoan translator is exciting," Lowry was saying. "Supposedly, they claim it can provide *direct* translation from the Builders' language and symbols to ours, but we have to be cautious."

"Why? You think the Minoans aren't being honest with us?" Matt asked.

"No, I worry whether they truly understand our semantics, much less the Builders. Our history with the Minoans is rife with misunderstandings."

"They've obviously been interstellar traders and peace facilitators longer than we can imagine," Ariane threw into the conversation. "It's hard for us to comprehend even the age of the Builders; didn't we date the creation of these ruins to between ten and fifteen thousand UT years ago?"

Dr. Myrna Lowry looked at her a bit sourly, as if she'd hijacked the conversation.

"We had to make a wide estimate because the Builders cleaned out organic matter and atmospheric gases that would oxidize metals. To make it even more difficult, many materials appear to have been imported to this system and we don't have references to calibrate nuclear decay. Hopefully, the *Minoans* can provide us keys to understanding the Builders." Dr. Lowry turned to Matt. "If their civilization has existed long enough to see both the rise and fall of the Builders, and if this translator is as old as they insinuate—well, that has amazing repercussions."

"How so?"

Ariane's eyelids drooped, although she kept half an eye on the others, tracking the conversation.

"Think about how *dynamic* human civilization is." Lowry became animated. Her hands unconsciously made symbols that were part of the Martian patois, even though she spoke common Greek well. "We've developed thousands of languages, only to cast them aside to be subsumed in the ice of Terra. Mankind has created symbols for at least nine thousand years—but if we believe the Minoans, the Builders civilization collapsed as we were just starting. I question how the Minoans could possibly produce an accurate translation from Builder symbols to ours if they experience the same dynamic change that we do."

"Maybe they don't. They make the distinction that we're an *evolved* intelligence," Matt said.

"Exactly! The Minoans seem culturally static, which is impossible from our point of view. We can't imagine keeping information over ten thousand years, without it drifting and losing integrity." Lowry's hands flitted about as she talked. "I follow xenologist publications, like David Ray, and a popular theory is the Minoans use some sort of mental telepathy. I hear the two of you came to similar conclusions after your time on the Minoan ship."

"David Ray told you that?" Matt sounded surprised.

"Not in so many words. He was telling one of his stories."

"When?"

"Um, can't remember. But you know how he gets."

"Yeah." Matt laughed. "Love the guy to death, but he does wander, doesn't he?"

Ariane watched this verbal dance through lowered eyelids. Dr. Lowry was vague about how she learned about Matt's time on the Minoan ship, while Matt was guarded about his experiences. Both Matt and David Ray had given statements about the isolationists to the ICT prosecution, but they didn't consider Matt's testimony relevant to the charges they were pressing against Rand and his men. *Hearsay! By the Great Bull's balls, one of those hearsay isolationists almost killed me*, Matt complained to her later. But, when it came to their observations of the Minoans, Matt and David Ray remained tight-lipped.

Matt's conversation with Dr. Lowry degenerated into polite small talk, such as the variety of cuisine available on Beta Priamos and whether they'd get anything other than prepackaged space rations down on the Priamos surface. Ariane dozed until the arrival chime yanked her upright. She rubbed her face, trying to massage herself awake. As she stood, she adjusted for Priamos's three-quarters standard gee.

"I'll meet you at Barone's quarters. Take your time—I have to check with the message center," Lowry said brightly, moving away, down the pressurized corridor.

This left Ariane as guide to Matt, a duty she didn't mind, although she wasn't the most informed choice. She led him down the corridor that connected the elevator to the alien archeological site. The temporary tube went gradually downhill and underground, where it curved and ended at another temporary airlock. It had just finished cycling; Dr. Lowry had moved through quickly.

Before the site-side doors opened, she told Matt about her first experience seeing the underground Builders' facility. "I never understood why the Minoans were paying Hellas Nautikos to document *human* reactions to the Builders' ruins," she said, as the site-side doors opened.

"Oh." His mouth fell open.

She gently pushed him forward, so he tentatively stepped onto the honed hard surface with irregular opalescent striations. They stood under an arch of the same material and on the edge of the glittering main hall, which reminded her of a jewelry box carved of translucent semiprecious stone. The hall was lit by glowing designs on the ceiling. Two rows of columns extended from their position to the end, creating an internal walkway with overhead ribs, like soldiers holding a ceremonial arch of swords. Behind them, the temporary airlock pressed into the arch like a plug into a bottle, closing with a huff.

"I thought the Builders didn't use ninety-degree angles." Matt looked about at the rectangular hall that measured approximately twenty meters by ten meters.

"This is the only space built in a rectangle, and all routes lead off it. Hellas Nautikos found that we humans are more affected by these shapes than we expected. They said video proved we gravitate back to this area for serenity and mental relaxation." She moved to the side of the arch and looked thoughtfully at nodes mounted on a thin metal structure built inside the arch. Their power was on, indicated by a tiny light on their edges. "I wonder if these are still recording. Abram and his band of thugs might have continued to use the Nautikos equipment for security."

"You're absolutely right, Major."

She jumped. "No rank, please. I'm not on active duty,"

she answered the voice that broadcasted from the disc-shaped node smaller than her thumb.

"Sorry, didn't mean to startle you, Ms. Kedros. Master Sergeant Pike at your service, representing the ever-faithful multidisciplinary Shock Force Command. We're responsible for security here on the surface."

"Autonomist Commandos, Matt. Here's where *our* guys are working." She smiled.

Matt nodded wordlessly, having moved to the closest pillar. He examined the symbols at the height of his head. They appeared backlit, made of worked metal embedded into what seemed to be polished, alien onyx.

"I assume you're here to take possession of the Nautikos facilities and data. We'll get you keyed into the system. Just go straight through the hall and turn right—well, angle toward the right through two branches," Pike's voice said.

She thanked the sergeant and tried to herd Matt through the hall. He resisted until she pointed out he'd have *plenty* of time to study this later.

"Do we know what any of this means?" he asked.

"No, but I have a feeling we'll figure it out." She gestured toward a linguistics team on the far side of the hall, working with slates and a big board that had fragmented pictures and symbols. The team stepped back from it as the graphics moved about, joined, and rejoined. The discussion was unintelligible, but their voices held excitement.

Ariane and Matt entered the hallways, turned sixty degrees toward the right, and he balked again. "Why does this place now feel oppressive? The ceiling isn't much lower than in the great hall."

"First, the dimensions don't feel right." She pointed out that the halls and doors were tall, but narrow for their height, violating what felt balanced to humans. The symbols and door controls were almost at her shoulder level. "Second, we've found these angles are disquieting to our minds. Third, their ventilation system automatically humidifies the air. The Builders liked their atmosphere a bit thinner, so when we push up the pressure from life support, it gets more dank than we like."

By now, they'd arrived at Pike's makeshift operations center, which also happened to be the message center. Abram had likewise chosen this room as his operational center. Ariane shivered, trying not to remember.

Pike introduced himself. "You've really stirred up the teams, Mr. Journey. When that translator downloaded a couple of hours ago, everybody was rousted, even the off-duty personnel. It's been a wild techno-clusterfuck ever since."

"That's good?" Matt's hesitancy with Sergeant Pike was understandable. Ariane hadn't been around shock forces much herself, and Pike's rough edges made Sergeant Joyce seem cuddly by comparison.

"Yes, sir, it is." Lines at the corners of Pike's eyes deepened, which might be as close to a smile as he'd allow. He put his broad hand on Matt's shoulder and gently pushed him toward the woman commando standing at a Builder console. "Why don't you have Technician Greco scan your palm so we can get you into the Nautikos rooms. I need to speak with Ms. Kedros."

There was no resisting that calm, authoritative tone. Matt went over to Greco, who gave him a wide natural smile, and Ariane followed Master Sergeant Pike into an interior room. He closed the door and cocked his head, telling her that he'd checked for listening devices. The room was secure.

"You've got your queue responding with a recording, ma'am," Pike said reproachfully, once the door closed. "And Sergeant Joyce says you don't often pick up your calls."

"Emergency calls come through. I figure I can handle all other calls later." She touched her implant panel on her inner arm above her wrist, but didn't change the settings. "Besides, there wasn't much comm support on the surface the last time I was here."

The lines deepened around Pike's eyes. "We've made improvements, Ms. Kedros. Emergency calls can be originated, and received, in the elevator. We've added nodes in the great hall, so you have mesh coverage for local calls. We even have an extra relay, but our bandwidth is being eaten

up by this R&D. You should check with the message center
regularly, particularly if someone must send you a large—
or classified—payload that has to be fragmented."

"Someone, like Sergeant Joyce?" She pulled out her
slate, showing its military encryption and secure-storage
identifier.

"Yes, ma'am." He nodded as she authenticated with
thumbprint and voiceprint, tapped the slate, and requested
the download. "I gave your sergeant a piece of my mind,
for swamping our comm."

"I'd like to have seen that." She couldn't imagine that
picture. The table of contents for Joyce's package displayed
on her slate, showing that she was scheduled to testify to
the ICT *tomorrow* from oh nine thirty to eleven hundred.
She'd give the testimony virtually, which brought up the
question: where?

"You'll have to give it from Beta Priamos, where they
have the equipment and authority," Pike told her.

*I can forget about doing anything useful during first shift
tomorrow*. However, her slate now contained Joyce's mission notes about Maria. Back on Beta Priamos, she'd be
able to make real-time calls if she had questions for Joyce.

Pike must have guessed her thoughts. "If you're going
back up to the station, you might make time to stop in at
the Terran Space Force brig. There's a prisoner, name of
Frank Maestrale, who wants to speak with you."

She sighed. Frank had been a friend she'd met in an
earlier solar system opening. But her most vivid memory,
now, was seeing Frank point a weapon at her, having been
seduced by Abram's cause.

"He's cooperated with the Terrans, and been helpful in
wiring more ComNet support into the station." Pike looked
sideways at her. "I think he's holding on to something, some
bit of information that he only wants to give to you."

"I'll think about it," was all she could say.

"And don't forget to keep a watchful eye, Ms. Kedros,
considering the recent attempts on your life. Any orders,
before I transmit the daily report to you?"

"Excuse me?" Then she remembered Edones saying

she'd have authority to take emergency mission command of the platoon, but this wasn't an emergency and— "What daily report, Sergeant?"

"With both the colonel and *Bright Crescent* offline, you've got command, as the local ranking officer." Pike didn't look ready to argue about this, adding a final punctuation of, "*Ma'am*."

"Er—I'm not—" She stuttered to a stop. She was, technically, on active duty. Not wearing her uniform for this covert operation didn't mean she could opt out of sudden administrative tasks. She wasn't risking her plainclothes mission—everyone on Priamos and Beta Priamos Station knew she was AFCAW. Reluctantly, she said, "I can go through whatever you're sending Colonel Edones. What kind of reports?"

"Security issues here on the moon surface. As well, the colonel wants us to keep an eye on the comm in and out of here *and* the station." Pike nodded firmly, as if to forgive her previous and un-commandolike indecision. He tapped and pointed his slate to directly transfer the report to hers.

"You can track the command post and out-of-system messages up on the station?" She brought up the report on her slate.

"Well, what we're allowed within CAW exploration law for open systems. And whatever TSF Ensign Walker lets CP give us. Surprisingly, the ensign has been quite generous. We get tallies of bandwidth used and gigabytes sent to other solar systems." Pike's gravelly voice became sterner, giving her the same prickles on her scalp as the sound of active armor tearing off a ship. "I'm sure Ensign Walker has noted the *interesting* distribution of outgoing comm this past couple of days."

Looking at highest recipients of data and messages, she was surprised to see District Six systems at the top of the list. She'd expected Autonomist solar systems, given that both Hellas and Konstantinople Prime had research centers and universities contracted to process data. The same went for the Sol system, with Terra and Mars supporting significant research, but *not* for New Sousse or Zhulong, the official seat for the Terran League's District Six. Frowning, she said, "This might be due to SP Duval's staff, or because the ICT defense—"

Pike stopped her with a tight negative nod. "That doesn't show out-of-system traffic originating from the *Pilgrimage* or its docked ships. But, keep in mind that the destination addresses can be forwarders or bouncers. We're not allowed anything specific about the receivers."

"Can you determine who sends each message?"

"Only that these transmissions originate from Priamos and Beta Priamos. Pilgrimage statutes don't allow anyone—including Ensign Walker—to monitor comm to that level of detail. To do that, we'd need authorization from a Pilgrimage command officer to install special software and equipment."

"Strange," she murmured.

"I figure the colonel would want someone keeping an eye on this, ma'am. Until he comes back online." Pike's shoulder, under his impeccably pressed uniform, twitched with a shrug. He didn't seem concerned about appropriating both her eyes for security issues beyond her civilian job.

Pike opened the door to the outer center, where Matt was playing with Builder technology, specifically the palm reader that extended a holographic four-clawed appendage. Greco was explaining how these readers allowed Builders, and now humans, to open doors within the facility.

Ariane said good-bye to Pike, as she thumbed off her slate and its puzzling report.

This was much worse than an operational readiness inspection, which was the only similar event Lieutenant Oleander had experienced. Normally, inspectors were uniformed military personnel with experience in the same operations they were evaluating. In this case, called the "Ad-hoc Senate Investigation into AFCAW Response to the Pilgrimage Mission 145 Crisis," the *Bright Crescent* crew had to deal with civilian auditors and data collectors.

After Myron pulled her from the *Pilgrimage* mainte-

nance shop, Oleander spent the next shift escorting auditors around the *Bright Crescent*, helping them collect logs
and recordings. She and Floros had this onerous task because they were Directorate personnel. The auditors were
Myron and two other politicians-in-training, a young man
and woman displaying severe deficiencies of humor or
even basic cordiality. When being audited, crew members
had to shut down their systems and remain at their stations
to answer questions.

By the time she could go off duty, she was exhausted
and filled with impotent ire at Myron and his two political clones. In her tiny quarters, as she unsealed her Alpha
jacket with trembling fingers, she tried to calm down.

There was a disturbing pattern to the questions Myron
and his lackeys had asked. They would ask what "decision
process" was performed before the task, even if it was
merely following orders to load missiles. The answer was
usually that the task was performed *rapidly* and *instinc-
tually*, because the crew member had performed the task
many times under training. This would elicit a look of con-
sternation and dismay, usually followed by a patronizing
comment about needing to fully analyze one's actions.

This was the antithesis of the military goal of a well-
trained crew. *Did they really want us to spend time dither-
ing?* She threw herself on her bed. Even though they hadn't
arrived in G-145 to do battle, there had been a ticking
clock: prevent Abram from detonating his stolen temporal-
distortion weapon.

The worst part had been Myron's interest in the early
casualties they'd had, right after dropping into the mine-
field. She tried not to blame herself; she'd been targeting
the mines with slugs to push them away. Several of the
mines had blown up, a statistical probability of one in ten.
Unfortunately, one mine damaged the compartment the
commandos occupied. One soldier was seriously injured
and one would never see home or family again.

She'd already gone over the logs herself, trying to convince herself that she wasn't responsible. The pilot who was
orienting the rail guns had also combed through the data

and had concluded that they couldn't have done anything different. Now, after seeing an uncharacteristic gleam in Myron's eye as he'd looked over the same log, she dreaded her upcoming testimony.

"Command: Display messages." She rolled over to face the bulkhead, expecting to see messages from Matt.

A view port opened on the wall with the error message, "Queue for Lieutenant Oleander is currently unavailable."

What did that mean? She called the comm officer on duty, luckily getting Lieutenant Kozel, who she knew better than the others.

"I'm sorry, Lieutenant, but you were off-ship when we made the announcement. They want to keep our queues and data cores static, so they diverted our queue traffic to the *Pilgrimage*. You won't lose any calls, but you'll have to use the *Pilgrimage*'s systems to go through them."

After concluding her call with Kozel, she lay on her back, feeling her eyelids droop. She was too tired to get dressed, get permission to debark, and process through security to get off the *Bright Crescent*. Now she *really* hated whoever was behind this audit.

Ariane looked down at the small packing crate filled with Mr. Barone's belongings. On top of his clothes, she'd laid a picture frame that cycled through still portraits of him and his family. The big, quiet man with the deep voice had left a wife and a daughter on Hellas Prime. She'd flipped through everything loaded in the frame, just to see the wide smile on his face. In the photos, there was artwork made by his daughter, who looked to be about six years old.

There was also a lumpy sculpture beside the frame, on Barone's working surface. It was a reptilian creature formed of polymer clay and painted with dabs of lime green, dark green, and yellow. When she turned it over, she saw "Pattie" scratched on its belly. She decided it was supposed to be a sibber, an amphibian that lived near the equatorial shores of a continent on Hellas Prime. Sibbers were smart; they were easily house-trained, loved interacting with children, and had quickly become domesticated pets after Hellas Prime was colonized. She gently laid the sculpture in the zero-gee shipping container and sealed it. The address of Barone's family residence on Hellas Prime brightened on the top.

Dr. Lowry stuck her head in the door. "Do you need any help?"

"We've finished all but one. You can help us with Peter Katsaros's quarters," Matt said, taking a last look around Barone's office.

"You said you were close to Peter. If you don't want to do this . . . ?" Ariane let her voice trail off into a question, remembering Lowry's stricken look when speaking of Peter.

"Yes, we were—starting to date." Lowry looked sideways, then cast her gaze downward. "But I can manage."

"This way." Matt led them to the next room down the hall. He eagerly held his hand over the glowing symbol, to meet the extended four-clawed holographic scanner. The door opened for him; the researchers figured the scanners performed sensitive topographic mapping and thus, one alien palm was as good as any other for identification.

Ariane smiled, standing back to watch. Despite the somberness of their task, Matt was still exuberantly interested in the novelty presented by the Builders' technology. Beside her, Dr. Lowry made an impatient sound under her breath and followed Matt into Peter Katsaros's quarters.

"Peter's things are to be sent to his older sister, it appears." Matt was reading his slate.

"No living parents? Any other family?" Ariane asked, watching Dr. Lowry rifle through Peter's work area and desk. She didn't get an answer.

Matt packed Peter's clothes, Lowry focused on his personal slate and reference library, and Ariane, to her surprise, got the most personal items. She picked up the frame next to the bed, turned it on, and flipped through the contents by pressing the arrow on the lower right-hand corner. There were stills of a couple with a son, perhaps Peter's sister's family, one with Peter alone and one with colleagues

in the Builders' great hall; she recognized Barone, with his
arm draped over the younger Peter. Lowry wasn't in any of
the stills, and she really didn't have time to run through the
videos in the frame.

"Dr. Lowry, you mentioned Peter was helping you research the buoy." Ariane turned off the frame and placed
it in the shipping container before turning to face the Terran woman. "I thought the Minoans had shown no interest
in the Builders' technology, in particular the dead N-space
buoy. Why would Hellas Nautikos assign him to your
team?"

"You military intelligence types are always suspicious,
aren't you?" Lowry's eyes glinted. "Aren't we supposed to
be working together under Pax Minoica?"

At the sound of her antagonistic tone, Matt's head
jerked around to watch them. She tried to defuse Lowry
with a mild tone. "I'm asking only because the artifact was
a topic of discussion when I visited earlier. Mr. Barone had
made a point of the Minoan's obvious lack of curiosity."

"I was the one who asked Hellas Nautikos for Dr. Katsaros's time, as a consultant. I needed his input."

"Because he's an expert on the N-space boundary? I've
read he's studied transition mechanisms other than the
Penrose Fold." Ariane smiled. "I try to keep up with the
field, in my own amateur way."

Lowry's eyes narrowed. "I thought you went through a
military academy."

"We could specialize on Nuovo Adriatico. My principal
course of undergraduate study was astrophysics."

"Ari's not your normal N-space pilot," Matt said. "Maybe
that's why the Minoans asked for her."

"Perhaps." Lowry didn't sound convinced.

"As for Peter—he helped you make headway on understanding the buoy, perhaps even operating it?" Ariane
asked. "How do you know that he wasn't helping the Minoans pass you information?"

"*We want you to be successful,*" Matt whispered.

"I don't know for sure whether Dr. Katsaros was providing his original thought and effort to the project." Lowry's

mouth shrunk into wrinkles as she concentrated. "My gut feeling is that he was honest with us. Even if the Minoans were trying to feed us information, we're still a long way from needing a pilot, regardless of what they inferred in the kick-off meeting. First, we need an expensive exploration-class ship and we're going to have to build a different referential engine."

Ariane opened a case that held several rings and wristbands. Peter Katsaros had a love of precious metals and metalworking, it seemed. She packed the case carefully with the picture frame.

"I'm sorry, but I have to go." Lowry sighed. "I need to send a report to Dr. Novak, so we can start translating the symbols on the buoy tomorrow." She nodded good-bye and abruptly left. Her footsteps faded away as Matt and Ariane exchanged a glance.

Ariane raised her eyebrows. "I don't think she found what she was looking for."

"What do you mean?" Matt surveyed the cluttered desk.

"She didn't pack anything and she looked through every slate, even the data stored in the desk."

"You *are* suspicious." Matt's head turned and he frowned at her over his shoulder. "This comes from being around that bastard Edones for too long. You can't trust anyone."

"This isn't about trust, it's just that I don't understand her," she protested, sidestepping the dig about Colonel Edones. "She says she was dating Peter Katsaros, yet she stayed away from his personal effects, like they carried a pandemic virus. There are no photos of her with him, and why does she keep calling him *Dr.* Katsaros?"

"So she's uptight about titles and degrees. Maybe she can't deal with looking through his belongings. Besides . . ." Matt ruffled his hair and grimaced. "I'll put this delicately: Do you think *you're* the best judge of a normal relationship?"

She was blindsided by his comment, made more painful by his honest tone. It hurt enough to make her blink hard and rapidly.

"I'm not qualified to make that judgment either," Matt added quickly. She looked away as he babbled. "I don't trust people, and considering how Leukos—"

Matt stopped. When she looked back at him, he had the glimmer of an idea sparkling in his eyes. Obviously, he'd forgotten what he'd just said, perhaps even the entire conversation.

"What's the matter?"

His eyes refocused on her. "Your Mr. Leukos. I think I just figured out how to fund an expedition vessel."

Her breath caught. "I'd prefer not to be in debt to Leukós Industries. I thought we already had this discussion."

"But we're not going to be the borrowers." His smile widened. "We'll introduce Mr. Leukos to the Minoans—actually, Hellas Nautikos. It's financial matchmaking, just like Carmen describes."

She nodded grudgingly. *As long as I don't have to talk to Brandon.*

CHAPTER 12

Today, the testimony covered what happened on the *Pilgrimage* when Abram Rouxe boarded. Tomorrow, they'll take the "unclassified part" of Ariane Kedros's testimony. Kedros is listed as a key witness for the prosecution. . . .

—*Dr. Net-head Stavros*, 2106.055.15.32 UT, indexed by *Heraclitus 11* under Conflict Imperative

The next day Ariane was to testify before the ICT. After she and Matt returned to the station, she made sure she got eight hours sleep in her quarters on the *Aether's Touch*.

Giving virtual testimony meant more than slapping on v-play equipment. She had to use verified equipment over a verified channel, under monitored conditions, meaning a representative of the court was physically present. On Beta Priamos, that representative was Ensign Walker, and she had to give her testimony in the security offices.

"Good morning, Ms. Kedros," Walker said brightly.

"Humph." She didn't want to be here, and perky young officers of the Terran Space League only made her mood darker.

"We've got everything set up for your session." Walker led her through workstation cubicles to a small room. Inside were two comfortable chairs with one set of v-play equipment. He added, "I have to stay here to verify you're the one using the equipment, you don't spoof the signal, et cetera."

"Like I'd try that," she muttered. The ensign's polite smile faded. "Sorry, I'm not looking forward to this."

"Well, today should be the easier of your two sessions." Walker pulled a slate from his pocket and consulted it. "I have to remind you that your testimony today is unclassified. If you feel your answer will involve information sensitive to the Consortium of Autonomous Worlds, it can be addressed in your second session, which occurs in three days."

"What if my testimony involves sensitive *League* information?" She cocked an eyebrow at him.

"Well." He floundered, then realized what she was doing. "Funny—ha, ha. You're not responsible for protecting our classified material."

No, that would have been Tahir's problem; an internal observation that was sobering as well as illuminating. She thoughtfully pulled on the long v-play gloves and the light visor, which plugged into her implant connector at the base of her neck. This interfaced *only* with her implanted mike and ear bug, because the Consortium had banned direct neural interfaces a long time ago.

There appeared to be no more v-play equipment other than her chair. Walker tapped his slate to bring up flat view ports, which he would use. She turned on her v-play equipment and looked down, seeing her simulated body. Symbols lit in the air before her, and she moved to tap them so she could log into the virtual session.

She heard Walker verify her status, and suddenly she was sitting in the witness stand in the amphitheater of the *Pilgrimage III*, if she could believe her eyes. She could put out her hand and "touch" the edge of the witness box around her chair, although if she tried to rest her hand on the box, the illusion from the gloves would be lost.

She looked to her right and scanned the audience. She didn't see a single AFCAW uniform, which told her how severe the ship's audit must be. Below her sat Rand and the other defendants, their faces tilted up to watch her three dimensional image, holding expressions ranging from disdain to hatred. Higher, to her left, sat the Interstellar Criminal Tribunal.

"Do you, Ariane Sophia Kedros, swear to ..." The court officer read some sort of mealy-mouthed oath to encourage truthfulness, weakened because it couldn't break her current military oath to her government. She listened carefully and then swore to abide by it.

The questions the prosecution asked her were predictable. She related how the isolationists had taken over the facilities on Priamos and imprisoned the staff. The prosecution asked her to describe the execution of Colonel Dokos, and to spare no details. She didn't, and her voice was unsteady by the time she finished. The prosecution paused and asked that a timestamp reference be inserted into the record. They could refer to this later, during the classified testimony.

"Ms. Kedros, you were taken aboard the *Candor Chasma* by Dr. Rouxe, Emery Douchet, and Julian Nikolov?"

"Yes, sir."

"Tell us what happened on that ship, but please avoid the subject of Dr. Rouxe's project."

That was the hint that she wasn't supposed to say *why* they took the ship near the sun, to avoid explaining how a stolen TD weapon could be armed and detonated. The Feed correspondents looked bored, but then, this line of questioning wasn't any more obscure than the celebrity trials they covered.

She kept the events as factual and dry as she could. Julian did the piloting and eventually his attention wandered. When she attacked him, Tahir stunned Emery. Then she left out a few details and said that Tahir wanted to leave the solar system (which was true). However, they were too far from the buoy to get a lock signal, so the ship would be lost in N-space (true again, but she glossed over the fact that Tahir had *armed* the weapon, still intending to turn tail and save himself). She had then knocked out Tahir and ejected the both of them in an emergency evacuation module, just before the ship entered N-space (taking the afore-*un*mentioned armed TD weapon with it). Without mentioning the weapon, how could any of this make sense?

"Thank you, Ms. Kedros."

"Does defense wish to cross-examine the witness?" asked the court official, who was from Pilgrimage headquarters and not a voting member of the Tribunal.

"We do." The Terran defense counselor looked down at his slate while the *Pilgrimage* defense counselor whispered in his ear. The isolationists had insisted that everyone representing them be male. The Terran attorney stood and as he did, he shot State Prince Duval a resigned look, as if to say, "I can't believe I'm doing this."

Ariane's heart sank.

"Ms. Kedros? Who programmed the N-space drop?" The Terran stood in front of her, wearing what must be common conservative court clothes, made of grayish brown material. The suit was unadorned and boring, from an Autonomist fashion perspective. Net-think had probably singled him out immediately for ridicule.

"I did," she replied. "But I could only do so with the referential engine's license crystal, which Dr. Rouxe had stolen. Abram had wanted the ship incapable of entering N-space."

"So you did this at Dr. Rouxe's request?"

"Yes, sir, but I'll have to elaborate on this during classified testimony."

"Noted. Timestamp reference inserted," the court official intoned.

"So you had the flexibility to program more time before the drop. Isn't it true that you could have saved more crew members, more than just yourself and Dr. Rouxe?"

"No, sir." Her voice became tense. "My time was limited."

"How?"

"I can't go into that until the classified session." She had to time the drop so the detonating weapon could be overtaken by the ship and, she hoped, sucked into N-space.

The court official came to her rescue. "Defense counsel is cautioned to stay within classification guidance. Please hold this line of questions for the classified testimony."

"Certainly, Your Honor." The Terran lawyer stilled, in

an unearthly manner, for less than a second. Then his eyes flickered and he became natural again.

She chided herself silently for not recognizing the counselor had *somaural* training. What better skills could a trial lawyer have? That look he exchanged with SP Duval was for her benefit.

"Ms. Kedros, you say you only had time to save one man. Please tell the court why you chose to rescue Dr. Rouxe."

"He defied his orders and helped me by stunning Emery. He also seemed less violent than the other two. I thought he'd be the best witness to his father's actions." Tahir had also masterminded the theft of the TD weapon, but she couldn't go into that.

"Wouldn't you consider this applying your own justice, Ms. Kedros?" The attorney's voice rose.

"I had only a few seconds to make my decision."

The Terran counselor faced her, now nearly shouting. "You testified that you saw Emery Douchet kill Colonel Dokos in front of you, in cold blood. Didn't that affect your decision?"

The Feeds were eating it up. Their cam-eye platforms focused on the two of them and the correspondents watched alertly. They loved drama and there probably hadn't been much on display in this court, until now.

"Of course it affected me," she said coldly. "I admit, I had no problems leaving him to die in N-space."

The audience erupted into applause and whistles. The court official called for order. There was no reaction from SP Duval or Commander Meredith, although Senator Stephanos's frown dug deeper into his bearish features. Perhaps she should have been more tactful.

"No more questions for this witness, Your Honor, until the classified sessions."

She saw the switch for ending the virtual session appear above her head, reached up, and toggled it. The sights and sounds of the amphitheater faded, the chair felt softer, and she was back on Beta Priamos with Ensign Walker.

"I admire your honesty, but I question your wisdom in showing it." He took the lightweight v-play helmet from her.

"Even if I acted with prejudice, it doesn't change what those men did. Besides, the important testimony is about the weapon. I'll do better in the second session, now that I know what the defense intends." She fluffed her loose curls with her fingers, removing the effects of the helmet. However, she was disturbed by the look between Duval and the Terran attorney, so obviously intended for her. It was a warning that her next testimony would be more difficult. Why was Duval even putting out the effort to protect these isolationists? After all, this tribe had been written off as worthless, long ago, by the Terran League itself.

"Perhaps you shouldn't have raised your net-think exposure, Major. It'll reduce your usefulness to the Directorate." Ensign Walker yanked her attention back.

Her stomach tensed as she shrugged nonchalantly. The Intelligence insignia on his TSF uniform was obviously more than garish adornment. Once he'd been assigned Beta Priamos security, he must have looked into the history behind unique situation in G-156, where Terrans, Autonomists, and even *Minoans* worked together in one of the first interstellar research efforts under Pax Minoica. Walker would have dug around, perhaps accessed classified reports, and figured out that Parmet had coerced the leases from her—thereby identifying her as a person of interest and in Walker's world, a possible enemy of the League.

She took the offensive. "It must have been tough securing this station, Ensign. Wouldn't you have preferred another assignment, perhaps under SP Duval?"

"I'll admit it's been challenging. Particularly when dealing with your Autonomist bureaucracies." He gave her his signature polite smile. "I've been learning a lot from SP Parmet."

I'll bet. She said casually, "You've got two State Princes here in this system, working for two different Overlords. Who gives the orders? What if they conflict?"

"I'm assigned to support SP Parmet." Walker's face became colder. He stretched his right shoulder and neck, a subtle indication of unease.

"But what if you can't tell which SP is *right*? Which one is supporting valid League doctrine?"

"We have directives—just as you do, I'm sure—and I'm not at liberty to talk about them." With a dark look that shut down this topic, Walker added, "By the way, one of our Autonomist prisoners has been asking for you. His name is—"

"Frank Maestrale," she said.

"That's the one." Walker gestured at the door. "Now, if you please, I have to set up for the next witness."

She stood and stretched. If she spent her on-station time visiting Frank and contacting Joyce, she could justify putting off a call to Maria.

In calling the brig, Ariane found that Frank wouldn't be off his work detail until thirteen hundred. That gave her time for a leisurely lunch and a tour of the small but growing commercial area of Beta Priamos Station. The Stellar Shield, the community bar, was being squeezed by commercial ventures such as Jeffrey Kuang's Kitchen and the Bosko Delicatessen. There was also an Aphrodite's, from a chain of salons pervasive in the Hellas Prime solar system. Now she knew where Sabina had gotten her skin-do.

After eating at the deli, she looked into the Stellar Shield but didn't enter. She felt a sharp urge to have a beer after lunch, but remembering Frank's vow of abstinence, she fought it off. She didn't want him to smell the beer and comment on her drinking.

"Thank you for seeing me, Ms. Kedros." Always meticulously polite—he'd always called her *Ms. Kedros*, even when he was shit-faced—Frank smiled as he sat down on the opposite side of the grille.

"Sergeant Pike convinced me that I should visit." She couldn't respond to his smile, and couldn't forgive his betrayal. This was a man who had worked as *space crew*, who supposedly had the code of the frontier embedded into him. Someone you drank with, someone you could *trust*.

Frank's smile slipped off his thin face. Even though there was no gray in his hair, he looked worn. Not tired, but eroded, like soft stone cliffs trying to withstand the sand-storms of Mars. He looked like a man who had tried to reinvent himself for the last time, and had given up.

"I know you don't care *why* I helped Abram," he began.

"You're right. I don't."

"Honestly, I didn't know his attitude toward women. Not until he slugged you. I'm sorry." Frank dipped his head and hunched his bony shoulders. "But there were other things I learned, that weren't so bad. See, he didn't have enough technical expertise down on Priamos, so that's why he kept me close."

"So you want to tell me something about Abram?"

"He really wanted to connect to his son, Dr. Rouxe. That's why he allowed you along, using that 'arc of retribution' line."

"It was a suicide mission, Frank. What kind of father sends his son on a mission of certain death?"

"One who fervently believes in the mission. Hey, I'm only saying that I understand bits of Abram. I didn't understand the whole package. Not by a long shot."

She suddenly felt tired. "So what's your point?"

"Abram was fallible and he could be *used*." Frank leaned forward.

Her interest flickered. "Who would have used Abram?"

"I set up a secure channel for him, and was sworn to secrecy about it." One thin shoulder raised in a shrug. "Threatened, actually, and told never to speak of it. He gave me a termination address for New Sousse."

This wasn't so interesting, after all. She made a dismissive gesture with her hand. "He was talking to tribal elders on his home planet."

Frank looked about the brig visitation area, ensuring it was empty, and lowered his voice anyway. "I disobeyed his orders and traced the termination. It was being forwarded to an unlisted address owned by Overlord Six—well, by the organization that's Overlord Six."

"You're saying a Terran *Overlord* knew what Abram planned for G-145?"

"More than that, I think Six called the shots."

She sat back and folded her arms. "You know how improbable that sounds."

"We had a dry run, you know. In J-132. I don't know how many system openings they shadowed and staged their people, their weapons, but J-132 was my first. We made sure we were in position, and we were contacted. Not by Abram. I didn't meet him until later. G-145 might have been an exercise, too, and then E-130 after that. I think most of the recruits outside the enclave, like me, thought of it as an exciting game—we didn't think anything could come of it. But we all knew it took a lot of money to run that operation."

The chair she sat in didn't feel substantial as Abram's plan ran through her mind, horrific in its interlocking details. Even now, it seemed impossible that they could have thwarted it. To stop that surreal feeling, she put her hands on the cool counter, pressing down to assure herself of the substantive world.

"I didn't think G-145 was a viable candidate, because it didn't have a habitable, temperate world. The Cause, we were told, was about finding a place where we could live without the interference of government." Frank's voice had fallen into monotone. "We could be free from the insanity of the Autonomist Consortium and the tyranny of the Terran League."

"But that's not what it was about." Her mouth was dry.

"No. I was one of the few who saw the strings of the puppeteer, and I became suspicious too late." For the first time, Frank's eyes looked anguished. "We got calls from that same address, twice, and I had to find Abram. In both cases, I think he was given orders."

"What kind of orders?"

"I don't know. The second time, his instructions didn't seem to sit well with him. He spoke for three minutes, with someone at the Overlord's address. That's why I couldn't talk to the Terrans running this station. I don't want this to get to the Tribunal, because Duval works for Overlord Six."

"But if Abram's plan worked, they'd have cut off this system. Why would any Terrans want to lose Builder technology?"

"That's another oddity. I came upon two of Abram's 'nephews.' One was talking about poor Mr. Barone, how he begged for his life." Frank's jaw became rigid. "How Barone said his people should be spared, that they could solve the Builders' buoy—then the other one laughed and said, *Too bad for them; we've seen this stuff before.*"

"What?" She blinked away the blur that rose when she heard Barone's name. "Are you sure?"

"That's a direct quote. When the guy saw me, he turned pale, and the only thing that ever scared those guys was Abram. They bullied me into silence—after that, I paid more attention to their behavior on Priamos. I'm sure the ones from New Sousse had encountered Builder technology before."

"Could you identify the guys who talked about it?"

"They're dead. Died in the takeover, by Sergeant Joyce's hands."

"That's convenient. You know how this sounds, Frank. As if you manufactured this for bargaining." When he shook his head and looked down, she sighed. "It's pretty thin, based only upon your opinion and this address. If you distrusted the Terrans, why didn't you talk to the Autonomist shock commandos when they came on-station?"

"I convinced Sergeant Pike to check out the address I memorized." Frank pointed at his head. "Unfortunately, it's been reassigned. To a toy factory."

"So you have no tangible evidence."

"Not a bit."

She stared at him, realizing how she'd avoided connecting the facts. Abram's takeover was well planned and executed, but she'd dodged any analysis other than anguishing over the needless deaths it caused. Spending all that time mourning, even blaming herself for the effects of the TD wave, had been a mistake. She should have been asking questions, such as, *where had Abram's money come from?*

"Did Overlord Six provide financing?" she asked Frank. "Is there a money trail?"

"I don't know. Some of Abram's men grumbled that the relief funds, sent to help those harmed by the Minoans, had all been funneled toward the Cause. I doubt Abram was able to finance everything with that charity, but I had no access to records—if there was anything of the sort."

She remained quiet, rubbing her upper teeth with her tongue, and Frank took his cue from her. He relaxed, his fingers tapping the arms of his chair.

Her thoughts ran through the possible connections. If Abram had been taking orders from Overlord Six, then the Interstellar Tribunal was a farce, because SP Duval was on Six's staff. But if the ICT had no teeth, why was Tahir killed? And why keep up the pretense of the Tribunal?

She took a deep breath as she widened the scope: If Overlord Six was behind the attempted takeover, then what about the other Overlords? There were plenty of Terrans in this system, predominantly from Overlord Three's district. They included SP Parmet and much of his staff, but they also had plenty of prior TEBI personnel—and Tahir's assassination smelled like a TEBI hit. Did that mean Overlord Three was behind Tahir's death? Were Three *and* Six trying to undermine the ICT? If these Overlords didn't support the ICT, then they might not honestly support the interstellar research in this system. Or Pax Minoica.

There was a whole spectrum of possibilities. On one end, Abram was an independent loose canon. At the other end, she envisioned a full-fledged Terran attempt to undermine Pax Minoica. Somewhere, along this sliding scale, sat reality.

"What are you thinking, Ms. Kedros?" Frank sounded hesitant.

"I'm wondering what you expect to get from telling me this."

Frank flinched at her hard voice. She wondered why she'd lashed out; was she really the sort to kick a man when he was down?

"I just wanted to warn you that there's still something

rotten in G-145. I know it, even if I can't prove it." He kept his gaze downward, not meeting hers.

She felt worse. He hadn't asked for anything and he seemed concerned about her welfare, considering the murderous attempts on the *Pilgrimage*. Wait—did Frank even know about those? She asked him, "Do you get to watch the Feeds?"

"No, but we did hear of Dr. Rouxe's death. That made those of us testifying for the prosecution pretty nervous." At least he was testifying against his cohorts.

She nodded approvingly and stood up. "Thanks, Frank, although I'm not sure what to make of your story. Yet." Just like Pike's report of all that data heading toward Overlord Six's territory.

"Ms. Kedros, wait—"

She did, watching him steadily. He appeared to consider his words, weighing them carefully and speaking slowly. "I've made some bad choices in my life. Joining Abram's Cause was one of them, and I'll have to pay for it. But there's one thing I can recognize, in myself and others, and that's *self-destruction*. Please, don't let yourself be overcome."

She wanted to walk away, but was caught by the grief on his face. "Is that why you stopped drinking?"

"I drank to stop myself from fading away."

Her face felt numb, so it was easy to hide her surprise. Sometimes she felt she was unraveling, like poorly woven cloth, so loudly that it would wake the ghosts in the back of her mind. If she drank enough, she stopped the internal unraveling and the rustling of ghosts—for Frank, it stopped the fading.

He continued. "I started a self-help group here on the station, if you're interested. Perhaps you can stop by, before you implode."

She shrugged off the quiver of recognition. Drinkers all had their reasons; just because Frank had seized upon her self-destructive streak, didn't mean he understood what was going on in her head. Besides, her rejuv didn't just give her an improved metabolism, it made her an ultra-rapid metabolizer of drugs and alcohol. She could handle her drinking without the self-help, the therapy, *or the therapist.* Major Tafani, her AFCAW-assigned addiction counselor, flashed through her mind.

"No, thank you, Frank." She tried for dignity, but it sounded more like outrage. "I doubt I'll have the time."

He nodded sadly. When she glanced back before going through the hatch, he was still watching her.

"I'm sorry I couldn't speak with you until now. It's been an exhausting day." Oleander spoke into her implanted mike while looking around at the busy cafeteria on the *Pilgrimage.*

"I sympathize, I really do. And you need to talk—things are going so well here on Priamos, I'd feel guilty about blathering on." Matt's voice sounded clear in her ear bug. The nodes were working well in the cafeteria, but the bandwidth charges on the *Pilgrimage* were so high that she and Matt had opted for audio calls only.

"Besides Senator Stephanos and his aides, we have to answer questions from two other senators." She was dressed in civilian clothes. The time displayed on her cuff in aquamarine blue, and she pressed her shirt's control to suppress the temperature readout. She had no need to monitor temperature on a ship the size of the *Pilgrimage.*

"They're representing all three major parties?"

"Looks like it. Senator Stephanos is running himself ragged, being on the Tribunal during most of first shift and trying to cover this investigation in second shift."

"Which parties are pushing this?"

"I don't know. But couldn't they have waited until we were in home port? It's not unusual to audit an expensive mission, but right now? And some of the aides are more than surly, they're sometimes disrespectful." With her peripheral vision, she saw Myron enter. She was sitting sideways to the entrance of the cafeteria and she shifted so Myron couldn't see her face. In uniform, she wore her long hair twisted into a coil at the base of her head. With her hair loose, he probably wouldn't recognize her from the back.

"I just can't tell you all the breakthroughs that have

started, entirely due to the translator the Minoans gave us."
Contrary to his earlier comment, Matt couldn't help gushing. "Of course, the Minoans don't have a good grasp on
our concepts, let alone the Builders' mental processes. . . ."

Across the room, Myron again moved into her range of
vision. He had a tray of food in his hands and he appeared
to be searching for a place to sit. Displaying his characteris-
tic pickiness, he turned down options of sitting with anyone
and ended up at an empty table.

"And I can't wait until the *Pytheas* arrives tomorrow
from J-132. It's supposed to be the tightest, best-equipped,
third-wave exploration ship around." Matt's voice had joy-
fully babbled beyond her attention span.

"The *Pytheas*? Who's going to pay for a third-wave exploration ship?" She'd missed something, since those ships
were equipped for terrestrial examination of habitable
planets, and no one had gone to the expense of sending
one to G-145. Smaller second-wave prospectors, such as
Aether's Touch, were for remote exploration and establish-
ing legal telepresence.

"It's owned by Leukos Industries. I—er—suggested that
Mr. Leukos get with the Minoan-owned Hellas Nautikos,
since they both seemed to be willing to invest in G-145."
Matt sounded embarrassed.

"I thought Leukos Industries did defense contracting."
Across the room, a Terran woman approached Myron's
table, obviously asking to sit with him. Oleander frowned.
Where had she seen that woman with short strawberry
blond hair?

"Apparently, he owns a small fleet of exploration class
vessels. Can you believe it?"

Her eyebrows rose at Matt's comment; how did he know
so much about the reclusive Mr. Leukos? At that moment,
she realized where she'd seen the woman speaking to Myron. Not currently in uniform, she was the Terran Space
Force lieutenant who had been in SP Duval's entourage.

Oleander tried to pull herself back to Matt. "Is this new
ship going to map Sophia Two? I thought they decided not
to put much effort into that planet."

Across the room, Myron played with his utensil in his right hand and made a gesture with his left that indicated he'd be leaving the table. He stood up and departed, leaving her standing. Oleander would have chalked this up to his inherent rudeness, except that the lieutenant remained standing and stared down at his tray. The lieutenant then put down her own tray, rearranged something on Myron's tray, and began to leave the cafeteria.

"Not Sophia Two—"

Oleander stood up, barely hearing Matt's next words. Something about getting the Builders' buoy working. This would have been heart-skipping news if she believed it could be possible within her lifetime. She made encouraging sounds of agreement as she casually walked over to Myron's table.

The departing TSF lieutenant didn't notice as she strode through the exit. Oleander looked down at Myron's plates, left for the bus-bot. There was thick sauce on one plate, where he'd scratched something in the viscous liquid. The smaller plate the lieutenant had placed on top hid most of the symbols, and the rest was disappearing as the sauce succumbed to ship gravity.

"I'm sorry, but something's come up." She cut through Matt's explanation as she followed the lieutenant.

"An emergency? Not more explosions, I hope." His voice sounded anxious. "Be careful, Diana."

"I will." At the cafeteria exit, Oleander looked both ways and saw the lieutenant's back. The hallways were crowded enough for her to follow without being obvious. "I've got to go, Matt. Miss you."

"I—I miss you, too."

"Right. Bye." She hurried after the Terran lieutenant.

CHAPTER 13

Our award for having the gonads to be *politically incorrect* goes to Reserve AFCAW Major Ariane Kedros, for testifying she *purposely* left isolationist scum to die. Bravo, darling—and isn't she a yummy morsel?

—Dr. Net-head Stavros, 2106.056.14.30 UT,
indexed by *Heraclitus 22* under Conflict Imperative

The *Bright Crescent* was still locked down and Colonel Edones was unavailable. When Ariane couldn't get through, she called Joyce and reversed the charges. Even now, comm was frightfully expensive in G-145.

"I hope I can get reimbursed for this," Joyce said dryly. He was in a private infirmary room, sitting up in his bed.

"It's good to see you, too." She meant it; his color was better and his profile said no more surgeries were scheduled. "Yes, this is business, so that's why I went full video."

"I've got no equipment, but I can give you a rundown." He shrugged. "I can't identify the person who held me down and drugged me, except he was a man and he wore a mask. *Pilgrimage* security can't find a used diaper inside a cardboard box, so I don't have high hopes of finding my assailant."

The attack had happened four days earlier, but it seemed so much longer ago. She nodded when he said he had *no equipment*, meaning he couldn't use military encryption. They were on an encrypted civilian line but according to regulations, they couldn't exchange classified information over it. Regulations absolutely forbade the use of personal codes and keywords to pass classified data—but she and Joyce had been on missions where they had to throw that rule out, or they'd never have survived.

"Give them time, Joyce. They're struggling with this."

"All I can say is I'm glad you came by. Otherwise, I'd be in an urn on my way home, and the crèche-get would still be wondering what happened." He snorted.

"Do I get points for protecting you, by sacrificing my body?"

"Nope." He grinned. "First, I wasn't awake to enjoy it, and second, it was really the Minoan warrior that sacrificed itself—or its gloves, I guess."

"I'll forgo the points, this time, since I got your package. I noticed it wasn't finished. Nice photos, by the way. How are Sara and the kids holding up?" As she said "package," she tapped her slate to start recording.

"Pretty good. I talked to them again today. Sara made an offer on that home, the one I told you about earlier?" He made a you-know-what-I-mean gesture. She *did* know: Joyce and his wife weren't looking for a new home. Joyce continued, "But the owners want too much. They won't budge unless they keep Autonomist citizenship and can raise their kids in the area. They also want a comfortable annual salary."

"Too bad. Did they mention what salary they hoped to get?" Obviously, the "owner" was Maria and even though this conversation might sound a trifle odd, the analogy worked.

"Eighty thousand HKD per year."

"Is the home still on the market?" She had almost everything she needed.

"I think so, but I won't be making another offer." He smiled wanly.

She stopped recording, because that was the end of the situation report. However, there were other particulars to address, such as what was happening on the *Bright Crescent*. "What's with the audit? Even for an HQ inspection, I've never seen a ship taken offline for more than a day. For that matter, I've never seen this happen at a nonmilitary facility."

"Yeah, a lot of 'firsts,' which make me suspicious. A team from the Headquarters Inspector General has arrived, comprised of a captain and two noncoms. When they came by to interview me, I got the scuttlebutt." He grinned in a predatory fashion, but quickly became somber. "They're just window dressing, to make the audit authentic. They've got no control in what they're privately calling 'the drubbing of the Directorate.' They say it's driven from the Senate."

"Stephanos?" She remembered the veiled threats. "But why would he take down the Directorate, when his committee gave us special projects?"

"You got it backwards, Major." Joyce scratched at a temporary implant in his neck. "They think this aims to discredit the senator and erode support for Pax Minoica, since he's such a staunch supporter. Of course, the colonel goes down as collateral damage."

Pax Minoica. She'd intended to tell only Colonel Edones about Frank's allegations, but the situation had changed. "Joyce, I got a lead that may be relevant, from a source who should remain anonymous."

"Is the source reliable?"

She paused to consider, and decided. "Yes. But there's no hard evidence."

"Remember, Major. We work in the intelligence field." Joyce sighed. "If we required hard evidence for following our leads, we'd be working in Justice."

"That's a good point. It's also corroborated by odd circumstantial data provided by Pike." She hesitated, thinking about the insecure comm, but her only classification guidance for this information was to protect the source. "My informant suspects Abram had funding, perhaps even direction, out of Overlord Six. Additionally, there's a suspicious amount of comm traffic going from Priamos to District Six worlds, although Pike cautioned me that this traffic could be misleading. The third oddity: Abram's men might have encountered Builder technology before they came to G-145."

She watched Joyce commit her words to memory. His eyebrows went up. "What about the other Overlords? Do we have an obligation to tell the Tribunal about this?"

"Don't know about the other Overlords. As for the ICT, we could insist SP Duval recuse himself, since he works for Six."

"Pax Minoica is really circling the crapper if this ICT is a sham."

"Our research push in this system might also be a joke if Six found Builder technology." She cocked her head as a thought zipped through her mind. "But I can't see the Minoans helping Overlord Six by handing over a translator. Maybe our alien oversight has been cooperative because they think we've finally got a true interstellar operation at Beta Priamos." Thoughts cascaded and sparked others. *If the Minoans wanted Aether Exploration before they'd provide assistance, then we employees looked like impediments to progress, at least while we sat on the* Pilgrimage. *Was that justification for someone to make attempts on our lives, or our ship?* That seemed ridiculous; more likely, Aether Exploration would be seen as a bunch of alien-loving traitors to the human race—once again, enough reason to plant explosives?

"Hmm—never credit Minoans with altruistic motives," Joyce said. "But what if the League is splintering? How will the Minoans react?"

"I don't know. I've been wondering how the TSF behaves during Overlord conflict. There's Space Force support for both SP Duval *and* SP Parmet—and which way will they jump?" She paused and Joyce waited. "At this point, let's keep each other updated and, when you get the chance, pass this on privately to the colonel. If not the colonel, perhaps the senator?"

"The colonel's restricted to the ship and the senator goes from the ICT hearings straight to the ship. Neither are approachable without going through some useless political straphanger," Joyce said. "And I don't think I can even board the *Bright Crescent*, under lockdown, without permission."

"Can you get a message to Captain Floros?"

"They've got her tied up on the ship for hearings, testi-mony, analysis, whatever. . . . Maybe."

"How about Lieutenant Oleander? Matt spoke with her recently, so they're allowing her off the ship."

"The weapons officer?" Puzzlement flitted over Joyce's face.

"The colonel appointed Lieutenant Oleander to a pro-visional spot in the Directorate." She realized Joyce had missed quite a bit while he was laid up.

"She's new to Intelligence."

"Yeah, but that might be why she's allowed to stroll off the ship, like the operations personnel. You got to work with what you've got, Sergeant."

After a bit of grumbling and symbolic back-slapping, they cut the call.

Ariane stayed in her quarters on *Aether's Touch* and jot-ted down some notes. She still had her original mission, the possibly defecting Maria. Joyce had given her the keys to Maria's demands, using the fake house-buying story. She tapped her console thoughtfully.

It sounds like Maria wants to have children. The back-ground file said Maria was bisexual, but that didn't affect the human urge to procreate and raise children. What did stand in Maria's way was the Terran League itself, which practiced strict eugenic controls. Accidental pregnancies were pre-vented by state-applied birth control implants that lasted years, with the additional threat of withholding citizenship from *unapproved* progeny. Citizenship was the only way to have health care, but it was that same health care system with which Maria had run afoul: She wasn't allowed to have children due to Tantor's Sun disease, which she'd contracted in a battle near Tantor. This disease incurred a measurable genetic mutation that would be found in all of her eggs.

On Autonomist worlds, the mutation was considered be-nign and could be removed from the egg, if parents wished, before fertilization. Besides, on any Autonomist world, Maria would be able to have her birth control implant re-moved and she could breed—like a bunny, if she wanted.

Ariane shut down her slate. This sleep shift she was staying in her quarters. *Aether's Touch* was home by now, and she sighed with pleasure as she got into bed.

As she drifted off to sleep, she considered Maria's hope for becoming an Autonomist citizen. Unfortunately, it didn't mesh with the Directorate's wish that Maria remain as an informant in place. Maria's double misfortune was that she'd kidnapped Ariane for torture and possible execution, so Ariane was the last person who'd sympathize with her situation.

The corridors were crowded on the recreation level of the *Pilgrimage*, so Oleander could be inconspicuous as she followed the Terran lieutenant. Luckily, she looked back only once, and Oleander drifted into another group of Autonomists, obvious by their bright clothes. This group of freighter crew members were clustered near the entrance of a rec room. They held drink packs and offered one to Oleander, but she shook her head with a smile.

The Terran lieutenant arrived at her destination, ducking into a package drop and storage center. A moment later, Oleander entered behind her.

Following Autonomist privacy laws, the *Pilgrimage* had opted to have no surveillance inside the center, other than at the doors. To Oleander's left, it looked like a miniature locker room, with lockers large enough to hang clothes or large packages. The other side of the center undulated with curved bays of smaller locked boxes. Half the bays were used by *Pilgrimage* crew members for physical post, such as parcels. The other bays held temporary storage and drop-boxes rented on a one-time basis or for as long as several years.

There were thirty people, maybe more, in the storage center. The Terran lieutenant stood in the first bay and, after noting the box location, Oleander walked past that bay into the next one. She roved along the wall, as if trying to find a box number and moved around the edge of the bay to peek at the lieutenant, who reached into a small box and pocketed something. Oleander turned back to peruse the storage wall as the Terran lieutenant left the center.

Oleander went to look at the box opened by the lieutenant. Whatever the Terran had picked up, it was thin enough to put into her stretchy jumpsuit pocket and yet not bulge. Any data storage could fit that requirement, being small, often carried subcutaneously—although the Terrans were only beginning to use implants.

The box could be opened by thumbprint, voiceprint, or by entering a code, since it could be rented for one-time use. She made note of the box number, but wondered what she could do with it. Even if she could prove Myron left something for the Terran lieutenant, she'd never convince the *Pilgrimage* crew to release records on the storage box.

She walked out of the drop and storage center, and turned into the shop promenade the *Pilgrimage* had established for the couple of years it would operate inside G-145. They had also upgraded this area with nodes and ComNet access. Walking slowly by the storefronts, she wondered if her suspicions were warranted and if so, whom she could burden with them. Her first thought was Floros, who was a genius with data systems, but she hadn't seen the brusque captain since the ship audit began.

Her ear bug beeped with a call. It was probably Matt; she pushed the switch behind her jaw to activate her implanted mike. "Lieutenant Oleander here."

"This is Master Sergeant Joyce, ma'am. I was wondering if you'd have time to drop by the infirmary."

She smiled at the convenience; her answer had actually called her. "Certainly, Sergeant. You're just the person I need to see."

Ariane was indulging in her wake-up cup of Hellas-grown Kaffi, savoring the aroma, when Matt's excited voice came over the internal comm.

"Hey, you got to see this!"

Her quick glance at system vitals, displayed above the galley's countertop, convinced her there was no emergency with ship. Combined with the fact that Matt sounded half his age, she continued to calmly sip her hot drink as she tapped a command on the bulkhead beside the system display.

"Ari?" Matt was in the protected array compartment, according to the ship's systems. "Look at this."

"What?" Her question was answered when she pulled up the displays Matt was browsing. "Has the *Pytheas* arrived already?"

"It docked at the *Pilgrimage* about four hours ago. It'll be here in about twenty hours, depending upon the crew rest they take. What a beauty—and is it equipped! It carries one of the largest ship-based telescopes available, as well as six specialized antennas."

A view port opened for face-to-face; she hadn't seen Matt bubbling with this much enthusiasm for a long time. Taking a sip of Kaffi to hide her smile, she stopped him with a dry comment. "Watch out."

"Why?"

"Your antenna envy is showing."

He chuckled. "I admit that I'm gushing like a kid with his first crush, but this ship is amazing!"

"It's a third-wave exploration vessel, so its price tag should be—"

"Yeah, it's three orders of magnitude over the value of *Aether's Touch*. It requires three crew members to run it in real-space, not counting the scientific mission crew." He whistled as he posted more schematics.

"I thought your finance *consultant* Carmen said nobody's making loans for G-145 research. How did Leukos Industries finance this, or insure that crew?"

"I didn't ask too many questions." Matt shrugged his shoulders. "Leukos himself is underwriting the life, medical, and disability insurance for the crew. He might be financing everything. Maybe it's because of you—but I don't care."

"Maybe you should care. Leukos isn't known for effusive acts of charity. He's been described as *ruthless* in his business dealings." She took another sip and watched Matt display more "beauty shots" of the *Pytheas*. It did look amazing and she hoped Brandon, aka Leukos, wasn't going to use it as leverage against her. She wouldn't be beholden to him and, in an effort to counteract Matt's giddiness, she added, "Too bad they're going to tear its referential engine out in the next couple of months."

"Could happen *much* faster than that. Come on, we've got briefings in less than an hour, followed by another scintillating meeting with Contractor Director." Matt winked and made shooing motions.

She cut the internal comm. Within twenty minutes, she and Matt were locking up the ship and walking quietly, companionably, down the halls of the Beta Priamos Station. She didn't like breaking up this comfortable moment, but she had to broach this subject before they were around any Minoans.

"Isn't this going a bit fast?" she started hesitantly. "Aren't you skeptical about the Minoans and their sudden insight into the Builders? They stayed quiet during our entry into G-145, and now they're helping us retrofit exploration ships, for Gaia's sake."

"Of course I'm suspicious." Matt's tone was casual as he strolled at an easy pace for her shorter legs. "Although I'll point out that they never entered this system, *to our knowledge*, until Hellas Nautikos asked for an advisor."

She noted the emphasis. "They also showed up in a vessel with some sort of cloaking. I noticed none of you who witnessed that, from you and David Ray to the crew of the *Bright Crescent*, have asked the Minoans to explain that capability."

"Because I don't want to remind them of what I know. Look at everything they've helped us with in the past twenty days, from squashing Abram to translating the Builders' language—so I'm just hanging on for the ride." Matt stopped and faced her, lowering his voice. "But I am wary of their agenda."

She nodded, relieved. However, once they'd entered Dr. Lowry's major laboratory, the sense of being drowned and tumbled about by a torrent of technological flux returned. "Our wayward bot is still transmitting?"

The two remaining members of the Artifact Analysis Team, Dr. Lowry and Dr. Novak, nodded.

Novak, a middle-aged man with a bit of excess weight around his waist, made a gesture toward the data on the wall, as a statement of the obvious. "We think it's in communication with the alien technology."

Matt had to be convinced. "How could that be possible, when I pulled its memory module?"

"That only held the temporary data we needed. The bot still had its processors," Ariane pointed out.

"We sent out other bots, keeping them suitably distant from the buoy. We captured data from five thousand kilometers, then moved closer. So far, we've been as close as two kilometers, without suffering hijacking attempts like— ah, your bot suffered." Novak brought up photos and video, showing the alien artifact that they now knew was an N-space buoy.

"It looks different," Ariane said.

Matt frowned, then saw the change as the video moved closer. "It didn't have those tails before. What are those?"

The fuzzy cylinder in the picture resolved into the familiar spindle shape of the alien buoy. What they hadn't expected were the three ribbonlike gossamer tails that extended from the "bottom," the narrow end. Before the tails, the spindle measured about forty meters long. Now they added another twenty, at least.

"Those appeared about a month ago," Dr. Lowry said. "They unfurled on their own and since we're nervous about letting a bot touch any buoy surfaces, we're unsure of the material."

"We think they're solar collectors. It deployed them once your bot gave it enough energy." Dr. Novak tapped the lab bench to bring up another picture.

"That's impossible. The bot's collectors are too small to charge—" Matt's jaw dropped as he watched Novak zoom in on the small bot, sitting on the sunward side of the rounded "top" of the alien buoy. "Is that part of my *suit*?"

Novak enlarged a picture of a jury-rigged connection

between previously unnoticed ports in the buoy and the bot's external charging cable. There, in the middle of the snarl, was part of the control harness for an EVA suit.

"I think I've been mugged," muttered Matt.

Ariane put her hand over her mouth, trying not to laugh. After their bot had started to misbehave, Matt had tried to retrieve it by exiting the ship, going untethered, and climbing around the artifact. The bot had resisted capture and he discovered that it had appendages sharp enough to damage an EVA suit. Moving about nimbly, it had sliced off wiring harnesses and punctured his suit. The suit sealant expanded so that Matt didn't have enough flexibility to move. Eventually, when his comm was cut, he was in trouble.

"We think it's been trickle-charging the systems on the buoy," Novak said.

"Hijacking—doing that—could only be considered—" Matt sputtered. "You're saying *something* had the intelligence to intercept our commands and hijack our bot, then figure out how to use the bot to power itself. That's super sophisticated."

"We realize that, Mr. Journey. But what other assumptions could we make, when looking at that?" Dr. Novak's voice was quiet as he gestured toward the picture of spliced wires wrapped with, of all things, shredded strips from Matt's EVA suit.

"What about DiastimBot Instrumentation? That bot's still under warranty, and I submitted a problem report to them." Matt's face was beginning to flush.

"Ah, we spoke with their engineers." Novak watched Matt's color with trepidation. "They sent us schematics and procedural code, with the primitive commands and rules. Of course, we had to sign nondisclosure agreements."

"So they helped?"

"As much as they could, Mr. Journey. The engineers told us the bot is custom-made—"

"And expensive. Don't forget that," Matt snapped. "I need it back."

Ariane put a light restraining hand on Matt's upper arm, to remind him that Novak wasn't responsible for the bot's behavior. Matt glanced sideways at her and his color began to fade. She gave his arm an encouraging squeeze before letting go, which reminded her how much muscle he had on his arms. Her hand fell to her side reluctantly—she wasn't the touchy-feely type, really, but she didn't want to remove her hand. Novak pulled her back into the conversation as he raised his voice.

"You should leave it in place," he protested. "The DiastimBot engineer said the license owner and parent ship had been 'burned in,' so we hope to get response from loyalty or ownership subroutines."

"Those subroutines didn't help us earlier," Matt said.

"At the time, you didn't know the bot was receiving other commands," Novak said. "We'd like to experiment with command sequences, but we think it's best if those commands come from its owner and parent ship."

"Well . . ." Matt was mollified; the chance to actively support the research overwhelmed his outrage and embarrassment, *temporarily*. But, from the set of his jaw, Ariane knew he wouldn't be leaving G-145 without that bot.

Dr. Lowry had let Dr. Novak take the lead regarding the bot. Now she took over the briefing, tapping commands to display images of symbols on the buoy.

"The translator hasn't helped us very much with these." Lowry stopped in an area that had a diagram of lines and dots, with symbols arranged around it. "We think this is a star diagram, so we're doing pattern matching against the stars as they look from the buoy's position. The symbols near this diagram have roughly translated to 'biological temple,' which is puzzling."

"Have you verified the buoy is anchored in N-space?" Ariane asked.

"It reads like any N-space connection would, from a gravity generator or buoy." Lowry shrugged. "Since it's fixed in real-space with no obvious means of station-keeping, which only Minoan time buoys can do—we're assuming it's anchored. What else can we do, given our level of technology?"

This, of course, was the gift the Minoans had given humankind: a way to have controlled entry and exit from N-space. Some considered it a yoke rather than a gift, because humans were still dependent upon Minoan-made buoys. Having conquered the creation of a Penrose Fold to transition into N-space, humans still needed references and a way to return from N-space at a specific *when* and *where*, in real-space. This *anchoring*, between real-space and N-space, still had to be provided by the Minoans. It was a bit humiliating, considering that humans had figured out how to use N-space for both dumping and building gee, as well as for signal transmission. As a result, humans built gravity generators as well as FTL data exchange relays—but still couldn't create their own buoys.

"Have you been able to determine what's inside?" Ariane asked Lowry.

"It's too well shielded. We've got some density readings." Dr. Lowry displayed a diagram, which showed them no more than they'd been able to get from Minoan-made buoys.

"Does it give off a lock signal?"

"Sure, it transmits several organized signals at specific frequencies." To supplement her answer, Lowry showed the spectral graph of electromagnetic transmissions. "And here's where we hit the wall."

And a big, thick wall it was. Ariane looked at the graph as she rubbed her chin, contemplating. Just knowing an organized signal transmitted on a specific frequency, was a long way from understanding the encoding, much less the data. This could take years, or decades, to understand.

"We're hoping that if the buoy was able to hijack your bot, it'll be willing to communicate with us through it." Dr. Novak sounded eager, but Dr. Lowry frowned at him.

"You're anthropomorphizing again, Oran," she warned.

"We could compare its interaction with the Minoan system buoy. After all, we have two—" Ariane stopped. *We have two buoys in this system.* She remembered Frank's earnest face, saying that Abram's men may have encountered the Builders' technology before.

"Yes?" Dr. Lowry looked at her with raised eyebrows.

"The temporal-distortion wave would have destroyed both buoys..." Oops, she was muttering out loud. She clamped her jaw shut as she thought about Overlord Six's mysterious involvement with Abram. Financing Abram's attempt would get rid of any connection to the Builders—possibly permanently, if the sun went nova, or putting it twenty-plus years away, if the sun survived. An aggressive Overlord such as Six, if he already had a Builders' buoy, might want to shut down the competition.

Dr. Lowry didn't notice that Ariane had stuttered into silence. "The Minoan buoys can't be destroyed, although they can be 'severed.' I suppose—"

"Destroyer of Worlds is correct." Contractor Director stood in the doorway to the outer lab. Its soulless voice, sounding neither male nor female, cut Lowry off. "The Criminal Isolationists could have severed both time buoys."

CHAPTER 14

Today we watched Garnet Tachawee and Sabina Cavanaugh, co-wives of SP Isrid Parmet. They described the execution of AFCAW Colonel Dokos and identified the executioners—one's now lost in N-space, and good riddance, I say. Another point: Who's dressing Terran women nowadays? They still have deplorable fashion sense.

—Dr. Net-head Stavros, 2106.057.14.30 UT,
indexed by *Heraclitus 6* under Conflict Imperative

Contractor Director startled everyone inside the small lab. Matt and Ariane recovered quickly, being familiar with the Minoan ability to move silently. Dr. Novak, however, had probably never encountered a Minoan this close and personal. His face paled and he dropped his slate. His foot caught on his stool and his arms flailed for support, pushing on lab equipment with shiny metal tubes sprouting from it. Dr. Lowry and Matt were nearest. Lowry jumped to save the lab equipment while Matt kept the cosmologist from getting a concussion on a lab bench.

Ariane was too far away to help. Distracted by the sudden use of that incriminating title, she turned to Contractor Director. "I prefer the title *Explorer of Solar Systems*," she said quietly, so the others didn't hear.

"We know," Contractor Director said. The Minoan stepped past her and a guardian followed, as she stood transfixed by the short and condescending answer.

"I could use some help here!" Dr. Lowry grunted as equipment began to tip. Ariane leapt to assist her, and they wrestled the equipment back onto the lab bench while Matt straightened out Dr. Novak.

"Sorry. Late." David Ray, gasping and puffing, appeared in the doorway. "Just notified of cha—change. Ha—had to run through two rings."

They all looked at the Minoan emissary.

Contractor Director dipped its horns. "I changed the meeting time and place. Dr. Novak has signed the Hellas Nautikos cooperative research agreements, and he will have need of this information."

This didn't seem to reassure Dr. Novak. Matt guided him to a stool, while everyone settled and the guardian moved to the hatch, ensuring they wouldn't be disturbed. As Ariane picked a stool to sit upon, she was reminded of her college science labs, except there had been a graduate student standing at the end of the two benches preparing to lecture, rather than a Minoan emissary. She leaned on her right forearm, which rested on the smooth and cool countertop made of synthetic soapstone.

David Ray sat down across the bench from her. Having caught his breath, he leaned over and whispered, "They have a good sense for drama, don't they?"

She nodded. By now, humankind assumed the Minoans *chose* to mimic a bygone civilization on ancient Earth. However, they didn't have to wear horned headdresses with cascading jewels, or flowing robes. Perhaps the cold air that moved their clothing was necessary, but they could just as easily walk about with tanks. That wouldn't make the same impression, would it?

"You may record this, since this information will be verified in the Builders' records on Priamos. This is not privileged information." Contractor Director allowed them to switch on recorders in their slates.

"We began observing the culture you call the Builders approximately sixty thousand UT years ago, when—"

David Ray's arm shot up for a question, and Ariane felt her life regress to secondary school. The familiarity deepened when Contractor Director sternly said, "Questions will be entertained later, General Counsel for Aether Exploration." David Ray lowered his arm with chagrin, as the Minoan began again.

"We waited about thirty-two thousand years to make contact with them and to forestall further questions, we will provide *exact* timelines to your xenologists below."

She watched David Ray, with a twist of anguish on his face, make notes on his slate. He probably wanted to explore each statement in depth. There was much more to ask the Minoans, now that they could *compare humankind's progress with another sentient species*. The ramifications, to net-think and popular culture, were both horrifying and exhilarating. This generated more questions: How long had the Minoans existed? How many species had they seen evolve to sentience? How had the Minoans managed to survive, over such a long time? After all, the universe was a very dangerous place.

"Mistakes were made with the Builders," the Minoan continued. David Ray was vibrating in his seat. "Over thousands of years, the Builders became hostile and what you define as 'xenophobic.' We watched their decline begin thirteen thousand years ago. They eventually withdrew from their outposts, such as this one here in G-145, to their home world systems. In an attempt to cut off contact with us and other possible spacefaring species, the Builders damaged the fabric of space and time."

"Meaning what?" David Ray couldn't stand it any longer.

Contractor Director's head turned to observe Ariane and David Ray. She shifted uncomfortably under the Minoan's silent scrutiny as previously unrelated facts crashed together in her brain.

"Temporal distortion," she whispered, her mouth dry. "They pushed temporal-distortion waves into N-space."

"They destroyed their own buoys?" David Ray sounded incredulous.

"No." She cleared her throat, staring at Contractor Director. "They damaged nous-space itself. That's why *you* can't travel to their worlds anymore."

The shock in the room was palpable. After a quiet pause, Contractor Director dipped its horns toward her.

"Correct," the Minoan said. "We could not survive the nous-transit, but *you* could, with the enhancements we provide."

"Do you seriously believe his death was due to 'natural causes'?" Joyce demanded.

Benjamin Pilgrimage, or at least his image in the view port, looked uncomfortable. "Our medical examiners can't identify the reason Dr. Rouxe's heart stopped. The Tribunal members are satisfied with the results."

"The Tribunal is satisfied that an effort was made, nothing more." Joyce was sweating, which he hoped Benjamin couldn't see. He'd increased the interval between his pain meds and he was paying for it. The right side of his torso screamed with every breath he took.

"I'm getting pressure to close the case. It's quite possible that Rouxe died from natural causes."

"We all know your medical staff isn't well trained in forensics. Nor are they up on the sophisticated multicomponent poisons used today."

Benjamin's face tightened. "What else would you suggest we do?"

"Send the body to Hellas Prime for examination by our people," Joyce answered promptly.

"We can't do that. Pilgrimage sovereignty—"

"Might have been what got us into this problem." Joyce's response was savage. "But I have an answer that can save your pride. Your offices on Hellas Prime enjoy extraterritorial status, so send the body there. It stays on sovereign soil and from there, you can ask for any experts you'd like."

"Dr. Rouxe was a Terran League citizen and the Terrans are asking for his body. They'll resist sending him to Hellas Prime."

"So ask them to provide their own forensics expert, who can observe and consult, under embassy jurisdiction."

Benjamin looked sour. "It would have been easier if your advisors had suggested this a couple days ago. What happened to all that promised help from your Directorate, anyway?"

"Sorry, those advisors were pulled into something more important," Joyce lied coolly.

He wasn't so calm and collected after he concluded the call. With shaking fingers, he adjusted the medication dosage from his implant back to the default programmed by the medics. *I was an idiot to assume I could get along without the pain meds so soon.*

The medication coursed into his blood, giving him immediate relief as well as sleepiness. He had to fight that. After speaking with Lieutenant Oleander, he'd looked into how the *Pilgrimage* staff had handled their recent cases. It was a travesty of investigative procedure and he wondered whether *Terran* advice had encouraged the absurdity.

Likewise, the investigation into the explosives had stuttered to a stop. *Pilgrimage* security decided they couldn't find the person who programmed the bot that had threatened *Aether's Touch*, and they realized their explosive sniffers weren't sensitive enough for the amounts used against Major Kedros, himself, and the intern who had the misfortune to trip the trap for David Ray. They told him the *Pilgrimage* would be retrofitted with better sniffers that were used for Autonomous security systems. That was good enough, right? Anyway, there hadn't been any more incidents and Benjamin had resisted buying portable EOD equipment. When Joyce had suggested renting Terran canines, which were still the best detectors around, he'd run up against crèche-get principles, sensibilities, and myths. They believed that dogs carried dust and dander and they smelled bad. . . .

Joyce's eyelids drooped. The damage might already be done, unfortunately. They hadn't stepped up background checks on incoming contractors. Since they were worried about the personnel shortage, they'd let more than a hundred Gaia-b'damned Terrans with spotty histories depart for the Priamos, Sophia, and Laomedon facilities. Joyce was less worried about Autonomist contractors, considering that it was almost impossible to work and live in the Consortium without leaving a ComNet trail.

Then there was this Senatorial audit, requiring a lock-down of the *Bright Crescent*. It came at the most inconvenient time and Joyce sensed the stench of false coincidence. He also smelled something wrong about that little prick, the senator's great-nephew Myron, who helped this charade along and gave something to the Terrans. Oleander was going to surreptitiously ask Captain Floros for help in checking Myron.

Joyce had to examine the background of every contractor who had followed Major Kedros to Beta Priamos. He'd have to coerce records from *Pilgrimage* security.... His eyes closed.

"We've got an exploration ship, provided by Leukos Industries, that we can enhance. They sent two support engineers who know the *Pytheas* inside and out." Matt's voice was eager.

"I don't think those are the only *enhancements* they're talking about." Ariane eyed the Minoan emissary. "Am I right, Contractor Director?"

"If the Penrose Fold is adequate for transitioning into N-space, then we only need to decode lock and destination information from the buoy network, Ms. Kedros." Dr. Lowry's voice was acerbic.

"What are you suggesting, Ari?" Matt asked.

"I'm saying there's a mental aspect to the nous-transit that we have to consider, not just the transition, the dropping out and in to real-space." She *knew* N-space piloting, and it involved more than plugging numbers into a referential engine; Lowry only understood the theory.

"Slow down, everybody. Please." David Ray made calming motions with his hand and tilted his head toward the Minoan, subtly reminding them to *wait*. Contractor Director seemed distracted, looking from Ariane to Dr. Lowry.

"Researcher of Astrophysics is correct in assuming your Penrose Fold is adequate for transition." Contractor Director finally nodded toward Lowry. "The locking by the buoy will be different, but we will provide engineering plans for the referential part of your engines, just as we did before."

As they did before? Ariane exchanged a confused glance with David Ray. Then she realized the Minoan was referring to their first contact with humans, near the end of the 1960s.

"What about compensating for other buoys in their network? Do you know their buoy topography?" Dr. Lowry asked.

"The Builders' buoys are simplistic derivations of ours. They provide single endpoint transits."

David Ray scribbled. Leaning over, Ariane saw "M's gave B's buoy tech?" written on his slate, at the end of a long list of questions. She doubted he'd get any of them answered soon.

Meanwhile, Lowry kept asking her questions. "You mean this buoy only allows us to go to one system?"

"Yes. You have translated the destination printed on the buoy. Soon, your automation will identify the solar system, as it appears from this position," the Minoan said.

"*Biological Temple*? That's what the symbols on the buoy translate to, literally. But what does that *mean*?" Lowry looked frustrated.

"We cannot apply nuance in the translation." Contractor Director made a gesture of helplessness, with a wrist rotation that looked *wrong*. Ariane shivered.

"What about Ari's question—can we get through to a Builders' system just by changing the *Pytheas*?" Matt frowned and watched the Minoan emissary carefully.

"No."

Everyone was quiet. David Ray shifted about on his stool, finally losing patience. "Throw the other boot, already."

"You mean 'drop the other shoe,'" muttered Matt.

"Whichever."

"Footwear is irrelevant," Contractor Director said, looking at Ariane. "I would speak with Explorer of Solar Systems alone."

"No. Not alone." Matt's jaw jutted out, promising a stubborn stand. "I'm her employer and I have to ensure her safety, according to our underwriters."

"I'm legal counsel to her, as well as part owner of Aether Exploration," David Ray said.

"And we—we have to stay," Dr. Lowry said, standing. "Right, Dr. Novak?"

Novak looked terrified. He hadn't said a word since the Minoan emissary arrived. When Dr. Lowry called for his support, he'd already been drifting toward the door. Novak's mouth dropped down. "Ah . . . I don't need to stay."

Contractor Director gestured and the guardian stepped away from the door, letting Dr. Novak escape. Dr. Lowry, however, stood firm.

"Explorer of Solar Systems takes the biological risks, as pilot," Contractor Director said.

"And what about the rest of the crew that goes with the pilot? Dr. Novak, or I, may be on that ship, with many others."

Contractor Director stood motionless and they waited. Then, with almost a peeved movement of its head, it said, "You may stay, but this information is protected, per your nondisclosure statement."

Lowry nodded and sat back down, taking Dr. Novak's abandoned stool.

"The risk of insanity to humans is high in damaged N-space." With a graceful twirl of a jewel, the Minoan displayed "Proprietary Information" in red letters on the bulkhead behind it. "If unconscious and under your delta tranquilizer, human passengers can make the transit safely. Obviously, the N-space pilot must stay awake and have special protection."

"Wait, please." Ariane extended her hand, palm out, having seen the Minoans make this same halting motion. Picking up her slate, she thumbed it into another mode. "I'm going to scan for listening devices."

Contractor Director nodded, but Matt groaned theatrically. "Don't you ever get tired of being so suspicious, Ari?"

"I've learned, the hard way, that I should never *assume* I'm having a private conversation." She walked about the room, thankful that she'd been able to keep her Directorate slate.

Matt changed his tune when she found recording pips under the two long benches, strategically placed across the room from each other. They appeared to be small raised bumps and when she peeled them off, they covered barely a quarter of her fingertip.

"Our lab was being monitored?" Lowry paled.

"Give them to me." Contractor Director extended a gloved hand.

Remembering Warrior Commander's treatment of equipment, Ariane peered at the pips carefully. Without a microscope, she couldn't determine if these were Terran-made. Figuring she'd never know for sure, she extended her arm as far as she could and dropped them in the Minoan's hand. She was right. Contractor Director's hand closed tightly and while there were no audible crunches, she knew the pips were destroyed. Matt flinched as the Minoan opened its hand, turned it over, and let the flecks fall to the floor.

"Do you think Terrans put those there?" David Ray asked.

"Possibly. They love to litter these things around." She looked down at the tiny flecks of metal and plastic while her mind went through the list: Ensign Walker had intelligence connections, Parmet used to run TEBI, and then there was Dr. Istaga, as possible super-spy Andre. The first two even had bona fide reasons for monitoring the lab, under the auspices of station security.

Contractor Director began again. "Damaged N-space will be dangerous for you to pilot, but not impossible. We can provide a better cognitive dissonance enhancer, one more effective in preventing dissociative insanity."

"Okaaaaaay." Ariane leaned against the lab bench and crossed her arms. Not so surprising, the Minoans had a better version of clash. This sounded *too* easy.

"The rips in N-space make the nous-transit more disruptive to the human brain and will require frequent dosage changes. A human with an ultra-fast metabolism would be the best candidate to use this drug."

She straightened, not looking at anyone else. The Minoans had guessed about her metabolism, or they knew about the AFCAW rejuv and its effects. Remembering how Warrior Commander had followed her around on the *Pilgrimage*, she figured it was the former, established through observation.

"Currently, we believe the safest route is to install a piloting enhancement, similar to your implants. It requires a candidate that can accept artificially grown tissues and Explorer of Solar Systems qualifies."

Ah, it won't be so easy after all. David Ray made a quiet gurgling sound and sent her a warning glance. Matt hadn't looked too surprised when the Minoans mentioned her metabolism, but now his eyebrows rose.

"How would you know that Ari—er, Explorer of Solar Systems—can accept vat-grown tissues?" Matt demanded. "Only about thirty percent of humans can do that."

"She works for the Intelligence Directorate," David Ray said in an undertone. "It's a prerequisite for that unit. It's listed in their public recruiting material."

"Oh." Matt was only now connecting facts, including Diana's recruitment and Sergeant Joyce's condition in his considerations. His frown deepened into a downright scowl. "That doesn't mean her body can accept *alien technology.*"

"I'm okay with—" she started.

"Not yet, Ariane. Please." David Ray stopped her with a distressed, sharp movement of his hands. He turned to the Minoan and said casually, "I'm wondering why you wanted to offer this, *privately*, to someone known for having a self-destructive streak."

Inwardly, she cringed. Externally, her face heated with embarrassment. She didn't have to wonder whether David Ray was correct; she already knew. When she binged beyond safe bounds, she didn't expect to wake up. There were all those dangerous missions she did for Owen, who had also offered her the risky rejuv that had destroyed Brandon's life. Owen knew her, but she didn't expect to be so transparent to David Ray, who had met her less than twenty days ago.

"Explorer of Solar Systems, based upon our observa-

tions, has the first suitable biochemistry we have found,"
Contractor Director said. "Of course, the candidate cannot
be averse to risk, and we evaluated the psychological urges
behind heroism and recklessness—"

"Hey! I'm right *here*." When the Minoan cocked its head,
she added, "It's rude to psychoanalyze someone in his or
her presence. And remember, *I'm* the one making this decision." She glared at David Ray, and Matt, who held up his
hands, palm outward, in front of his chest in surrender.

"Ariane, they're banking on your acceptance," David
Ray said, not taking hints as well as Matt. "They've stacked
the dice against you."

"The *deck*. They've stacked the deck of cards," Matt
muttered.

David Ray was right again, despite his butchered idiom.
As the others waited for her to speak, she regarded Contractor Director in somber silence. The Minoans knew
about Ura-Guinn; they'd seen how Abram's stolen weapon
had affected her and brought back her ghosts. Was it beneath their dignity to manipulate her with her guilt? *Apparently not.*

She took a deep breath. "We have to research the contractual and legal ramifications, because we're talking
about opening a new solar system." David Ray nodded
approvingly and she continued. "Acceptance of this work
is contingent upon having a medical doctor, *of my choice*,
examine your drugs and your proposed implant. We just
moved Dr. Lee Pilgrimage and her lab to Beta Priamos
Station, so I'll ask her for consultation."

"Of course." Contractor Director bowed its horns. "It
will be appropriate to continue under CAW exploration
law. Aether Exploration is taking the risks and will be identified as Major Prospector to your S-triple-ECB, so you will
be primary holder for claims in the new solar system."

"That's if this 'Biological Temple' system isn't inhab-
ited," Matt muttered.

"We are absolutely sure the Builders devolved, Owner
of Aether Exploration. There are no sentient species in
that solar system."

"You're being generous with money *and* technology." Matt's tone was suspicious. "What are you getting out of this?"

That was a very good question, and they looked to Contractor Director for the answer. "We will discuss reciprocity for our enhancements later, when we draw up the contract."

They got nothing more than that slippery assurance, because the Minoan ended the meeting.

CHAPTER 15

State Prince Isrid Parmet, the man who reviled CAW after the war and reportedly sent "reprisal" hit squads against our officials, gave his unclassified testimony this morning. I mention his history, because he hardly seems the same man. Even knowing what skillful actors the Terrans can be, I couldn't help tearing up when he described how the isolationists tortured his son.

—Dr. Net-head Stavros, 2106.058.14.30 UT,
indexed by *Heraclitus 9* under Conflict Imperative

Lieutenant Oleander flagged down Captain Floros near the galley hatch, before the first-shift review board.

"Hey, Captain," she beckoned, offering an open steaming drink pack of Kaffi. "Buy you a coffee?"

Floros checked the time and stepped into the galley. She took the drink, sniffed, and had a long savoring sip.

"Hellas Kaffi." The burly captain sighed. "You must have gotten this on the *Pilgrimage*."

"I figured you'd like something better than generic." Oleander glanced meaningfully at the nearest node, and gestured toward two counter seats. Floros joined her and laid her slate on the counter.

"These boards have been brutal." Floros's mouth twitched, but couldn't manage a smile. "I'm barely getting enough sleep these days."

"Almost by *design*, isn't it?" Oleander said, jokingly, as

she pressed her wrist implant interface and casually put her hand on the counter, next to Floros's slate. "I've been called in front of the board at ten thirty. They're going to ask about the missiles we shot off during the mission."

"Don't worry. You followed orders and checklists—so just tell the truth. Once I finish up this morning, I'll finally get some shore time." Floros never looked down at her slate, where Oleander was using near-field transfer of a message from her implant. It was the low-tech equivalent of passing a note in class and Oleander hoped she didn't look like a guilty schoolgirl.

"Thanks for the coffee, Young Flower." Floros held the coffee up. "Got to go."

"You're welcome—ah—Prickly Cactus," Oleander called to Floros's broad back as she hurried away.

She grinned as she walked to the kiosk and got herself a fruit juice. Sergeant Joyce said they had to get Captain Floros on the job, because if Myron made extra copies of data from the *Bright Crescent*, Floros might be able to track it. The message she'd loaded on Floros's slate explained their suspicions and asked for her support.

There was something else Sergeant Joyce needed. Oleander headed for the day officer, from *where* all administrative and mission orders emanated.

"Hello, Lieutenant." Chief Master Sergeant Serafin stepped out of the hatch that read DAY OFFICER, as Oleander arrived.

"On control deck today, Chief?" Oleander said. Serafin ran the tactical assessment station.

"Haven't you heard? We've been taken off op-status." Serafin ran her fingers through her short salt-and-pepper hair. "I've got some unhappy people downstairs in Tactical and Weapons."

Oleander nodded in sympathy. Everyone took a pay cut when taken off operational status, but the noncoms and soldier-grade were the hardest hit. And being here in the boondocks, where nothing was cheap, was even more punishing.

"Congratulations on the career move, although I'm sorry to see a good weapons officer go to the black and blue." Serafin smiled.

"Can I quote you when I see Colonel Edones?" Oleander laughed. "I'll be going into the conference room."

"You certainly can—he knows my feelings. If you really do speak to him, tell him his ops crew stands by him." Chief Serafin's face sobered as she bid Oleander good-bye.

Before entering, Oleander squared her shoulders and took a deep breath to calm her stomach. She wasn't going to be lying as much as stretching the truth, but it was scary to try this with AFCAW officialdom.

The person who could cut admin orders, the sergeant on Day Officer duty, listened to her story with a skeptical squint around his eyes. "If Master Sergeant Joyce wanted a change in status, why didn't his doctor call?"

"We're on lockdown," she reminded him. "No calls are coming in."

"Right, forgot that. Hell, it's been four days now. Plenty of time to finish their audit," the sergeant muttered. He pointed to a leaning stack of slates in front of him. "I'm backing up, sitting on orders to transmit to HQ Personnel."

"Sergeant Joyce wants to be put on restricted admin status. He feels he can do his administrative work if he has an issue slate with secret-level access and crypto." This was the crux of the request and she tried not to hold her breath as she waited.

"Hmm. I'd have to end his sick leave. Is he up and about?"

"He can get around and work for a couple hours a day. That's why he wants restricted status—he's not a hundred percent yet." This was an understatement, not a lie, she told herself.

"Really." There was a bit of a drawl to the Sergeant's voice and his eyes narrowed. Oleander tried to look as innocent as possible as they locked gazes. "If you say so, Lieutenant. You'll go down as the releasing authority for the change of status." He reached for a slate and made out the orders, sending her a local copy for ship's supply and storing a copy for HQ. "You'll have to figure out how to get him the slate."

"Thank you, Sergeant."

She left for her appearance before the board. It might be third shift before she got the slate to Joyce. She'd lose rack time, but it'd be worth every minute of lost sleep if Joyce could figure out who was behind this audit.

Myron sat at one end of the conference room with another aide. Open view ports behind him showed two other representatives of the board. During first shift, the aides asked questions, arranged data, and dug up information, until fourteen thirty hours. At that point, there was a break while the ICT concluded and Senator Stephanos appeared. Another session continued until twenty hundred, where the *real* audit board members, the senators, looked at the notes prepared by their aides and asked their own questions. Oleander had joked about this audit intentionally running the crew ragged, but the senators themselves weren't holding up well under the brutal schedule either.

Colonel Edones, as mission commander of the *Bright Crescent*, and Lieutenant Colonel Aquino, as operational commander, sat to one side behind a small table. She thought they looked inspiring in full dress under the AFCAW crest, a stylized Labrys Raptor printed on the bulkhead. They looked the picture of military experience—*too bad these sessions are closed to the public.* Aquino's red-and-gold dress coat upstaged Edones's black one, edged with light blue, with blue and gold epaulets. On the other hand, the left side of Edones's chest dripped with shiny medals and colorful ribbons, surpassing Aquino's awards. Those decorations on Edones's full dress were a reminder of his wartime assignments. She looked around. Colonel Edones was probably the only person in the room who had been on active duty during the war with the Terran Expansion League.

It was break time and there was a busy hum as personnel changed. Some were leaving, having given their statements; others, like her, were just beginning the process. She pushed through the small throng to the table where the commanders sat.

"Chief Serafin sends her regards, sir," she said to Colonel Edones. "She says your crew stands behind you."

"Thank you, Lieutenant," Edones replied. Aquino nodded.

She went to her seat on one of the benches and watched the two commanders. Aquino was the younger, but he appeared ground down by this audit. Edones looked his usual cool and alert self; perhaps he wasn't as affected by politics as Aquino. She'd seen Edones look much worse, particularly when he was evaluating the casualties and destruction wrought by Abram.

"Attention please, let's begin." Myron sounded more self-important than the last time she'd spoken with him. "Calling Lieutenant Diana Oleander to the stand for a formal statement."

Pompous little prick. That was Joyce's name for Myron and they'd never even met. She tried to suppress the words and couldn't, so she had a smile on her lips as she swore to abide her oath as an AFCAW officer.

"Please state your position and responsibilities on the *Bright Crescent* during your entry to G-145."

"I was the senior weapons officer, responsible for planning weapons loads, as well as targeting, firing, and launching weapons."

"Lieutenant, when you planned the mission weapons loads for entering G-145, did you consider the costs of comparable loads?"

Senator Raulini's aide asked the questions from her offices on Hellas Prime. Her image on the bulkhead looked outward with a severe expression that suggested she carried many burdens.

"No—but first, I must point out that this was a joint mission with the TLS *Percival*, so we had to coordinate with the Terran crew to avoid duplication of weapons coverage. Second, we don't know the price tags of weapons. We plan weapons loads against the threat that Intel gives us." Oleander had a sinking feeling in her gut.

"You don't ever consider cost? For instance, you must know the Assassinator missile is several orders of magnitude more expensive than a load of swarm missiles. You know that, don't you, Lieutenant?"

"Yes, but I can't use that as the basis for my decisions. In this case, we knew there might be *one* ship with an armed TD weapon and we had to—"

"Do you think you *should* consider cost, in retrospect?" The woman coldly cut her off.

Opinion, apparently, even the retrospective kind, was more important than fact. Oleander's stomach started churning. She knew any questioning that required hindsight could only get worse.

Isrid was pleased with his testimony this morning in front of the ICT. He'd identified the two technicians who had tortured him under Abram's direction, although they were only lackeys. Being an expert in the discipline of torture, Isrid knew the responsibility lay with the architect who controlled the drugs, technique, and tone of the interrogation. He wished he could have meted out justice, personally, to Abram.

He knew the audience had responded emotionally to his story. The crèche-get were the most influenced; they loved and prized their children, even if they came out of birthing chambers. The Autonomists and Terrans, who initially had wary, closed faces, were still carried away by the account of torturing a child to extort his father. The exception had been SP Duval. Isrid saw hostility and doubt shouting from the other SP's body language. Thus, after ICT adjourned for the day, he wasn't surprised to hear he had a call from Duval. This would be their first face-to-face direct conversation and before he answered, he tapped the RECORD-AND-SAVE command.

Duval appeared in a view port on the wall, and bypassed any pleasantries. "You put on quite a show for the Tribunal, SP Parmet."

"I described what happened, SP. Did you expect something else than the truth?" He used a casual tone as he saved an entry on his slate with a tap of the stylus, taking his time. He could analyze Duval's reactions later.

"This is an unusual situation for me and my staff. Our Overlord doesn't like working with Autonomists." A greasy smile slid across Duval's face.

Isrid nodded politely. "It's unfortunate that your delinquents reared their ugly heads again. Weren't you asked to take care of this isolationist problem a long time ago?"

"We don't refer to them as the 'isolationist problem.'"

"My apologies." Isrid *sounded* unrepentant, while looking apologetic. Sending conflicting signals made the recipient uncomfortable. "You haven't explained the purpose of this call."

"We thought it polite to warn you of an intelligence leak." Duval's smile moved askew. "The Directorate is running *Kressida* in G-145—ah, I see you recognize the name. We think they're turning someone in your area of the solar system, someone on your staff, or Ensign Walker's."

"What's your source?"

"We've got a Directorate file that references the operation as being current, but no other details."

"Really? You're sure . . . ?" Isrid showed his doubt that Duval could put his hands on actual Directorate files, although he wasn't blindsided, not in the least. Dr. Istaga suspected such an initiative and was now evaluating loyalties. In fact, yesterday he'd given Isrid a list of personnel he thought were intelligence risks, having chinks in their loyalty or "issues rendering them susceptible to Autonomist manipulation." These were valuable people, ones the Overlord couldn't afford to lose, and ones who should be watched. *Maria's name was at the top of the list.*

Duval defended his statement. "*My* TSF intelligence staff is trustworthy. They claim it came from the *Bright Crescent.*"

Isrid knew about the audit on the AFCAW cruiser. Duval was hinting he'd found a leak, possibly due to that audit, but why did he emphasize the trustworthiness of his Terran Space Force? "Ensign Walker appears to be doing well with station security."

"The TSF has its uses, but I wouldn't be too dependent upon your ensign. Major Kedros is obviously running this Directorate op, but she's integral to the Priamos R&D efforts, is she not? So the TSF won't do anything about her, not openly."

"We're watching Kedros."

"She's probably behind the threats sent to you and your family." Not trained in *somaural* projection, Duval couldn't hide the faint downward waver of his gaze. *He was lying.* Of greater significance, he shouldn't know about the threats.

"Why would Kedros threaten me?" Isrid trolled for more information. Luckily, Duval couldn't envision a world where Isrid had confronted Kedros, or believed her innocent.

"Revenge, perhaps? For your offenses last year." Duval cocked his head. "Vengeance can only be satisfied in one way, regardless of what the Autonomists say. That's why Pax Minoica can't last. And when it blows apart, only the nimble will survive."

"I appreciate the heads-up." Isrid smiled politely. A warning, yes, but Duval wasn't just passing it on; he was adding a threat. Isrid filed this away in his memory, as well as the hint that Duval knew how and why Kedros had signed over the G-145 leases. Most intriguing, because this was a fact in pursuit of both relevance and context, was that *Duval didn't want the League in G-145.* His body language made that obvious. But why, when the League was benefiting from this research?

After Isrid finished the call with the odious Duval, he checked with his personal security. Flynn had sent out his right-hand man, a husky no-neck sort named Zheng, who had been on Parmet's security for years.

"Yes, SP?" In the view port, Zheng looked up.

"You said you traced the threats down to a specific port on the *Pilgrimage*?"

"To a public kiosk, with no surveillance." Zheng agreed with the rest of his security staff; Pilgrimage had too many places on their habitat that needed security upgrades, and he'd be happy to talk to them about it.

"No way to figure out who sent the message?"

"No, sir." Zheng's face held self-inflicted misery of failure. "And we've only got the two messages."

"But they definitely came from the *Pilgrimage*?"

"Yes, sir."

"Well, here's another twist. SP Duval knows about the threatening messages. He might have gotten the info through TSF, or not—can't tell." After relating the relevant information to Zheng, he called Maria.

"I need you up here," he said after she answered. His fingers flickered and added, *Espionage*.

"Same old stuff?" Her fingers and wrist asked, *Autonomist?*

"Not necessarily. I'm worried about Six, which is your specialty." He remembered a night many years ago, when she'd asked to take the lead on coordinating surveillance on Overlord Six—the same person and staff as today—being the only Overlord still in power since the end of the war sixteen years ago. *After all, I have a personal interest in how they allocate childbirth licenses. If I can get approval, I'll transfer,* she'd said, rubbing her long leg over his. At the time, he'd held her tight and immersed himself in the smell of her hair and the feel of her skin—knowing he'd never let her leave. He gave her the assignment and as it happened, she had less chance of having offspring in District Six than in Three.

"I've been trying to stay in the scientific research biz." Her smile was slightly sad.

"This could shut down the 'biz' in G-145. It's that important."

"The *Pytheas* has docked. A mass posting came out, saying the Minoans are sponsoring its next mission to the Builders' solar system. They're taking applications for crew. I can qualify for the copilot and sensors position." She looked stubborn and signed in Martian patois, *Chance of a lifetime.*

She'd named her "price" for coming back to staff work. He watched carefully, knowing her skills with *somaural* projection. Maria had worked for him since the end of the war and he'd never heard her talk about such a goal. However, he'd rather have her up on the station near him, than down on Priamos with Sergeant Pike and his AFCAW commandos. She'd be closer to Major Kedros, who certainly *was* running the Kressida op, but he knew how much bad blood came between those two women. Besides, Maria would be near two former lovers, him and Sabina, and that'd make her less of a "loyalty risk."

"I suppose we could make that happen," he said slowly. "What about your medical records? Will they be a problem?"

Her laugh sounded brittle. "They'll never see them. I'll be up on-station in four or five hours, SP."

Ariane looked about Dr. Lee's lab, noting the prominent birthing chambers bolted to the bulkhead, trying to ignore the question the older woman had asked. Unfortunately, Dr. Lee wasn't so easily put off.

"You do realize you're being used, don't you?" Lee asked again. "The Minoans are trying to manipulate you."

Ariane sighed, staring at the shiny chambers. They had placards covered with legible names, date of fertilization, and gender. She read them in turn: Nigel, Peter, and Charlotte Anne, all of whom would soon be a month into their development. Finally, she said, "Does it really matter?"

Dr. Lee, frail, yet oozing forceful opinion, came to stand beside her. "Of course it matters," she said. She gestured toward the end chamber that held Charlotte Anne. "Abram said he needed *sons*, so I purposely misinterpreted his orders when I realized one fetus would be female. Unfortunately, I didn't know Abram's men considered him childless, or that they often murder first-born females. In the end, my assistant Allison paid *for my selfish decision* with her life."

"So I'm making a selfish decision. Now who's trying to manipulate me?" She turned to look at the doctor, thin and graceful, but with paper-thin skin and puffy white hair that showed her true age.

Lee only raised an eyebrow.

"Using hindsight, would you change your decision?" Ariane asked, pointing toward Charlotte Anne.

"Hindsight doesn't help." Dr. Lee smiled sadly. "An idealistic person might believe that dice are rolling randomly in their heads, so if they have a chance to make a decision again, they might go a different route. A practical individual, like me, would say I would never make a different decision, given my knowledge and emotions at the time."

"You sound pretty confident of that. What if you can manage to be less cautious, more perceptive, or whatever?"

"How much *more* or *less*, of anything, would be required to change your decisions? Can you honestly expect things to be different if your basic nature doesn't change?" The older woman's words were clipped.

Her words also caused disturbing thoughts. Ariane had already run her second life off the rails, but what could she have done differently? According to Lee, she'd take the same route, in every time and in every world. Of course, Lee was speaking rhetorically. She didn't know the woman standing next to her had *really* been given a second life, another identity, and a chance to start over.

Breaking the silence, Lee said quietly, "I'm guessing hindsight won't give you any clarity."

Ariane took a deep breath. "I know the Minoans are manipulating me, leveraging my guilt. They're giving me a chance at reparation and redemption."

"What—" Dr. Lee seemed taken aback. Whatever she expected, it wasn't this. "What could you have possibly done?"

"You don't know my past, Doctor." Ariane's voice was level and unyielding. "You've signed nondisclosure agreements, you know there's secrets here. Many of them have to do with me, and why the Minoans chose me. You're going to notice my biochemistry and cellular metabolism are enhanced, although I can't tell you why."

Lee's jaw went slack. Then she closed her mouth with a snap and her dark eyes glinted. "That'll teach *me* to stick my nose into somebody else's psyche." She straightened her lab coat with a snort and turned toward her lab equipment, beckoning Ariane to follow. "I totally missed the mark with you. Let's get to work. I'll need fluid and tissue samples from you."

Ariane sat on a stool beside her and couldn't contain her curiosity. "How did you miss the mark?"

"I'm a bit embarrassed." Lee's eyes slid sideways to look at her. "I thought you were doing this for Matt. I'll need a good amount of blood, so stick out your arm."

"Really? But, why—when Matt's so devoted to Diana?" She thoughtfully watched the doctor check her implant, before using it to sample blood.

"Yes. Well." Lee looked away and changed the subject. "I'll also take tissue samples, about biopsy size. These tests are similar to evaluating which of these tissue types, if artificially propagated, your body would accept in a graft or transplant."

"The military already did those tests; I can accept most of my vat-grown tissues."

"But they weren't checking to see if you could accept one of *these*." Dr. Lee leaned across the lab bench to tap a command on what looked like an oven or incubator, and a display of the interior incubation chamber appeared on the side.

Ariane gulped. "That's what they call *implants*?"

The display showed a flat nutrient dish, with a length scale beside it. Inside the dish lay what first looked like two thin columns of muscle tissue approximately thirty centimeters long, which made them about as long as her forearm. The tissue columns narrowed to filaments at the ends, so they looked like complete muscles from—well, from a human, except the fluorescent yellow streaks and olive green blotches indicated the contrary. The yellow streaks bunched and twisted at two distinct bulges midway on each length of tissue. But the worst, most gruesome aspect that made her brain gibber was that they *moved*, undulating slowly in the thick nutrient broth, leaving rippled impressions that slowly faded as the liquid leveled.

"Reevaluating your motives?" Lee asked dryly.

"Ah." For a moment, her mouth wouldn't form words. "It'll take more than a *few* tests to convince me to put one of those in my body."

Lee chuckled as she sealed and removed the bag of

blood from Ariane's arm. "I'm impressed. You took that pretty well. David Ray, my sweet hero, nearly fainted when he saw them. Matt became positively ill."

"Are they *alive*? Why two?" She couldn't take her eyes off the things in the display.

Lee shook her head. "Those are only our test models. I'm going to use grafts to see how compatible your tissues are with one; leaving the other as a control. The Minoans will examine them after I'm through. As for whether they're alive? I don't know. I've asked that masked, horned mystery to give me more documentation."

"Contractor Director, you mean?"

"That's the one. I was sent a hefty file that looked like an operating manual, but they might be instructions for assembling a glider, for all I could understand." Lee strode across the room to put the blood in a storage unit. "I told the emissary I needed something better. It said, *You need simplification, Physician of Pilots?* and I nearly decked it, regardless of its big bad bodyguards."

The thought of Dr. Lee punching out Contractor Director distracted her, and she was still chuckling as Lee came back with a row of big biopsy needles on a tray.

"You'll have to lie down on the cot over there. Let me get the topical anesthetic." Dr. Lee pointed to the curtained area in the corner. "I have to get samples big enough to graft onto the sample—er, equipment—and view the results."

"I understand. And please, please make sure we understand how it works." Ariane tried not to shudder as she took a last look at the wiggling implant.

"Don't worry. We're in uncharted territory and nobody's putting this thing into your body until we do every test we can think of—and some we've never thought of before."

After Dr. Lee had used what seemed like every needle and knife in her lab, she declared she had enough samples. Granted, she had a skillful touch, but Ariane still felt like a pincushion when she was finished. As she pulled her coveralls on, the doctor made a comment that sounded shrewdly casual. "Before you volunteer, remember that we're all concerned for you. Especially Matt. He's twisted up with worry."

"I think he's more excited than worried. After all, exploration is his calling." Ariane glanced over her shoulder. She saw Lee's ramrod-straight back, as the doctor fussed with samples at her bench.

"Well, he'd do *anything* to ensure your safety or your happiness. Remember, he's known you far longer than Diana." The doctor turned to look at her.

Ariane looked away. *Old busybody—she's trying to make mischief, mess up my working relationship with Matt.* He was her employer, making him the civilian equivalent of her commander. Besides, he was crew. She knew, from experience, how fast romance or sex could break up a crew. In fact, she was reminded of this every time she saw the Leukos Industries logo.

She left Lee's lab quickly. It seemed inevitable that her feet would lead her by the Stellar Shield. She'd kept away from bars and hadn't had even one drink since Matt had retrieved her on the *Pilgrimage*. She walked in.

CHAPTER 16

Forget Major Kedros! My vote for hero of the millisec-
ond (the average net-think attention span) is Master
Sergeant Alexander Joyce. The man went head-to-head
with Abram and took a full flechette blast in his side.
He's been through transplants, tissue grafts, and surgeries as they've rebuilt half his abdomen. Today, he testified from his clinic bed. . . .

—*Dr. Net-head Stavros*, 2106.059.14.30 UT,
indexed by *Heraclitus 5* under Conflict Imperative

Ariane was intent upon controlling her drinking that
evening, and circumstances helped her. Hal, her usual
drinking buddy, wasn't in the Stellar Shield. When she
looked around, a group of maintenance workers hailed her,
but she declined with a smile.

The cheerful noise in the bar bothered her, seeming
overbearing and artificial. Her mind kept repeating Lee's
words, and she wanted that *stopped*. She drank a beer at
the counter, but it didn't make her feel any better and it
didn't stop her thoughts. Where did Lee get the idea she
was attracted to Matt? Well, "attracted" was the wrong
word—"smitten," perhaps? "Infatuated?" *Impossible*.
He now had Diana: young, beautiful, smart, and *unbur-
dened by demons*. There was no way she'd mess that up
for Matt—no matter what. She decided to order a pint of
liquor to take with her.

The bartender looked skeptical. "Ms. Kedros, you know

we don't carry good stuff in pints. We've got the tasteless and odorless rotgut—leastways, that's what I call it. Then we've got two others, called 'rum' and 'whiskey,' but you got to be wasted to believe those names."

She ordered a pint of rotgut, because it had the highest proof. The bartender looked away with a vague expression as she slid the pint into the pocket of her coveralls. It came in an unbreakable zero-gee container so it could be sipped almost anywhere. She wasn't the first, and certainly wouldn't be the last person to buy this sort of comfort on a rough, lonely, frontier outpost like Beta Priamos Station.

When she came through the airlock on *Aether's Touch*, she asked Muse 3 whether Matt was on board. Now that he'd initiated the licensing process, Matt had taken to leaving Muse 3 enabled. However, Muse 3 had strict instructions on whom it could initiate speech with, or answer.

"No, Ari. Matt said he will be on the surface of Priamos moon until next first shift."

"The entire night? Sorry, let me rephrase that. Does he intend to spend his sleep cycle down there?" Being planet-born, what Matt called a "grav-hugger," Ariane often reverted to planetary rotation terms. Even her phrase of "down there" could be misleading, but at least Beta Priamos Station orbited Priamos.

"Yes. Matt is staying in Visitors Quarters and will return to the ship around zero eight thirty."

She immediately pulled out the pint, popped the top with her thumb, and took a deep swig. It burned like hell going down, but she loved the warming calm she felt spreading from her stomach. As she walked past the control deck and checked status panels, she took a few more sips. By the time she climbed down to the galley and her quarters, the sound of unraveling was gone from her head.

There was a message from Joyce in her queue. She lay down on her bed and played it, hoping there'd be good news about the audit of the *Bright Crescent*. Joyce only indicated it was still in progress; he spent more time on the investigations into Tahir's murder and the explosives.

Joyce was brutal about *Pilgrimage* security. *They can't*

even qualify as a clusterfuck, Major, with so many blind groping the blind, was his deadpan and dead-on assessment. She smiled as she sipped her pint. It was good to see his face and hear his voice, even if it was only a recording. His irritation proved he was getting better.

Joyce had a right to be vexed. They'd given up on finding Tahir's cause of death and Joyce managed to get Tahir's body sent to Hellas Prime, where he hoped he could convince Pilgrimage HQ to call in forensics experts. Inquiry into the explosive attacks had hit an even thicker wall.

She chuckled when Joyce said, "I'm pushing to have Benjamin order canine teams—I get such a kick seeing these crèche-get shudder when they think of hairy, drooling beasts running around their habitat. However, they could be the best solution, low-tech or not, to my problem."

At the end of his message, Joyce asked for updates. She knew he was referring, obliquely, to the Maria mission. *No need to call him back, because I haven't done squat.* With a pang of guilt, she took a long sip.

Ariane woke to the sound of her alarm. Her head was clear, surprisingly so, when she looked at the pint and realized how much she'd drunk. Last night had only been about the alcohol; she couldn't even justify her drinking as socializing. This was another line her addiction counselor, Major Tafani, had warned her not to cross. She stuffed the pint of rotgut into her locker in the hygiene closet, behind one of her soap bottles. Leaving it beside her bed, or even in her quarters, was too close and personal. It nagged at her, but she couldn't throw it away, not when it still had a third remaining.

She checked Matt's schedule. At the moment, he was coming up on the elevator, climbing the stalk in the long trek between moon and station. She considered calling him, but hesitated. Looking at his and her schedules, side by side, she decided that she wouldn't call him under normal circumstances. Which made her pause; why was she so worried about normalcy? Her schedule had visits to Dr. Lee's lab, as well as Novak and Lowry's lab. She decided she didn't want to face Dr. Lee so soon, and moved that session to after lunch.

After devouring a big breakfast, she decided she couldn't put off her mission much longer. She had to speak with Maria, but when? There wasn't time for a trip down to Priamos, not for several days. On impulse, she called Maria, audio only.

"Yes, Ms. Kedros?" Maria's voice was chillingly polite.

"I was given a package to hand carry to you, from the *Pilgrimage*." She kept her voice relaxed.

"I see. You're the last person I'd expect a favor from."

"Agreed." Ariane responded in an equally cool tone. "But a mutual acquaintance gave me an antique document you ordered, and told me to be careful with it."

Maria didn't miss a beat. "It might be something I ordered more than a month ago."

"It's a play titled 'A Famous History of Troylus and Kressida,' printed on paper, so I'd prefer to deliver it in person. Unfortunately, I don't know when I can make the trip down to the surface."

"I'm working up on-station for a while," Maria said. "I can meet you on Ring Three, near Maintenance Equipment and Supplies."

"How soon?"

"Immediately." Maria hung up.

Well. Ariane grabbed the sealed box that Edones had given her. It contained, surrounded by inert gas, a certified copy of the play she mentioned—not an original, of course, but a one-hundred-and-fifty-year-old limited print.

She was off the ship in what she considered record time, but she didn't beat Maria to the maintenance equipment office. As she approached, she saw the tall leggy blonde leaning against the side of the corridor, staying out of the way of maintenance carts and personnel departing for jobs. Maria had cleverly picked a high-traffic area with no Com-Net nodes installed.

"You have it?" Maria pushed away from the bulkhead and smoothed her cap of chin-length hair. Her eyes were focused on the package. "What about the price?"

"I was given latitude to negotiate a few points. You can take possession of the document now, if you wish, and deal with details later." Ariane handed her the package carefully. The package was the important part of their interchange, because an observer would concentrate upon it. And it was totally meaningless.

"Details later, hmm? I can read your body language, Ms. Kedros, and it bodes a high price for me."

"We'll talk." She shrugged uncomfortably under Maria's knowing glance. The Directorate had made itself perfectly clear, through written orders and Edones's verbal instructions. AFCAW wasn't going to pay for Maria's defection unless they got decent intelligence from several years in place.

Maria would also have to take risks. It was customary for the Directorate to promise "protection" to an informer, but this was unrealistic for deep cover operatives. If Maria backed out of this, Ariane would understand, but she'd also have to pressure Maria to stay the course. She took a deep breath. "We can meet at the end of this shift. I assume we're both hip-deep in this expedition."

"I'm applying for the copilot and sensors seat." Maria sniffed. "Sent in my records and recommendations this morning."

"I suppose I—" Ariane had to lean in to the bulkhead to avoid an elbow from a lab technician. More than station maintenance streamed by; the R&D laboratories had to requisition equipment through this office, also. This tech was Terran, with a loose lab coat over his tight jumpsuit. She caught a glance from angry blue eyes under a mop of straight caramel-colored hair. Someone was having a bad day. She finished with, "I should wish you good luck."

Maria watched the back of the tech with a strange expression, shook her head, and murmured, "I hope luck has nothing to do with it, Ms. Kedros." She held the package close to her body as she strode away.

Ariane watched her weave through the crowd in front of the maintenance office toward the other end of the hall. After passing a knot of people having an impromptu but heated discussion, a shorter figure with burgundy hair darted from behind the group to intercept Maria.

Great. Sabina might have been shadowing Maria. Ariane watched the two greet each other, neither showing surprise. Maria bent her head to listen to the psychotic bitch but they both turned away, so Ariane couldn't see their expressions.

She sighed. This mission might be going sour, but that was more Maria's problem than hers. She had physicists to consult, with hopes of kick-starting an ancient N-space buoy.

After Maria entered, Sabina stood in the doorway until Isrid sent her off with a flicker of his hand.

"Is *she* going to be a problem?" Isrid raised an eyebrow. Maria and Sabina had openly been lovers; Sabina herself had shown him video, for some purpose she wouldn't divulge. Sabina didn't know how to interact with people, other than to try manipulation. When Maria had distanced herself from everyone on the station, his wife had probably been hurt, but she'd responded by stepping up her machinations against everyone around her.

"Not at all." Maria responded blandly. She dropped a light carton, made for the protection of old paper documents, onto the table.

Isrid shrugged. Maria had been forthcoming about her bisexuality, but she'd never publicized her relationships, nor acknowledged Sabina's jealousies. He didn't understand her reticence, and probably never would.

"Let's get to work." Isrid rapidly filled her in on the many disparate facts. First, Andre Covanni was on-station, carrying out orders from Overlord Three. Second, threats were made against Parmet's family that mentioned retribution for letting Major Kedros live, yet were referenced by Duval, who then blamed the threats on Kedros. Third, Duval's information gathering had expanded to include the AFCAW Directorate of Intelligence, and he now had the balls to throw his weight around with Overlord Three's staff, insinuating that Pax Minoica would be falling and taking all supporters with it.

Maria zeroed in on Andre. She knew the code name, but she couldn't know Andre's identity as Dr. Istaga. "What's Andre doing here?"

"Cleaning up embarrassing loose ends, like letting somebody steal a TD weapon. He's also inventorying Overlord Three's assets, assessing loyalties, et cetera."

"Oh." Her eyes flickered. She'd been his best intelligence analyst, so she probably just accurately surmised that Andre had executed Dr. Rouxe. "Did Andre have anything to do with the explosive grenades planted on the *Pilgrimage*?"

"He denied any involvement. Seemed rather offended by the insinuation, in fact."

"And Duval knows what was in the threats you received," she said. "But only your personal security knew about them, and they say you allowed a *destroyer of Ura-Guinn* to go free."

He sighed. "So I always come back to the basic question: How did our kidnapping of Major Kedros become common knowledge on Overlord Six's staff? That doesn't make sense. Neither does Duval's absurd attempt to blame Kedros for the threats."

"Who, on the Terran side, knows who Kedros is, and what she did?"

"You, me, my wives—although they insist it's gone no further. Andre knows, but he's only briefed Overlord Three and his closest advisors. Some of my security know, generally, that I came in contact with someone responsible for Ura-Guinn, but they can't know it's Kedros, specifically. That still keeps it within Three's sphere—"

"You haven't mentioned Nathan," she said.

Nathanial Wolf Kim had been one of his close advisors, responsible for torturing Major Kedros, until Isrid stopped him. Nathan couldn't handle the transition from military intelligence to industrial and economic espionage, or that's how Isrid phrased it. In other words, Nathan couldn't let go of the war. The irony was that the Overlord was pushing Isrid to be more flexible about his own attitudes, so Nathan became an anchor he couldn't afford.

"Nathan resigned, of his own free will." Isrid had tried not to take it personally. "I ensured he got a job elsewhere with Overlord Three, a high-profile, career-building position that would help rebuild Terra."

Maria snorted. "You give him too much credit, SP. Nathan never wanted to build, or rebuild, as much as he wanted to destroy."

"He didn't take the job?"

"I don't know." Maria paused. "But we should find out. This morning, I suddenly thought I saw Nathan's posture and walk, but it wasn't."

Isrid got up to stretch his legs. "You'll get the same access to records as Ensign Walker's people have, so if Nathan's here, you can find him."

"Who's on the trusted list?"

"You and I. Right now, we can trust only each other."

Maria flinched, minutely, at his words. Someone untrained in *somaural* reading wouldn't have seen it, but he did. "I'll get started immediately," she said quietly.

"Sure, I'm getting around." As he spoke into his mike implant, Joyce eyed the torture implements near his bed, all designed to help him "get around." There was the standard old-man walker that, even though it punctured his pride, turned out to be the most useful. The anti-grav harness was hard to strap on and caused nausea. There were various types of canes, all of which required more coordination than he could summon. Luckily, Matt Journey was a cheap bastard who didn't want to pay for video, so he couldn't see Joyce's state.

"That's good," Matt said. "I'll tell Ari that you're getting some exercise."

There was a pause. Joyce rolled his eyes. *Wait for it . . .*

"Is Diana there? Will she be visiting in the next hour or two?" Matt asked.

"No, Mr. Journey. Lieutenant Oleander has started her testimony before the board. From what I've seen, they'll suck away everything but minimal rack time."

"Is she in trouble? Why are they allowed to do this?" Matt sounded plaintive.

"I don't know that any one person is targeted, but they do seem to be trying to find inadequacies in the *Bright Crescent*'s performance. And *they* can do it, because *they* are senators and apparently we taxpayers have hired them to do this." Joyce was getting tense, because this was pinging the last working nerve he had and making it raw.

"If you see her, can you tell her to call me? And have you heard anything about that bot that tried to take out my ship? *Pilgrimage* security isn't taking my calls." He sounded so miserable that Joyce felt a spark of compassion, which didn't happen very often.

"Sorry. Nothing on that bot problem either." He wouldn't talk down *Pilgrimage* crew members to another crèche-get, so he left it at that.

After Matt hung up, Joyce stood up and rearranged his bed, pillows, and blankets. He stretched and tried to settle in a more comfortable sitting position on the bed. Just that little bit of exertion made him tired. Not only that, he was depressed. He wasn't recovering as fast as he wanted.

With lukewarm enthusiasm, he picked up the civilian slate. He'd hoped to get a military slate with crypto today, but Lieutenant Oleander hadn't showed up, probably for the very reasons he'd explained to Matt Journey.

Surprisingly, with that slate he found a few answers in publicly available records, although he was no Captain Floros when it came to data digging. He concentrated on discovering who was really behind the senatorial investigation, and why. Two powerful senators, Stephanos and Raulini, who sat at the helms of opposing parties, were driving this board of investigation. Why? Even more puzzling, why *now*? It wasn't the best time for Stephanos because he had to sit, concurrently, on the Interstellar Tribunal. Raulini was distracted in a likewise manner, spearheading some legislation that would soon be discussed on the Senate floor on Hellas Prime. In fact, these senators were so busy that their aides had to stand in for them during most of the board's proceedings.

That was the clue that finally helped Joyce; that, and his natural suspicion of anyone who wore suits like Myron's.

When he couldn't find anything by sifting through the public correspondence between senators, he dropped into the aide and staff level. *Pay dirt!* He gave a little whoop as he marked his sources with his stylus.

"Good to see someone's enjoying the ComNet experience." Captain Floros stood in the doorway and held up a military-issue slate. "But I think this should help." She tossed it to him.

"Come in, Captain, and shut the door, will you?" Joyce happily turned on the slate and started the sweep tool. He held it out to Floros, meaningfully.

She nodded. After closing the door, she swept for the listening pips that Terrans littered about, and found none. "I'm sorry to say that you're important enough to blow up, Sergeant, but not important enough to monitor."

"I'm not offended a bit. Thank you, Captain, for bringing the slate. How is the Lieutenant doing?"

"Well, our Young Flower is sweating in front of the board. I've already been grilled, on anything and everything, it seems," Floros said, sitting down beside his bed. "Mornings are the worst. That's when we get in the junior varsity, the snobby aides who think we can't do anything effectively, efficiently, or legally. They're excessively rude, as well. The senators, at least, are respectful of rank and military experience."

Joyce chuckled. "That fits my hypothesis perfectly." He held the two slates and transferred his data to the military slate. Then he tossed the civilian slate to Floros. "Take a look, Captain. I've found these suspicious memos between aides which provide information that appears, in coordinated fashion, within point papers for their senators—all building a case that each senator's opposition is using the recent military mission in G-145 against them."

Floros looked skeptical, but started scrolling through the data on the slate. He gave her time to absorb it. Finally, she nodded with grudging admiration. "Sergeant, this is good. You should be working for me."

"Aw shucks, ma'am." He grinned.

"Don't let it go to your head. Besides, there's nothing

concrete here. For decades, there's been professional, but nonelected, staff that's acted as a behind-the-political-class class. They know how to cover their tracks with innuendo and senate gossip."

"A behind-the-class class? If you say so. Whoever they are, they're capable of sending these senators stampeding into a panicked audit."

"Maybe," murmured Floros. She transferred the information to her slate and proceeded to wipe the civilian slate of any evidence of Joyce's searches. "So Myron and others, on several senator's staffs, manufactured a need to dissect our mission. How does this fit with Myron passing something to the Terrans?"

"I have no idea," Joyce admitted. "Have you been able to trace what the dear nephew has done on the *Bright Crescent*?"

"Myron is Stephanos's *great*-nephew," Floros said primly. "And while he's pulled every possible log and setting from the *Bright Crescent*'s systems, I can't prove that he's done anything hinky with them. There's classified data in those logs which could compromise the ship, but if he's provided copies to somebody, we won't find evidence on the ship."

"Too bad we can't set up a sting to—" Joyce stopped at the strange sounds in the hallway. Floros cocked her head as they heard clicks and loud snuffles, combined with muffled commands in a male voice. Shrieks in both male and female voices followed.

Floros stood up, opened the door, and jumped out of the way of two huge furry animals. They headed toward Joyce's bed, panting and making clicking and scrabbling sounds with their four feet. Joyce flung himself backward and hit his head against the bulkhead behind his bed.

"Scarier than you thought?" Benjamin had followed the beasts in the door. He cocked his head and said mockingly, "*Dogs are what you need, Benjamin. They're supposed to be great at finding explosives, even after the explosives have been moved.* Do you remember saying that, Sergeant Joyce?"

Benjamin had been unexpectedly creative in getting payback for a flippant remark—*Okay, I was being a smart-ass*. The dogs were loose and moved around the room, panting. Long moist tongues lolled out over sharp white teeth that seemed to grow longer as their jaws came close.

Joyce moved away as they put their huge heads on the bed, sniffing. "I didn't think they grew so big."

"These have been bred large." Benjamin waved and the dogs' handler came in. Once he collected their leashes, the dogs calmed down and somewhat resembled the sole canine that Joyce's old aunt had imported to Hellas Prime. That one had been frightfully expensive, fluffy, barkless, and couldn't reach above his aunt's knees in the video without jumping. These dogs were more sturdy, bigger, and, to be truthful, more obedient than his aunt's.

Joyce's medic hadn't calmed. "They're filthy, they smell, they drool—*eeeeew*—they can't be in here!"

"They can be cleaned. They've been cooped up in their cages for the last ten hours," the handler said. The nurse immediately began arguing with him, so Floros herded them toward the door, canines included.

"I'm surprised at you, Benjamin," Joyce said.

"Why?"

"First, you took my advice and second, you're willing to get covered with dog hair."

Benjamin looked down, shuddered slightly, and surprised Joyce with a lean grin. "Actually, I kind of like them, although we *have* to do something about the smell. After that, I'm taking them through the visitors' quarters." He glanced at the handler, standing in the doorway and defending his wards against the medic. "I've heard some great things about Sammy."

"Sammy?" Joyce noticed Benjamin seemed a bit giddy. Had the *Pilgrimage* security officer discovered he had a deep love for hairy four-legged animals, or was he just allergic to their dander?

"Sammy's the explosives dog. The other one, Xena, can follow people's scents and special identifiers."

"Xena and Sammy. Sure. Thanks." When Benjamin

showed no sign of moving, Joyce added gently, "I could get better rest if you and the dogs left."

"Wait. I've got an idea." Captain Floros smiled.

Dr. Lee Pilgrimage walked through artificially dimmed and quiet hallways. It was the middle of third shift on Beta Priamos Station and as always, humans tried to maintain a universal diurnal schedule. Lee, however, hadn't slept very well and she'd quietly left David Ray in bed, still snoring faintly.

Late yesterday, the Minoans had delivered a *simplified* copy of the "manual" for their implant. Ariane Kedros had come by and helped her peruse it. They finally found out how to install an implant; it could attach to a chemically tagged long muscle or ligament in Ariane's body. From there, it interacted by introducing biochemical signals into the muscle and blood—so its location with respect to arteries and veins was important.

Lee had also started tests with Ariane's tissues and blood, trying to figure out what the implant was doing— biochemically, at least. This morning, she'd have some results that would indicate whether the implant could be easily removed. The information about the removal procedure might be the tipping point for Ariane's decision to allow the implant. So far, Lee couldn't tell which way the young woman was leaning.

Her lab was darker than the corridor and, like this entire part of the station, it didn't have full node coverage. She couldn't display anything on the walls yet, but she could use the ubiquitous plasticlike covering on the ceiling for light and she had minimal audio support.

She frowned. On her lab bench, she saw one of her slates brightly displaying something. There was also a view port open on the counter-height surface of the bench. She hadn't left any displays running; even so, they would have dimmed by now. Reaching beside the door, she tapped a command.

Sudden, bright lights showed an empty lab. The corner with the hospital bed had closed curtains that hung, knee-height, above the floor. No one's feet showed. She couldn't see behind the lab bench, so she moved to the displays and leaned over to look behind the bench. There was no one there. Her slate displayed the results of a tissue test—

She was grabbed from behind, a hand pressing over her mouth with iron control, an arm wrapped around her waist and pinning her arms. It was a tall, strong person who must have stood on the bed. She should have checked the patient area first.

"Stop struggling, Doctor, or I'll break your neck." The voice, close to her right ear, was male.

She stopped. The grip on her mouth pressed her head back against his chest, while the arm around her waist loosened. She heard a *snick* as something was unfastened from a clip. Her eyes widened as he held up a tube-shaped instrument longer than his hand. It had multiple prongs that ended in delicate wires. She recognized it: a portable neural probe.

"You and I are going to have a discussion about your work. Don't worry—you're not going to remember a bit of this."

CHAPTER 17

Once the ICT began closed sessions, our correspondent in G-145 has covered only side-interest fluff. Our editor has asked her to remain for the final judgment of the ICT, as well as the results of the Senate's inquiry aboard the *Bright Crescent*. . . .

—*Editorial Board Minutes, Interstellarsystem Events Feed*,
2106.060.09.58 UT, indexed by *Heraclitus 21*
under Conflict Imperative

Ariane walked into the meeting in time to hear a dispute between questionable authorities on idiom history, regarding "waiting for the other shoe to drop."

"I should be able to use 'boot.' The style of footwear shouldn't matter," David Ray said.

Matt leaned forward in his chair. "It's from a time when people were squeezed on top of one another in multifloor residences. When someone above them was undressing and dropped a shoe—"

"Or boot," David Ray interrupted. "It was a time when people wore *boots*. It indicates anticipation of an event that everyone believes will happen."

This was a regularly scheduled status meeting with their management. Contractor Director and its guardian stood in front of a small audience seated in semicircle of chairs. Matt and David Ray sat in the center, debating casually and ignoring the motionless Minoans standing a few meters away. On Matt's far side sat Dr. Novak, who was still intimidated, frozen into stillness with only his gaze moving between the two aliens. Beside David Ray sat a man in a jumpsuit made in the Consortium, given its colorful combination of red and black. He watched, bemusedly, the discussion between David Ray and Matt, although he kept glancing at the Minoan emissary—suitably awed, but not in Novak's catatonic way. On his upper sleeve was a patch showing a shield and stars, with the word "Pytheas" underneath.

He could have been Brandon's older brother. She stared at him, but revised a few assumptions. He could have been Captain Brandon Lengyel's brother sixteen years ago, before the Ura-Guinn mission, before the disastrous rejuv attempt, and before AFCAW made him Bartholomew Leukos.

The subject of her interest turned in his seat, and offered a handshake. "Hello, I'm Dalton Lengyel, mission commander of the *Pytheas*."

It took a feat of mental strength not to answer, "Of course you are." She shook his hand, leaning downward. He kept smiling in a puzzled sort of way. "Oh—I'm Ariane Kedros," she said quickly. "I'll be the pilot if we get this expedition off the ground."

"Glad to meet you."

As she sat down next to Dalton, Matt grinned at her. He didn't connect Dalton with Leukos, not knowing how Leukos looked when he was healthy and young.

"Your ship's time and crew are on the payroll of Leukos Industries, so we have Mr. Leukos to thank for this, I guess," she said.

"I've never met the big guy." Dalton shrugged. "I don't ask where the money comes from; getting research fellowships or grants aren't my business."

She smiled politely. Dalton had to be related to Brandon, who was helping his old family, regardless of secret identities. AFCAW would certainly disapprove, but it didn't seem to harm Brandon's identity as Mr. Leukos.

Dr. Lowry appeared in the door, late and rushed. This was the signal to Contractor Director to start the meeting.

The guardian closed the door and positioned itself in front of it. Contractor Director immediately had everyone's attention.

The Minoans were using a three-pronged onslaught: equip an exploration ship, equip a human N-space pilot, and get the Builders' buoy working so that the first two could use it. The three efforts were somewhat related; for instance, the *Pytheas* would probably need a few changes to be able to use the Builders' buoy lock signal. The pilot, aka Explorer of Solar Systems, had to also be *upgraded* to use the buoy and ship, according to the Minoans. That work was ongoing, as was the research into the buoy.

"Additionally, you must ensure Pytheas-ship is capable of defending itself," added Contractor Director.

"And the other boot is dropped," David Ray muttered. He was right, because a miniature tempest ensued.

"I thought you told us the Builders no longer existed," Matt said.

"Defending against what? Are we talking about weapons?" Dalton asked. "The *Pytheas* isn't fitted with anything but rail guns. We don't have a crew position to run weapons."

Eventually, everyone quieted when they realized the Minoan would only answer questions in its own way, and in its own time. Beside Ariane, Dr. Lowry fidgeted as the silence wore on.

"We explained the xenophobic nature of the Builders. They protected their home world by damaging N-space, so they have surely installed real-space protection." Contractor Director made a gesture as if to say, *Isn't this obvious?*

"Please, Contractor Director, we need more explanation. The timeline you gave our researchers states the Builders became extinct approximately seventy-five hundred years ago," David Ray said. Ariane raised her eyebrows, impressed that David Ray was following the xenology studies as well.

The Minoan emissary stayed motionless, until David Ray remembered that he had to ask a question. "You can see why we're confused, can't you? We wouldn't expect space-based defenses to be working after thousands of years, so we question equipping the *Pytheas* with defense systems. Why should we go to the effort and expense?"

Contractor Director cocked its head. "The Builders shut down their facilities on Priamos, but have you not seen them to be in almost perfect operating condition?"

There was silence. She saw her own thoughts on Matt's face, and in the incline of the Minoan's head. Silly humans! *Because our own artifacts and creations rarely last thousands of years, we can't comprehend planning or engineering on that time scale.*

"I don't know about the rest of you, but I feel humbled," David Ray said in a low voice.

"We need to know more about the threat," Ariane said. "Will they have atmospheric, orbital, or space-based platforms? Will they be mobile? What about missiles? Active or passive targeting? Can you answer any of those questions for us, Contractor Director?"

"No. We have not observed the Builders recently."

David Ray choked a little at the word "recently."

"Maybe our xenologists have amassed enough background on Builder technology to make educated guesses. I'll start working with them," Dalton said. "And I'll consult the military advisors we have at our disposal, to see how we can give the *Pytheas* more defensive capabilities."

"We'll continue working on communicating with the buoy," Matt said.

The meeting started to break up until Contractor Director said, "I must speak with employees of Aether Exploration separately."

At which time, Dr. Lowry crossed her arms and sat back down. "We need open R&D for the exchange of ideas and technology—having secrets only privy to Aether Exploration is unhealthy."

"We will discuss a private contract between Hellas Nautikos and Aether Exploration." Contractor Director's words didn't budge Dr. Lowry.

Dr. Novak and Dalton Lengyel left, with barely a shrug of dissent. Dr. Lowry, jaw clenched, remained and tried to engage Contractor Director in a silent battle of wills. This was extremely difficult because Minoans had no face to focus upon, only the dark contours under the horns. Ariane was puzzled by the depth of Lowry's stubbornness, but to her surprise, the Minoan emissary broke first by making a fluid gesture with its index finger. The guardian stepped toward Dr. Lowry, who paled and stood up.

"Okay, I'll leave," she muttered, making a wide berth around the guardian as she left.

The guardian closed the door and on the wall behind Contractor Director the word "Proprietary" displayed. Ariane pulled out her slate again to scan for monitoring devices.

"You did that two days ago, Ari," Matt said. He sighed when she held up the recording pip she found under a chair.

"You have to remain vigilant in the secrecy business." She dropped it on the floor and crushed it.

"Is there any way to figure out who planted that?" David Ray asked. "Or why they're so persistent?"

"Doubtful. It might not have come from the same people, this time." She shook her head as she sat down. The face of Terran intelligence was fracturing. The TEBI that Parmet built, that trained Maria, that gave Andre his missions more than fifteen years ago, might no longer exist—which might be the message behind the explosives on the *Pilgrimage*, built with old TEBI-issue grenades.

Contractor Director began. "As Explorer of Solar Systems has stated, we cannot survive a nous-transit to the Builders' world. Hence, our hiring of *Aether Exploration* and our support of your expedition."

Support? How about *insane acceleration*? Without the Minoans' translator and other insights into the Builders, they wouldn't have considered an expedition for decades. Ariane saw David Ray and Matt exchange a glance. Matt looked as if he said, *Don't go there*, and David Ray wasn't taking the advice.

"Can you explain why *you* can't survive, but *we* can?" David Ray asked.

"No." It sounded like a case of *I can, but I won't*, and David Ray looked about to ask another question, but Contractor Director continued rolling. "We do require reciprocity for our pilot enhancements and must draw up a contract. Explorer of Solar Systems will retrieve and return our property, which the Builders stole from us."

Stole? This was intriguing enough to keep everyone's mouth shut.

"After we made contact with the Builders, we tried to encourage their development by seeding their technology. Admittedly, we made mistakes regarding which technologies to encourage, but we always told the Builders the seed must be returned."

"You're speaking metaphorically?" Ariane had a visual picture of the Minoan holding a huge nut or kernel between its gloved hands.

"No, Explorer of Solar Systems. This is concrete, something you can touch, *must* touch. Perhaps you should think of a seed crystal, which acts as a nucleus for crystallization. In this case, our seed can grow an archive of information."

That helped, because humankind had progressed to crystal data storage. "So I'm looking for something that looks like one of our crystal vaults? That could be pretty big." She exchanged a look with Matt. They carried sapphire-protected crystal storage on the *Aether's Touch*, more than a vault's worth. "What will it look like?"

"We cannot describe the physical characteristics of the archive grown by the seed."

"Is it still useable?" she asked.

"Of course. The Builders received the seed from us a few thousand years after first contact with us. After ten or eleven thousand years, we decided they misused the technology and formally requested its return. They responded by preventing us from physically repossessing the seed for their archive."

Ariane raised her eyebrows. Two important tips: The Minoans had a very long memory and, apparently, they held grudges for just as long.

"How did they misuse your—your gift? And was it a gift, freely given?" David Ray asked.

Contractor Director paused far longer than the Minoan norm, which was already long. Beside her, Matt fidgeted, but they all waited.

"This will be difficult for you to understand, because the Builders had different concepts and traditions around 'gifts.' In particular, the receiver had obligations to the giver, with respect to the gift. The gift had to be respected." Contractor Director spoke carefully.

"So they didn't have a 'no strings attached' clause?" Matt asked.

"If I understand that clause correctly, Owner of Aether Exploration, the answer is no. We were within the traditions, rules, and laws of their society to ask for the return of our seed."

Ariane had another problem. "You want me to retrieve this 'seed,' but you can't even describe it. Where's it located?"

"We do not know."

"This is ridiculous!" She forgot the warnings about raising your voice to Minoans and speaking too fast, which was considered disrespectful. "How the hell do you expect me to find something in a great big solar system, without a location or even a description!"

Contractor Director went motionless. Matt and David Ray had wide eyes, looking between her and the Minoan. She realized she'd better control her temper, fast. "I apologize for my outburst, Contractor Director. But how will I find this article?"

"With your implant." The Minoan bowed its horns, perhaps excusing her behavior. "It will help you home in on our technology. You will be able to sense direction—"

Emergency calls always sound obnoxious. David Ray suddenly received one of those calls, with alarms that everyone else could hear. He started in his seat and answered, pressing his implant mike.

"David Ray. Yes?" He listened, his face serious, and then said, "I'll be there in a few moments."

"They found Lee unconscious, collapsed in her lab." David Ray headed for the door and the guardian moved out of his way.

"I'm right behind you," said Matt, rising.

"I should go also," Ariane said to Contractor Director, receiving an acknowledging nod. The discussion about the implant would have to wait.

Dr. Lee was sitting on the bed in the patient area. Two Terran Space Force medics attempted to treat her, but she wasn't a cooperative patient. One side of her face had swelled and promised a black eye with bruising down to her neck. A medic was applying a cold pack to the area.

"I only fainted. Really, I don't have time to visit your clinic," she was saying irritably as David Ray hurried across the lab to kneel in front of her.

"What's the last thing you remember?" David Ray asked, holding both her hands in his.

"I started logging the results of the tissue tests. I opened the incubator, I remember feeling woozy . . ." Lee pulled one of her hands out of David Ray's and took over holding the cold pack to the right side of her face. "I'm quite capable of holding this, thank you."

Ariane went around to the other side of the lab bench, where the door to the incubator hung open. The interior tray had fallen to the floor and bent. Puddles of nutrient solution lay about, splashed out when the tray fell, and there was only one implant.

She picked up the tray gently, trying not to rock the remaining implant. Its streaks were faded and she wondered if it had gotten too cold on the floor. As she fit the misshapen tray back into the incubator, the implant suddenly rippled and one thin end rose to wrap lightly around her thumb. She nearly dropped the tray, but its soft, comfortable feel against her skin stopped her revulsion. It felt like a baby curling its hand around her thumb; now she could believe the Minoans had designed the implants for her body.

With as light a touch as she could manage, she peeled the implant off her thumb. She closed the incubator door, noting it was set to human body temperature. Matt came around the end of lab bench and stopped in surprise at the sight of the mess on the floor.

"What happened here?" He stood about two meters away and he bent down to view the floor from a more acute angle. "Did something drag liquid over there? There's a dried trail." He pointed at two vents in the floor behind him.

"One of the implants is missing." Ariane exchanged a glance with him, and they both ran over to the vents.

"Could it squeeze through these grates?" Matt poked at the finger-size holes in the grates. The larger grate was for air exchange between the lab and utility area between decks, and it was fastened down onto the raised floor structure. He pulled off the smaller vent cover, for distributing pressurized gas.

"Maybe." She bent down and looked into the small vent, which was nano-manufactured pipe. "This should have a one-way valve, to prevent backflow. I can't see all the way to the valve because it curves."

"If it went into the subfloor area, it could be anywhere."

"This doesn't make sense." Ariane shook her head. "I didn't think these things could travel, much less motivate themselves for—for *escape*. Even if they have rudimentary brains, I don't think they can live long in low temperatures. Why didn't they try to get back to the incubator, which is warm enough to keep them alive?"

"Beats me. I'll call maintenance," Matt said grimly, his hand going to the base of his jaw. He turned away as he quietly made the call.

She frowned, looking down at the grates and hearing Dr. Lee repeat her story again, word for word. Sighing, she put in a call also, to Beta Priamos Station security.

"There's a Minoan-made *worm* loose and running around the station?" was Ensign Walker's first response, and she had to calm him down. His second response was to get to the lab as fast as possible, followed by a TSF noncom, who started helping Matt and the maintenance tech remove the grate to the subfloor area. Causing Dr. Lee more irritation, Ensign Walker made her go through her story again.

"Are you sure you weren't attacked, maybe stunned?" Walker was poking at his slate as he asked the question, so he didn't see Lee's eyes flare.

"I can tell the difference between feeling light-headed and having a couple hundred thousand volts applied to my body," she said scathingly.

"I still think we should have the medics do a scan."

"I'm a medical doctor, and I haven't suffered any serious injury. As I said, I opened the incubator, I remember feeling woozy—"

"Then there's no harm in letting the medics—" Walker tried again.

"No!" Lee's eyes widened into a glare and she started shouting. "Who do you think you are, young man?"

David Ray flinched and pulled back. Ariane's frown grew deeper; Dr. Lee always mixed her wise-old-lady tartness with warmth and humor, but now she just seemed like a crusty old witch. To be fair, she was hurt and tired, but this intense anger made her unrecognizable.

"I *think* I am *Ensign* Walker of the Terran Space Forces, entrusted with the security of this station." Walker glared right back at her. "Do I need to arrest you, Dr. Lee, or will you go willingly to the clinic?"

"Please, Lee." David Ray's voice was hoarse, obviously fighting tears.

They took her, but she didn't go willingly. Luckily, Lee wasn't strong enough to make too much of a scene. Ariane beckoned to Walker and pulled him aside.

"Does the clinic have any way to check for use of a neural probe?" she asked the ensign quietly.

"You're pretty quick on the uptake. I'll ask the medics if they've got the equipment to check for that."

"I can recognize the signs: fanatical adherence to a word-for-word story, anger and subconscious distress when the story is questioned. Even worse, personality changes— can you find out who could have been in this lab in the past few hours?"

"ComNet hasn't been activated on this ring yet. We'll look into it, Ms. Kedros, and you'll be third, maybe fourth, to know. After the SP and his staff, of course." Ensign Walker gave her a tight smile.

"Better consider the possibility that one Minoan device was stolen." Matt walked up, wiping his hands on a towel. "We can't find any nutrient solution on the grates, so it probably isn't wandering about in the dark empty spaces of the station."

"Can anyone use those Minoan—things, or just you, Ms. Kedros?" Ensign Walker asked, revealing the reach of the Terran intelligence-gathering machine. He was probably only a shift behind her and Matt, reading reports on their meeting—and whatever Ensign Walker knew, SP Parmet knew.

"I don't know." Ariane glanced at Matt, who was frowning. Perhaps he was wondering where Walker got his information. On the other hand, it wasn't a bad idea to have an informed Walker doing the investigation. "I need to speak to the Minoans, as well as go through Dr. Lee's notes."

Ensign Walker walked off with Matt to examine the vents and the trail of nutrient solution. When they were on the far side of the lab, she tried to call Owen Edones. His queue was still blocked for the audit. She tried Sergeant Joyce next. His queue wasn't blocked and by his status, he shouldn't be out of his clinic room, but all his calls were going directly to recorded queue. Where was he?

She chewed her lip. She'd like some advice because she was flying blind here, but leaving information on his queue was unwise. "Call me when you can, Joyce," was all she said.

Joyce had purposely put his calls on hold. He was casually sitting on a bench outside Recreation Room Three, with his hated walker to his left and burly Captain Floros seated on his right. Neither was in uniform and they blended in with the off-duty crowd, which was restive because the ICT sessions were now closed and they'd lost their free entertainment.

"Why do you think he's going to pass on information this afternoon?" Joyce asked, watching a Feed correspondent try to provoke an "emotional" moment out of some hydroponics workers.

"Because he just discovered the Weapons Demand Schedule Backup." Floros's voice was silky with satisfaction.

Joyce squinted as he pushed his brain. "I don't remember that one. It's a log? Of what?"

"Of nothing. But what sort of Ships' Information Control Officer would I be if I didn't point out to the auditor the *lack* of a Weapons Demand Schedule *Log*, when there was a backup with that name?"

Joyce laughed. "Myron immediately assumed incompetence or treachery. Someone must have erased the original, right?"

"After Myron checked his list of logs, he fell for it, hook, line, and sinker. He demanded a copy and I said I wasn't familiar with this log, but I suspected it contained ship—"

"Performance data? You're scary, Captain, when you set your sights on someone. But what if they don't use the same drop as before?"

"That's where the dogs come in—and Myron's stinginess," Floros said. "There's only one medium he can be using. Crystal would be outrageously expensive, the log is too big for implants, so that leaves portable discs and sticks. I know Myron uses ship's stock for the audit copies, but I suspect his own copies go on stock also, so he doesn't have to buy his own. I've carefully contaminated the supply discs and sticks with one of Xena's special colognes."

"He could have his own stash. They're pretty small."

"Granted, I'm taking a chance. I checked supply and found he's requested a couple discs here and there, but he's kept the number small, hasn't even requisitioned a whole box. When he's making the official audit copy, he asks his escort for a disc—and I handed him one with a drop of the scent on it."

Joyce frowned. "So you're contaminated."

"I beg your pardon, Sergeant." But Floros smiled. "I rubbed myself down with a soap the dog handler recommended, and I've changed clothes. That scent sticks to everything, your hands, your pockets, anything you touch—so I spent a long time steaming."

"Hope Myron takes the bait."

"And soon. With the ICT and audit both winding down, we don't have much time."

CHAPTER 18

Neural probes were first used, near the end of the war, by the fledgling Terran Bureau of Intelligence [*link to TEBI, under leadership of Isrid S. Parmet*]. It's difficult to detect use of neural probes after the subject's tissues have healed in the area near the brain stem. . . .

—*Dr. Diotrephes*, testimony to Senatorial Subcommittee on Intelligence, 2105.302.10.05 UT, indexed by *Democritus 8* under Metrics Imperative

After Lee Pilgrimage was taken to the clinic, Ariane tried to go through her notes with the help of a battlefield medic, courtesy of Sergeant Pike. Specialist Dimitriou didn't have an advanced medical degree, but he had a pragmatic, unassuming manner and a quick mind.

"I'm better at immediate aid and trauma surgery, ma'am," Dimitriou confessed. "This xenografting is beyond me."

"The fact you know the word 'xenograft' puts you ahead of all of us." She smiled at him. "I hear you trained with one of the manufacturers of *our* implants."

"This is way ahead of stuffing a chip or mike or ear bug under your skin."

With Dimitriou's help, she located the tissue grafting test results, which looked quite successful. Only one implant had been used for tissue grafting. The other was the control, and was now missing. But was it even usable?

"There's not going to be a problem with your body rejecting their implant." He glanced at the display of their surviving visitor, looking healthier every hour and starting to ripple, and a queasy expression settled on his face. "Are you sure you want to put that thing in your body?"

Following his glance, she said, "No, I'm not sure. But right now, I'm more worried about getting it *out* of my body. I asked Dr. Lee to look into that, specifically."

"I think I saw some log entries about removal. Maybe I can find them." He went back to digging through the lab's data stores. Because the Beta Priamos labs were to be used by separate companies, each lab had independent processors, data stores, and security protocols, all firewalled away from ComNet.

Ariane looked through logs tracking usage, trying to see if anyone other than Lee had accessed the lab data in the past few days. She found no evidence the system had been hacked, although it had been used early on first shift—but Lee had been in early. Unfortunately, she was no Captain Floros and she might not see the subtle signs of infiltration.

Time had marched on; it was well into second shift and she needed some sleep. "I have to testify tomorrow before the ICT, so I've got to get rest. You're welcome to keep looking through this data," she told Dimitriou. "Remember that it has to be protected under the nondisclosure agreement you signed."

"I'd like to dig through Dr. Lee's earlier notes and compare them to the work she did today, before her seizure." Everyone now referred to today's episode as Lee's "seizure." Then Dimitriou reminded her of Lee's other duties. "I also have to run periodic checks and tests on the birth chambers and their contents."

Their contents. Ariane nodded, feeling disconcerted. They were both Autonomists, so they weren't used to seeing past the shiny machine fronts to the human beings that would emerge, but at least Dimitriou hadn't forgotten their presence or Dr. Lee's paramount duties.

As Ariane left the lab, she knew she'd have to challenge Contractor Director about the gray areas of using their technology, and she needed to do it without Matt or David Ray present. Her instincts told her the Minoans were less likely to hedge when they were alone with her. However, she didn't know how to make an appointment with Contractor Director, who resided in an amoebalike ship that suckled at one of the station's class C docks. Setting a destination of "Knossos-ship," she sent a message asking Contractor Director to meet her near its dock at oh eight hundred tomorrow, well before her testimony. She hoped the Minoans would receive and understand her message.

The next morning she cautiously approached the dock that supported Knossos-ship, having not received any answer. The docking ring, in this area of the station, was silent and deserted. As she walked over the ring rise and came in sight of the dock, she saw the tall red figure standing patiently, its robe slowly stirring. Initially, she thought the emissary was alone, but saw two guardians several meters away, watching the docking area.

"I await your questions, Explorer of Solar Systems." The Minoan emissary bowed its horns as she approached. It sounded slightly smug.

She sighed and looked about, uncertain how to start the conversation. The docking area behind Contractor Director gave her shivers, because the Minoan ship had forced fleshy extensions into and out of the station's airlocks. Through the open airlocks, she saw the wall of "solid soup" that Matt had called the Minoan mechanism for containing pressure. Of course, Matt would disapprove of her meeting the Minoans alone.

"Perhaps you've heard of the problems that Physician of—of My Choice encountered, and the disappearance of one of your implants," she began, warily steering her way through the pitfalls of Minoan interaction.

"We are aware of the replacement of Physician of Your Choice. Will you need another implant for testing?"

She paused in surprise; they could flip around pronouns in long names correctly, but they couldn't handle short names like "Lee." She shook her head. "I don't know if we need more implants for testing. I'll check. More important,

I have to ask you if *anyone else but me* can use one of these implants?"

"You mean another human?"

This conversation was already proceeding at the speed of oil spreading in the cold of space. She repressed a childish urge to stomp her foot. "Yes, I mean another *human*, different from Explorer of Solar Systems, with different DNA coding and biochemistry."

This seemed to cause some thought on Contractor Director's part, as the tall figure went still for several moments. It finally stirred and said, "We project disastrous results if another human, other than Explorer of Solar Systems, attempts to pilot damaged N-space with the implant."

She didn't bother to explore the disastrous projections, since she was well aware of the hazards of N-space. That wasn't the important issue. "What about the homing functions for finding your 'seed' archive?"

"We are uncertain that the function will work correctly in another organism." Contractor Director cocked its head slightly, although the movement increased at the tips of its horns and caused the cascading ropes of jewels to sway and sparkle. "If you suspect the missing implant may be found and used by another human, I remind you that the final implant will have adjustments for your biochemistry."

"What if the implant isn't missing, but *stolen*?"

"Then you have a competitor for finding our property, and this concerns us," Contractor Director said gravely.

"Can we scan for the implant?"

"It will appear similar to human muscular tissues, whether it's been implanted or not."

She chewed her lip. Biological matter was hard to detect and *differentiate* with stationary scanners, let alone portable ones. She knew, from personal experience, that Minoans and their weapons defeated human scanning devices all the time—perhaps for this very reason.

Of course, she might be worrying for nothing. The Minoans weren't sure that anyone else could use it, and the implant was useless unless it got to the Builders' solar system. They could physically search the *Pytheas*, do background checks on the final forty people chosen to crew it, and perform tedious physical searches on everything loaded on the ship. That assumed the person hadn't already put it inside their body.

"Does the implant have a limited lifespan? Maybe it'll be dissolved into the body? If so, then all we have to do is wait."

"No. If the implant is kept under optimal conditions, it can live as long as its host. Besides, we cannot afford to wait." Contractor Director's voice, neither female nor male, was uncharacteristically forceful.

"Live as long as its host, huh?" She caught that, as well as the comment on waiting. Closing her eyes for a moment, she remembered the feeling of warmth she had when the implant had touched her skin, almost a welcoming feeling, like she was encountering a part of her separated self. "If I choose to install an implant, how difficult will it be to remove?"

"Section 241.55 in the manual describes removal."

"You're avoiding the direct answer." She stared up at the mask of darkness under the headdress. "You're required, under our contractual law, to provide me an assessment of risk. That includes an evaluation of successful removal."

It took another invocation of Autonomist law to finally get a grudging response from the Minoan. "There is a ninety percent chance that biochemical responses will inhibit the host's urge for removal, and a forty-one percent chance that surgical removal, the preferred method, will not adequately remove all the implant's cells."

She took a moment to digest this, her jaw tightening. "You're saying I probably won't *want* to remove it—but even if we try, we might not remove it entirely?"

"An imprecise summary, but yes."

There was no sound of human life in that part of the station. Command Post had put the Minoans on the opposite side of the docking ring from everyone else. No one wanted to be near them, or to have their ships near them. The creaks and pops of the station's structure became much more obvious as her brain wound through arguments, pro and con, regarding the Minoans' offered technology.

"This would be the time to tell me the *real reason* why I should risk using your implant." Her voice was tight. "You've tried to motivate me through the reward of exploration and the thrill of risk—what *else* do you want to lay upon me? What are you hiding?"

"You cannot pass on this information, even to Owner of Aether Exploration. We need your most solemn oath."

Barely holding on to her temper, she made the promise, unwisely and flippantly. "By Gaia and by my oath as an AFCAW officer, I swear I will not pass this information to anyone."

Contractor Director bowed its head. "The seed contains very dangerous knowledge. We didn't know how dangerous it could be and we didn't predict its devastation."

"Your gift caused the destruction of the Builders." She wasn't surprised that the precious "knowledge" the Minoans sought was related to weapons. "What'd they do? Blow themselves up?"

"That might have been a far easier death than seeing each generation devolve, trying desperate experiments to reverse the changes in their reproductive code, until their basic cognition and sentience evaporated. When we determined the cause of their devolution, we decided an evolved intelligence could never be *given* this again. Perhaps, if the Builders had developed the knowledge on their own, they wouldn't have misused it."

"I wouldn't be so sure." She threw out the caustic comment while her mind went into overdrive. She'd assumed Gaian-based life-forms *always* evolved toward higher organization, specialization, and intelligence. The Builders had obviously messed with their natural reproductive process and encoding. That sounded a lot like the function DNA played for humans, although human genetic technology was obviously way behind the Minoan understanding of— Her breath caught.

"You're talking about technology to make weapons like those *you* used at Enclave El Tozeur, on New Sousse. The ones that affected Abram's people." Her lips and face felt numb.

There were people who would *kill* to get their hands on that "seed" from the Minoans. Several examples came to mind: angry isolationists who had suffered from the Minoan genetic weapons and other Terrans under Overlord Six, such as SP Duval. Then, there were the Terrans under Overlord Three, including SP Parmet and Dr. Istaga, aka Andre Covanni, who might want weapons technology that would be superior to the Autonomists. Of course, there were plenty of power-hungry Autonomists—the Terrans didn't control the market on people with Alexander complexes. No wonder the Minoans wanted to keep a lid on this.

"Yes, the Builders developed that kind of weapon and used it against one another." The Minoan emissary ignored her mention of New Sousse. "If it had been possible for their culture to overlap with yours, they would have used their weapons on humans."

"I understand your guilt, believe me, but if you just wanted to make sure *we* never get our hands on it—why help us explore the Builders' system?"

Contractor Director was silent.

Rubbing her temples with her fingers, she knew she was missing something. The Minoan standing in front of her was either testing her, or waiting for her to have an epiphany. She pressed further. "All you had to do was leave well enough alone, and it'd be decades before we got their buoy to work."

Or would it? Suddenly, she saw Frank's face as he said, *I'm sure the ones from New Sousse had encountered the Builders' technology before.* At the time, she'd passed over his comment in favor of the tangible connection of following the money. Then she'd been hit with a clue club and ignored it: David Ray asked Contractor Director, *You encountered the Builders elsewhere?* And Contractor Director said, *Certainly.*

Instead of calling herself stupid and running headlong into a bulkhead, she took a deep breath and said, "We need to get to the Builders' system before someone in the Soussen System gets there? *That's* why you say we can't afford to wait."

She watched the slow nod of Contractor Director's horns with horror. "But you've helped them, don't you understand? Everything we've translated or uncovered here in G-145 has been sent back to Overlord Six's territory. I need to tell—"

"You swore not to pass on this information, using the name of your deity and your oath as an AFCAW officer."

"Yes, but . . ." She hadn't expected to stumble over vital intelligence about a Terran Overlord. This raised serious questions regarding Six's support of Abram; was he hoping that Abram would get rid of a pesky competing Builders' buoy with the stolen TD weapon? If a couple of thousand people died in the process, it apparently didn't matter. But, since Abram's plan was thwarted, what was Overlord Six's backup plan? Was Six, and his SP Duval, behind the "competitor" the Minoans feared?

"We decided we could wait no longer. We observed you, and selected you because of your many titles, Ariane-as-Kedros." Now the emissary was putting the pressure on, as much as it could with its soulless voice, even using her name—which didn't happen very often. "You know the duties required of a *Destroyer*, who must ensure restitution, reparation, and, when necessary, take action to restore order."

You cold, inhuman, manipulative bastard . . . and she meant that in the worst way possible. Her hands clenched and she bit back her first response. After a deep breath through her nose, she said, "Are you Minoans admitting to being 'Destroyers of Worlds' also? If you understand restitution and reparation, what about *redemption*?"

She didn't expect an answer, and she didn't get one. After several long moments of silence, her timer went off. Glancing at her sleeve, she saw she had ten minutes before she had to give testimony.

"Will you assist us, as Explorer of Solar Systems?"

Her mind flailed about and stumbled upon a bargain. "Basically, it's your *property* that must be kept secret. Once it's returned, do you care how many missions we launch to the Builders' solar system? Do you care who knows the locations of the other Builders' buoys?"

Contractor Director replied, "If you successfully return the seed, the answer is no."

"Once I return it," she didn't dare say *if*, "I want the location of the other buoy and the permission to release that information to whomever I wish."

She watched two minutes tick away on her sleeve while Contractor Director considered. Finally, it lowered its horns. "Agreed. However, we cannot have a record of this agreement."

Looking about at the unfinished, unwired, and un-noded station, she shrugged. "Verbal agreement's fine. *No* handshake necessary," she added, leaving a possibly bemused Minoan standing alone in the corridor.

"Is Ariane coming today?" David Ray's face peered at him from a view port.

"No, she's testifying to the ICT—and I don't envy her that." Matt was having his Hellas Kaffi on the control deck of *Aether's Touch*. "I hear Duval's getting pissy because there's no *direct* proof there was a stolen Terran TD weapon, now that Dr. Rouxe is dead. He's avoiding the inconvenient fact that a temporal-distortion wave can't spontaneously appear, not as a natural physical phenomenon."

"He's playing up the uncertain *source* of the weapon and who controlled it. I'm even beginning to wonder if the prosecution will get their convictions. Lee sends her regards, by the way."

"She's back to her old self, I hope," Matt said.

"Maybe." David Ray shrugged and Matt knew enough to drop the subject. "When do we leave?"

"I've got permission to disconnect in two hours—we'll be gone about four hours. The station hasn't moved that far away from the buoy."

"Good." David Ray rubbed his head. With such a short haircut, it was easy to see his scalp wrinkle up on his head. "You've talked to your AI so it'll stay quiet while Lowry's around?"

"Don't worry." Matt signed off.

Just to be sure, he had another talk with Muse 3. Even

though Matt had started the licensing paperwork, he was worried about exposing the AI to a Terran scientist, and this wasn't just military paranoia rubbing off from Ari. Everyone was beginning to get their first glimpses of Terran standards of living—and they didn't live up to their political hype.

The Terrans had no equivalent to ComNet and the Autonomist Worlds' huge crystal vaults of data. They certainly never developed AIs to sift through data and do objective indexing. The Terrans were enamored with the Heraclitus and Democritus models that indexed the minutiae collected every minute of every day—although Matt wouldn't give it such a pretty name. The darker side of Terran interest was their requests for "copies" and their failure to grasp that each AI model number actually had *rights* and couldn't be copied or dissected, by Consortium law. Matt didn't want to deal with requests or demands to access his AI, from Lowry or the Terran State Prince who currently administered this station.

"I understand I cannot let the Terran scientist suspect my existence, but can I remain operational while she is aboard?" Muse 3 asked.

"Certainly, since your interpretation routines might help us speak to the bot on the buoy."

"I do not think the bot will understand your speech," Muse 3 said cautiously.

"I mean I'd like to try to interpret its signal—remember I asked you to analyze its command set?"

"Yes, Matt. I have developed some routines for you, accessible on the console. Please look at the far left comm panel."

He looked over the smooth console of displayable material, configured with touch squares. To the upper left of the console was the comm panel, using orange squares, which was how he and Ari configured the commands on the *Aether's Touch*. There were three new squares, titled BOT COMMANDS, BOT RESPONSE VARIANT, and BOT RESPONSE ACTUAL.

He tapped BOT COMMANDS and a view port opened, displaying a menu. As he read it, he nearly choked on his Kaffi. "There's more commands here than in the bot's operational manual. How were you able to put these together?"

"The standard commands are marked, but they're too limited. The bot's situation has changed and it may now interpret an aggregate command. I sliced up the standard commands and ran a random aggregation routine to see if anything useful appeared." The AI sounded smug and, just like a pet, it hoped for feedback.

"This is great, Muse. We can query 'friend or foe,' and ask for general cooperation, assuming the bot considers itself the interface for the buoy." Matt got excited, scrolling through the lexicon. He opened view ports for the other two functions Muse 3 had provided, discovering a routine for attempting response interpretation directly, and one for breaking a response apart into original primitives.

"I suspect the bot has become responsible for providing an interface. Your original video makes its intent fairly clear." Muse 3 used a satisfied tone.

Matt remembered Muse's interest, or *obsession*, with the video he took with his EVA suit on that day. He'd nearly lost his life, because the bot was slicing his suit apart while he pigheadedly told Ari he didn't need rescue. But he did, and he didn't realize his dire circumstances until the bot had cut his communications with Ari and the ship. Lucky for him, Ari didn't always obey orders and she was on top of the situation.

"How did you get this done so fast?" Matt asked, then wished he could take it back.

"I have had no other duties for six days," Muse 3 said reproachfully.

"Sorry, Muse. Life can be boring sometimes, when you have synapses that run near the speed of light." According to Ari, however, human synapses were necessary for piloting N-space and human heads contained quantum devices, blah, blah, blah. Matt didn't want to discuss any of these subjects with Muse 3. "Now stay quiet while I go through this undocking checklist."

Everything was prepared and requisitioned by the time

David Ray and Dr. Lowry stepped through the passenger airlock. *Aether's Touch* could support a two-person crew for a real-space voyage of sixty days. Matt didn't consider it risky to take three people on a little jaunt within an hour of rescue from Beta Priamos Station and the Laomedon mining operations.

Lowry had effusive praise for the bot command testing routines; her face became animated and cheerful, making her seem positively friendly.

"How did you have the time to do something like this?" She scrolled through the interactive tests, almost chirping when she saw an interesting command.

"Oh, I ran a random aggregation routine to see if anything useful appeared," Matt said modestly.

David Ray, standing on the other side of Lowry and a little behind her, rolled his eyes. Matt hoped Nestor hadn't programmed Muse 3 with pride of ownership. Was it possible to offend an AI by taking credit for its work?

Matt didn't wait to find out. "Everybody get webbed into their seat." He shooed David Ray toward the jump seat, and pointed Lowry at the other control deck chair. David Ray gave him an annoyed look, but started webbing into the seat.

After doing his system checks and ensuring his S-DATS display was working, Matt got clamp disconnection verification and departure approval from Command Post. He boosted away from the station efficiently. Even though Ari had more real-space hours and gave him gas about his piloting experience, he was a safe real-space pilot.

They spent at least an hour on transit, including boost and braking time. During that time, David Ray and Lowry chatted about the Minoans and their substance, background, and technology. The Minoans were one of David Ray's favorite subjects and one he'd studied extensively. Matt had heard plenty of David Ray's opinions and theories, so he stayed quiet. He also noticed David Ray was trying to draw Lowry out of her prickly shell and elicit her opinions.

"The Minoans build and sell us N-space buoys—but did

they do the same with the Builders?" David Ray gestured at the pictures Lowry displayed above the console. "That buoy looks like it might have been manufactured by the Builders."

"The shape is similar to ours—the ones we pay the Minoans to build, that is. The physical differences may be superficial. It's the functional difference, the fact it only goes to one place, that intrigues me." Lowry zoomed in and displayed the baffling text that translated to "Biological Temple."

"You think the Builders designed their own time buoys?"

"An aggressive, xenophobic species wouldn't leave their buoy manufacturing to aliens," Lowry said. "We just happen to be okay with having them build our buoys for us."

"So you're not happy with the status quo."

"Do *you* think the Minoans are inherently benevolent?" Lowry asked David Ray.

"Absolutely not. On the other hand, I don't assume they're opportunistic and greedy, just because I don't understand their agenda."

"And they *do* have an agenda. I just wish I knew what it was," Lowry grumbled. "What bothers me is that humans are taking all the risks in this venture."

"All the *physical* risks, but not the financial ones." Matt finally piped up.

"But they're still pretty careful with their money." She looked thoughtful. "That matches with their unwillingness to provide us with a new buoy."

"You asked them for one?" David Ray raised his eyebrows. "Only the generational ship lines are allowed to transport buoys."

"It made sense. Why not do the same job as a generational ship?" She blew out her breath in annoyance. "But they hid behind the contractual issue you mentioned—only generational ship lines have the necessary neutrality, et cetera, et cetera."

"We're coming up on the buoy," Matt said. He brought up an external cam-eye view of *his* exploration bot, sitting serenely on top of the long cylindrical buoy.

"Now we'll see if your bot can communicate for us. Is it possible to get a copy of your routines and commands?" Lowry asked Matt. She waved her slate, prepared to copy immediately.

"I'll have to make sure they don't contain proprietary code from the ship," Matt said. "If not, I can get you copies."

Lowry seemed too excited to notice his reluctance. While he started a careful approach, Lowry started scrolling through commands. "First we establish ourselves as a friend, not a foe," she muttered. "Let's begin by . . ."

"You're cutting it close, Ms. Kedros." Ensign Walker, as representative of the court, was starting to panic.

"What's the matter? We've got four minutes." Since they both knew the drill, she was ready in two.

Before Walker took his place beside her, he hesitated. "We haven't told Dr. Lee yet, but we found tiny channels from the leads inserted near the base of her head. Someone used a neural probe on her."

"Will she be okay?"

"Maybe. The brain doesn't like having its memory changed, dealing with the conflicts, so to speak. And whoever did this was a pro; they left hardly any physical trace. If we'd waited longer to scan her, we wouldn't have found anything."

She nodded. "Thank you, Ensign."

"They've finished crew selection for the *Pytheas*." He still stood. "I expect you'll be delaying the expedition?"

"We can't. The Minoans won't wait." Until the words were out of her mouth, she hadn't realized she'd made her decision.

"Ridiculous! You've got someone loose on this station, someone who has a neural probe and isn't afraid to use it. Even on nice old lady doctors."

"But we weren't supposed to find out about *that*—we're just supposed to continue on with the mission. That's what'll draw out this lowlife." This felt right. She hadn't played the part of bait, in so many of Owen's plans, without learning a thing or two.

Walker gaped. "You're putting the crew and ship in danger."

"Everyone on this habitat will be in danger until we find who did this. If we delay the mission, the perpetrator could get bolder or more desperate. Either possibility is perilous."

"But—we need to check if other people have had memory lapses, or have mysteriously passed out."

Good point. She gave the Ensign credit for thinking around the angles. "You should do that. And you're going to help me go through the backgrounds of everyone who will be on the *Pytheas*, as well as everyone who applied for crew positions."

"I'll have to clear that with Leukos Industries, as well as SP—crap!" He whirled to tap a command on the tabletop. "You've got video-play appearance in front of the ICT in five, four, three . . ."

Symbols lit in the air before her. Ensign Walker and the Beta Priamos security office faded from her sight. She logged in and the *Pilgrimage* amphitheater appeared, with three grim members of the Tribunal sitting above her.

CHAPTER 19

While waiting for the ICT to complete their closed sessions, net-think has spawned a Voice of Concern regarding the sentencing. The accused may be remanded to Terran League courts, which have the death penalty. Interested activists should visit "Isolationist Advocates," at virtual address . . .

—*Interstellarsystem Events Feed*, 2106.061.09.03 UT, indexed by *Heraclitus 14* under Conflict Imperative

If Joyce had anything to say about his future, and he usually did, he was never getting this damaged again. When the medics first helped him walk up and down the corridors, saying it was good for him to get up and about, he'd joked with them. But, as each day went by, he didn't seem to be getting better. When he tried to use his walker, the whole side of his torso felt like it was on fire. If he saw one of those medics now, he'd snarl, *Up and about, my ass. Speaking of which, I can barely drag it along.*

He'd hauled his pain-racked carcass out again today to sit beside Captain Floros on their favorite bench. The advantage of this bench was that it had a line of sight to the *Bright Crescent*'s dock area, through the central docking ring. It was early second shift, when almost fifty percent of the *Pilgrimage* came off shift, and the busy foot traffic was good cover for Joyce and Floros.

"There he is," Floros said.

Myron, dressed in his dapper designer suit, stood out

from the crowd as he nodded to the dock perimeter guard. Before Myron crossed or turned onto the docking ring, he stopped in front of a kiosk panel and called up a cam-eye view of himself, turning and evaluating the fit of the suit. He fiddled with the suit's color, finally choosing a dark gold thread mixture that blended well with the *Pilgrimage* monochromatically yellow crew overalls and ship decorations.

Frowning, Joyce could only guess Myron was considering evasion or disguise. As someone who either put on the same uniform every day, or wore bland civilian attire, Joyce could only label Myron's behavior as narciss—narcissis—*the man is obsessed with his appearance, okay?* Joyce's sole amount of preening was shaving and keeping his mustache clipped within AFCAW regulations.

Myron was finally satisfied with his appearance and turned off the kiosk "mirror" view. He strolled onto the docking ring and to their surprise, turned *right*.

"He's not using the same drop." Floros eyed Joyce's walker as she stood up. "I'll follow him while you call for Xena, the wonder hound."

And a wonder Xena was, after smelling the sample of specialized scent. While Floros followed Myron, Joyce started Xena back at the *Bright Crescent* airlock and ramp to see whether they could trail the contaminated discs. Xena snuffled at the railing of the ramp, and "went ballistic," according to her handler. He let Xena off her lead, making Joyce nervous. But he quickly got over his worry, after laughing at crèche-get hugging bulkheads to get out of the dog's way.

Xena led them to the kiosk where Myron had brought up his image and adjusted his suit color. When the handler looked at Joyce inquiringly, he said, "Yup, he was touching that."

"Good girl, Xena!" exclaimed the handler, and the dog barked twice in excitement or pleasure. "Now, go get him!" She bounded into the ring corridor, following Myron's trail.

Joyce paused at the sound of her bark. Before this, he'd heard her make semi-articulate sounds from her throat, and she'd snuffled, panted, whined, but she hadn't barked.

His aunt's dog could find a piece of cheese blindfolded, but its bark had been bred out. That'd been a disservice to the breed, because the bark was such an *honest* exuberant sound. At that point, Joyce decided he wanted a dog in his household, provided he could convince his wife it'd be worth the expense. *For the kids, of course.*

This was also the point he lost sight of Xena and her growing entourage. A loose furry mammal on four legs was hardly ever seen on generational ships, where crews "raised" yeast mashes, fungi, and fish for their protein and generally eschewed transporting life-forms other than humans. Xena attracted attention from visitors and crew alike, although the crèche-get gawked in horrified, wide-eyed, space-wreck-watching fashion. Joyce could follow Xena's paw-steps by homing in on the furor.

He was panting with pain by the time he regrouped with Benjamin, Xena, and her handler. They were outside one of the package drop centers. Benjamin called Floros, who still shadowed Myron, and checked against his notes.

"Yes, we got that. V-play equipment at station eight in rec room four. Then she homed in on locker 223; pawed at it. I agree." Benjamin broke off his call and started speaking to Joyce. "Amazing. Xena picked up on every one of Myron's stops. He had crossed his path once and she got the stops out of order, but I'm still impressed."

"What do we do now?" Joyce knew what he'd do, but this was sovereign Pilgrimage territory, and Benjamin wasn't doing this because classified *Bright Crescent* data was at stake. Benjamin had been swayed by Captain Floros's argument that Myron's secret maneuvers, besides flouting Pilgrimage line neutrality, were ultimately endangering the Interstellar Criminal Tribunal proceedings. It was now a Pilgrimage op, so to speak.

"We wait." Benjamin gestured toward a bench against the wall of the crowded public area. Joyce gratefully eased over and seated himself. Xena and her handler, however, set up as a sort of carnival exhibit near the door of the package drop lockers. As people slowed to watch, her handler started putting her through some tricks.

"Do you think that's a good idea?" Joyce pointed at Xena, who had crooned a short bar of a song from her throat, and garnered applause. "Will that scare our suspect off?"

"Smith knows what he's doing." Benjamin referred to the handler, who was casually steering everyone who entered and exited the package drop lockers past his wonder dog. "After all, these animals are so rare outside the Sol system now . . ."

Benjamin had become a dog lover and Joyce actually *listened* to his impassioned speech on the many fine qualities of canines, storing away wife-convincing facts for later use. Due to selective breeding, dogs now lived longer and healthier lives. They didn't provoke as many allergic reactions in humans and their longer lives helped improve their intelligence. Wasn't it amazing that today's dog had three times the vocabulary of its ancestors? Joyce rolled his eyes, but Benjamin continued without pause. The dog's scent processing was superb and trainable; they could even diagnose human health problems. Of course, when used for finding explosives—

"Have you taken the other dog through the station for explosives yet?" Joyce interrupted Benjamin's info dump.

"The dog triggered on your old clinic room and the bot storage bay. It's a big ship, so we're just getting to—"

"Visitor quarters?"

"They're next. Sammy will be taken through in an hour or so." Benjamin checked the time on his sleeve.

"There she is." Joyce focused on a passing Terran woman. Her closely cropped blond hair had a reddish tint. She wore a TSF lieutenant's uniform with intelligence insignia, but had no nametag, as was often the case with Terran military uniforms. The Terran Space Force rank structure derived from old Earth naval organizations, meaning this lieutenant was equivalent to an AFCAW captain such as Floros. Joyce immediately raised his estimate of the woman's age and experience.

Like several other "grav-huggers" who were more comfortable around animals, the lieutenant stopped and exclaimed over Xena. Benjamin and Joyce watched as she talked to Smith, bent down, and stroked the dog's head.

"Why, thank you, Lieutenant," Joyce drawled. "For giving us a perfect before and after comparison."

Looking up at the lieutenant with large brown eyes, Xena patiently accepted the admiration as her due. Then the lieutenant disappeared into the package drop and locker area. Benjamin stood up and Joyce followed suit, although it took him much longer. The lieutenant appeared and Xena became excited, with her hindquarters trembling, her neck elongated, and her nose stretched outward with her ears forward. Smith looked over at Benjamin, who gave him a nod. Xena moved in front of the lieutenant, impeding her, and tried to paw at an area near the lieutenant's hip.

"What the—?" The lieutenant spun, trying to avoid Xena, and backed into Benjamin.

"Will you empty your pockets, Lieutenant?" Benjamin asked politely, having reached the group.

Her blue eyes cooled as they flickered from Benjamin over to the approaching Joyce, whom she had to know, because of recent events. She had the regular bland features that all Terrans had, but the light freckling across her nose and cheekbones gave her an engaging, wholesome look that most Terran women lacked.

"I have diplomatic immunity. You have no right to search me," she said.

"Nice try, Lieutenant . . . ?" Benjamin matched cool for cool.

"Lieutenant Tyler, of the Terran Space Forces, escorting State Prince Duval."

"Claiming diplomatic immunity doesn't work in our ship's public areas, particularly when we're investigating crimes such as theft, murder, bombings, or the interference of interstellar justice." Benjamin tapped the small badge on his upper right chest. "This badge, plus probable cause, allows me to search your pockets."

"What's your probable cause?" The lieutenant was composed and levelheaded; Joyce gave her credit for that. She ignored the moist, warm nose that snuffled at the side of her hip. Could there really be a pocket there? The Terran uniforms looked skin-tight and smooth—Joyce had to wrench his gaze away.

"We contaminated a stolen disc with a scent."

"Oh. Then you must be looking for this." Lieutenant Tyler ran her finger along the seam on her hip and a pocket opened. She slid her hand in and removed the disc that excited Xena so much. It was smaller than a commemorative coin, thin and flexible as display plastic; she held it between her long fingers and gave it to Benjamin with a graceful flourish. "Of course, I have no idea what's on it," she added. "I was only picking it up."

Of course. Joyce asked, "By whose orders?"

"We were following an anonymous tip." She gave Joyce an arctic glance, daring him to object. At this point, he couldn't.

The three of them became silent, each with an impassive expression, perhaps evaluating their options. Finally, Benjamin cleared his throat and held out his slate toward Lieutenant Tyler. "Your diplomatic status doesn't prevent me from marking you as a witness and person of interest. For the time being, you're not allowed to leave the *Pilgrimage* until I'm satisfied with your story. Please indicate your understanding with a thumbprint."

After they finished and the lieutenant walked away, Benjamin said softly, "I'll let you observe our interviews, but there's nothing we can do about her or whoever holds her leash."

"I didn't expect to—it's Myron I had to stop first. Wait a minute, please." Joyce took a call from Captain Floros.

"I've detained Myron just outside the ship." Her voice was small and clear in his ear bug. "The ICT will be letting out in an hour."

"Right." He looked at Benjamin. "I'd appreciate having you and Xena available when we face Senator Stephanos."

Luckily, Benjamin agreed. Joyce managed to get to the *Bright Crescent*'s slip on his own initiative; either he was getting stronger or he was learning to use his walker. At the bottom of the ship's ramp stood Floros, Myron, and two members of AFCAW security force.

"Captain, you've overstepped your authority so far that *no one* will have heard of the post you're going to—" Myron was running off at the mouth, but his jaw dropped as he saw the dog.

Xena, of course, went off on Myron's pockets and hands, which he quickly held up at chest height. "What's going on?"

"I think you lost this." Benjamin held up the disc, almost under Myron's nose. Xena had to be pulled away from the ramp.

"Where'd you get that?" Myron stood his ground.

Joyce put his hand on Myron's shoulder—to be honest, he had to lean on the slight man. "Son, I don't think you're going to need designer wear anymore, not where you're going."

"I haven't done anything wrong." Myron didn't manage to look as confident as he sounded. "Plenty of Autonomist senators exchange data with Terran Overlord staffs."

"They don't release *classified* AFCAW ship specifications." Hissing his words softly, Joyce leaned closer, his hand tightening on Myron's shoulder. Myron paled. "Here's a piece of free advice: Never believe a Terran Space Force officer, particularly if she wants to sleep with you."

Myron's mouth closed with a snap and his nostrils flared. Joyce shook his head; *done in by the oldest trick in the book, pardon the pun*.

Captain Floros motioned to the SF, having them arrest Myron. He'd be under AFCAW control, not Pilgrimage, and would be detained on the ship. Joyce watched the young man's jaw clench as his wrists were put in a manacle and he was marched through the airlock.

"The Colonel wants to be briefed, of course." Floros looked at the time, then nodded toward the departing Myron. "You expect we'll get anything useful from him?"

"Yes, if he helps us identify every system, and every function, that may have been compromised on the *Bright Crescent*. As for the important questions—why target Myron, why compromise this ship, what did SP Duval want, specifically, if he's the one who ordered this . . ." Joyce shook his

head, thinking how TSF Lieutenant Tyler would respond
to—or coolly misdirect—Benjamin's friendly interrogation
methods. "Only that Terran intelligence officer can answer
those, and I don't think she'll talk."

Ariane felt as though the ICT had lost its way. Everyone
seemed on edge and the Tribunal members exhibited rancor
toward one another. Senator Stephanos looked exhausted,
Commander Meredith seemed like all he wanted was to
get the others *off* his ship, and SP Duval had captured the
market on spite and hostility. Duval's eyes seemed to burn
whenever he looked at her.

The prosecution's case was in a shambles, due to the loss
of Tahir's testimony. For two hours, Ariane was asked to describe what the isolationists had done with the TD weapon,
how they released and detonated it, and how she'd sent a
ship after the detonating weapon to take it into N-space.
After a break, the Terran defense counsel cross-examined
her.

"Ms. Kedros, please tell us again how you verified the accused had a temporal-distortion weapon at their disposal."

"Tahir Rouxe showed me an image of the warhead in
its container. TD weapons have a distinctive geometric
shape, usually employing a great stellated dodecahedron,
for bringing together exotic matter. The case was the type
necessary for shielding exotic matter and it had the Terran
designation of—" she closed her eyes "—TDP-dash-two-
one-oh-two-dash-oh-one-two-slash—"

"That's fine, Ms. Kedros." The defense attorney overrode her. "Were you aware of Dr. Rouxe's previous occu-
pation?"

"He said the weapon was a 'gift' to his father, so I assumed he worked in a weapons depot or maintenance
facility."

"Since you made that assumption, Ms. Kedros, didn't
you consider he might have taken that picture at a Terran
depot before coming to G-145? Why did you assume a *picture* was enough evidence that Dr. Rouxe had a weapon in
his possession?"

"I didn't—not until I was thrown into a cell with State Prince Parmet—"

"Stop, please." The defense attorney turned to the bench. "Motion to strike this—considering that SP Parmet's testimony regarding his knowledge of the weapon was thrown out."

Her eyebrows shot up. Thrown out?

One of the prosecuting attorneys popped up and said, "Objection to motion. Ms. Kedros didn't have reality-distorting drugs in her system. She can accurately describe what SP Parmet told her."

"She would be repeating a drug-induced hallucination," responded the prosecution.

"Agreed, but only with respect to Ms. Kedros's conversations with SP Parmet," Duval said primly.

Ariane couldn't believe this was happening. She watched Senator Stephanos roll his eyes and say, "I disagree, so you can't abstain, Meredith."

Commander Meredith sighed and said, "For the sake of consistency, I will agree with SP Duval."

She realized now how her actions would sound on the court record. The conclusion would be that she was a loose cannon, making improbable presumptions, and inclined to take justice into her own hands. As a result, when asked to relate what happened on the *Candor Chasma*, she tried to orient on the interface that the isolationists had rigged to the weapon. They discredited her again, using her insistence that Tahir had a Terran weapon and she was an Autonomist.

"I agree your records show appropriate experience, Ms. Kedros." Luckily, her false military records listed maintenance time with a TD weapon system. "But, have you ever actually *seen* a *Terran* interface to a *Terran* weapon?"

"No—"

"Then I would say you can't be credible witness to what the ship carried."

"Objection!" The prosecution popped up again. "Defense is making conclusions. This should be saved for closing argument."

Well, that *really helped!* All three Tribunal members sustained this objection, but she felt frustration growing in the pit of her stomach. They were avoiding the point: a lot of people had died because of Abram and his weapon.

"I can't be a witness to each of the one hundred and ten deaths from radiation, *but they still happened!*" The words burst out of her and her voice cracked in anguish at points. The defense attorney tried to override her, but she just kept raising her voice. "The sun suddenly spouts mass emissions, flares, and radiation—and you want to ignore the *cause*? The cause was those men and their weapon. Are you going to pretend it didn't happen? The measurements show the residual temporal-distortion wave going through the sun. Perhaps you don't consider science to be *credible* in this court."

She was yelling by the end of her tirade, and so were the defense counsel, the defendants, and SP Duval. Commander Meredith wouldn't look at her. He kept his gaze down, with an expression of misery. Senator Stephanos was shaking his head; *not a good idea to lose your temper*, his face said. After Duval said something about "contempt of court," she quieted.

"My questions, Ms. Kedros, are exposing Abram's secretive methods and how he tightly controlled information about the weapon." The prosecuting attorney's tone was acidic. "Even *you* didn't physically see the weapon. While you can testify to the actions of Dr. Tahir Rouxe and his father, can you produce any proof that my *clients* knew about that weapon?"

She looked at each defendant's face. Most tried to appear detached, but Rand smirked back at her. "No," she said grudgingly.

The attorney allowed a climactic pause, then continued. "Let's talk about what *you* did with the alleged weapon, Ms. Kedros. Are you familiar with the TD Testing Treaty, signed in 2092, where signatories agreed to stop all testing? Specifically, pushing TD detonations into N-space was prohibited, was it not?"

Oh, for Gaia's sake. Her jaw set, due to the unfairness

of the situation. The Minoans had pushed that treaty because the *Terrans* had been the biggest transgressors, but that fact would be in testimony the Tribunal threw out: the conversation she had with SP Parmet after he was tortured. Tensely, she answered, "At the time I pushed the ship and detonation into N-space, I was trying to prevent the sun from going nova. Adhering to the Testing Treaty wasn't foremost in my mind."

"Were you aware the Minoans initially intended to charge you with treaty violations?"

Confused, she hesitated. These questions weren't going where she expected. Remembering the name "Breaker of Treaties," she tried to recall who had told her about the possible charges. She shrugged. "I think somebody told me about the possibility, but I don't remember who or when."

"Can you explain *why* the Minoans suddenly withdrew their charges, directly *after* your company accepted a lucrative contract from them?"

At the time, she'd thought the charges might be coercion, ensuring she'd work the contract. She decided to go with an incomplete, but truthful, answer. "I assume the Minoans researched the matter and decided the charges were invalid."

"You didn't provide the Minoans with information that made the treaty irrelevant?"

"No."

"The Minoans didn't uncover evidence that suggests the weapon didn't detonate?"

"No. I told you, there's scientific proof the temporal-distortion wave leaked back into real-space." The absurdity of this made her want to laugh hysterically; she, of all people, was having to prove how dangerous TD weapons could be.

The defense attorney turned to the bench, perhaps feeling he'd pushed this obscure and irrelevant point as far as he could. Addressing the Tribunal members, he said, "The Defense wishes to enter the timeline for this Aether Exploration contract into evidence, as exhibit one-two-seven. We'll address this again, under credibility of the witness."

Ariane kept her mouth from opening in dismay. Duval nodded sharply to the court recorder. Meredith agreed also, although he seemed sulky and resigned. Stephanos looked asleep and when he didn't object, the court recorder added the data to the ICT records.

Could this cross-examination get any worse? Yes, it could.

"Ms. Kedros, would you say you're a heavy drinker?"

"What?"

"Do you ever drink to excess?" The attorney rephrased the question patiently.

"I've been known to tie one on, every once in a while." She tried to smile naturally.

"But is it true that your employer had to—"

"Excuse me. Hold, please." The court recorder held up his hand, while looking at his slate. He was the only one in the amphitheater allowed to have one, or to receive calls. "*Two* members of the tribunal, Senator Stephanos and State Prince Duval, have emergency calls from their staffs. I suggest we adjourn this session, since we're only thirty minutes away from the scheduled end."

The defense attorney looked sour, but acquiesced. A set of doors across from the witness stand opened, and against a bright light she saw a TSF uniformed woman run down the aisle to go to Duval. Behind her hurried someone in a black Directorate uniform, perhaps Sublieutenant Matthaios. The lighting contrast caused problems for her v-play helmet and the amphitheater was fading. She hadn't toggled the switch, so Ensign Walker was pulling her out of the virtual session.

"I didn't think you'd mind." Ensign Walker looked worn, as if someone had mopped the floor with him. Of course, he'd been watching this ridiculous charade day after day.

"How can you stand this?" she asked, running her hands through her hair and rubbing her head.

"Today, the political pack ravaged you. A few days ago, they ravaged State Prince Parmet. Even he couldn't opt out of this unpleasantness."

"So Parmet's out of the loop?" When Walker looked

at her warily, she added, "If I were an average net-rat, I'd wonder if the ICT was being pushed around by the Terran League."

She could see Walker weighing his two possible responses: close ranks and patriotically stonewall, or open up to an Autonomist intelligence officer, at the expense of SP Duval. Surprisingly, he decided on the latter, saying, "Whatever's afoot, particularly with SP Duval, is a mystery to me. There've been no changes in policy at *the League level,* so my orders remain. I'm here to support SP Parmet and this multi-stellar research station."

"If the Overlords were fracturing, would you be told?" she asked.

Ensign Walker shrugged, avoiding an answer. Instead, he picked up his slate. "While you were giving testimony, I got permission for you to see our background investigations, such as they are, of everyone selected to go on the *Pytheas.* Ms. Guillotte was chosen for the sensors and weapons position, given her experience. At the SP's request, she has also looked over the backgrounds."

Meaning, even Parmet was nervous about the people recently arriving at this station. Ariane picked up her slate as Walker thumbed his. She saw his package arrive on her queue. "Did Ms. Guillotte have any concerns?" she asked blandly.

"She didn't find anything definitive, but she wants to speak with you privately."

Of course she does. Ariane nodded.

"I still recommend you delay the expedition. Everyone would support you, including the crew. We all know this is going too fast."

Except the Minoans. Drained of energy and emotion, she said good-bye to Ensign Walker. She was juggling too many missions, hiding too many secrets, and knew too much about all the wrong people. She had just been maligned in front of the ICT as a greedy drunk turned vigilante. Now she was going to let the Minoans implant their technology in her, just so she could pilot a crew infiltrated by unknown treacherous persons to a solar system that contained a civilization-destroying time bomb. Paying her debt to society was getting more difficult every day.

As she exited Walker's security offices, she wondered whether she'd *ever* been in control of her life. Outside Security, where the corridor met the ring, a small crowd had formed.

"Ari!" Matt turned and, before she knew it, enveloped her in a tight hug. "We did it! We got a lock signal that we can use. There's a viable N-space path."

Regrettably, the hug had to loosen, but he kept his arm around her shoulders as he twisted her around to look at the cluster of people. "Here's our pilot!"

There were cheers and suggestions of celebration as Matt said in her ear, "Meet the new exploration crew of the *Pytheas*." As his arm pulled her against his side, she felt she was coming home to where she belonged—an *impossibility*, for her, for more than sixteen years. Maybe this trouble was worth it, after all.

CHAPTER 20

Shocking, just shocking. We all know, by now, the isolationists stole a TD weapon and intended to use it in
G-145. They wanted to drop out of the civilized galaxy or
go out in a nova. They'd have been successful if not for
the heroics of Major Kedros and Master Sergeant Joyce.
This morning the ICT dropped all charges associated
with the weapon, leaving only the wimpy indictment of
violating the Phaistos Protocols. . . .

—Dr. Net-head Stavros, 2106.064.09.58 UT,
indexed by Heraclitus 12, Democritus 3 under
Conflict, Cause and Effect Imperatives

*A*ren't you afraid? Owen had asked Ariane this morning. *Yes, Owen, I'm frightened. I'm sorry I couldn't admit that to you.* She watched Dr. Lee pick up the Minoan
implant with forceps. It hung in the cool air of the lab and
writhed. She stiffened, her belly feeling like a rock, and
time slowed.

Earlier that morning, Edones had finally called, via encrypted comm. He looked better than when he'd taken
back the *Pilgrimage*; the man seemed to thrive on politics.
Or, perhaps she should consider the sympathetic corollary:
When thousands of human lives hung in the balance, decisions weighed more heavily and sapped his life force. Regardless, he looked his politic and chipper self this morning,
even though he was delivering bad news about the ICT.

"They say there wasn't enough evidence for Article Five

charges of isolating and enslaving a population. But they did rule that Rand and his men are guilty of violations of Article Two, for breaches of the Phaistos Protocols."

"That's nothing to message home about. And the sentences?" She was mildly disappointed and surprisingly overwhelmed by the relief that she wouldn't have to testify again.

"They haven't an 'accord' yet on sentencing, according to SP Duval, who took the brunt of the Feed correspondents' attention. Senator Stephanos is just hanging on for the ride, since he's involved in damage control right now." Edones went on to describe how Myron, with the help of aides for two other senators, had managed to concoct a political struggle around how AFCAW had handled "the G-145 situation." Several senators were realizing they'd become far too dependent upon their staffs for political threat and public opinion assessments.

"What about the bombing attempts? What have you gotten from the lieutenant?" She frowned. The TSF intelligence officer might be able to dig up an old APG-3034, but why?

"We can't connect anyone to the explosives—we're having trouble proving the Terrans knew they were getting data from Myron. The lieutenant's initial story is that she received anonymous tips for the pickups. She won't answer, yet, any questions about her superiors, such as SP Duval." One of Edones's eyebrows twitched; he didn't have to tell her that he wasn't finished with the TSF lieutenant. "As for the explosives, we suspect the grenades were stored in the visitors' hostel on the *Pilgrimage*, but only for a short period of time. Four Terrans selected for the *Pytheas* crew stayed in that hostel. I've sent you their names."

She'd check out those people as soon as she could. Right now, she wanted to know more about Edones's situation. "What harm has Myron done, besides wasting time and attention on this audit? I'm worried that Overlord Six's staff is involved—Joyce told you about my informant, right? Six may have been behind Abram's botched attempt to sever this solar system."

"We won't know the full damage until we look through everything Myron passed on. We've demanded they return the data, but Duval and his staff are being a tad obstructive. I'm hoping the TSF, on its own, will be willing to work with us." Edones grimaced. "The capabilities of the *Bright Crescent* have been compromised, of course. I've ordered an entire overhaul of the ship, but we have to wait until we're at Karthage Point or another depot-level facility. Oh, another caution—there were references to Directorate case files in the data Myron passed—your current mission might have been jeopardized."

"And what about Overlord Six?"

"Hmm. Yes, all leads point to Six, don't they? Who's your informant?"

"Frank Maestrale, an Autonomist who's detained on Beta Priamos for helping Abram." This was a secure session, so there seemed little harm in passing Frank's name. "All he can give us is hearsay. You might want to look over Sergeant Pike's report on the comm traffic as well."

Edones made a note on his slate, then asked the question she'd been dreading. "How's our friend doing?" Even over encrypted comm, he was careful when he referred to Maria.

"Have you seen the crew selections for the *Pytheas*?" After Edones nodded, meaning he knew Maria would be on the crew, she continued. "Everything's on the back burner until we finish the first exploration mission."

"Just remember that we have no funds for relocation—our friend must stay in place."

"That may be a deal-breaker," she said.

Edones shrugged, his face frigid with indifference. *So much for Maria's wishes.* Meanwhile, Edones said, "I suggest you find a way to delay the exploration mission."

"Not so easy. The Minoans are champing at the bit."

His blue eyes became even cooler. "I think they might listen to *your* cautions."

"The TSF security manager, Ensign Walker, has already let me look through everyone's background investigation. All the Terrans look innocuous." Even Maria. Knowing Maria's TEBI background, she'd had a laugh at *that* harmless-looking dossier.

Edones sighed. "You know the Terrans don't have reliable tracking systems. Those investigations are fantasy."

They stared at each other in silence. A strange expression crossed Edones's face; he looked away, and when he focused upon her again, his eyes still seemed remote. "Please, Ariane. Delay the launch. You're risking too much. Besides the possible saboteurs, I've heard you're going to use enhanced piloting drugs and Minoan tech. Is that true?"

The shock of Edones using her first name hit her like a cold shower. She shivered, suddenly recognizing what had briefly shown on his face: worry and fear.

"I can't delay." She tried to talk around the secrets, which was dangerous to do with Edones. "The Minoans have good reasons for this schedule. They've got a slightly better clash for me to use—" She drew a big breath to hide her hesitation. "And they'll be adjusting my body's drug levels through—some equipment."

"Equipment?" His voice was sharp.

"They're, sort of, inserting something under my skin. That's privileged information, per our Minoan supervisor." Although most of Parmet's staff, and only Gaia knew who else, were aware of the implants.

He blew his breath out in exasperation. "I can tell you've made up your mind and you're hell-bent on doing this. You're always so—so—"

"Stubborn?" she said.

"*Self-contained.* Closed."

"That's rather ironic criticism, Owen, coming from you."

"Aren't you afraid?" He looked at her searchingly. "Because you should be."

She couldn't answer. Owen wasn't exactly emoting all over his screen, but she had to wait for him to transform back into the "calculating, manipulating bastard" that she thought she knew, and who had earned Matt's antipathy.

Owen's parting words had been, "Please keep yourself safe." With those words echoing in her head, Ariane watched the Minoan implant struggle against the forceps.

"This is a new implant that Contractor Director says is tweaked, based upon the test results we gave them." Lee looked dubiously at the yellow and green implant, then at Ariane. "Last chance to back out."

Ariane sat at the lab bench, her left arm extended flat over the bench top. Specialist Dimitriou, who was now working full time for Dr. Lee, had carefully injected the chemical marker between the sheath of the brachial artery and the triceps in her upper arm. Likewise, tiny amounts of marker had been put on the input and output points of her drug implant, located on and under the skin of her inner forearm. Dimitriou held a cauterizing scalpel hovering over the anesthetized inner part of her elbow, ready to make a longitudinal cut for entry of the Minoan implant.

Impulsively, she held out her free hand, remembering how the implant had wrapped around her thumb. "Let me hold it."

"I hope you know what you're doing. We can't chase this all around the station," Lee muttered. She dropped the struggling fibrous thing into Ariane's hand, where it wrapped itself around her wrist and then wove through her fingers, almost lovingly.

"Do it." She nodded at Dimitriou and looked away.

She didn't feel the scalpel cut, but she saw it well enough when she turned back. Holding the implant over the incision, she hoped it would "know" what to do. Indeed, it slid into her arm, causing a strange sensation that abruptly stopped.

She waited several minutes. "Well. I don't feel any different."

Lee and Dimitriou leaned over her arm, inspecting it. Dimitriou said, "The incision looks like it's closing by itself."

The implant shifted and she felt a wave of nausea. She turned away from Dimitriou and suddenly vomited. "Sorry," she said as she coughed. "I didn't consider the 'ick' factor."

Then she fell backward off the stool. Dimitriou caught her, as she saw his worried face fade to gray.

When she woke up, she found Dimitriou had put her on the patient bed in the corner of the lab and was hooking her implant—her normal Autonomist-designed one—to a monitor. She tried to sit up.

"Hey, be careful. Let's see how you're doing first," he said, pushing her back.

Matt came running into the lab, followed by David Ray. "Is she okay? What happened?" They circled her bed anxiously before Lee calmed them down.

"Don't worry, her vitals look good." Lee turned back to the displays.

Ariane watched David Ray watch Lee, and sympathized with the older man. He was worried, but tried not to show it as he hoped his familiar Lee would return. This was a different Lee; the spark was gone. Every once in a while, she shied away from a shadow or flinched suddenly, with no provocation. The medics said that deep emotional memories of her attack remained, even if she had no sensory or narrative memories of the event. In a sense, Lee had lost her confidence, but had no idea why.

"If you're ready, Ms. Kedros, we'll do a few tests," Dimitriou said.

"Let's go."

First, they did the standard pilot clash-resilience tests. With these tests, they'd compare her responses against the averages and assess her required dose—which would be high, because her ultra-fast metabolism processed it quicker than normal. Like any N-space pilot, she hated the standard eye response and attention tests, as well as feeling of the clash when she wasn't in N-space.

Clash was the name pilots gave the cognitive dissonance enhancement drug. It kept N-space terrors at bay by dulling the pilot's emotional response and helping maintain "distance," while keeping her reflexes sharp and thoughts clear. After transitioning to real-space, she was always hypersensitive and irritable, every sound and sight seemed to have jagged edges. Clash, however, was well worth the bother; it kept the pilot sane and had no lasting effects. The removed and distant N-space pilot who was unable to empathize was a v-play stereotype, claimed every medical trial report. *Hmm*. Those reports did nothing to quell the conspiracy theories about clash on net-think. *No worries here; I've harmed my body more with alcohol and recreational drugs than with anything I've taken for work*. After all, she was already the result of a medical experiment, that classified military rejuv—

"We're starting the enhanced clash, so go through it again." Dr. Lee's voice, small but clear in her implant, grabbed her attention. She acknowledged and performed the same tests again, under the enhanced clash designed by the Minoans. She didn't feel the same pressured feeling behind her eyelids but otherwise, the Minoan clash felt about the same.

Trying to rub away the sharpness in her head, she heard concerned murmurs over at the display bench. She unhooked the leads from her implant—her Autonomous one—and decided to internally call the Minoan implant a *parasite* to differentiate it from all the other subcutaneous Autonomous equipment in her body. "Parasite" made sense, didn't it? At her spiteful thought, it stirred and she had momentary nausea.

"What's the problem?" She walked up behind everyone and looked at the graphs. All showed early and precipitous drops in drug concentration. This was more than an ultrarapid metabolic response. Lee sat to one side, frowning and scrolling through a document. The others turned to face Ariane.

"You need to keep higher levels of clash in your bloodstream," Matt gestured at the graphs. "It looks like the Minoan implant will *prevent* you from piloting N-space."

"Perhaps we need the conditions of N-space to test my little parasite."

Matt's face turned pasty. "Dropping into N-space, without knowing whether the clash will kick in—"

Lee yelped, "Hah! She's got it right."

Turning to survey the three men, Lee added tartly,

"Those responses were what the Minoan manual said would happen. It looks like only the women in this room have got Gaia's common sense."

Now *that* sounded like the old Lee. Ariane smiled. The others followed suit and David Ray smiled so widely, he showed teeth.

Lee looked at them suspiciously and snapped, "Why are you all standing about and grinning? We have work to do if we're getting this launch off the ground—metaphorically speaking."

Isrid looked at the forty view ports of faces on the wall in front of him, one for every member of the *Pytheas* crew, and sighed. Sometimes he regretted the end of the war; otherwise, he could pump everybody full of drugs and interrogate them. "Let's go through them again, but not through their superficial background records. This time—no holds barred—we identify *who* knows *what* about *whom*."

"Yes, SP." Maria Guillotte and Ensign Walker nodded, although Walker double-checked the secure status display on the tabletop in front of him. Isrid approved. *A survivor, if he continues to pay attention to details.*

"Start with the auxiliary members who'll be near the buoy," Isrid added.

Walker displayed two more view ports to the side, under a label of "Aether's Touch." The faces belonged to Mr. Matthew Journey and Dr. Myrna Fox Lowry, who would be controlling the bot that ended up being their exclusive interface to the buoy, as well as relaying comm through to the Builders' solar system.

"From the top and no holds barred," she said with a warning glance at Walker. "Ariane Kedros, which we know isn't her original name, is the N-space pilot chosen by the Minoans. I'm using her as the central starting point. The Minoans say she's the key to a successful N-space drop, because she's using their enhanced drugs and tech. I also suspect most of the security risks for this mission are related to her."

Maria didn't add, *because Kedros helped detonate the*

weapon at Ura-Guinn sixteen years ago, since Isrid had used the highest TEBI restriction he could on that information. That was part of his agreement with Kedros, for getting control of the leases on G-145. Walker knew about the involuntary and unpleasant ride Kedros had upon Isrid's ship, but he couldn't know why.

"Yes, everything connects to her." Isrid stared at Kedros's official portrait, with which he was so familiar. It showed a waiflike face with sharp cheekbones and loose curls framing dark eyes that held tormented knowledge. A true *Destroyer of Worlds*, as the Minoans had named her.

"The entire crew has now met Ms. Kedros, but here are the people who might have had some connection to her *before* the *Pytheas* entered the system."

About half the view ports became highlighted, showing people who knew the civilian Kedros before G-145 was opened, or had met her during Abram's takeover. Ensign Walker immediately homed in on the one exception.

"What's the connection between Dalton Lengyel, the mission commander, and Kedros?" Walker frowned. "I don't remember reading anything in his background that connected him to her."

"That's marked TEBI-Restricted." Maria looked at Isrid. "However, my research indicates that Lengyel himself might not be aware of the connection, so I doubt it's relevant."

Walker raised his eyebrows, but said nothing.

"We could concentrate on who knows Kedros's history." Maria tapped a command and three view ports became highlighted: hers, Journey's, and Lowry's. She made the Martian patois sign for *frustration*, and added, "There's our problem. We're looking for someone who'll be on the *Pytheas*, and it looks like I'm the only suspect."

"Let's try this differently." Walker tapped for control of the displays. "Let's assume that Kedros's background is common knowledge. If so, who'd want her dead or harmed?"

Maria snorted and Isrid said, "Better light up every Terran. That's half the crew—by design. And since we don't keep a tenth of the data the Autonomists do, all Terran backgrounds are suspect. That's too many threats to monitor."

Walker held up a cautionary finger. "But let's apply a *familiarity* factor. They say 'familiarity breeds contempt,' but it also blunts the passions. Many of you who now know Kedros—as a real human being—are less likely to fly into a vengeful rage. Am I right?"

Maria sneered, while Isrid returned to contemplating Kedros's face. Walker was right. Isrid had known he wouldn't kill Kedros from the moment he saw her loyalty to her commanders, new and old, even under torture. At the time, he couldn't admit he *admired* the fact that Nathan couldn't break her.

"If we remove Terrans who have worked with her or might thank her for being saved from Abram's weapon, we end up with fewer people upon whom to focus." Walker tapped and only nine faces remained.

Isrid stared at those faces, but he'd spent hours already going over any video and photographs, trying to see if he recognized Nathan in any of them. Unfortunately, appearance was meaningless, particularly through cam-eyes. Don't like the texture or color of your hair or skin? Salons had both temporary and permanent fixes for that, as well as the ability to hide, change, or create birthmarks. Don't like the color of your eyes? The possible changes ran from full-fledged transplants to injected dyes to thin, difficult-to-detect contacts. Shape of eyes? Facial features? Plastic surgery had advanced, even on Terran worlds, to perfection. Weight could be changed and height could be fudged, given the nebulous Terran records. However, one thing that wasn't as easy to hide, even by those knowing *somaural* projection, was muscle memory and unconscious body language. That was why he and Maria had looked through hours of ComNet video collected though the newly installed nodes on the station, hoping to catch a glimpse of Nathan—but to no avail.

Perhaps Nathan wasn't here, but Isrid couldn't prove he was anywhere else, either, after searching through Terran governmental records. Nathan had vanished. The Autonomists would say he was "out of crystal," although they were referring to the act of avoiding ComNet records.

"SP, Colonel Edones of the AFCAW Directorate of Intelligence wishes to speak with you, face-to-face," Walker said.

"Clear the displays," Isrid said.

Ensign Walker did so, and then let Edones's call through by dropping the privacy shield. The wall displayed the head and shoulders of Colonel Edones, whom Isrid considered the most dangerous intelligence controller in AFCAW. Unfortunately, and perhaps by intent, the view port didn't display Edones's lower arms or hands, which would have given Isrid a *somaural* reading advantage.

"Glad to finally meet you, SP Parmet," Edones said. "Greetings, Ms. Guillotte and Ensign Walker."

Maria returned a cold nod. Edones had connected to a conference room that contained several people, so the node automatically gave him multiple views of the room. This was something Autonomists expected, but Terrans had to think twice about, so Isrid was relieved he'd cleared the displays.

"Likewise, Colonel. How may I help you?" Isrid asked.

"I have information for your security. These four Terrans stayed in the *Pilgrimage* Hostel A, in a room that also held explosives within the past ten days."

Walker nodded and displayed the list, bringing up photo and records. They were, indeed, three men and a woman who were on the crew of the *Pytheas*. Latecomers to G-145, they were also among the nine Terrans who hadn't ever worked with Kedros.

"There's no proof any of these people carried explosives onto the *Pilgrimage*," continued Edones. "But someone's baggage inside that hostel contained explosives. Unfortunately, nonresidents also stored luggage inside that room."

"This may be helpful, Colonel. Thank you," Ensign Walker said.

"For the next topic, SP, I'd like to speak with you privately."

"Certainly." Isrid dismissed the others with a hand signal.

Maria stood up with composed movement, but her gaze lingered on Colonel Edones. As Parmet watched her walk out, he remembered another list, more distasteful, that Dr. Istaga wanted him to keep in mind.

Edones cleared his throat. "I hope you're devoting resources to protecting Ariane Kedros, SP. Her safety is paramount to the success of this exploration mission, which I suspect is a test."

"A test? By the Minoans?"

Edones's eyes narrowed at his tone of false naiveté. "What better way to test Pax Minoica than to dangle a solar system full of goodies and see who behaves themselves?"

"You think the Minoans are waiting for one of our governments to take over."

"They left their warship sitting in this system." Edones shrugged.

"We're committed to the cooperative research programs here at Priamos."

"Nice statement, but how far does your royal 'we' extend? To other Overlord staffs?" Edones glanced downward with his frigid eyes, and then returned to making eye contact. "Ensign Walker will be receiving some news about a surprise arrival to this system. Don't be too hard on him; our TSF source was blindsided as well."

His Terran Space Force source? Isrid saw a square brighten on the table surface in front of him.

"You'll want to take that," Edones said. "I'll wait."

Isrid put Edones's call on hold. He was irritated, but his *somaural* skills allowed him to appear unruffled as he shut off the cam-eyes in the room. Once he had no witnesses, he jabbed the smooth surface that looked like a red blinking button. "Yes, Ensign?"

"The TLS *Ming Adams*, under Soussen Port Command, is docking with the *Pilgrimage III*. Sorry for the late notice, SP. We should have been told as soon as it dropped into real-space, but even Lieutenant Tyler wasn't given appropriate notice—she's been confined to the *Pilgrimage* and SP Duval won't take her calls." Walker's voice was tense.

"Get me all the information you can on that ship and why it's here. I don't like playing catch-up with the Directorate's golems. Send an immediate recall to the *Percival*. I want them back at this station, using best speed."

"Yes, SP."

Isrid composed himself. Walker worked quickly, because a view port opened right beside Edones's image, showing a photo of the TLS *Ming Adams* with specifications. The ship was a frigate, like the Defender-class TLS *Percival*, but was a lighter and older Atlantic-class ship with less advanced weapons.

What is Duval doing? When Isrid looked at the ship specifications, he realized Duval might have violated their tonnage limitations set in the Status of Forces agreement with the Pilgrimage line. Of course, that depended upon what weapon loads the ship was carrying, which Duval wasn't likely to reveal. The tonnage limitations in that SOF agreement were the source of Edones's problem as well. His AFCAW Fury-class cruiser, the *Bright Crescent*, had longer range, better armor, and more brute firepower than the Terran frigates, but that extra tonnage meant he couldn't call in anything more than a corvette if he wanted to stay within the Status of Forces agreement.

"Caught up now?" Edones gave him a perfunctory smile when taken off hold. "I see you weren't forewarned about the *Ming Adams*."

Although it was obvious, Isrid wouldn't own up to being unprepared. "Why aren't you asking SP Duval about the ship, since it's out of his district?"

"Oh, I will, after he's finished answering Commander Meredith's questions. I hoped to first have a civilized and informative conversation with you."

"Flattery won't get you anywhere, Colonel."

"No insincere praise intended, I assure you," Edones said blandly. "I just wanted to check, as of this moment, whether you thought Pax Minoica was still in force."

"Would I say anything *but* 'yes,' with a Minoan warship in the system?" Isrid responded, just as dispassionately.

"But, can a State Prince push the Terran Space Forces in

his or her district? Duval can't order the crew of the *Ming Adams* to violate Terran treaties, correct?" Even though Edones tried to hide it, this was the crux of his call.

Isrid looked at the other view port, where Walker was displaying data, estimates, and intelligent guesses. The *Ming Adams* was indeed docking at the *Pilgrimage*. Ensign Walker, perhaps with the assistance of his superior on the *Pilgrimage*, Lieutenant Tyler, was estimating the armament, weapons load, and crew. As Isrid noted the crew composition, his heart sank and he figured Lieutenant Tyler was the one who had warned Edones. Tyler and Walker estimated regular TSF makeup at less than ten percent. The remaining crew members were classified as "local irregulars," which meant different things to different Overlords.

"The TSF won't violate a treaty unless they receive an order validated by the entire League membership." Isrid made sure he sounded confident.

"What if Duval's Overlord makes unilateral decisions?"

"Then I would need instructions from my Overlord." Isrid could outbland Edones forever if he needed to. There was silence as they eyed each other.

"I'm disappointed, SP. You know how long it would take to get decisions from your Overlord's staff. I had hoped you'd commit to protecting this expedition, and Pax Minoica." Edones's eyes became colder, which didn't seem possible. "I think you'd better recall the TLS *Percival* from its patrol, because you might need it."

"Until we speak again, Colonel." *Which might be sooner than you think*, Isrid thought as he signed off.

Ensign Walker came back in, once he saw the call had finished. "Maria had to leave. They're doing a test drop with the *Pytheas*."

"Can the *Ming Adams* reach us, or the *Pytheas*, before the exploration drop?" That was the important thing to remember about space: It was *big*. Big enough to prevent surprise moves at sub-light speeds, that is.

Walker's face paled as he realized what Isrid implied. "Depends upon what they're doing at the *Pilgrimage*, and how much crew rest they take."

"Call Officer Zheng. I want your people working tightly with my civilian security staff. I want redundant comm through command post, with twenty-four-hour coverage and a Feed into this room, starting now. I want scenarios plotted out with timelines, taking into account all players and pieces. I'm going to speak with SP Duval, but I don't expect to get any answers."

Ensign Walker nodded. He knew the players and pieces to plot: the *Pilgrimage*, Beta Priamos Station, the two buoys, TLS *Percival*, *Bright Crescent*, *Pytheas*, *Aether's Touch*, TLS *Ming Adams*, and what should never be forgotten, the shadow-wrapped Minoan warship.

The N-space test drop went like a dream. Ariane had positioned the *Pytheas* in the farthest corridor from the Minoan buoy, only a couple of hours from Beta Priamos Station, at the exploration ship's best speed—which was considerable. The *Pilgrimage* had issued them a key for the short N-space trip. As usual, the "briefest" estimated N-space transit from G-145 had no relationship to the "closest" solar system via real-space. The *Pytheas* dropped to Ephesus Point, a habitat in the quiet New Ionian solar system.

"That's the easiest nous-transit I've ever made," Ariane said, as soon as Maria opened her eyes. This was also a chance to test the systems that commanded the crew's implants to put bright into their bloodstreams.

"Good—rail guns online!" Maria snapped, looking over her console and starting her checklists.

"Chaff ready to deploy. How's our targeting systems?" asked Dalton from the seat behind them. He sounded like Brandon had, sixteen years ago.

Ariane sat quietly while Maria, Dalton, and the engineering team ran through checklists and scenarios designed to avoid whatever might come at them when they entered the Builders' system. When they were done, she said, "I don't see why I couldn't operate one of the sensors or weapons."

"Just because this drop was easy, doesn't mean you'll react the same to damaged N-space," Dalton said absently, as he checked the status of all stations.

She turned and watched the back of Dalton's head with a smile and a touch of melancholy, thinking of Brandon, until she realized Maria was watching *her*. She cleared her throat and displayed the results from her implant, saying, "I'll have Dr. Lee look at this, but I think the enhanced clash worked quite well."

"Certainly," Maria murmured, turning back to her console.

The shakedown of drop procedures went well. They docked at Ephesus Point for four hours of crew rest and extended diagnosis of ship systems. They then undocked and returned to G-145.

One of the more unpleasant parts of N-space piloting, for Ariane, was the transition to real-space. She usually had intense nausea coming off the high clash dose and as she moved into real-space, she had to get reacquainted with her senses. This was when light, sound, touch, smell, and taste seemed too intense and unpleasant for her brain to process. But the combination of the enhanced clash, her metabolism, and perhaps her friendly parasite, made her feel almost normal. Maybe this new clash could help other N-space pilots.

"I'll check in with CP." Maria had come off the D-tranny, and now had bright being pumped in by her implant. She chatted with Beta Priamos Command Post while Dalton did a systems check.

Even though Dalton and Maria were qualified to pilot in real-space, Ariane put the *Pytheas* on docking approach, using the S-DATS information.

"That's odd," Maria said quietly. "Command Post just moved our departure up, giving us a green light for tomorrow morning at oh-six-hundred hours."

"Woo-hoo! I'm ready." Dalton's exuberance was infectious.

Ariane smiled as he announced their departure time over the ship intercom. But, as she glanced at Maria in the copilot seat, she sternly reminded herself that someone on this ship had a different agenda.

CHAPTER 21

Remember that ICT in G-145? I know, yesterday's news
is old news for net-rats, *but* ... did you see the snag
they ran into with the sentencing? The Terran member,
State Prince Duval, has demanded custody of the prisoners, which doesn't sit well with half our Senate. Angry
rhetoric directed at Overlord Six ...

—Dr. Net-head Stavros, 2106.067.11.24 UT,
indexed by *Heraclitus 21* under Conflict Imperative

"Good luck, Ari, To quote St. Darius, 'May you be
always shielded from the solar wind, but avail
yourself of its power.'" Matt's voice wasn't compressed
and processed by relays, because *Aether's Touch* was close
enough to see on her real-space view, hovering within a ki-
lometer of the Builders' buoy. Matt and Dr. Lowry would
be there for this entire mission, which they all hoped would
be completed within seventy-two hours.

"Thanks, Matt. I've double-checked the lock signal
you're transmitting. It looks good and this is last voice
transmission before drop. *Pytheas* out."

"See you in a day or so. *Aether's Touch* out."

This was the time she loved, when systems were shut
down and she was truly *alone* on the ship. Most people
couldn't handle a solitude where they couldn't call someone using their implants and the nearest node couldn't be
activated with an emergency call. But when a ship dropped
out of real-space, one human mind had to stay awake and

strangely enough, only one. Multiple minds could lose the ship.

Surprisingly, she felt no more anxiety than for a normal N-space drop and her attitude had rubbed off on Matt and other crew members, to good effect. This was familiar ground and her checklists reinforced that feeling. Before switching off crew status, she ran through the names and readouts from their implants. No one could be awake or cognizant under those amounts of D-tranny. The Minoans had insisted that all passengers take excessively strong doses because of the possible effects from damaged N-space. Beside her in the copilot seat, Maria was webbed in, her body loose with sleep—or an enforced half sleep, if her body tried to rebel. Likewise, Dalton was webbed into the mission command chair behind her.

Selecting the suspicious four names provided by Edones, she double-checked their doses. She had no doubt they were under, particularly after the warnings the Minoans had given them regarding N-space psychosis and how the damaged N-space "fabric" could be worse. Two men and one woman were on the mission crew, while the last of the "suspicious four" was an engineer. She'd met them, pored over their backgrounds, and watched Ensign Walker put them through additional interviews. SP Parmet and Maria had also observed the subtle interrogation designed by Walker. If one of these four was behind the bombings on the *Pilgrimage*, he or she was an incredibly adept actor.

She shut down all the systems requiring sequential Neumann processors and verified the licensing crystal was in the augmented Penrose Fold referential engine. Then she let her webbing wiggle tight and checked her clash levels as a matter of habit. That wasn't necessary, she reminded herself, because her friendly parasite was monitoring things now.

The twitching heartbeat signal, the evidence of a valid lock signal from a buoy, displayed on her console. The estimated drop time, which the Minoans said might not be accurate, was five hours. For her, the transit might feel short, or it could feel agonizingly long.

She put on a visor that was an imitation of v-play equipment, although it only displayed unprocessed external cam-eye circuits. Leaning back, she put one hand on the N-space control and sent the drop command to the referential engine.

She felt the familiar feeling of slipping into a pool of oil and losing sensation. For her, N-space piloting felt like steering a sensory deprivation tank through a shark-infested canyon with nebulous terrors hiding in shadowy vortices. The test drop had been good, meaning she'd felt insulated from the nightmarish storms she saw in N-space. This was different.

The navigational "path" is different for every pilot, but it's usually obvious. Not this time—*Gaia, where's the path? There?* She dodged flashes and discharges of energy. Usually those were encased within shadows. She never peered into the maelstroms, because faces would appear and hungry flickers of energy could reach out, but this time she was *inside* the storms. Struggling not to panic, she tried to steer along the dark thread of a trail.

Isrid watched the track of the TLS *Ming Adams*.

"They're following their filed flight plan," Ensign Walker said again.

"I know, but after taking on those prisoners, why would they want to head out to this station? We all know they have no reason to check on the alien buoy." Isrid didn't add: *And Duval isn't taking my calls.* That might sound trivial or even juvenile to Walker, but it was the most troubling indicator of all. The League was heavy with overhead, which meant it had an oversupply of bureaucrats that justified their positions through talk, talk, and more talk. Politics could only form through discourse. When the talking stopped, when a bureaucrat refused to jaw about himself or herself, that was the time to start worrying.

"The Directorate is obviously suspicious," murmured Walker.

Isrid nodded, watching the FTL data. Shortly after the *Ming Adams* had filed their abbreviated flight plan and abruptly undocked from the *Pilgrimage*, the *Bright Crescent* had done exactly the same. Using top boost, the *Ming Adams* should be able to stay ahead of the *Bright Crescent*, which was heavier but had more firepower. Surprisingly, the *Ming Adams* was letting the AFCAW cruiser gain to within a couple hundred kilometers. Isrid looked to the other side of the diagram, where he could see his station (*his* station?) connected to the Priamos moon, and orbiting the gas giant Laomedon. Coming round that gravity well was the TLS *Percival*, starting its braking and hell-bent for Beta Priamos.

Across the table, Zheng looked at his slate. "SP, there's a Dr. Istaga who's demanding to enter. He insists he needs to speak with you, face-to-face."

Walker looked inquiringly at Isrid, with caution obvious in his eyes, even if he didn't use *somaural* signals. It appeared that Walker knew Istaga was more than he seemed.

"Blank all the displays. Then let him in." Everyone complied: Zheng, his female security compatriot, Ensign Walker, and his petty officer, with such a smooth scrubbed face that everyone wondered if he met the TSF age requirements when he enlisted.

"SP, thanks for seeing me." Dr. Istaga hurried in, but his glance was sharp and he'd left his soft academician voice behind. This was Andre, unvarnished.

"Yes?"

To answer, Andre used quick Martian patois in *somaural* signals. He did it all with his left hand and arm, the one that couldn't be seen by the others in the room. *Important news. May require unilateral decisions. Can you trust your TSF?*

Isrid hesitated. The problem with a federated force, like the Terran Space Forces, was what to do when the leadership fissioned—so to speak—and splatted everywhere. Whose orders should they follow? On paper, the TSF was here to support SP Isrid Sun Parmet, but under contradictory orders, there was always a small chance that Ensign Walker would abandon him. Of course, that was why some

SPs relied upon irregular militia, even though they were little better than mercenaries.

"Go ahead. We all need to hear the news." He made a sign that Andre should continue, although the flash in the master spy's eyes told him that his decision was unwise. However, Isrid had learned much during his leadership of TEBI. One point was that loyalty could often be bought by trust, and the corollary was that if he showed distrust toward Walker, he increased his chances of losing the TSF.

"Very well." Andre's voice was clipped. "My source says a declaration of war, upon our Overlord Three, just arrived from Overlord Six."

There was stunned silence. Then the young petty officer whispered, "What does that mean?"

"It means civil war," Zheng's assistant replied, before her wide eyes moved to Zheng, then Isrid. He knew his civilian security would always look to him for command. But would the TSF?

"SP, we have no idea how Three will respond—it may not be civil war that spouts from the multiheaded creature that's our Overlord and staff. At our level, we may only see a change of policy." Andre spoke quickly. "You must tread carefully, SP, until you get guidance."

"When would that be?" Ensign Walker asked sharply.

"Hours, maybe a day—"

Isrid cut off Andre and turned to Walker. "There will be a lag while the highest members of the staff consult with the Overlord. However, as Assistant for the Exterior, I'll be at the top of the message list, once they've drafted a response."

Ensign Walker calmly met his gaze. "And until then, SP? What will you do?"

Again, Walker rose in his estimation. *Most TSF officers have been prepared for this moment, but as a bureaucrat, I'm on my own.* Isrid said, "I'll honor my prior commitments to running this station and supporting an interstellar exploration mission. Any use of Terran Space Forces or TSF weapons will be considered exactly as they would have been yesterday; all in support of Pax Minoica. Are you with me, Ensign?"

"Yes, sir." Walker snapped back the reply, and the petty officer beside him straightened unconsciously.

"Raise the threat-ready level for the operational crew on-station and notify the *Percival*. However, *no one*, repeat, *no one* is to take action, even defensively, without my approval."

"But what about the exploration mission?" Andre pushed forward, his eyes wide and his face flushed. "You can take control, SP, or order the Autonomist commander replaced. You should press for an advantage right now."

Before anyone else added their advice, Isrid raised his hand and signaled for quiet. He watched Andre's face, remembering how the master spy thrived during wartime. He also recalled phrases from field commanders, such as "loose cannon" and "uncontrollable," being thrown about with Andre's name.

"What *should* we tell the exploration team?" Zheng asked.

"Nothing," Isrid said. "That includes all the R and D teams on Beta Priamos and Priamos. There's nothing they can do, anyway, so let them work in peace."

Ensign Walker and Isrid both looked at Andre, who tried to forestall what was coming. "SP, any decision you make could be permanently attributed to you, or merely blamed upon a faceless committee or group. You need me *here* as advisor, for your protection."

"I'll accept the responsibility, thank you, but I'll need to keep you incommunicado for a while, for *your* protection." Isrid smiled. "And Ensign Walker, make sure your security personnel institute full chemical protection protocols, to protect against multicomponent poisons."

Andre sighed as two tough-looking TSF guards appeared in response to Walker's call. Looking at Isrid, he shrugged and said, "Exactly what I would do. Bravo, SP."

He was quickly transitioning to Dr. Istaga as he walked out between them.

*   *   *

"I'm going to catch a few hours of sleep," Dr. Lowry told Matt. "Nothing's happening for a while, but wake me if we get surprised."

Matt nodded as she left the control deck, wishing he could address her as Myrna, but she was so formal. He certainly hoped they weren't surprised and everything happened the way they *trusted* it would. That was the whole problem: They had to put their faith in experiments and alien assurances. The Minoans had run experiments against the bot-plus-Builders' buoy and proclaimed that there *was* an operating buoy at the other end and that it would probably carry comm and provide a lock signal. If not, the Minoans provided some equipment, that *they just happened to have lying around*, which could relay comm and *maybe* coax a lock signal from the buoy on the Builders' end. *So . . . this is all going to work, right?* He was asked to believe this, coming from aliens who refused to take the risk of traveling themselves.

He stood and stretched. Ruffling his short hair, he wondered how they had managed to get this far, based on Minoan smoke and mirrors. And why was he getting jitters *now*, after he had watched the *Pytheas* drop out of real-space? Maybe he was just worried about Ari and the others.

His glance fell on the small FTL data diagram of G-145. Once the *Pilgrimage* had installed more buoy relays, the faster-than-light data coverage was good over most parts of the solar system. He frowned, seeing more symbols and movement than he expected. He tapped the console to enlarge it and translate call signs to ship names. The *Pilgrimage* was still near the system buoy. Leaving the *Pilgrimage*, heading vaguely toward Beta Priamos, was the TLS *Ming Adams*, followed by the *Bright Crescent*. Their headings were unclear when Matt eyeballed the diagram, but when he ran the vectors, those ships were heading toward his ship and the Builders' buoy, *not* the station.

There was movement near Laomedon and Priamos as well. The TLS *Percival*, on a patrol that *should* have positioned it far on the other side of the gas giant Laomedon, was streaking toward Priamos and the Beta Priamos Station. He whistled; "streaking" wasn't an exaggeration. It looked like all three military ships were either at full boost or full braking, and that wasn't just disquieting; it was frightening.

Time to call Diana, who was probably on the *Bright Crescent*. He waited for either an answer or her queue, but finally got the response, "Unable to complete call. If you wish to leave a message on station *Pilgrimage*, please . . ."

Matt recorded a simple statement like, "Diana, please call me," but for a different purpose. He then commanded a reverse trace of the package he had just sent, including a download of the routing table. He examined it, frowning.

The call had been correctly routed through two inner-system relays between him and the *Bright Crescent*, but the message didn't make the final hop to the ship. The errors indicated transmission failure or interference, causing the call to be rerouted back through a relay to the *Pilgrimage*. He called Beta Priamos Command Post, asking for security, and was quickly transferred to Ensign Walker.

"What, for Gaia's sake, is going on with the *Ming Adams* and the *Bright Crescent*?" Matt demanded.

"Mr. Journey." Ensign Walker seemed uncertain and looked to his right, out of Matt's view. The ensign was in a big room, and there seemed to be movement about him, perhaps of other people. Colorful graphs and displays were on the bulkheads, but Matt's view port didn't show them clearly.

State Prince Parmet stepped into cam-eye range, causing it to refocus. He stood half a head taller than the ensign. "May I help you, Mr. Journey?"

"Certainly, SP." Matt dialed back his smart-ass setting. He didn't like Parmet because of what he had done to Ari, but it wouldn't be wise to offend the State Prince—in this situation. "Perhaps you should tell me why the *Ming Adams* is boosting toward me at top speed, and why it seems to be jamming my messages to the *Bright Crescent*."

Parmet had a face of stone, but Ensign Walker didn't. He raised his eyebrows and looked impressed, perhaps of Matt's assessment, or of Matt's audacious tone.

Parmet paused, appearing to weigh options. Finally, he said, "Ostensibly, the TLS *Ming Adams* is here in G-145 to take custody of the isolationists and transport them to New Sousse. Two hours ago, they left the *Pilgrimage* with this station filed as their destination."

"They're a little off course," Matt said. "And what about the jamming?"

"In their flight plan, the *Ming Adams* stated a deviation to collect data on the alien buoy. As for their active jamming, perhaps they're using the recent compromise of the *Bright Crescent* as a way to tell them to back off." If Parmet was trying to calm Matt down, he was failing. Matt noted the language—why refer to "they" and "them" when speaking about another League ship's crew? Why use the patronizing tone, as if speaking of obvious fabrications? Unfortunately, Parmet seemed to know no more about the crew's intent than Matt.

As for the "compromise" of Edones's ship, Matt had gotten the gist of what happened from Diana. The Terrans had taken a gander at ship specifications, and might have reverse-engineered security algorithms that did everything from comm frequency hopping to missile-avoidance flight patterns. What Parmet didn't point out was that *Edones would rather suffer active jamming of his comm than let his ship fall too far behind the faster Terran ship.* Now *that* was scary.

"Remember, there's a Minoan warship sitting near the *Pilgrimage*," Walker added. "We're watching the situation carefully, and nobody's gone into Minoan-provoking behavior. For instance, boarding actions would indicate piracy, unless accompanied by a declaration—"

Parmet put his hand on Ensign Walker's shoulder, gently shutting him up. Matt glanced at the FTL diagram, which now had vector information about the ships. The *Bright Crescent* was a cruiser, and it was barely keeping up with the *Ming Adams*, which was a lighter and faster frigate. Of course, the frigate could continue to jam all comm going in and out of both ships. That would be the equivalent of a tantrum-prone kid stuffing fingers into his ears and humming, refusing to listen to reason.

Matt frowned and said, "I see you've recalled the TLS *Percival*. You're responsible for the security of Beta Priamos station and its occupants, SP; did you decide your ship might be needed?"

"There's an old adage that says no one may listen to you unless you're carrying a big stick." Parmet paused, looking intently at Matt. "For instance, a club or weapon. In whatever's happening between those ships, I want my voice to be heard."

In whatever's happening between those ships. Matt's stomach tightened as he thought of Diana. However, he had the *Pytheas* to think about; its thin thread of communication back to human civilization hung on a fragile bot clinging to this buoy and a second-wave *weaponless* prospecting ship. The Builders' buoy, like the Minoans' buoys, would withstand all sorts of weapons fire, but not the bot or *Aether's Touch*.

"What about my ship and our interface to the *Pytheas*? We're sitting ducks out here." Matt clenched his teeth and felt his jaw muscles bulge.

"Are you asking me for protection, Mr. Journey?" Parmet became almost deathly still.

Matt checked the FTL display again. In solar-system distances, nothing happened quickly. The TLS *Percival* was a newer type of League frigate and might get to his position within six hours. That could beat the *Ming Adams*.

He took a deep breath and hoped he wouldn't regret this. "Yes, SP, I'm formally requesting protection."

This was like no other nous-transit Ariane had experienced. Usually, there were indications when you approached your destination and here's where all pilots agreed: Minoan buoys looked the same in N-space as they did in real-space and you steered toward them before initiating the drop into real-space.

But Ariane saw no buoy, no artificial structure. Instead, there appeared to be a rending or tear in the darkness ahead. There was bright, piercing light and she hesitated. Should she push the ship through? Behind the light, she thought she saw a huge rounded form. She drove the ship forward and squinted at the light, through which there was obviously a solar system. She pressed the switch to dissolve the Penrose Fold and drop into real-space.

She would have screamed if she could have handled the noise. Instead of the gradual unpleasant transition, her body's nervous system was promptly battered by input. Curling into a helpless ball was the only response she could muster. She had more to do after pushing the switch, and her hand flinched from the burning cold of the console as she shut down the referential engine. She slowly began sifting the light, sound, temperature, and pressure through correct sensory paths. The gravity generator must have been turned on—did she do that? The voices were tense; they began to separate, into male and female, rattling off tight but incomprehensible strings of words.

"Incoming kinetic—maneuver—"

"Avoid them—farther away—"

"Need chaff, releasing at—"

"Disable that platform to port before—"

Eventually, the alarms quieted down, as did the voices. Someone asked, "Ariane? Can you hear me?"

She flinched. When the question was repeated, she tried to answer, but only a groan came out. They removed her N-space visor and gave her a drink pack of sweet concentrated juice. She began to feel better. With trembling fingers, she lightly stroked her temples and came away with hair. Obviously, this had been a hard drop.

"You're going to need quite a trim." Maria's face came into view. She was smiling. "But you got us here."

"Wea-weapons?" Ariane's mouth and tongue were still relearning how to speak.

Maria nodded. "Automated weapons platforms for protecting against incoming ships. They did extremely well, for only having solar power for the past couple thousand years. Unfortunately, they damaged one of our antennas before we disabled them—but we can get on fine without it."

"You need sleep, Ariane, but I don't want to send you to quarters before you see this." Dalton leaned over her chair and turned her around to face a view port on the bulkhead. She gasped. She'd seen a lot of planets that supported Gaian-based life, so it wasn't the hovering green-blue-white ball that amazed her, so much as the *thing* that orbited it.

"Yes, it's as big as rocks we've called moons, but no, it's not natural." Maria immediately answered some of her questions, while she zoomed in on the orbiting body. "At least, we can't see how it *can* be natural."

The object couldn't be described with ordinary station structural engineering terms, like wheels, struts, modules, and shielding. From their distance, even given the attempt to enlarge their picture, the object looked like a cracked red egg, with the shell expanding about, and not quite hiding, a glowing green core. Periodically, green light moved along and shot out the longitudinal axis, which paralleled the rotational axis of the planet.

The seed is there. Her Minoan parasite stirred. Ariane tried to sit up and say something, but became dizzy. The N-space drop had affected her more than she realized.

"Don't worry." Dalton smiled. "As soon as we've established a comm relay back home, we're heading toward that station—habitat—object."

"I'll get her to her quarters," Maria said firmly.

She protested, but in the end, Maria had to help her. She nearly couldn't manage the vertical tube descent by herself. Maria opened the hatch to her quarters and helped her step inside.

"Listen carefully," the tall woman said quietly, while holding Ariane upright against her side. "The entire crew is now awake. After I close this hatch, I want you to throw the disablement switch and lock your hatch manually. *Do you understand, Major?*"

"Yes," she gasped. It took almost all her strength to get out that word.

"Good." Maria opened the panel for her and leaned her against the bulkhead. "Don't trust anyone," she said as she closed the hatch behind her.

Ariane pulled the disablement switch and then locked

the hatch, before stepping backward and falling on her bunk. She let the darkness of deep sleep take her.

Matt was watching the FTL data diagram obsessively, and the faint noise coming out of the comm panel nearly caused him to jump out of his skin.

"Calling *Aether's Touch*."

Did he really hear that? He'd been playing music because it had only been three hours since the *Pytheas* had left. He shut off his music and moved closer to the comm panel.

"*Aether's Touch*, this is *Pytheas*. Do you copy?"

He whooped. It *was* Dalton's voice, and *not* his imagination. "Yes, *Pytheas*, I can hear you," he answered eagerly, throwing protocol out the airlock.

"We're here and our N-space pilot is resting. We've suffered minimal damage, which shouldn't stop us. We'll make another comm check in thirty minutes. *Pytheas* out."

"Acknowledged. *Aether's Touch* out."

Before he registered what had happened, Matt realized he'd gone through the first comm check and hadn't even notified Dr. Lowry. Besides that, he hadn't gotten any details—Ari might be resting, but was she really okay? What was in the new solar system, besides a buoy? He called Beta Priamos Command Post to tell them the news, and then woke Dr. Lowry over intercom. She wasn't happy.

"That's impossible!" She was irate as she stepped out of the vertical tube to the control deck, stomping as she walked. Perhaps she was one of those people who was always grouchy after waking from naps. One side of her face had a crease pattern that looked like it came from the piping of her sleeve, although she was now wearing a loose equipment vest over her tight Terran coveralls. "The Minoans said nous-transit would be *five hours*."

"They also said that was an estimate."

Dr. Lowry turned and saw the large FTL data diagram that Matt had left displayed, near the jump seat behind the consoles. She frowned, causing the fading crease to bend as it went by her eye. "What's going on?"

"Oh." Matt didn't want to frighten her, but she should know what was going on. He walked back to the diagram so he could point at the ships between their position and the *Pilgrimage*. "We've got two ships, one from the Terran League and one from AFCAW, that might be involved in some sort of altercation—perhaps even wanting to do something with us, or the Builders' buoy. Don't worry, though, because I called for the *Percival*, which should be here before the others."

Matt's pride over mitigating a dangerous situation evaporated at seeing a stunner in her hand.

"You idiot," she said levelly. "You've ruined everything."

His gut twinged in reflex. He shuffled through his brain in panic for tips on dealing with stunners. The one Dr. Lowry held wasn't a mini-stunner, so it definitely had the range needed for the two meters that yawned between them. *Get as close as you can*, Ari had told him, *because stunners are difficult to use in hand-to-hand.* That sounded good, in theory, but not so much when actually facing a stunner.

"Mayday! Mayday! We've got—" Dalton's voice came suddenly from the comm panel and was cut off.

Matt moved, before he decided to go for the comm panel or for Dr. Lowry, and she pulled the trigger. He *hated* stunners, he thought, as he twitched into unconsciousness.

CHAPTER 22

Although Senator Stephanos has been surprisingly silent, we've got exclusive interviews from his staff regarding the scandal of indicting his own great-nephew, Myron Stephanos Pulnik, for treason. These interviews can't be found anywhere else. . . .

—*Interstellarsystem Events Feed*, 2106.068.12.01 UT,
indexed by *Heraclitus 11* under Conflict Imperative

When Ariane woke, she knew something was wrong. It wasn't the silence, because she knew her quarters would be quiet due to their location. As she started to stir within her webbing she realized what bothered her. The gravity generator was off, which was an unusual situation for a civilian crew.

"*Command:* Lights, slow." The lights came up. She loosened her webbing; she must have dragged it over herself at some point, by instinct.

"*Command:* Call Maria." All she got was Maria's message queue. She remembered the whisper as darkness overtook her: *Don't trust anyone.*

Where was the ship? If they were using boost engines, she shouldn't feel zero gee, unless they were in free fall around a planet. When she'd left the control deck, Dalton had said they were heading toward the egglike station—she felt a jolt of excitement when she thought of visiting it.

As she tapped the bulkhead for a command view port, she noted the time on her sleeve. She'd been asleep about two hours. She felt much better, but as usual after a drop, she was hungry.

Requesting exterior views proved that they'd moved and suddenly there was the object, hanging over the planet. Her breath warmed, her heartbeat quickened, and she felt the blood pound in her neck. *There it is.* The Minoans hadn't been able to describe how the "homing" function would work, but the intense spike of excitement and anticipation she felt whenever she saw the Builders' station was obvious. Her parasite quivered and she knew the seed she had to retrieve was *there.* She fought the impulse to immediately push out of her room and find a way, any way, to get to the station that had the glowing green light at its core.

First, she had to talk to Dalton, the mission commander. She lightly pushed across the room to her hygiene closet and inside found dried ration bars and a drink pack she'd stashed there. Their flavors were pungent, tangy, and tastier than she remembered; the crunchy texture of the bar felt stimulating—something she'd never noticed before.

Glancing in the mirror, she almost didn't recognize herself. Her hair had come off in clumps, mostly on her temples and over her ears. Too bad she didn't have time to get the rest clipped short—her pulse pounded, reminding her. *Hurry, hurry.*

Remembering Maria's caution, she paused at her hatch. She tapped for the intercom and listened. No chatter. She pressed her ear against the hatch, and heard faint clicking. It didn't trigger any memory of ship machinery and every once in a while, there was a disturbing irregularity to it. *Hurry, hurry.*

She unlocked her hatch quietly. Opening it required pushing hard on the frame with one hand while she kept her body close to the heavy hatch as it swung. When it opened, she smelled a strong and familiar metallic odor. Blood. She could almost see the stench riding the air, moving lazily through the corridor, until she felt something dial back her sense of smell. The quivering sensation in her arm made her wonder if the parasite was increasing and decreasing her sensitivities, as necessary. *Hurry.*

After looking around, she floated out into the empty corridor. When she turned to close the hatch, she saw the source of the smell. Bloody handprints covered the access panel, hatch handles, and both the inside and outside of the mechanical disablement panel and pulls. However, since she'd already disabled the door from inside and locked the hatch with steel bolts, whoever had left this panicked, bloody trail couldn't get inside. Were they trying to warn her or harm her?

The scent trail of blood went both ways from her door. Only the N-space pilot and mission commander were housed on this deck; to the right she could climb to the control deck and to the left was the engineering control center, from where she heard that insistent clicking noise. *Hurry, hurry.* She pushed down the nagging urges of the Minoan parasite to get to the alien station. *No. This is important.* She moved down the hall toward engineering, using handholds to control her short movements.

The hatch to the engineering center hung halfway open. Beyond the hatch was darkness. She hesitated, because the first rule for space crew was *secure everything.* The joke was that the second rule was *secure everything again.* Hatches could be secured open or shut—who'd forgotten their most fundamental training? She opened the hatch wide until it fastened to the bulkhead. Leaning in, she asked for lights and recoiled as they came on.

Jonathon Fitzroy, an engineer in the "suspicious four" that Edones had identified, had been garroted so violently that his head floated grotesquely above him. He was against the bulkhead, just opposite the hatch where she stood, and remained hovering there in the zero gee. Pools of blood floated to the side of his head and neck. He'd obviously been killed a meter away from his current position, where there was blood spatter clinging through surface tension to walls. The killer had then moved him out of the way of the consoles.

Although she'd privately viewed Fitzroy with suspicion, he'd seemed friendly and eager to help. Now she felt a spike of sorrow and anger—which suddenly smoothed out to blandness. Was this the parasite again, adjusting hormones and neurochemistry? *Let me feel!* she thought viciously and applied coercion with doubt: *Otherwise, I can't do my mission.* Immediately, sorrow tightened her chest again, but not with the original intensity.

She pushed to the consoles, grabbing a corner. This engineering control center was probably where the gravity generator had been taken off-line. The console was covered with bloody fingerprints. She dragged the command view ports over to the side that was easier to use, but her fingers still ended up with pungent blood on the tips.

Calling up status, she saw that environmental support—specifically, heat and air—had been shut off in the lower levels, where the scientific mission crew worked. She immediately restored life-preserving service throughout the ship, not knowing where people were at the moment. She started the gravity generator up, which would initialize and slowly apply force. She unlocked the interlevel airlocks. She saw the intercoms light up but before she listened in, she saw another problem. No one was responding from control deck.

Carefully, because the gravity generator was going to gradually ramp up to a half gee, she worked her way out of the engineering control center toward the bow, and the control deck. By the time she was going up the vertical tube and open airlock, there was partial gee. The devastation on the control deck had settled, under half gee, by the time she arrived.

Mission Commander Dalton Lengyel's body had crumpled awkwardly, his throat cut military style, by stabbing sideways and pushing the blade outward. He had a defensive cut on his forearm, probably made before his throat was sliced. He'd bled out and died quickly. Maria must have been on duty in the copilot and sensor seat, but there was no sign of her. However, some massive hand-to-hand battle involving a knife had occurred. She saw slashes in seats and heavy gouges in the display plastic on the copilot console and next to the exit. On the floor were pieces of webbing and in the far corner lay a TEBI-issue stunner that she guessed had been Maria's. She put it in the pocket of her coveralls.

Where was Maria? She considered what was available on this level and the one below, since they'd been sealed off from other levels. There were emergency escape modules for the control deck further aft. Turning that way, she smelled blood and started running.

The corridor came to a T, with the escape modules to her left. She didn't find Maria, but she smelled blood and sweat near the control panel and one module had been ejected. Running to the panel, she punched for comm. "This is *Pytheas*, calling . . ." Who?

"Kedros?" It was Maria, floating out in space, inside an escape module. Her voice sounded weak. "I'm still bleeding. He has a knife."

"Hang on, we'll get you back to the ship. Who attacked you?"

"It was Nathan . . . we should have warned you."

Ariane displayed the location of Maria's module, which had been ejected about an hour ago. The ship had moved since then, leaving Maria halfway back to the buoy. Meanwhile, in her mind, she ran through the crew members on the *Pytheas*. "I don't remember a Nathan."

"His cover is Hanson, the Terran xeno-archeologist. But he's really Nathan—Nathanial Wolf Kim," Maria said. "And he's insane. He didn't recognize me, but I know his muscle memory, his moves in hand-to-hand. He smashed up the comm console."

Ariane paused. She'd gotten complacent, letting her guard down around Parmet and Maria, almost thinking of them as coworkers rather than *enemies*. "You knew Kim was on board?" she asked, her voice low and dangerous.

"No. I suspected. We looked, we really did," Maria's voice faded. She was either tired or wounded, or both.

Hanson? She searched her memory, recalling a Richard Moki Hanson. A Terran, but not one of the "suspicious four" identified by Edones. Perhaps someone else had unknowingly transported his explosives. Hanson was new to G-145 and had been on the *Pilgrimage* for a short period, coinciding with the bombings. She tried to connect the picture she remembered of Hanson with Kim's face. It seemed unbelievable, after going through the crew herself. She couldn't have missed Nathanial Wolf Kim, the man who tortured her, could she?

Her implant vibrated, reminding her that she had another mission to complete. "We've lost the mission commander and at least one engineer. Once I can get the crew together, they can retrieve your module."

"I think he did something in the clinic, maybe harmed a medic. He was obsessed with getting to that orbiting monstrosity," Maria said.

No! Don't let him. Hurry, hurry—must get there first. She gasped at the intense anxiety the parasite let loose in her body. She signed off with Maria. Going back to the control deck and no longer worried about running into Kim, she got some answers from the second-shift medic and engineer, who were in their work centers and trying to get operational again.

"Hanson killed Sapphira." The medic, who had been locked below, had arrived in the clinic to find their Autonomist medic, who was also their xenobiology expert, dead. "Crazy—what a waste."

Yeah, *crazy*. Considering the chemicals pouring into her bloodstream and the anxiety her parasite was invoking, she figured this was why Kim wasn't behaving sanely. He must have installed his own parasite—the missing one from Lee's lab—despite the fact that it was experimental and designed for her biochemistry. Now there were three dead, on the *Pytheas* alone, to lay at Nathan's feet.

The engineer had been crying, obviously close friends to the man Nathan had killed. She'd escaped the carnage by being off-duty in her quarters below, and then had been saved from a cold death when Ariane restored life support.

"He took one of the exploration skiffs, so we can use the other one to get—"

"No. I'm taking the other one," Ariane said. "You'll have to turn the ship around and retrieve Ms. Guillotte. Use the manipulator arms."

"But—what about you?" The engineer was aghast.

"I'll get back to the ship in the skiff. Don't worry."

When Ariane arrived at the skiff docking area in the aft section behind engineering, she knew she was on the right track. She bared her teeth, feeling a primitive excitement surge through her body. *Hurry, hurry.* She ensured the skiff had its environmental suit, air, and power. As she climbed in, she felt the parasite in her upper arm vibrate. *Yes—yes—yes—yes—yes....*

Matt woke up, feeling like he had a hangover. He was in the common hygiene closet of *Aether's Touch*, which wasn't an immediate problem, because he had to relieve himself. As he did so, he surveyed his situation and his attitude sputtered into hopelessness.

Dr. Lowry had locked him in, but he tried the hatch anyway. Worse, she'd smashed the nodes inside the closet—that bitch must have used a heavy wrench to break them, then pulled the node assemblies out of the bulkhead and cut them off, leaving the microwire harnesses dangling without their connectors. The damage enraged him and cleared the last vestiges of fuzziness left by the stunner. It also dispirited him, because she'd cut him off from communicating in *any* way with the rest of the ship. The nodes brought in comm, controlled the displayable surfaces, and operated as sensors. Any hopes he had of contacting Muse 3 or causing emergency alarms, via smoke or chemical vapors, died a quick death.

However, growing up on a generational ship, he'd been trained to handle emergencies since he could walk. The first step was always to inventory everything you had available, meaning food, tools, and resources. Sometimes he thought this first step was just a mechanism for calming down. He looked through everything secured, either through webbing or magnetic surfaces, inside the lockers. There were various cleaners and personal toiletries, as well as a small one-third-full pint of liquor with the Stellar Shield's logo slapped on it.

He squeezed some air out and sniffed. His eyebrows rose. Rotgut—it couldn't even qualify as artificially flavored liquor. Was Ari starting to drink in the mornings as she got ready? He sighed. Whatever problems Ari had, she was in much deeper trouble now, considering the mayday he'd heard.

Surveying the wealth of hair and body care products, he decided that none of it would be useful. He looked up, thinking through the ship's structure. Considering that a second-wave prospecting ship was defined by its customizations, and the fact that he'd overseen every upgrade, addition, and alteration, he knew every bolt, strut, and level of his ship.

Above this hygiene closet was an air duct that ran above the central corridor all the way to the passenger airlock. It pressed against the ceiling, so it probably could work as a sound conductor—but only on this level, which was insulated from the control deck level. Unfortunately, this was just a normal-size air duct. He wasn't in a v-play where one could watch actors, or co-opt an actor's part, and escape evil through absurdly *huge* vents that ran through *all* parts of a ship or habitat. No, sound conduction through this level's central corridor was all the conduit could provide, but that might be good enough.

Standing on the closed head and twisting his neck, he could get his ear pressed against the vent opening. He heard nothing but ship hum, so he figured Lowry wasn't in the central corridor.

"Muse, can you hear me?" He started at a whisper, but had to go to a conversational tone before he got a response. This was an uncomfortable process, having to speak into the hole, then twist his head sideways to hear.

"Yes, Matt, I can hear you near the passenger airlock, but I cannot see you." Muse 3 sounded clear, but he could tell that the AI had pushed its volume up.

"I'm in the hygiene closet. You haven't identified yourself to Lowry, have you?"

"No. I have followed your procedures," Muse 3 said primly.

"That's good—but now we might have to violate those rules."

"I have already run through scenarios to see how I can assist your escape. Unfortunately, Dr. Lowry has exhibited what Ari would call 'controlling behavior.' She has turned every system to manual and cut off all automated input."

Did Lowry suspect the existence of some agent like Muse 3? With everything set to manual, Muse 3 couldn't do anything small, like open doors, adjust temperature, or answer calls—nor could Muse 3 perform larger actions, like control parts of the ship. The AI had only been able to pilot the ship, following Ari on Abram's fateful mission, because a ship at dock was left "asleep" so that someone, *with proper authorization*, could remotely control systems.

He asked Muse 3 about Lowry's actions after he'd been stunned. She hadn't reported the mayday from *Pytheas*; apparently, she'd expected some sort of problem. She'd given Beta Priamos Station an imaginary update that everything was going well. However, after waiting an hour, she'd tried to raise the *Pytheas* herself and seemed puzzled when there was no answer.

"That smacks of mutiny aboard the *Pytheas*," Matt said, looking at the time on his sleeve. Almost two hours had passed since he'd been stunned.

"Smacks?"

"Has the flavor of—er, we're equating taste with—so when will the *Percival* arrive?" Matt didn't have the patience for a lesson right now. Besides, he needed to step off the head, and stretch his neck.

"Expected ETA is four hours and seven minutes," Muse 3 said. "From the way she is pacing, I think Dr. Lowry is worried about their arrival."

"Keep me apprised of her actions. I need to think for a while." Matt stepped off the head and stretched. He wished he had room to pace. There was little he could do, no matter what creative ideas might hit him. Lowry had to make the next move.

The exploration skiff was designed for real-space, but not for long trips. After undocking, Ariane put the boost engines at full burn and realized it'd take her almost an hour to get to the alien station. *Hurry, hurry*. Her fingers shook with anticipation.

She left the *Pytheas* behind her and, though she had no formal training in biofeedback, she tried to influence and calm the Minoan parasite. *My body can't take this*, she thought—which seemed to mitigate the tension and adrenaline. She also tried to assure herself she wouldn't become a murdering monster like Nathanial Wolf Kim, if that was who she was pursuing. Of course, Kim had already been a sadistic bastard who jumped at a chance to take out his revenge upon her. Now he was well beyond state-sanctioned execution and had become insane, probably from putting the implant in his body. She hoped she wouldn't suffer the same fate, but it begged the question as to what sort of "tweaks" the Minoans had put into this second implant.

She tried a comm check with the *Pytheas*, but there was no answer. Maria had mentioned a damaged comm console, so maybe they were doing repairs. She passed time by doing things the skiff *should* be used for, namely recording data through its host of sensors. The planet was going to be a dream for biologists and naturalists of all types, but she was more concerned with the approaching artificial satellite.

It turned out to be smaller than most moons, but still huge for an artificial object. It measured about two hundred and fifty kilometers in height, by about two hundred and thirty kilometers in diameter. This made it similar in size to Phoebe, a natural moon in the Sol system that orbited the gas giant Saturn. However, there was no confusing this thing with a natural satellite. As she came closer, the cracked egg illusion turned out to be the result of many large, separated plates that allowed glimpses of the glowing green core between their irregular edges.

Following the urge of her Minoan parasite, she homed in on the sunward side. The dark red surface of the large plates began to resolve into large rectangular sheets of some substance, with obvious seams. Soon she saw large circular iris diaphragms, with thin overlapping plates that looked like they could expand and contract like a lens.

Hurry, hurry. She headed slowly toward the one that *felt* right, trying to follow the signals of adrenaline that sped up her heartbeat. Her instruments indicated gravity, so she aligned the skiff with its belly toward the iris.

The diaphragm began opening when her skiff came close. At its widest, it was near thirty meters across, allowing plenty of room for the skiff. It closed above her, and she continued to descend into a cavernous space dimly lit with red light.

She directed the skiff's spotlights downward and could make out a floor, along with something bright yellow—it was the other skiff, although it hadn't made a controlled landing. The boom and antennas along its dorsal side were twisted and bent. The nose area appeared to be crumpled. Some bits of yellow farther away indicated that delicate equipment had broken off when it hit the bottom.

Landing her skiff lightly, she watched for movement in the wreckage of the other skiff and saw none. The environmental readings outside her skiff were interesting; the atmospheric pressure was about twenty-five hundred meters, like high altitude on Terra, and was quite warm. There was enough oxygen in the air to sustain humans, but what worried her was the amount of "unknown constituents" the sensors read. These were complex gaseous organic compounds and even though they were present in low concentrations, she didn't trust them.

She put on a light environmental suit and a small self-contained breathing apparatus. She wouldn't be able to withstand vacuum for more than a minute or two, but she didn't expect to encounter it. Although the station had initially looked "broken," that had been an illusion of the zig-zagging plates; in general, the station looked to be in good condition.

Despite feeling anxious and driven to move away from her skiff, she spent time examining the wreckage of the other one. She had a tight spotlight on the chest of her suit, so she examined the cockpit area, marveling that Kim had managed to get out alive, as it appeared he had. There were bloody smears where he'd dragged himself out of his cockpit.

After twisting and turning, she determined which direction excited her parasite the most. She walked quickly but didn't run, not until she felt comfortable in the slightly heavy gravity. Beneath her feet was the same smoothly designed surface that she'd seen in the Priamos ruins. She was approaching a tunnel, which had familiar inlaid ornamentation and glowed in the dim red light. When her spotlight hit it, she drew in her breath, distracted by the arching roof of the tunnel, inlaid with glowing symbols.

Suddenly, she was grabbed from behind. A cold knife blade pressed below her jawbone. Her first instinct was to freeze. Beside her ear, a tortured voice whispered, "Why am I here?"

About two hours later, Muse 3 reported to Matt. "Dr. Lowry seems increasingly anxious, but her patterns suggest a plan."

"What's that?" Matt asked. At least this discussion took his mind off what might be happening in the Builders' solar system.

"She copied the commands for controlling the alien buoy. After that, she examined the instructions for operating the manipulator booms. Perhaps she intends to remove the bot?"

"*Remove* it from the buoy? You mean disconnect it." Matt put his hands over his face and rubbed hard, stretching the skin. "That'd leave us with no way to talk to the *Pytheas*—and they might get stranded. What are the chances of initiating nous-transit without that bot?"

"There is not enough information for a hypothesis."

"I have to stop this woman."

CHAPTER 23

I knew it was too soon to forget G-145. This time, I'm not talking about isolationists, or an ICT, or even the exploration of a new solar system launched from Beta Priamos. No, this time it's about old enemies: Overlord Six has been given an ultimatum [*link to statement by rivals Stephanos and Raulini*]. With Six's approval, apparently, SP Duval has violated agreements with Pilgrimage by deploying another warship to G-145, in addition to the Terran Space Forces already in that system. Our Senate has given him a deadline for withdrawal. . . .

—*Dr. Net-head Stavros*, 2106.068.21.00 UT,
indexed by *Heraclitus 9* under Conflict Imperative

The blade moved up Ariane's cheek and with a quick movement, Kim cut off her mask. She took a breath of thin, fetid air and started coughing. When he loosened his grip, she elbowed him sharply and twisted out of his grasp. As she whirled to face him, she saw why she had escaped so easily.

Kim stepped after her, shambling, but she easily stayed out of his reach. His right ankle and leg twisted strangely; he could barely put weight on it. He held his left arm tight to his chest and she drew breath in her nose sharply, smelling the blood. He had various wounds, probably from fighting his victims on the ship, but his upper left arm looked like *he had gouged and wounded it himself*. There was a lump under the skin on his left shoulder, which extended to the base of his neck. As she watched, the lump shifted. The parasite? Had it escaped self-surgery by moving?

"I'm here for a weapon." Confusion crossed Kim's face, or rather, Hanson's face. She couldn't even recognize Hanson, much less her torturer, Kim, whose face she still saw in her nightmares. After all the bruises, blood, and swelling, this man didn't even look human anymore.

"Are you Nathanial Wolf Kim?" she asked. There was no response, no flicker of recognition in the strange blue eyes. Kim didn't have blue eyes, which was why Maria didn't recognize him. She tried the name Maria used. "Nathan? You planned to use the implant and you *killed* people to get here. You're working for Duval, right? Overlord Six?"

He tilted his head, looking wary. "Do I know you?"

She slowly backed away, down the tunnel with the arched ceiling, because her parasite wanted her to go that direction. Having lowered the intensity of the spotlight on her suit, she could almost see the layered air currents, with different scents, moving sluggishly. Kim had already come down this corridor, at least once, because she smelled his blood when she turned her head.

"I recognize you." His voice changed, became sharper. "You were on the *Pilgrimage*."

"Yes. You tried to kill me, using antipersonnel grenades," she said steadily.

He smiled in a sickly way. "Orders, you know. The Aether Exploration personnel named in the contract. Get them off the *Pilgrimage*, or kill them. Nothing personal."

Nothing personal? *What about breaking my legs during a torture session, to make me say Ura-Guinn was an unauthorized mission?* Her voice shook as she said, "What about Ura-Guinn? What about the threats against Parmet?"

Kim seemed surprised. "What about Ura-Guinn? What matters is now, and what we're after. *You're* going to get the prize for me." He gestured with his right hand, the one that held the knife, because his upper left arm was mutilated. That was when she noticed his right hand was blistered and swollen. She realized with a start that he'd already tried to take the seed.

She turned and began running, her parasite sending exhilarating chemicals into her blood. She could smell traces of Kim's blood, from his first trip down this corridor. Behind her, Kim shuffled faster, but couldn't keep up.

"Get it and I'll spare your life!" More inanities followed: "There'll be war when we return! I can protect you!" His voice faded behind her.

The strong gravity and thin air made her puff harder and breathe deeper. She wondered if there were mind- or behavior-altering drugs in the air, because Nathan hadn't killed her immediately and *he could have*. She hoped she could handle all these "unknown constituents."

The high arched ceiling of the corridor suddenly disappeared, and she staggered, unbalanced, to avoid stumbling down a steep slope. Below her was a bowl of coliseum size. Above, the ceiling rose to heights similar to the landing area under the iris, but this ceiling allowed light from the Builders' sun to enter.

She was looking at a garden, crowded with varied colors of vegetation that fought one another to get toward the light. How could these plants continue to live, over so many years, with no one to tend them? Moreover, how did the material above filter out harmful radiation? There was heat here, as well as robust water and air recycling—provided by systems that could last thousands of years. Obviously, human technology could benefit from the Builders.

There was a path to the center of the bowl and she walked along it slowly, occasionally passing under looming vegetation, trying to make sense of areas that looked more like displays than planters. Something kept the plants from encroaching into the path, but she didn't know what— Was that movement? Were there animals here?

Biological temple. That was the direct translation of the name of this solar system, according to the Minoans. Was it possible the Builders kept the reproductive codes of their planets enshrined here? Surely, this garden was only one of many; huge as it was, it couldn't contain enough plants and animals to represent the planet below. She couldn't imagine species sustaining themselves here, even with the possibility of perpetual power. There were plenty of puzzles here, and she wasn't the one to solve them. Given time, a host of other people could explore this solar system in detail.

She was here for only one thing and she felt it as she came to the center of the bowl. The path intersected another, the two of them cutting the bowl into quarters. Their meeting place was round and flat, with what she assumed were benches around the periphery. She'd already seen the inhuman dimensions of benches and doors on Priamos. From here, the wild jungle could be seen climbing up all parts of the bowl.

What held her attention was the column at the very center of the bowl. Smooth, made of a material that had glittering veins, its circumference was so large that she couldn't put her arms around it. Her parasite vibrated with excitement; the seed was within this pillar, which supported nothing and had nothing on its flat top, which was level with her eyes.

She felt the urge to touch it, although that's probably what Kim did, and he got a blistered hand. She held her hand near the column and felt burning heat, even in her environmental suit, which had thick protective gloves. This was probably a security feature by the Builders—so her Minoan parasite couldn't help her. Or could it?

She decided to shed the entire suit. As she pulled it off, she realized she still had Maria's stunner in her coveralls. She circled the pillar, feeling the seed calling to her, making her parasite thrum. No matter which way she turned, or how she held her arm, she felt it pulling her in all parts of her body. But when she drifted close, the heat pushed her back.

Surely the Minoans knew something like this might happen. If nothing else, the seed would have "grown" an archive and been buried within it. She stopped. If the seed called to her, couldn't she call to it? Extending her hand, but keeping it from touching the pillar, she concentrated. Called. Cajoled. Urged. Cried out with *need*.

Crack! She jumped as pieces fell off the pillar. It split along the veins, from the top toward the bottom. As chunks fell away, she continued to pull at the seed, mentally. It flew out of the heart of the pillar and she grabbed it. A clear crystal was in her palm, almost small enough to wrap her hand around. It looked similar to, but much smaller than, their crystal storage on *Aether's Touch*.

She grinned. It seemed like magic, although she knew it was merely advanced technology. *Hurry, hurry*. Her parasite wanted her to rush this crystal back to its masters. She looked around at the peaceful garden. If this was a v-play drama, then this whole station would start imploding, right? Nothing happened. She put the cool, almost cold crystal into the pocket that didn't have the stunner, and sealed it tight. She ran back up the incline, out of the bowl, at a sustainable pace. There might not be imminent danger of station destruction, but she'd left wounded people on the damaged *Pytheas* and the Minoans wanted this crystal— *badly*, according to her parasite.

When she entered the tunnel, she smelled Kim before he accosted her, but she was surprised by his strength and tenacity.

"I need it!" he seemed to be screaming, although there were some inarticulate sounds mixed in. He tried to wrap himself about her, his hands finding the outside of the pocket with the crystal.

She twisted violently and pushed him away. With a feeling of careless familiarity, she pulled the stunner out of her pocket and pressed the trigger. Surprised by the speed of her reflexes, she resisted the urges of her parasite and stopped. The *sizzle-pop* sound of the stunner ceased and she smelled the ionized air mixing with his sweat, blood, and pain. She could *smell* his pain. Amazed, she stepped back.

"Nooooo," wailed the thing that hunched against the wall. He should have been twitching and helpless from the stunner, but he wasn't. His Minoan parasite might be helping him, but at least he seemed to be tiring.

"Do you know who Major Ariane Kedros is?" she asked.

He muttered something about Ura-Guinn, but the visceral hate that Kim had previously displayed toward her wasn't there.

"What about those grenades you used?" She started backing down the hall toward her skiff.

He launched himself toward her again. She stunned him. Again. He still crawled after her as she tried to back down the hall. Suddenly angry at the deaths he'd caused, the pain he'd inflicted upon the girl who made the mistake of opening David Ray's door, the neural probe he'd done on Dr. Lee, for all the crimes he'd committed for Overlord Six—she lashed out with her foot and kicked him in the torso. He howled, curled up, and she did it again. *What am I doing? How is this different from torturing someone?* Ashamed, she dialed up the stunner's power and finally had him twitching into unconsciousness.

"I just don't know what to do with you," she said aloud, looking down. "Maria could be wrong. Maybe you're not Kim, maybe you're just Hanson."

She thought she would have enjoyed taking out her revenge on Nathaniel Wolf Kim, who'd tortured her, but this thing that curled in front of her wasn't that man. He didn't look like Kim, with a thick mop of caramel hair; she realized that he was the person who'd bumped into her while she spoke with Maria near the maintenance office. Looking at the broken man, she tried to convince her emotions that this was Kim, but the niggling doubts only grew. What if Maria, for some strange reason, had lied to her? No, the only thing she'd do *to* this man, or perhaps *for* this man, was to leave him.

The skiffs could only hold one person, anyway, and his was no longer operational. She wouldn't be sending someone to his death—remembering Duval's accusation, which still rankled her. Kim, Hanson, or whoever, could be retrieved during another mission, in a day or two. She checked the wreckage of his skiff and pulled out the emergency supplies: four days of minimal water and rations, plus some first aid supplies. Making sure they were in plain sight, she added all the emergency food and water from her skiff. Surely, eight days of supplies was enough. Provided they could find him later, he'd face justice for his crimes when he returned.

The iris opened as she lifted off. She felt wonder at the Builders' technology that let her skiff through yet kept the station pressurized—but shelved all her questions as she set her course for the *Pytheas*.

"Dr. Lowry is having difficulty using the manipulators to retrieve the bot," Muse 3 told Matt. "I cannot provide input to the manipulators directly, but I have slowed the interface between her controls and the actuators by several seconds. The lag is making her more distressed, because she cannot catch the bot."

"Good job." Matt chuckled. "Hopefully, that'll delay her until the *Percival* arrives."

"The *Percival* has arrived and hailed us already. It is standing by. Dr. Lowry has told them you are unavailable. She also said that the bot requires maintenance."

"They accepted that?" Matt started cursing under his breath. Of course they did; they didn't have any reason not to believe her. He stepped down from the head. Too bad Dr. Lowry didn't need to use this facility—for the first time, Matt regretted the convenience of a small hygiene closet off the control deck.

"Your bot and my algorithm have thwarted her, Matt."

He could barely hear Muse 3, so he stood on the head again. "What's that, Muse?"

"It appears that she must physically retrieve the bot. She's told the *Percival* that you—" Muse 3 stopped and Matt heard footsteps. Lowry was walking down the central corridor. Was she coming to let him out? Going into space with only a vacuum suit to protect you was always risky, but doing it without someone to watch you, or run your ship, was highly perilous. Using autopilot algorithms to keep the ship nearby was dangerous, particularly in this case, because the buoy had gravity generation through its N-space connection. They all had to hope that its "gravity" would remain stable.

Matt pushed his ear nearer the ceiling, to try to pick

up sounds. The footsteps faded. Finally, Muse 3's voice came down the vent. "She has entered the equipment bay and put on a suit. However, she told the *Percival* that you will be going EVA and to perpetuate this deception, she is broadcasting to the *Percival* from the ship's transmitter, but through her suit. She put the ship on automated station-keeping."

Matt suddenly realized what had just happened. By using the autopilot to keep the ship on its position close to the buoy, she'd given Muse 3 its "back door" into the ship systems. *Click*. He heard Muse 3 unlock his door—thank Gaia that Lowry hadn't decided to manually disable his door.

"Has she left the airlock, Muse Three?" Matt was out of the hygiene closet and sprinting toward the control center. Lowry wasn't a professional ship hijacker or she would have taken the gravity generator down to make it more difficult to retake the ship. Of course, having been raised on a generational ship, Matt didn't have as many problems as a grav-hugger under zero gee.

"Yes. She left the airlock before I hacked into the control routines."

Matt paused. Even though this had worked in his favor, he was somewhat uncomfortable with Muse 3 "hacking" into his own ship's security. He'd have to revisit this issue with the AI—*later*.

"We've got to stop her from damaging the buoy interface, or stealing the bot." He climbed the vertical tube to the control deck, and slid into his seat. Checking the comm channels, he turned on monitoring as he looked at the FTL diagram.

"Holy Great Bull-shit," he muttered as he considered the situation.

The TLS *Ming Adams*, perhaps after seeing the TLS *Percival* leave Beta Priamos Station, had apparently decided that getting to the buoy was more important than staying within jamming range of the *Bright Crescent*. His call log now showed unacknowledged calls from Edones's ship, but he pushed them to the bottom of the priority list. The *Bright Crescent* was too far away to be of help; the

Ming Adams had outrun her and was now less than five thousand kilometers away and closing fast. Dr. Lowry's collusion with the *Ming Adams* was obvious on Matt's comm panel, where he saw she'd made good use of the starboard beam antenna, the one with the signal strength needed for second-wave prospecting. She was on a directional, non-standard channel with the approaching *Ming Adams*, while the *Percival* sat nearby, having no reason to suspect she was engaged in any duplicity.

"He suspected they'd be bringing back an artifact, but I can't wait any longer," she transmitted. "I'll have the interface package soon. Lowry out."

"Good. We'll—"

Matt cut in on the *Ming Adams* response. "I'm not so sure of that, considering the package is a real scamp. Isn't it, Dr. Lowry?" He watched the bot slice the leg of Lowry's suit, this time in what he considered justified self-defense.

"Matt? No, you're making a mis—" He cut off her horrified voice, hoping the bot could defend itself until he figured out how to help. He called the TLS *Percival* on the Beta Priamos channel, which the other ships could easily monitor. "TLS *Percival*, this is the *Aether's Touch*. Disregard everything Lowry's been telling you. We lost contact with the *Pytheas* hours ago—"

There was a brilliant flash of light that usually occurred when a referential engine wasn't tuned correctly. Or, in this case, when a human-made referential engine was trying to sync with an alien Builders' buoy. The *Pytheas* was back, its ID transmitting in emergency mode.

Ariane needed to make an immediate nous-transit back to G-145, because when she returned to the *Pytheas*, she found dire circumstances.

"We're not equipped for this type of surgery, nor am I trained for more than initial triage and trauma," explained the second-shift medic, who was now their *only* medic. He eyed her askance as she tore into another rations pack, munching on the bars as if they were ambrosia. She felt strong, but she was voraciously hungry.

"Ms. Guillotte is the one I'm most worried about," he continued, as she also opened a juice pack. "When we get her to G-145, the only facilities that can handle her are on the *Pilgrimage*. Ms. Joy is stable but she needs more surgery. Dr. Novak just needs recovery time."

Eva Joy had been the comm engineer on duty when Kim, or Hanson, went on his upper-level rampage. She'd been found, barely alive, stuffed in a locker. The only person who had escaped injury on the top two levels had been Ariane, only because Maria had told her to disable her hatch after locking. That, and the fact she'd slept through everything; she might not have survived waking up to do hand-to-hand with the deranged Kim.

For everyone trapped in the lower levels, it was the psychological stress of dealing with no environmental support for thirty or forty minutes. There were several panic attacks and Dr. Novak's was the worst. He'd hyperventilated, fainted, and hit his head in the process. Now he was in sick bay, under observation.*

"We have to get back to G-145," Ariane said.

"If you're up to doing the drop so soon," the medic said. "Remember, better to lose two patients than the entire ship and crew."

"I'm fine. Just need one more ration pack." She winked. After all these years, she knew nous-transits always got better. Plenty of people who trained to be N-space pilots quit after their first few drops, convinced they couldn't face the nightmarish transits, over and over. Experienced N-space pilots tried to tell them the transits *could* get better, particularly when you made the same nous-transit again, between the same buoys.

In getting the *Pytheas* back to G-145, they ran into a few more glitches. The operational crew that ran the ship was distinctly different from the mission crew, responsible for collecting and analyzing data. The operational crew still had its N-space pilot, but had lost its primary members for the captain, comm, engineer, and copilot seats. Kim had also damaged equipment, including the interface to their transmitters. They had lost their primary antenna during the weapons platform battle, but they still had secondary antennas, just no way to control or use them for the comm.

"I'm replacing damaged parts with spares, and trying to bring basic comm online," the second-shift comm engineer said. "We don't have data or voice working yet."

"I assume our ID transponder is working," Ariane said. Civilian transponders were extremely difficult to disable, meant to operate independently, and located in out-of-the-way, secure places. It was illegal to purposely damage the black box that squawked your ship ID.

The comm engineer nodded and said, "We can put it in emergency mode." That would cause the ID to flash red on other consoles, the universal indicator of a comm-out situation.

"What about the buoy lock signal?" This, of course, was crucial to getting back and doubly important now, since they hadn't been able to call for help.

"That runs through a different transceiver, with different routing—looks like it should still work." The secondary comm engineer looked tired. "For once, I think I'll appreciate being knocked out by D-tranny."

The nous-transit, this time, took less out of Ariane. She suspected her parasite was finally hitting its stride, so to speak, and adjusting her clash doses more effectively. Her resistance to the damaged N-space was stronger; she'd already trod this nous-transit path before, and she knew how to steer for the strange-looking rift into G-145. After she hit the switch to push wake-up bright into the crew members and restored ship gravity, however, she pulled a juice pack out of her coveralls and contemplated the scene in front of her. *Hurry, hurry. Return the seed*, urged her parasite, but she had to ignore it. Something serious was happening in G-145.

"What's going on?" asked Elias, the secondary copilot seat, who was also responsible for sensors. He had opened his eyes, brought up sensors, and stared at the same display. As a civilian, he didn't jump to bringing up the newly attached weapon systems, like Maria would have.

"My first guess is that we've interrupted a standoff. We have two Terran League frigates and an AFCAW cruiser, all squaring off, if you'll excuse the geometric oddity of that statement." She focused on the three large military ships separately with cam-eyes, then on *Aether's Touch*, which was hovering close to the buoy. Was someone working on the buoy? She zoomed to try to see the white-suited figure, who was waving frantically. Was that Matt? Probably not, because he'd be smart enough to move into the full sunlight.

"Which means . . . ?" Elias, an Autonomist, wasn't used to thinking about self-protection.

"It means you should get the weapon systems on line, Elias, while Brooke takes over sensors," Ariane said severely, as she opened the intercom to engineering. "I need *comm* as soon as possible."

There was grumbling from the comm engineer, something like "I'm working as fast as . . ." which she overrode with an announcement to the entire ship.

"*Pytheas*, we apparently have a *situation*. There are three military ships at the buoy and some of them may no longer be our friends. Someone may shoot off weapons at us—and without comm, I'm making a run toward the *Pilgrimage* and hoping I get an escort."

The intercom lit up after her announcement, but she shut off the audio. Elias muttered about training as he tried to assess the weapons systems. Brooke appeared capable of handling sensors and Ariane had moved targeting over to Elias.

"I wish we had FTL data." Ariane ran her fingers over her head, shedding more hair. Unfortunately, the damage to their comm systems also prevented them from getting buoy data, so all she had was what Brooke could get from their light-speed sensors. For the benefit of the others, she quickly listed the players. "The *Bright Crescent* is an AFCAW cruiser, with the most firepower. It'll probably escort us, but it's still too far away to really help protect us. The TLS *Percival* is a fast frigate, crewed by TLS regulars, and it helped us get rid of Abram. The TLS *Ming Adams* is older, and an unknown; I'm not sure if it's crewed by regulars or not."

"We've still got chaff and one volley of swarm missiles," Elias announced. "And why does it matter whether there are 'regulars' on the League ships?"

"Brooke, you're Terran, so you tell him," she said grimly, before calling engineering. "Do we have comm yet? Emergency—broadband—anything?"

"No comm," came from engineering, followed by choice and colorful expletives.

Brooke gave her a cautious look, then said to Elias, "I think Ms. Kedros is referring to the possibility that the ship may be more rogue than TLS, meaning they might not be operating fully within Overlord law or following treaties—"

"Like the Phaistos Protocols?" Elias blanched.

"Let's get going. I hate doing this with only light-speed data, but we've got wounded." Ariane set a course and started moving the *Pytheas* away from the buoy. "We can go the speed of the frigates, but I want to give the *Bright Crescent* a chance to catch us. Stay ready on weapons, Elias, and give me continuous updates, Brooke."

Brooke complied by shouting, "The *Bright Crescent* is changing direction, moving toward escort position, but the *Ming Adams* is moving to block us!"

Ariane winced. "Dial down the volume, please."

"The *Percival* is holding her position." Brooke's pronunciation became staccato, but softer. "*Ming Adams* still moving in front of our bow."

Moving to *block*? Ariane couldn't believe a League military ship would try such an inept maneuver. Space was three-dimensional and required at least that many dimensions in its tactics. Maybe whoever was commanding the *Ming Adams* thought they were dealing with a civilian real-space driver. *Fine. . . . Wait for it. . . .*

"*Ming Adams* still moving to block." Brooke couldn't help herself—her voice was tighter, higher, and louder.

At the last possible moment, the *Ming Adams* started veering starboard to avoid collision, like a driver stuck in two dimensions. Ariane dove the *Pytheas* under their ventral area, flipped, and yanked hard to port, knowing the *Bright Crescent* would track them easily from far escort position. They ended up above the planetary plane, or below it, depending upon viewpoint. Actually, the point was that a pilot shouldn't consider *above* or *below*. The *Ming Adams* scrambled to follow.

Elias made a gurgling sound as he unnecessarily gripped the arms of his seat.

"Don't look at the cam-eye views," Ariane advised him.

"*Bright Crescent* is following, but *Percival* is obviously hanging back. *Ming Adams* is catching up." Brooke reiterated what Ariane's screens showed her, but that was fine. It helped her concentrate. She wished she knew who wanted what—and why was the TLS *Percival* staying out of the scrap?

"What the hell? The *Ming Adams* is firing rail guns—"

"Thanks." Ariane turned the *Pytheas*'s ventral side toward the firing frigate, and tried to angle the bow area out, since the referential engine was nearly indestructible. "Next time, tell me sooner."

"We've been hit!" Elias panicked for a moment. "Thank Gaia, we've got smart armor and there's hardly any damage. Good move—"

"Elias, be ready to fire swarm missiles. Brooke, I expect the *Ming Adams* will move closer."

"You're right."

"Fire swarm missiles," Ariane said grimly.

"At a TLS frigate? Are you kidding?"

"*Now*, Elias!" Ariane shouted. "Otherwise, they'll think we agree to being grappled and boarded."

While Elias hesitantly moved the target-tracking missile array, the *Ming Adams* pulled back and let loose a cloud of expanding chaff on their dorsal side. The swarm missiles detonated in the chaff. Of course, Elias wouldn't know that unless he was very lucky the missiles couldn't penetrate the ship's smart armor. This salvo was mostly a statement of "Stay away!" Unfortunately for the *Ming Adams*, staying away from the *Pytheas* might open it up to fire from the *Bright Crescent*.

"Tell me if the *Bright Crescent* fires," Ariane told Brooke.

"You mean they might *not* help us?" Elias sounded plaintive.

Ariane was busy trying to stay away from the *Ming Adams*, whose pilot had finally woken up and shown some focus. If someone on the *Ming Adams* wanted whatever she brought back from the Builders' station, their only option was to grapple and board the *Pytheas*. Under Pax Minoica, that would be an act of piracy upon a civilian ship, or it could be considered an act of war if the *Pytheas* qualified as a combatant—all of which was questionable because it did have weapons.

"If the *Bright Crescent* fires on the *Ming Adams* before it grapples us, then they'd be blamed for initiating warfare. If they fire *after* grappling, they take the chance of hitting us." In explaining this, Ariane had an idea. "I'm speeding up and leaving the *Bright Crescent* behind. Now, it's just between us and the Terran frigates, which simplifies the rules of engagement."

"We don't have any more missiles." Elias's face wrinkled with fear. "And why are you worried about *rules*?"

"Wake up, would you? There's a Minoan warship sitting near the *Pilgrimage*." Brooke's scoffing words came out just as the intercom light lit up.

"Control Deck, you've got comm on the standard emergency channel," the engineer said.

"Thank Gaia," Ariane breathed. She changed her course to a straight vector toward the *Pilgrimage*, glancing at the others. "And thank you, Brooke, for reminding me of another option."

With a puzzled line between her eyes, Brooke continued to provide status. "The *Bright Crescent* is falling behind, and the *Ming Adams* is moving into grappling position. The *Percival* is moving up. They're firing their rail guns, but only as warning, I think."

"Elias, will you swear that you're not trained to operate weapons?" Ariane asked. "Particularly if you're questioned by Minoans?"

"But that's the *truth*," Elias said. "Isn't it?"

She had stopped accelerating the ship and their velocity was steady. Their diagrams showed the *Ming Adams* setting up for grappling. This was always a dangerous proposition, but Ariane was going to make it riskier, and not in the way they expected.

"Exactly." She turned and began to broadcast on the emergency channel. "This is *Pytheas*, calling Knossos-ship. This is *Pytheas*, calling Warrior Commander and reporting an act of piracy. The *Ming Adams* is attempting to board *Pytheas*, which is a civilian exploration ship."

She paused and they waited.

"Nice try, *Pytheas*, but you fired on us." This male voice came from the *Ming Adams*. She winced, knowing this was the hole in her plan, but she could hope.

"Acknowledged, Pytheas-ship. This is Knossos-ship, Warrior Commander speaking." The Minoan voice she was waiting for came over the emergency channel.

Meanwhile, she realized engineering had comm working with the buoy relays, meaning her FTL diagram was working. They were still several hours from the *Pilgrimage*. The *Pilgrimage* was stationary, but a tag that read "(Minoan)" was beginning to move away from its position near the generational ship.

"Is this some kind of joke?" demanded the voice from the *Ming Adams*. "Besides, we're entitled to defend ourselves in time of war."

In time of war? She broadcasted again. "I repeat, to Knossos-ship and all ships in the area. The *Pytheas* is a civilian research vessel."

Another voice piped up on the emergency channel and said, "Knossos-ship, this is the TLS *Percival*, notifying you that Overlord Six has filed a formal declaration of war against Overlord Three, as well as Three's allies from the Consortium of Autonomous Worlds. However, the *Pytheas* is classified as noncombatant by Overlord Three."

"Knossos-ship, this is AFCAW ship *Bright Crescent*. CAW also classifies the *Pytheas* as noncombatant." Edones's voice was crisp, but notably, he didn't specify which Overlords were allied with the Consortium. He probably didn't know yet.

"But *we* have not, ah—Knossos-ship. Not only did the *Pytheas* target us with swarm missiles, they're carrying stolen materials. Items that are archeological contraband—er—which gives us the right to board." The male speaking for the *Ming Adams* couldn't be military; he wasn't following proper comm protocol and he'd just prevaricated on interstellar treaty law in front of a Minoan warrior.

Brooke exchanged a puzzled look with Elias, who said, "I feel like I'm in kindergarten, trying to please our favorite teacher."

"Elias, the Minoans are *nothing* like your favorite teacher. They don't give anyone second chances." Ariane broadcasted Minoan-style into her mike, "Pytheas-ship to Knossos-ship. We have wounded and under Phaistos Humanitarian Directives, we request safe passage to Pilgrimage-ship. We are a civilian research vessel, and the only material we transported into this solar system is *owned by Hellas Nautikos*. This is Pytheas-ship, Explorer of Solar Systems speaking."

This time, the answer came more quickly. "Your request for support under Phaistos Humanitarian Directives is granted, Pytheas-ship. This is Knossos-ship, Warrior Commander speaking."

"Look at the speed of that thing," whispered Brooke, pointing to the Minoan warship on the FTL data diagram.

After hearing Warrior Commander's response, the *Ming Adams* gave up on talking and broke off. Ariane kept a cam-eye on them as they first tried to stay close to the *Percival*, then the *Bright Crescent*, but they were anathema to the other ships. For self-defense, the military ships scattered. At that point, the *Ming Adams* tried to run for it.

Unfortunately, they had wasted time and couldn't get within lock-signal distance of the buoy to drop out of real-space. In a last ditch effort, the TLS *Ming Adams* unwisely fired every missile it had while wildly attempting to outmaneuver the shadowy Minoan ship. Neither produced a reaction from the Minoan warship as it bore down on the frigate.

The directed energy beams overwhelmed the cam-eyes and sensors for a moment, but after clearing, the cam-eyes showed beams *slicing* through the *Ming Adams*. Secondary fires and explosions blazed into violent life before their air dissipated. Titanium and magnesium sparked, burned, then fizzled. From the *Pytheas* deck, they watched, their jaws slack; humans still couldn't make directed energy weapons with enough power to slice through a ship.

As the *Pytheas* continued speeding toward the *Pilgrimage*, she silently continued to display the cataclysm behind them, using the control-deck view ports. The TLS *Percival* and the *Bright Crescent* were moving in to rescue survivors, while the Minoan warship pulled back and then remained stationary.

"Gaia protect us," Elias muttered.

"And Gaia have mercy on their souls," added Brooke.

"They're fools," Ariane said flatly. Her exhaustion crashed down on her now that the adrenaline surge had subsided. She sighed, looking at her S-DATS display, which she could use now that she had FTL data.

"*Pilgrimage*, this is *Pytheas*." Her voice was hoarse with fatigue. "We have two critically wounded casualties, and six others with minor wounds. We need morgue support for three fatalities."

"*Pytheas*, this is the *Pilgrimage Three*. We have medical staff standing by," Justin answered, his voice warm. "Come on home, Ariane."

CHAPTER 24

We're at war again, but with a twist. This time we're on the sidelines, watching the Terrans have a go at one another. Yes, it still means using our money, weapons, and people [*link to report of our commitments*]. I hope we picked the right side. . . .

—Dr. Net-head Stavros, 2106.074.09.20 UT,
indexed by *Democritus* 7 under Metrics Imperatives

Matt ended up watching the episode helplessly, as he rescued someone he wasn't sure deserved the kindness. He had intended to follow the ships pursuing the *Pytheas*, but it was Muse 3, of all things, that reminded him of his duties.

"You cannot leave Dr. Lowry unprotected in space, Matt. Does that not violate the Spacecrew Code of Ethics, written by St. Darius?"

Matt gritted his teeth. "I need to make sure Ari and Diana are safe."

"What can we do, that the *Bright Crescent* cannot do better?"

"We're faster than Edones's ship," Matt said.

"But we have no weapons. You requested protection from State Prince Parmet for the same—"

"Be quiet, Muse." He pounded the arm of his chair to keep from saying something nasty to the AI. But he'd rather face the Great Bull itself, before he'd allow a Gaia-b'damned piece of software call him on his ethics!

That meant he answered Dr. Lowry's pleas, to her great relief. Even though she could keep herself safe from the bot, which was physically tied to the buoy, she'd panicked as she watched her oxygen levels fall. She expected to be abandoned, and Matt told her just how close she was to being right. "If you want rescue," he'd said, "tell me who's giving you your orders."

He'd been uncompromising and ruthless, getting Lowry to confess everything before he moved the ship close enough so she could get into a bay. As he recorded her babble, he watched what was happening to the *Pytheas*, powerless to help. When the FTL diagram showed the *Bright Crescent* falling behind, his turbulent feelings nearly tore him apart. Was Diana safe? Could he lose Ari?

Instead of listening to Dr. Lowry, he followed Ari's appeal and the arguments on the emergency channel, heard about Overlord Six's withdrawal from the Terran League, and watched the *Ming Adams* make lethal blunders with the Minoans—then the inner system lit up. Energy beams exposed ship positions to the naked eye as the TLS *Ming Adams* was lanced by the Minoan warship, wrapped in its defensive shadows. Matt was speechless. *I won't make fun of the Minoans' inflexible adherence to rules anymore.* He'd just been reminded of their power. He'd become complacent, assuming the Minoans were no different from eccentric human bosses—he should never forget they were aliens, with alien beliefs and logic.

To get back on board, Dr. Lowry told a simple story. She'd taken bribes from Overlord Six's staff ever since she'd arrived in G-145. The payments were for leaked research data and reports. After the Minoans had hired her by name, she was contacted by Hanson, a Terran xeno-archeologist, who had identified himself as a compatriot and asked questions about what the Minoans were doing. She'd been instructed that after Hanson snatched an important piece of technology and sabotaged the *Pytheas*'s mission, she was supposed to seize the interface to the Builders' buoy.

The appearance of the TLS *Ming Adams* came as a surprise to Lowry, although it made sense, in retrospect, to send someone to collect the bot, which was extremely interesting to Overlord Six. To Matt, the fact she'd done it for money made her pathetic, even less forgivable than someone like Abram.

"I'm nothing like those isolationists! If things had gone smoothly, no one would have been harmed." Now that Lowry was safely inside the bay, she tried to justify her actions. "And I needed the money. You Autonomists don't know what it's like; surrounded by wealth and you're—"

Matt shut off her intercom. *Try having a debt-load of eighty-five years, you bitch, and watch how you respond to somebody smashing equipment on your ship.* Instead, he watched the FTL diagram and tracked status, as he headed his own ship toward the *Pilgrimage*.

The first thing Ariane had to do upon returning to Beta Priamos, a day later, was to deliver the "seed" archive to Contractor Director.

"You're sure that's what they wanted returned?" Matt frowned at the crystal in the case. "That can 'grow' an archive of information? I can't see the Minoans obsessing about *that* for ten thousand years."

"I'm sure." Her parasite thrummed with impatience and set her on edge. She put the seed into the small lockbox, keyed to her thumb- and voiceprint, so she could appease her own worries and secondly, subdue her parasite's jitters. When she closed the lockbox and believed the seed was secure, the parasite calmed.

"They never told you what this archive would contain, once grown?"

"No, and I don't want to know." Years of hiding her history made her a facile liar, even more convincing when she rationalized that she was protecting Matt. A secret known by more than one person might not be considered a secret anymore—not by alien thinkers as literal as the Minoans.

Matt shrugged, apparently believing her, and turned back to the control console. They'd just docked at Beta Priamos and he was paying their lease and maintenance fees. He pointed at their operations account, where the balance blinked because it was entering a dangerously low bracket. "Remind them that this is a contract deliverable, will you? They're prompt with their payments, so I might not have to grovel, yet again, for a loan."

"Yes, boss." She stood and slipped the fist-size lockbox into the large pocket on the side of her coveralls. That put it right at the tip of her fingers; she could tap it and feel its form against her thigh.

"*Boss?* As if I control what happens around here." Matt hunched over the control panel, grousing. "Now I have to figure out how much hacking Muse has done to my security systems."

She grinned, leaving him to deal with Muse 3. She'd climbed down the vertical and started down the corridor to the forward airlock when Matt yelled, "Remember to get a receipt! And ask them about removing that worm from your arm; maybe they'll do it for free."

Luckily, she was far enough away, opening the airlock, that she could ignore him. When she stepped out on the ramp, facing a new and underused station, she ramped up her senses and enjoyed a rebirth of her first introduction to Beta Priamos. The few commercials displayed on the walls were brighter and the smells of construction added color. Everywhere, she inhaled newness and cleanliness.

Matt didn't know the pessimistic prospects of actually removing the parasite, nor did he know that the Minoans had correctly anticipated that she'd want to keep the parasite in her body indefinitely. Her enhanced sense of smell had saved her life and she now depended more and more upon it. Her reflexes were faster and her movements more accurate. She tested them by jogging over the curved decks in station gravity to where the Minoans were docked, to find Contractor Director waiting for her.

Any hopes that she'd be treated like a triumphant hero, returning the stolen elixir, were crushed when Contractor Director immediately displayed a copy of the contract on the nearest bulkhead. Then, with a swirl of red robes, the emissary held out a long slim hand, palm up. She placed the lockbox, closed, on the palm area of the hand, taking care not to touch the alien. Suddenly she felt exhilarated, suspiciously similar to a sudden release of endorphins after winning a boxing bout or race.

I'm not a trained pet, performing for rewards. She forced a savage spike of anger and the feeling of elation faded. Whether the reward was the result of her parasite's automatic programming, or Contractor Director's doing, she didn't know. The Minoan was currently scrolling through the contract and didn't seem concerned with her.

"Aether Exploration will receive the verified payment in a few hours." Contractor Director marked something on the contract before hiding the lockbox within its voluminous and shifting robes. She noticed it had no concern about the *locked* aspect of the box, either.

"We—er, Owner of Aether Exploration would like a receipt for your returned property," she said.

Contractor Director nodded in approval. "Of course."

After looking over the receipt on her slate, she had to ask for more. "Remember our bargain? The location of the other Builders' buoy?"

The Minoan emissary paused, perhaps hesitating. She hoped she hadn't been irritating, but they'd had an agreement and she would make them stick by it. However, Contractor Director might be reevaluating the scope of their agreement. "Would you prefer only locations of buoys, or locations of all known edifices in mundane space?"

"There's more? Of course. I'd like all locations." She didn't want to look surprised and she certainly didn't want to seem grateful. She'd gone through a lot to get this information, and the Minoans preferred a businesslike approach.

Contractor Director extended a single finger, while it twirled a gem on the glittering chain that cascaded from one of its horns. "Your slate, please?"

It touched her slate and transferred three real-space coordinates. She recognized the first two coordinates as being in the New Sousse system, but the third was surprising. She didn't immediately recognize the solar system, but she could tell that it was Terran-controlled space, which was discouraging.

"Per our agreement, I'm free to release this information to whomever I wish," she said cautiously, testing.

"No, because circumstances have changed." Her stomach tightened in dismay, but eased as the emissary continued with, "Having carried roles of Treaty Compliance Officer and particularly, Breaker of Treaties, we would expect Ariane-as-Kedros to restrict the information to adherents of Pax Minoica."

"I understand." She could live with that.

Although she didn't want to address removal of her parasite, *yet*, she still had questions. The improved clash could be used by other N-space pilots, of course, but could parasites, or implants, be designed for other humans? *Maybe*, said Contractor Director, although she sensed reluctance in that answer.

This led the Minoan to another point, one she wanted to avoid: her ultra-rapid metabolizing of alcohol. She would metabolize alcohol even faster and if she enjoyed the effects of alcohol, she would see that diminished.

Great. "By how much?" This was important.

"Your sense of taste will be enhanced, but you must take warning. You will not experience the depressive or relaxing effect of the alcohol *until it's too late*."

"What?" Her face prickled with embarrassment. "Are you trying to 'fix' me?"

"That was not our intent. You may still harm yourself with alcohol consumption if you wish," Contractor Director used a helpful tone. "An excessive amount will be required to overwhelm the implant, and it *will* result in brain damage or death."

The earnestness of the Minoan, who obviously didn't intend to humiliate her, angered and embarrassed her even more. Her cheeks felt like they were on fire because, apparently, she cared about what the aliens thought of her. She abruptly bid Contractor Director good-bye, hoping it'd be a long while before she encountered the emissary again. Besides, she had a duty to perform and she couldn't be late.

*   *   *

Ariane sat on her bunk in her quarters on *Aether's Touch*, smoothing the gloves in her lap and emptying her mind of aliens and their pesky parasites. Yes, it was wartime again, but it wasn't going to be her war. Her war had lasted for decades and the hostilities had mostly occurred in space, often leaving civilian populations unaffected.

The Terran League's civil war would be different. *This* war felt like the chaos and fragmentation that had happened to Earth when the Minoans arrived. Give mankind a chance at some alien tech, and watch them fall upon one another like savages, every time. She snorted, finally pulling on the gloves.

She was wearing her dress coat, black edged with light blue, with blue and gold epaulets and stripes about the cuffs. It was longer than her Alpha Dress, reaching the midpoint between the tips of her relaxed arms and her knees. Her trousers had a sharp crease and a blue stripe down the side. Her white gloves added the final nuance to her purpose.

"Ari, Sergeant Joyce requests an encrypted face-to-face session," Muse 3 announced.

She took the call. The turnaround at the *Pilgrimage* had been too quick; she hadn't had time to debrief Colonel Edones. Joyce was probably doing follow-up.

"You clean up pretty good, Major." Joyce looked impressed.

She smiled. "Expressing AFCAW condolences and, since there wasn't a TSF officer available on the *Pilgrimage*, escorting the remains."

"Hmm. About that ... The colonel's pretty pissed. With both of us."

"I'm the one who takes the responsibility—for violating orders and not taking the mission to completion," she said.

"No doubt about that. It's why you're paid the big bucks." Joyce joked, meaning she was the *responsible officer* in charge of the case. "The colonel's slightly appeased by the information Dr. Lowry has given him. And he's getting tidbits from our new TSF ally."

"New ally? You're not talking about the traitorous great-nephew."

"No, Myron still claims he was only helping his uncle by negotiating, on his own but in good faith, with Overlord Six. Instead of insanity, he's going for the idiocy plea." Joyce shook his head. "However, when SP Duval departed in a highly vexed mood, he wasn't interested in taking his TSF intelligence aide. Lieutenant Tyler has decided to cooperate with AFCAW, Overlord Three, and Pilgrimage HQ. She's waiting to see whether the TSF agrees with her decision and is temporarily suspended from duty while they review her case."

"Too bad they couldn't keep Duval from leaving." She tugged at the white gloves, adjusting their fit.

"Commander Meredith had no choice; the *Pilgrimage* had no means to detain his ship, and neither the *Bright Crescent* nor the *Percival* had time to prevent it. They were cleaning up the Minoan mess and, believe me, no one wanted to ask the Minoans if Duval's diplomatic privileges from the ICT still held water. Speaking of which"—Joyce's voice became more casual—"you wouldn't care to tell me what you gave the Minoan emissary, would you?"

"It was only a contract deliverable." She laughed.

"And it was the property of Hellas Nautikos, about which you broadcasted to the entire solar system?"

"I'm prohibited from talking about it, per my contract. But the Minoans *did* tell me where there were other Builders' buoys or outposts, and I'm allowed to share this with all our allies under Pax Minoica. I'm sure the colonel will be interested to see there's one location in Overlord *Five's* district, besides the two in Six's district. So we have even more interest in how the League fragments." She tapped and sent the file.

"Can I pass a recording of this call to the colonel?"

"Be my guest."

After concluding the call, she checked that the necklace was in her inside breast pocket and she opened her locker to get the sealed ceramic box. It wasn't big, but its weight required two hands to lift it out. "Maria Rose Guillotte" was engraved on its flat top, above another line that read, "August 18, 2072—March 10, 2106."

Taking a deep breath, she left her quarters and was surprised to see Matt waiting for her at the passenger airlock.

"You own a suit?" She raised her eyebrows. The coat and trousers were subtle, as Autonomist clothing went, by being dark gray with metallic silver pinstripes. The suit's cut was clean and sophisticated, with a cutaway and slight tails, like an old-fashioned morning coat. Under it, he wore a dark red shirt.

"Carmen ordered it for me. I never know what's in style." He shifted awkwardly. "I thought I'd accompany you, since Maria helped me, also."

"Thanks, I'd like that," she said. "But I warn you, this may get emotional."

The warning stood for her as well, because it made no difference that Maria Guillotte's ashes weren't really in this box. The pain, to Maria's friends and family, would be real and powerful. The Maria who had lived and worked on Mars was *no more*—and that was a hard thing to accept and understand, even to a relocated Maria with a new life and identity. She couldn't claim her wartime medals, her civilian service, and everyone in her new life was an uncaring stranger. Maria's life, as it was defined, had truly *ended*.

Of course, no one but Ariane, Joyce, and Colonel Owen Edones knew the truth about Maria. Ariane wasn't supposed to approve relocation, much less deliver the defector to the *Pilgrimage*. Given Maria's medical situation, as well as the chaos in Directorate leadership and funding, Joyce was easily able to whisk Maria out of G-145. She'd been badly injured, which helped the story work. Joyce was the one who *made* it work, of course, by getting the certificate of death endorsed by a Pilgrimage medic and substituting a body from the *Ming Adams* for cremation—what was one more "rebel" militia irregular lost in space?

The service was held in the little generic chapel on Beta Priamos Station. Ariane walked the box of ashes through the doors to Ensign Walker, her shoes clicking sharply on the deck while a French dirge, traditional to Maria's background, played. She gave the box to Walker, stepped back, and saluted the ashes in respect. Before she did her about-face, she caught sight of Parmet's family. Sabina had given up any *somaural* control; her face and eyes were puffy and red. Ensign Walker, as ranking Terran Space Force officer on the station, walked the rest of the aisle and set the box on the low generic alter, draped with TSF and Terran League flags.

State Prince Parmet gave an excellent and moving eulogy. Even though Ariane knew his acting abilities, she couldn't help but feel that *this time*, he spoke from the heart. He would be sending Maria's ashes home with a Terran Space Force escort.

After the service ended, Matt stayed with her as she did her last duty. She worked her way through the press of people and tapped Sabina on the shoulder.

"I have to give you something," she said. Someday, she would pay back Sabina for attacking her one night on this very station. However, today would not be the day.

"Yes?" Sabina said dully.

She pulled the necklace that Maria had worn out of her pocket. It had a well-wrought chain and a small precious stone hanging from it, but it didn't appear to have a high value or any obvious message. *You can't give her anything that tells her you're still alive*, she'd warned Maria. No, Maria insisted, this was only a necklace that Sabina had given her earlier. Ariane had believed her, or perhaps, wanted to believe her.

"Before she died, Maria asked that I give you this." She dropped the necklace into Sabina's hand.

"Thank you, Major Kedros." Sabina's words were solemn, and her fist closed tightly over the necklace.

"You're welcome." Ariane studied Sabina's face, but she saw nothing but loss.

"Ah, Major Kedros. So good to see you. Sad, sad affair." Dr. Istaga appeared at her elbow, on the other side from Matt.

She tried not to sigh. "Yes, Doctor?"

"I read the autopsy report. That *Pilgrimage* crew can

work quickly, when it wants to. Did you see my message asking you to wait for my examination, before cremation?" Istaga smiled his ingratiating smile.

Cautioning herself not to get irritated, she gave him a slight smile. "That's not my area of responsibility, Doctor."

"My request for hold was ignored, so I wanted to speak—"

"Will you just leave it be?" Sabina's voice was anguished as she erupted. "Let Maria rest in peace, will you?"

Her voice sounded so pained that even Ariane's eyes teared up. Parmet followed the sound of his wife's voice and put an arm around her as she started sobbing. Over Sabina's head, he glanced at Ariane. She felt a shock run up her backbone. Parmet *knew*.

If Istaga, aka Andre, had doubts about Maria's death, then he must have warned Parmet that Maria might be a defection risk—that would have been within his duties as Andre Covanni. Yet, Parmet had endorsed Maria's work history and applications for a position on the *Pytheas*; Ariane had read the file. He must have suspected what Maria was planning.

The glance Ariane exchanged with Parmet told her everything, although later, she'd wonder how she read him so well. Sabina's grief, on the other hand, was genuine. Garnet arrived to comfort her co-wife. Chander, Sabina and Parmet's son, hovered behind the group. Dr. Istaga was pushed out of the area by the flow of the emotion, and Ariane and Matt made their escape.

"Well, that's my last task," she said. "I'm off active duty once I shed this uniform."

"Good." Matt smiled. "Looks like we'll be able to pick up Hanson with another exploration drop, scheduled in another twenty hours. This time, however, I'm coming along. I've had enough of sitting helpless while I watch others—I care about—risk their lives."

He was probably talking about Oleander, who was leaving G-145 with the *Bright Crescent*. "I guess Lieutenant Oleander will soon be at Karthage Point. You guys going to try the long-distance relationship thing?" She kept her voice light.

"We'll give it an honest try. We have incompatible professions, so I'm being realistic. And, like I said, I've had my priorities rearranged in the past couple of days." His brown eyes softened and he looked away.

"Oh." She liked walking companionably beside him and wished it'd never end, but it had to. "There's something I should do right now. Meet you back at the ship?"

"Yeah. I'll want to go over your meeting with Contractor Director."

"You read the Minoans right—they approved of documenting my delivery with a receipt. Here I thought I'd be a triumphant returning hero, and Contractor Director turned it into a business exchange. Humbled me right up." She smiled as he patted her shoulder. This being all the thanks she'd get, she'd better savor it. She'd tell him and David Ray about the locations of the other Builders' structures later.

After she parted ways with Matt, though, her thoughts sobered. The crystal seed could build a civilization-destroying archive, according to the Minoans. They indicated it would initiate their genetic weapons technology, but could it be used otherwise? Had she handed over the means to cure humankind's genetic disorders? Possibly. However, the shortsightedness and greed of Overlord Six was a timely reminder that humans undoubtedly had the same flaws as the Builders. Was it fair for the Minoans to judge humans by the past actions of the Builders? Probably not—but Ariane Kedros didn't have the qualifications to second-guess Minoan decisions regarding material that was rightfully theirs.

Overlord Six apparently thought he did. Initially, Six and his staff hoped to solve the Builders' puzzle by themselves, for themselves. That's why Six had supported Abram's attempt to blow G-145 off the N-space map, although he'd backed his bets by bribing Dr. Lowry for reports and keeping up with her research. Lowry was still trying to grasp the unpleasant truth that she'd worked for *Abram's* overseer. When Abram failed, a different strategy became necessary.

That's why Nathaniel Wolf Kim had come back into her life, if Maria was right about his identity. Still having doubts, Ariane internally named the strange man Hanson/Kim. He had used the grenades on the *Pilgrimage* against all the Aether Exploration personnel in the Minoan contract, which had been publicly posted by the CAW SEEECB. They already had Lowry working on the contract, so killing, wounding, or terrorizing Aether Exploration personnel were all useful results. Hanson/Kim was trying to get the contract to *move*, one way or the other. Once they were on Beta Priamos and the Minoans had produced the implants, Hanson/Kim had gotten enough information from Lowry and poor Dr. Lee to decide there was good reason to join the expedition and use an implant himself.

In the future, when they managed to retrieve Hanson/Kim and examine his Minoan implant, Matt would again ask her what she intended to do with hers. She had no idea how she'd feel about the parasite by then. She did know, however, that she had to address her drinking *now*. Contractor Director's warning about her parasite had been humiliating and *necessary*, which was doubly embarrassing. Then there'd been her testimony in front of the ICT. *Do you ever drink to excess?* the defense attorney had asked her. Her drinking reduced her credibility and, if the ICT hadn't already failed, could have affected the final ruling. To add to her shame, she knew Matt had found her pint of rotgut during his incarceration in the hygiene closet, though he'd been careful not to mention it—he'd also been careful to throw it away.

All this had led to her appointment this afternoon. She found the maintenance break room, but hesitated. Finally, she went through the door. Three people sat inside. When they looked up at her, she saw open expressions on the faces of hardworking space crew. Unlike the one other support group she'd tried, these people wouldn't judge her and they weren't here to psychoanalyze her. Each one of them looked like they understood her demon, because they lived with similar ones. Frank was dressed in clean prisoner coveralls and his lean face lit with a smile.

"Is this the place for someone who doesn't know what to do about her drinking?" she asked. This time, she didn't suppress her hope.

"This is it," Frank said. "Have a seat."

ALSO AVAILABLE

Laura E. Reeve
Peacekeeper

A Major Ariane Kedros Novel

**First in a new action-packed
military science fiction series**

Fifteen years ago, Ariane Kedros piloted a ship on a
mission that obliterated an entire solar
system. Branded a war criminal, she was given
a new identity and a new life in order to
protect her from retribution.

But now, twelve of Ariane's wartime colleagues are
dead—assassinated by someone who has uncovered their true identities. And her
superiors in the Autonomist army have placed her
directly in the assassin's line of fire on a
peacekeeping mission that will decide the fate of
all humanity...

**Available wherever books are sold or at
penguin.com/scififantasy**

R0039

ALSO AVAILABLE

Laura E. Reeve

Vigilante

A Major Ariane Kedros Novel

Amidst an uneasy peace between the
Autonomists and the Terrans, Major Ariane
Kedros and her partner, Matthew Journey, have
discovered alien ruins on a remote planet—ruins
that bear evidence to an ancient and highly
advanced technology. But their discovery has
drawn the interest of high stakes players from
every corner of the universe—including that of
the rogue leader of a fringe Terran sect. Ari must
find a way to stop him, before they all become
ancient history...

**Available wherever books are sold or at
penguin.com/scififantasy**

R0040

THE ULTIMATE IN
SCIENCE FICTION AND FANTASY!

From magical tales of distant worlds to stories of
technological advances beyond the grasp of man, Penguin has
everything you need to stretch your imagination to its limits.

penguin.com

ACE
Get the latest information on favorites like
William Gibson, T.A. Barron, Brian Jacques,
Ursula K. Le Guin, Sharon Shinn, Charlaine Harris,
Patricia Briggs, and Marjorie M. Liu,
as well as updates on the best new authors.

ROC
Escape with Jim Butcher, Harry Turtledove, Anne Bishop,
S.M. Stirling, Simon R. Green, E.E. Knight, Kat Richardson,
Rachel Caine, and many others—plus news on the
latest and hottest in science fiction and fantasy.

DAW
Patrick Rothfuss, Mercedes Lackey, Kristen Britain,
Tanya Huff, Tad Williams, C.J. Cherryh, and many more—
DAW has something to satisfy the cravings of any
science fiction and fantasy lover.
Also visit dawbooks.com.

*Get the best of science fiction and fantasy
at your fingertips!*

PO # 4500305027